The Perfect Bou

Zoe came over to examine the bouquet. "How did you know to pick those exact flowers?"

Lara bent down and tucked a curl back under the knitted brim of the little girl's hat. Zoe smelled of outdoors and chocolate cereal. There were bread crumbs clinging to the front of her coat. Up close, her eyes were the pale green of myrtle leaves.

"You want to know a secret?" Lara whispered. Zoe nodded. "I don't pick the flowers, they pick me! Now"—she stood up and held out the vase of free flowers—"let's see which one picks you."

The *Flower* Arrangement

ELLA GRIFFIN

BERKLEY
NEW YORK

BERKLEY
An imprint of Penguin Random House LLC
375 Hudson Street, New York, New York 10014

Copyright © 2016 by Ella Griffin

Library of Congress Cataloging-in-Publication Data

Names: Griffin, Ella, author.
Title: The flower arrangement / Ella Griffin.
Description: Berkley trade paperback edition. | New York : Berkley Books, 2016.
Identifiers: LCCN 2016020083 (print) | LCCN 2016028227 (ebook) | ISBN 9781101989739
(softcover) | ISBN 9781101989746 (ebook)
Subjects: LCSH: Florists—Fiction. | Interpersonal relations—Fiction. | Dublin (Ireland)—
Fiction. | BISAC: FICTION / Contemporary Women. | FICTION / Romance /
Contemporary. | FICTION / Family Life. | GSAFD: Love stories.
Classification: LCC PR6107.R52 F58 2016 (print) | LCC PR6107.R52 (ebook) | DDC
823/.92—dc23
LC record available at https://lccn.loc.gov/2016020083

First Edition: October 2016

Printed in the United States of America
1   3   5   7   9   10   8   6   4   2

Cover photo of woman by Nora Dal Cero / Plain Picture
Cover design by Sinem Erkas / Orionbooks; image retouching by Cathal O'Flaherty
Book design by Laura K. Corless
Title page and chapter opener art © JJ-Whic/Shutterstock

For my beautiful sister, Frances.
And for Neil with love and Avalanche Roses.

I am the lover's gift; I am the wedding wreath;
I am the memory of a moment of happiness;
I am the last gift of the living to the dead;
I am a part of joy and a part of sorrow.

—KAHLIL GIBRAN
"SONG OF THE FLOWER XXIII"

When you have only two pennies left in the world,
buy a loaf of bread with one,
and a lily with the other.

—CHINESE PROVERB

IVY

Femininity. Tenacity.

Dublin was deserted at 7 a.m. on Saturday except for a pair of die-hard Friday-night clubbers kissing in the doorway of the antiques shop at the corner of Pleasant Street. Three purposeful seagulls flew along the curving line of Camden Street, then took a sharp right along Montague Lane. Gray clouds were banked above the rooftops but the heavy rain had thinned out to a fine drizzle, and a slant of weak sunshine cut through the gloom and lit a shining path along the drenched pavement ahead of Lara. She stepped into it, luxuriating in the faint prickle of heat on the back of her neck.

This was her favorite time of the year. The madness of Valentine's Day over. Mother's Day still a month away. The wedding season a dot on the horizon. Spring blooms had been coming in from Holland since December, but now flowers from Irish growers were arriving. Daffodils with their frilled trumpets and tissue-paper-delicate anemones and the first tulips with sturdy stems and glossy, tightly packed petals.

She made her way past the shuttered shops and the boarded-up stalls, heading for a tall, slim slice of pale pink in the line of red and gray brick facades. Phil, her younger brother, had painted the exterior of Blossom & Grow. The slapdash blobs and trickles he had left in the paint were, she thought, rummaging for her keys, part of the charm, like the swags of realistic-looking painted ivy that seemed to trail up the outside of the three-story building, curling around the drainpipe and the windowsills. Lara had painted the ivy herself. She had always loved ivy for its tenacity and determination, for the way it pushed through tiny cracks and crevices to reach the light.

She had spent weeks making sketches, teaching herself trompe l'oeil techniques, and then conquered her fear of heights to balance on a ladder with her paintbrushes and palette. No two leaves were the same. Even now, five years later, looking up, she felt as if she knew every single one.

She shifted the armful of damp greenery she'd cut from her garden and unlocked the door. The Chubb lock stuck the way it always did. The Yale turned with a soft click and the six Thai temple bells that hung above the door rang out a soft jingle of welcome.

The wildflower man had already been here, she saw. He had his own key and would have driven up from Wicklow before it got light. He had left a huge bucket of narcissi beside the door. The tiny white flowers had been picked before dawn and they glowed as if they had been drenched in moonlight. A second, smaller bucket was packed with bluebells and Lara could smell some hyacinths in there too. She bent down and felt around for the little waxy blossoms, and their fragrance rose up to meet her. If perfumes were the feelings of flowers, as her mother used to say, then the hyacinths were as happy to see her as she was to see them.

"You want to open a flower shop?" Her husband's jaw had dropped when she had told him, five years ago. His voice, usually so calm and quiet, had been sharp with anxiety. They had always come to decisions together, careful of one another's needs, but the truth was that deep down they had both wanted the same thing. Then they had lost their baby and instead of turning toward one another they'd turned away.

Lara, who didn't have the energy to shower, who could not find a single reason to get dressed, stayed in bed for weeks. Michael could not sit still. He spent whole days out in the garden bent over his spade, digging beds that didn't need digging, reseeding the lawn, replanting the Chinese camellias he had moved the winter before.

He held Lara when she cried. He reached a hand out to squeeze hers when she lay awake, her knuckles pushed into her mouth to choke back her grief. He told her the pain wouldn't go on forever, that life would return to the way it had been. But everything had changed, and Lara knew that the only way she could get through it was to change everything.

"Lara, listen to me," Michael said. "Floristry is not about floating around arranging flowers. You have no idea what you'd be getting into."

"I can learn." She'd hoped he'd be happy for her.

"You don't understand. It's backbreaking work. You'll be on your feet all day, every day, sweeping, cleaning, hauling water around. That's not what you need, not after what you've been through. You need to think about this carefully."

"All I've been doing is thinking and it's killing me. I thought it would get better when I went back to work, but it hasn't."

Michael ran his calloused thumb over her palm, following the lines that trailed across it. The head line, the heart line, the health line, the life line.

"Throwing away a career you love is not the answer. Give yourself time. Stay at Green Sea for a few months; then, if you still need a change, set up a design studio at home. Go freelance."

She shook her head. "I can't. I've made up my mind about the shop." She hadn't quite, but she did in that moment.

"Well, you don't need my opinion then." He let her hand drop. "But for what it's worth, I think it's a mistake. Retail is tough, and a luxury business in a recession, with unreliable suppliers, difficult customers, perishable stock . . . I just hope you're not going to regret it."

Michael had been trying to protect her, she knew that. He knew what he was talking about. He had run his own landscaping business for eight years. She did trust him, but in some stubborn place deep in her heart, she trusted herself more.

He had been right about some things. It had taken Lara two years to find flower sellers she could trust, and second-guessing how much stock she'd need a week in advance was still a leap of faith. Flowers were expensive and they had a short shelf life. After five years, she had developed better instincts about ordering but there were disasters along the way. The first Mother's Day she had run out of flowers with half the orders in the book unfilled. Three years ago it snowed for two weeks before Christmas and she had to throw away over a thousand euros' worth of stock. The work was, as Michael had said, backbreaking.

There were late nights, and early starts for weddings, sixteen-hour days in the run-up to Christmas and Valentine's Day. The shop had to be kept cool because the flowers liked it that way, and no matter how many layers she wore, Lara was always cold. Her hands were ruined. Standing all day made her bones ache, and there was a pale blue hashtag in the soft hollow of skin behind her left knee that she thought might be the beginnings of varicose veins.

But Michael had been wrong about the customers. They weren't difficult at all; they were a joy. Lara had known since she was a child that flowers were a language, but what she hadn't realized was that she was a natural translator. That she could help another person to find the flowers that expressed the feelings their words were too flimsy or too worn out to hold. "I love you" or "I'm sorry" or "I'm happy" or "I'm grateful" or "I'll never forget you."

She straightened up and looked around. She loved this small shop, and in a way that she could not explain, it seemed to love her in return. Phil had helped her to strip the walls back to bare brick and to paint the floorboards French gray. They had found the wooden counter in a salvage yard. It had dozens of cubbyholes and drawers for wraps and wire and scissors and ribbon.

The walls behind the counter had deep floor-to-ceiling shelves for vases and jam jars and scented candles, and there was an old wrought-iron revolving stand for cards. But most of the space in the long, narrow shop was taken up with flowers and plants.

Today there were fifty-two kinds of cut blooms, from the tiny cobalt-blue violets that were smaller than Lara's little fingernail to a purple-and-green-frilled brassica that was bigger than her head.

The flowers were set out in gleaming metal buckets and containers of every shape and size. They were lined up on the floor three deep and stacked on the tall three-tier stand in the middle of the shop.

The plants, huge leafy ferns and tiny fleshy succulents, lemon trees and jasmine bushes and freckled orchids, were displayed on floating shelves that were built at various heights all the way up to the ceiling.

Lara had spent weeks getting the lighting right. There were a few soft spotlights above the flower displays, and an antique crystal chandelier hung low above the counter. There were strings of fairy lights and dozens of jewel-colored tea lights and tall, slender lanterns dotted between the buckets. When they were lit, they cast star and crescent moon shapes along the walls and the shop resembled the courtyard of a Moroccan *riad*—a tiny walled garden right in the middle of the city.

She put her bag and her greenery down on the counter, lit the candles and switched on the fairy lights. Then she took off her coat, pulled her old gray cashmere cardigan off a hook and put it on over the two long-sleeved T-shirts she was already wearing. She went out into the cluttered galley kitchen and filled the kettle. While the water boiled, she rolled forward slowly, loosening up her spine, one vertebra at a time. Her long hair fanned out around her on the worn wooden floorboards. Through a gap in the dark curtain her hair created she spotted a little drift of leaves and petals by the skirting board. No matter how often she cleaned, there was always more to sweep.

She swung her head from side to side to stretch her neck. Then she stood up and spooned loose-leaf peppermint tea into her flask and filled it with boiling water, inhaling the cloud of warm steam.

Opening Blossom & Grow had not been a mistake. No matter how tough it had been, she had only one regret. That she hadn't been able to persuade her husband that it was the right thing to do.

Even now, he didn't seem to understand that the shop had been her lifeline. It had carried her away from the empty space in her own heart and into the lives of thousands of strangers.

When she worked as a graphic designer, the only display of feeling she had seen was when a client who owned a pizza franchise had a meltdown because Lara refused to copy the British Airways corporate identity when designing his logo. Now she was surrounded by feelings every day—joy, sorrow, gratitude, regret, lust, hope. And the one feeling that seemed to underpin them all—love.

She carried her flask and her favorite mug out to the counter, flipped open the fat leather-bound order book and fired up her laptop. She turned on the radio and a Bach cello concerto poured out of the small speakers, the simple, fluid notes weaving around the sounds of the sleepy city waking up outside her window. The rattle of the shutter going up on the betting shop next door. The distant rumble of a Luas train pulling into Harcourt station. The hammering, drilling and whistling from the building site a few doors away. The shouts and laughter from a group of Italian students gathering on the steps of the language school across the street.

A withered petal from the kitchen floor was caught in Lara's hair. She picked it out. It still held its heart shape and an echo of fragrance. She tucked it between the pages of the order book. It was only March but the book was already satisfyingly fat both from daily use and occasional, accidental dousings. The pages were densely covered in a jumble of her assistant Ciara's loopy scrawl and doodles and Lara's copperplate handwriting. Lists of flowers that had been ordered to check off against deliveries. Reminders of the chores that had to be done daily and weekly. Special requests from customers. Bookings that came in on the phone.

Today there were regular orders from two restaurants and a hotel, a dozen small table centerpieces to make up for a charity dinner, and bouquets for the maternity hospital on Holles Street, a house in Kilmacud and an eighteenth birthday party in a tapas bar in Donnybrook.

Lara read the message that Ciara had scribbled on a Post-it and stuck crookedly to the page:

> *It seems like only yesterday that we brought you home, 6 pounds 3 ounces of joy wrapped up in a pink blanket. We felt like the luckiest people alive that day and every day since. Happy 18th birthday to our lovely and amazing daughter Ailish.*
>
> *Love,*
> *Mum and Dad*

A thirty-euro bouquet. Lara picked up a pen to start planning it, then gathered up her long dark hair and used the pen instead to fasten a bun at the back of her neck. She rested her chin on her hand. She tried to imagine an eighteen-year-old's cluttered bedroom. The blinds still drawn. A tumble of hair on a pillow. A girl still fast asleep on the day she would take the last few steps across the bridge from childhood to adulthood. She might be given dozens of flowers in her life, Lara guessed, but these might be the very first. And she would remember them twenty, forty, sixty years from now—long after her parents had gone. They would have to be perfect.

By eight thirty, Lara had changed the water in every bucket and checked over all her stock, carefully picking out any blooms that wouldn't last for the next seven days. She had trimmed the rejects and popped them into a vase on the counter with a chalkboard sign that said "Please take one home." She had turned the wildflowers into a dozen ten-euro spring bouquets wrapped simply in brown paper for men who might feel shy about carrying a larger bunch of flowers. She had sterilized the jam jars for the table centerpieces, made up a rainbow of tissue paper and cellophane wraps, soaked twenty blocks of Oasis and fed the orchids. Ciara had gone away for a romantic weekend with her husband, Mort, so Lara would be in the shop on her own today. It was a good idea to get a head start.

Mondays were her biggest delivery days. She'd arrive to find huge boxes, fresh off the Dutch transporters that had rolled into Dublin port the night before. She always held her breath as she slit the tape and pulled back the corrugated-cardboard flaps. Ordering online was all about ticking boxes. Species. Color. Size. Number. Grade of quality. Degree of openness. But there was something miraculous about seeing the flowers she'd imagined brought to life. Roses from Colombia. Chrysanthemums from Ecuador. Orchids from Thailand. Anemones and agapanthus from Spain. Stargazers and parrot tulips from the vast Dutch flower fields.

The shop was usually quiet on Mondays, so she and Ciara could take time to condition everything properly. Stripping leaves, removing thorns, rehydrating the flowers, separating any blooms she'd ordered for weddings or events from the stock for the shop, and filling the tiny cold room.

Tuesdays were catch-up days. Between the phone and walk-in orders, they'd give the shop a proper clean—dusting shelves, polishing vases, replenishing cards and ribbons, tissue paper, cellophane, wire and sterilizing fluid.

Midweek there would be a steady flow of customers and some early orders for the weekend. If stock looked as though it was going to run out, there was still time to put in an order.

Fridays were frantic. Men rushing in to buy flowers for their wives and girlfriends. Women looking for last-minute plants to take to dinner parties. Single girls who were going to spend the night in treating themselves to a bouquet on the way home.

Saturday was Lara's favorite day. The shop was busy with strollers and browsers, families out for a walk, loved-up couples in town for brunch, local people who emerged on the weekends to take the streets back for themselves. A Saturday could be even more hectic than a

Friday, but it felt more chilled out because everyone had time to stop and, literally, smell the flowers.

Just after nine, the door opened and her first customer came in: a man in his twenties in jeans and a very crumpled shirt carrying two cups of takeaway coffee and a plastic bag full of croissants. He winced when the wind chimes tinkled, and Lara turned the radio down in case his hangover was as bad as it looked. "Good morning."

"Very good night!" He grinned sheepishly. "Not sure about the morning yet."

He rambled around the shop for a while, muttering to himself, apologizing to a bucket of stargazers when he bumped into it. Lara asked if he wanted any help, and five minutes later he left with a glorious bunch of white narcissi tucked under his free arm.

A stressed-out woman in her thirties wearing pajama bottoms under her coat and Velcro rollers in her hair double-parked her Mini on the street right outside and rushed in looking for twelve gifts for a hen party.

"Perfect! Sorted! Done!" She swooped on the line of jam jar arrangements that Lara had just finished. And Lara, who had seen the traffic cop go past a minute earlier, didn't have the heart to tell her that the twelve miniature bouquets were meant for the charity dinner.

The shop was busy for the next two hours; then there was a lull. At about twelve, a man in his forties in a light green linen jacket, with thinning hair carefully spiked up to hide a bald patch, ducked in to avoid a sudden shower of hailstones. He cursed under his breath as he shook little nuggets of ice off his shoulders. He looked around at the fairy lights and lanterns and finally at Lara, who was working under a circle of soft light cast from the chandelier.

"It's kind of dark in here." He sounded disapproving.

"It is." Lara gave him a quick smile. Choosing flowers, deciding what to write on a card, these were personal things. A little mood lighting didn't hurt.

Hailstones were flinging themselves against the window like

handfuls of gravel. "Bloody typical." The man rolled his eyes. "I'm going on a blind date. Better hope she's actually blind if I have to walk to Duke Street in that!"

"Why don't you wait it out?" Lara smiled. "It won't last long." She went back to work on a new set of mini bouquets for the charity dinner. She had panicked when she found she didn't have enough jam jars, then decided she could use a dozen mismatched china cups she had picked up in a charity shop at some stage. They were turning out better than she had hoped.

She heard, rather than saw, the man's mood change as he wandered around the shop. He began to whistle, out of tune, to the aria playing on the radio.

The reason people loved to give and receive flowers, Lara thought for the hundredth time—the truth, the root that ran deep beneath the bouquets for birthdays and anniversaries and births and even deaths—was that human beings were changed by flowers. Even when they were not aware of it, some part of them basked in their beauty. They slowed down. They took deeper breaths. Their faces softened.

"It's stopped." The man was standing by the counter now. Lara looked up and saw that the sun had come out. The light catching in the drops that clung to the window cast tiny darts of rainbows that danced around them.

"Spring is the sun shining on the rain and the rain falling on the sunshine," she quoted.

"Seamus Heaney," the man sighed. "One of our greatest poets. Hard to believe he's gone. Nobody could say it the way he did."

"True," Lara agreed tactfully, although the quote was by Frances Hodgson Burnett, the author of her favorite childhood book, *The Secret Garden.*

The man was staring out the window. "I thought I was ready to go out there." Lara had a feeling he wasn't talking about the weather. "My girlfriend left me after Christmas," he said glumly. "Everyone says I should make an effort to meet someone else, but I haven't been on a

date since 1998. I'm not even sure what you're supposed to talk about."
He frowned at the vase of free flowers Lara had left on the counter.
"Isn't that bad for business? Giving flowers away?"

"It's better than throwing them away," Lara said. "Help yourself."

"No, I don't want to look like I'm trying too hard."

"How about a buttonhole?" she said. "It'd be something to talk
about."

"Oh, go on then!" he sighed. "Maybe it'll distract her from the fact
that I'm not George Clooney."

Lara picked out a white rosebud. She snipped it below the head, then
picked out a stem of *Alchemilla mollis* that was the same color as his jacket.
She twisted it deftly around the bud, secured it with an inch of wire,
slipped in a pin and handed it to him. He fixed it onto his lapel.

"What do you think?" she asked him.

He looked down at the flower and then up at her with the beginning of a smile. "I think I've been very rude and that you've been very
kind." He pointed at the flower. "What do *you* think?"

"I think you should forget it's a date," Lara said, "and just enjoy a
nice lunch."

As she swept the floor for what must have been the tenth time that
morning, Lara wondered if she'd see him again. Customers were like
flowers: they had their seasons too. Some only appeared once, but there
were regulars who came in every other week. Alfredo from Havana, who
bought his wife, Dominga, exotic plants that reminded her of home—
succulents and orchids and kumquat trees. Dermot, a perpetually love-
struck pensioner who hobbled over from Donnybrook on his Zimmer
frame for a single red rose every time a new female guest arrived at his
retirement home. Ciaran, who was waving at her through the window
right now. He had been coming in to Blossom & Grow with his daughter
pretty much every Saturday since the shop had opened.

Lara had met Zoe when she was only five days old—a tiny bundle strapped to her dad's chest in a sling, her face tightly furled, like a rosebud. Zoe had loved flowers when she was still too young to see more than blurs of color. She would drum her tiny heels in her stroller until her dad took her out and held her up—a flying baby above the buckets of roses and irises and lilies. Once she was old enough to know not to eat it, Lara had given her her own flower to take home every week. A purple iris or a yellow parrot tulip or a bird-of-paradise cut short and wrapped in cellophane and tissue and tied with a ribbon.

Lara had watched Zoe grow up, week by week, year by year. Seen her take some of her first tottering steps. Now Zoe was the same age as Blossom & Grow. A skinny, long-legged five-year-old in stripy red and black tights and a navy duffle coat. She still had something of a rosebud about her. A saffron-tipped, creamy-centered Leonidas, Lara thought, with her milky skin and her coppery corkscrew curls escaping from under her bunny-ears hat. Seeing her warmed Lara's heart the way the sunshine had warmed the back of her head first thing that morning.

"Well, look who it is!" she said, leaning on her sweeping brush. "I told the flowers you'd be dropping in this morning."

"We're late"—Zoe hopped from foot to foot in her scuffed black patent shoes—"because we had to take a long time feeding the ducks. We have to do everything extra slowly this morning because Mummy needs a long lion."

"Mummy needs a whole pride of lie-ins." Her dad yawned and rubbed the coppery stubble on his jaw. "She was up with Bugs Bunny here at the crack of dawn. Can you make us up a fifteen-euro bouquet, please, Lara?"

It was what he asked for every week, and Lara had already set the flowers to one side. Three deep-pink anemones with sooty centers, a single full-petaled ballet-slipper-pink Antique rose, half a dozen blue-bells, a pale pink hyacinth, a spray of freckly green hellebores.

She made a circle with her thumb and forefinger and began slotting the flowers into it, spiraling the stems so they wouldn't break when she tied them. She watched Zoe out of the corner of her eye. The little girl stopped to gaze up at a bright pink orchid, squatted down to sniff the narcissi and stood on her toes to touch the inside-out trumpet of a calla lily with her red-mittened fingertips.

"Careful there, butterfingers!" her dad warned her.

"It's okay." Lara smiled. "She knows not to squeeze them too hard." She tied the bouquet with a pale green ribbon the same shade as the hellebores.

Ciaran whistled. "Wow! That is something else. You're a genius, do you know that? It doesn't seem fair that you make that amazing arrangement and I take the credit for it."

Customers were always telling Lara that she had a gift, that nobody arranged flowers the way she did. Three years of graphic design college and seven years poring over a Pantone color chart had probably helped. The course she'd taken at the London School of Floristry had taught her the basics of conditioning and arranging. But the truth was that Lara was as amazed as anyone at how instinctive it felt, how easily it all came to her. She rarely had to think about what she was doing. Her eyes and her hands took over, weaving the flowers together, layering color and texture to create something beautiful and unique every time.

Zoe came over to examine the bouquet. "How did you know to pick those exact flowers?"

Lara bent down and tucked a curl back under the knitted brim of the little girl's hat. Zoe smelled of outdoors and chocolate cereal. There were bread crumbs clinging to the front of her coat. Up close, her eyes were the pale green of myrtle leaves.

"You want to know a secret?" Lara whispered. Zoe nodded. "I don't pick the flowers, they pick me! Now"—she stood up and held out the vase of free flowers—"let's see which one picks you."

The small red mitten hovered over the vase and then settled on a bright pink gerbera. Lara folded a sheet of pale pink tissue into a fluffy froth and tied it with a snippet of pink ribbon.

"What's the magic word?" Ciaran asked when she had handed the flower over.

Zoe thought for a moment, then waved the flower like a wand. "Abracadabra!" she said imperiously.

After they'd gone, Lara stood at the counter for a long time, twisting a stray length of ribbon around one finger while her mind probed nervously at the ache in her heart the way a tongue explores a broken tooth. Seeing Zoe every week was always a blessing, but sometimes it was a cruel reminder too. Five years, she thought, staring down at the ribbon but not really seeing it. Seeing, instead, the life she and Michael could have had if things had turned out differently.

The sadness didn't mug her the way it had in the beginning. Then it had knocked her down every day, worked her over and left her limp and shaking. Now it could leave her alone for a week, then suddenly slide up behind her, pull and prod at her, looking for a way to drag her down.

She forced herself to pick up the phone and make some calls, then check her emails. She swept the floor again. She moved some of the flower buckets around and organized the counter and replaced the till roll. Then, when there was nothing else to do, she dug out the squeegee mop and marched herself outside to clean the already clean window.

One of the girls from the betting shop next door stopped to say hello. A chef from Pizza Heaven who was having a quick smoke by the Dumpster bins in the lane gave her a wave. Ketut, the solemn Balinese man who owned the furniture store two doors down, emerged and asked in his elaborately polite way for Lara's advice about his window display. She spent a few minutes pointing and nodding and shaking her head while he rearranged the gilded Buddhas and the intricate shadow puppets and the brightly painted wooden gods and goddesses who had found their way from Indonesia to keep watch carefully over this tiny corner of Dublin.

As she went back to Blossom & Grow, she glanced over at the Camden Deli across the street and saw the owner behind the gleaming plate-glass window. Glen was fortyish, with a closely shaved head and a mid-Atlantic accent. He had gone to the States on a J-1 visa when he was twenty and come home a year ago when he'd inherited the café from his mother. He had transformed the place from a greasy spoon to a glossy black-and-white-tiled New York–style deli. Brought in real American bagels and French pastries and Italian espresso and a coffee machine as big and complicated as Lara's brother's motorbike.

Lara raised her squeegee to wave at Glen, but he turned away quickly, in a way that seemed almost deliberate, and ducked out of sight. He used to call over to Blossom & Grow at least once a week, bringing Lara chocolate and raisin twists and cappuccinos with flower designs traced in chocolate dust on the foam. He'd hung around admiring the flowers, complaining good-humoredly about Dublin's lack of decent baristas and gay bars. But it was at least a month now since he'd dropped in. She tried to think back to their last meeting, hoping that she hadn't said anything to offend him.

A flurry of customers arrived, and by the time the shop emptied out again it was after two o'clock and there was still no sign of her brother. She usually liked to do her own deliveries, but today, without Ciara to look after the shop, she'd asked Phil to do the run.

His phone was about to ring out when he picked up. "What?" He sounded groggy.

"Please tell me you're not still in *bed*."

"Oh shit! I said I'd come in, didn't I? I forgot to set the clock." His voice was husky. He'd sounded like this every morning since the age of thirteen, when his voice broke: as if he'd been drinking whiskey and smoking cigarettes in his sleep. "I decided to take a run down to Kilkee on the bike last night."

"Why?"

"I don't know. Because it was there. At least I think it was there. It was too dark to see it properly. I could hear the roar of the Atlantic, though."

"You took a six-hundred-kilometer round trip just to hear the sea?"

"It was only five hundred and eighty-four kilometers," he yawned. "And it's an ocean. I'm not sure I'm in a fit state to drive around Dublin."

"I'll do the deliveries if you look after the shop."

"Any chance Michael could do it?"

"He's working on a job in Howth all day."

Michael had started taking on freelance projects after Lara opened the shop. He worked in his corporate landscaping business Monday to Friday, designing rolling parklands around newly built apartment blocks, dreaming up streams and waterfalls to break up the concrete jungles of business parks, color-coordinating plantings of shrubs and bushes to create pleasing harmonious blurs on the hard shoulders of motorways.

At the weekend, he went back to what he'd been doing when they met—landscaping gardens. Digging out borders, building rockeries and raised beds. Moving earth. Losing himself in activity. Trying to fill the same aching space that she was. She sighed.

"Lara! Stop," Phil grumbled.

"Stop what?"

"Stop giving me those sad puppy-dog eyes!"

"You can't see my eyes!"

"I don't have to see them to know they're doing that big brown pleading thing. I'll come in for an hour. One hour only, Lara. Then I'm going straight back home to this lovely bed."

Lara managed to get the delivery bouquets finished between customers. She was about to nip out and load them into the van when she noticed a man in a high-visibility jacket and a hard hat walking purposefully past the window. A moment later, he walked past the other way. Then the door opened a crack.

"Hello," Lara said.

A head appeared around the door, then the builder edged into the shop in his large dusty boots, looking mortified. He pointed at the flowers in the nearest bucket, some yellow chrysanthemums that Lara kept for funeral wreaths because they were cheerful and because they lasted if not for eternity, at least for a few weeks.

"I'll take ten euros' worth of them," he mumbled.

"They're a lovely color, aren't they?" She came out from behind the counter. "But have you seen these?" She pointed at the bucket of sunflowers that blazed in the corner. "They'll really light up a room."

He nodded. "Okay, those then."

He retreated to the door while she wrapped them, his tattooed arms crossed on his chest, his jaw clenched as if he was waiting for a filling rather than a bunch of flowers.

"Why don't you pick a card to go with them," she suggested. "It'll make the flowers last longer."

His eyebrows, caked in dust, disappeared up under the yellow plastic brim of the hat. "If she puts the card in the water?"

"If she puts it in a drawer or tucks it into a book." He looked confused. "Women don't throw cards away, you know. She'll find it a year, two years, ten years from now, and remember the sunflowers you gave her."

The builder took a few tentative steps toward the counter and turned the revolving stand slowly, then furtively picked a card and held it out.

"Probably best if you write it." She slid a pen over to him. It stayed where it was for a long moment, then a huge hand snaked out and took it. The builder hunched over the card, nibbling his knuckles.

"I can't think of anything to say."

"Just say whatever you'd say in a text." Lara put the finished bouquet on the counter. "A romantic one. I just need to pop upstairs for a minute. I'll leave you in peace."

She went up to the workroom and spent a minute checking over a vase of Memory Lane roses she'd left to open by the window. When she came down again, the builder and the bouquet and the card were gone and there was a pile of change on the counter. She smiled to herself as she put the money away.

It had taken careful nurturing and tending and six days of her life every week for two years, but despite the recession and all of Michael's worries, Blossom & Grow had broken even two years ago and had been in profit ever since. Lara was still only earning half the salary she'd made as a graphic designer, but it was enough to cover the mortgage and her share of the bills and to pay back the six thousand euros her father had lent her to start the business, though he always insisted the money was a gift, not a loan.

She and Phil joked that they had to be careful what they said to their father. If Lara mentioned on the phone that she was thinking of repainting her living room, he was quite likely to be at the front door with paint and a ladder before they'd finished the call.

Families fell apart when mothers died, especially when the children were young, but theirs had grown closer, held together by the glue of their father's love and determination. Overnight, his Dick Francis and Stephen King novels had disappeared and were replaced by dozens of books on parenting. He had taken a two-year sabbatical from his marketing job until Phil was old enough to go to school. Walked twelve-year-old Lara down to the local hair salon and asked the hairdresser to teach him how to French-plait her hair. Brought Phil to the toddler playgroup, sat cross-legged on the floor playing patty-cake and singing "The Wheels on the Bus," not giving a damn that he was the only man there.

He had never missed a school concert or a parent-teacher meeting or a hockey game. He had done the washing and the ironing and the vacuuming. Checked their homework every night. Taught both of them to play golf and to fish and to name every plant in the garden. Turned himself, after a rocky start, into a fairly decent cook, though he had never got the hang of baking. Lara remembered coming down in the middle of the night for a drink of water when she was fourteen and finding him in his dressing gown in a blizzard of flour on his third attempt to master a Victoria sponge for her school cake sale.

When Phil arrived, Lara left him propped up at the counter with his leather jacket zipped up, complaining about the cold. She made him a cup of strong coffee and told him to call her if there was anything he couldn't deal with. But her brother was good with flowers, she thought, loading bouquets into the back of her pink van, and with people.

Every light seemed to be green, every loading bay had a free space and she flew through the deliveries to the restaurants and the charity ball. She drove through sun and rain out to Donnybrook to drop off the birthday flowers, making sure that the manager of the restaurant found a champagne bucket to keep them in so they wouldn't wilt before the party started. Then she got into her van again and headed on to Foster Avenue, taking the long way along the Goatstown Road so she could see her favorite tree, a rare magnolia Genie that had taken over the entire garden of a suburban house. The tree was ugly in winter, a tangle of twisting branches like scrawny limbs, but in March it was covered in heart-stoppingly lovely pink and cream flowers the size of teacups.

She had delivered lilies and twisted hazel to that house once, and an elderly woman in a dressing gown with a hot-water bottle tucked under her arm had opened the door and burst into tears when she'd seen the bouquet.

"I'm sorry," she said, after Lara had found her a tissue and brought her inside into a hallway that felt colder than the doorstep had. "They're from my son in Sydney. I don't know how to tell him . . ." She sat down on the bottom step of the stairs and began to cry again. "I don't need flowers, I need money to pay the gas bill."

Lara had given her the money her son had spent on the flowers and left her the bouquet as well. She hadn't told Michael. He had warned her many times that she'd have to separate her heart from the business, but how was she supposed to do that when the flower business was all about heart?

She took a left onto the Kilmacud Road and then another right onto Sweetbriar Grove. She pulled over and opened the back of the van and took out the anniversary flowers. A sullen woman in her thirties with her hair scraped back in a severe ponytail opened the door. "Can't you read?" she snapped, pointing at a printed sign over the letter box. "No junk mail, no sales calls, no—" Her eyes widened, her hand floated up to her mouth and here it was, the tiny gap between the moment a woman saw the flowers she'd been sent and the moment when she said "Ah" or "Oh" or "Wow" or, in this case, "Are they for me?"

And maybe Lara was just imagining it, but it always seemed to her that the relationship between the woman and the person who had sent her flowers fit into that gap somehow, in all its beauty and complexity, the way the magnolia tree fit into the tiny suburban garden.

Her heart lifted as she walked back to her van, then sank a little as she began the drive back into town to make the final delivery. The one she had left till last.

Her dad had taken her for an extravagant lunch to celebrate after Lara had paid him back. She had wanted to invite Michael and Phil along but he was having none of it. "Bring that pair into a Michelin-starred restaurant? Don't be daft. Michael would trample mud all over the carpet and Phil would show up dressed like a bloody Hell's Angel. Anyway, it'll do my street cred some good to be seen out in a posh nosherie with a glamorous woman."

"Hardly glamorous, Dad," Lara had sighed, but she had dressed up for the occasion, the way her mother would have. Swapped her shop thermals and jumpers and jeans for an elegant blue jersey dress, worn high shoes.

Afterward, they walked across Merrion Square to where she'd parked, stopping to admire the flowers in the brightly planted beds. Her dad walked her to the Holles Street gate, then stopped and took her arm and gently turned her around to face him.

For a long time he had looked years younger than he really was. Then, in his mid-sixties, he had started to look his age. Now, every year, her brother looked more like the dashing dark-haired father she remembered from her childhood, and her father looked like her grand-father did in photographs. His hair was thinning on top, silvering at the temples. His skin, always tanned from the golf course, was deeply lined. Only his eyes were unchanged. Dark as her own, sparkling now with the wine he'd drunk at lunch and a touch of mock annoyance. He'd been trying to persuade her for most of the afternoon that the money she'd paid back was a gift.

"Make an old man happy." He put his hands on her shoulders. "Let me put it into a deposit account with your name on it."

"We've been through this," she sighed. "And you're not old! You're mature."

"Like a cheese, and you, you're like your mother." He shook his head. "You won't do what I want but you give me the brush-off so elegantly that I'm happy anyway. I suppose the money doesn't matter. All that matters is that you're happy. You *are* happy"—he looked at her closely—"aren't you?"

"Of course I am." She smiled. "I wake up wanting to go to work. I think that's about as good as it gets."

"You've done a great job with the shop. You should be very proud of yourself." He cleared his throat, a signal that he was straying onto uncomfortable ground but that he was determined to give it to her straight—the way he had when he told her about periods, and later, when he asked her if she needed to go on the pill. He had never shied away from any of the conversations she would have had with her mother, no matter how hard they were for him.

He looked pointedly at the maternity hospital across the street and Lara felt a flutter of anxiety. Please! No! she thought.

"Work is all very well, but it isn't enough. Kids are what give life meaning, Lara. I wouldn't have wanted to go on if it hadn't been for you and Phil. I hope that's not, what do they call it these days, too much information?"

Lara shook her head, hoping that was it, but he went on.

"I know you had your heart broken into a million pieces over there." He nodded at the hospital. "I know the last thing you want to do is talk about it. But some women are meant to be mothers, and what happened doesn't change the fact that you're one of them. You know, when your mother and I were dragging our heels about having another baby, you invented an imaginary one of your own." He looked wistful. "What did you call her again?"

Lara had called her Lily, but she couldn't say that. If she tried to say anything, she would start to cry. She held her breath and managed a jerky shrug.

"Well, I've said my piece." He tucked a strand of hair behind her ear. "I'll shut up now and get out of this lovely hair of yours." He gathered her into a fierce hug. "*Ti amo molto.* You know that, don't you?"

He was the straightest talker she knew, but there was one thing he had never been able to say. Phil still teased him about it. "Come on, Dad, it's three little syllables. You can do it!"

But the words caught in her dad's throat. His face would flush, his hands would flap in frustration. He could say "I love you" in French or Danish, or Creole or Esperanto. But he couldn't say it in English.

He hailed a passing taxi, and as he opened the door, Lara heard the driver singing along to the radio. George Michael's "Faith." She waited until the taxi had disappeared around the curve of Mount Street, then she let her breath out in a little ragged sob and looked up at the elegant facade of the hospital. The red brick glowed in the afternoon sunshine and the windows were full of sky. She wondered which was the room where she and Michael had been told that Ryan was gone.

Faith was not enough: Lara could have told the taxi driver that. She'd had faith through the three years it took to get pregnant. Through the false alarms and the dashed hopes and the fear that it was never going to happen. Through those first three months of her pregnancy when she was terrified that she would do something wrong. Through the scare at ten weeks, when she'd had spotting.

She'd still had faith the afternoon of her twenty-four-week scan, when the technician's smile had frozen and she switched off the machine.

And even after the doctor had told them that she was sorry, really sorry, but there was no fetal heartbeat, Lara had faith. There must be something wrong with the machine, she'd said. She'd felt Ryan moving that morning. Michael was holding one of Lara's hands and the doctor had taken the other one, and she explained that what Lara had thought was kicking was just a uterine contraction, her body reacting to the loss of her pregnancy. Their baby had been dead for days.

Lara felt then the way she thought people must feel when they realize that the car they are traveling in is about to crash, frozen in the moment between impact and aftermath. Believing even as the car swerves crazily into the path of the oncoming traffic that it can somehow be stopped. She turned to Michael, wanting him to tell her that this could not be happening, but all the color had drained from his face. His mouth above his neatly trimmed dark beard was a thin, shaky line.

She felt as if she was watching herself from a distance as she was admitted to the hospital to be induced. As she had a shower in a tiled communal bathroom, soaping her swollen stomach for the last time. As she lay on a bed in the pre-labor ward hooked up to an IV of Pitocin.

She listened to groans and the restless pacing of the other women on the ward, who were going to deliver live babies. Now she could only remember one of them, a dark-haired girl called Rebecca, very young, very overdue. Sixteen, she heard one of the nurses whisper, unplanned pregnancy, no boyfriend.

Rebecca sobbed all night and Lara was grateful to her for that. She was so stunned by the violence with which her future had been ripped away that she couldn't cry at all. That night, it was as if the girl was crying for both of them.

But in the weeks that followed, all she could do was cry. Everyone said that she would feel better after she went back to work, and she wanted to believe them. But when she finally returned to her office on the top floor of an elegant Georgian house on Leeson Street, Lara felt worse. Everything looked unfamiliar. Her shelves of design books, her framed typography posters, even the weekly work list, written on the whiteboard in her own handwriting. It all belonged to a stranger—the person she had been before she lost her baby. The only things in the room that she felt any connection to were half a dozen flower postcards pinned to the wall above her desk.

The red and white tulip by Judith Leyster. The vase of white lilac by Manet. The bowl of blowsy roses by Henri Fantin-Latour. The vase of tumbling blooms by Brueghel—lilies and tulips, fritillaries and daffodils, carnations and snowdrops, cornflowers and peonies and anemones. Those flowers had all died four hundred years ago, but that first week back at work, they planted a seed in Lara's heart. Flowers had healed her before, when she was the child who had lost her mother. Maybe they would heal her again now that she was a mother who had lost her child.

"Lara, you do realize," Michael had said gently, "that people send flowers to mothers when a baby is born. You'll have to go to maternity wards every other day. You'll have to go back to Holles Street. Have you thought about how hard that will be?" It had been his last attempt to get her to reconsider and the only thing that could have changed her mind, but by the time he said it, it was too late.

She had already resigned. Told her boss, Frank, that afternoon that she was leaving. Blurted it out in a traffic jam on the way home from a meeting because they were friends and because she felt like a fraud taking a brief for an annual report that she was never going to design. He had looked sad and shocked but not surprised.

"When do you want to go?"

"As soon as you can do without me."

He had helped her clear her desk and driven her home. Her things were still in the boxes, lined up in the room that should have been Ryan's nursery.

Lara parked on Holles Street and unloaded the last delivery of the afternoon, a frothy arrangement of white agapanthus and lisianthus with the faintest blush of pink.

Two overdue women in slippers with fleece dressing gowns pulled around their enormous bumps were smoking on the steps of the maternity hospital. "Jesus," one of them said, turning to look at the bouquet as Lara passed, "I'd have to have triplets before me fella gave me a bunch like that."

"I'd have to have the winner of the Grand bloody National," her friend snorted, "and the Cheltenham Gold Cup."

Lara was smiling as she crossed the marble floor of the entrance hall, but her throat tightened as she took the stairs to the third floor, where she had given birth to her own baby on a sunny spring morning sixteen weeks before his due date.

The first time she had delivered a bouquet to this hospital she sat outside for nearly an hour trying to talk herself into getting out of the van. She'd only made it as far as the hall, where she dropped the flowers on the porter's desk and bolted back out. But she'd forced herself to keep coming back until she could bring the bouquets all the way up the stairs to the nurses' stations on the maternity wards.

She had learned to distract herself, to fill her mind so there was no room for the memory of the day she'd walked down these same stairs without her baby. Today, she made a mental list of flowers for next week's order, moving on to foliage as she hurried along the corridor, past the closed doors of the private rooms. She handed the bouquet over to the nurse at the desk, then started back the way she'd come.

"Nurse!" A voice called from behind a closed door as she passed.

Lara looked up and down the corridor. It was empty.

"Please?" The woman sounded frantic. "Could someone help me?"

Lara hesitated, then walked back and opened the door.

A pale, exhausted-looking woman was propped up on the pillows in the bed, a baby in a blue blanket in her arms. "Please!" she gasped, pointing at a stand near the door. "Can you get me that bowl?"

Lara picked up the plastic bowl and crossed the room quickly.

"Can you hold him for a second?" The woman held up the bundle. "I need to be sick."

Lara froze and looked down at the baby. He could not have been more than a few hours old. "I can't," she said. But the woman was already thrusting him into her arms.

Nothing Lara had read in her "what to expect" books had prepared her for the tiny body of her dead son, so small that he fit into her cupped hands. He weighed exactly two hundred and forty-one grams. He was the color of a ripening plum.

She had returned to the hospital and brought Ryan home the night before he was buried. Michael could not bear to look at him but Lara could have looked at him forever. His eyes sealed closed beneath the finely traced eyebrows. The smooth whorls that would have become his ears, the mouth like a puckered flower. She had sat up all night holding him in her arms, learning him by heart.

"It happened for a reason," Michael kept saying. But when Lara asked him what that reason was, he couldn't tell her.

The postmortem showed that their son had died prematurely because of a rare chromosomal problem. The chances of it happening a second time were minimal. The doctor said they could try to get pregnant again whenever they were ready, but a year had gone by, then three, then five, and Lara still felt that having another child would be a betrayal, that they would just be trying to replace Ryan.

Lara braced herself as she took the baby from the woman in the bed. She had not held a baby in her arms since that night she had held Ryan. She waited for the usual tsunami of grief to slam into her, but it didn't come. Instead she was overcome with something that was almost joy. He was small and helpless, but he was so alive. She could feel his warmth through the blanket. He squirmed against her chest and let out a small, scratchy little cry.

The woman finished retching into the basin. "God! Sorry!" She wiped her mouth with a tissue. "He was two weeks overdue. They had to induce me last night. The stuff they gave me was awful." Lara nodded; she remembered it. "I keep getting these waves of nausea, but it's worth it! I still can't believe he's here!" She held out her arms.

Lara handed the baby over, carefully. "Does he have a name?"

"My husband thinks he's a Daniel"—the woman settled the baby gently into the crook of her arm—"but I like Ted."

"Me too!" Lara smiled. "It's my dad's name!"

"Seriously?" The woman looked up at her. The color had come back into her face now. She still looked exhausted, but her eyes were shining with happiness. "It wasn't just a coincidence that you came to our rescue. It was a sign!"

Lara leaned over and touched the baby's cheek. Felt the velvet of his skin beneath her fingertip, softer than the petal of any flower.

She had the strongest feeling that maybe the woman was right. That maybe this was a sign for her too. She was forty, but it wasn't too late to try for another child. There was still time.

PANSY

Remembrance and Unfading Love.

He opens his eyes again and she is still there, between the sink and the bin with the biohazard sticker on it. He blinks at her in amazement. "Jesus, what are you doing here?"

"Nice to see you too." She laughs and peels off her leather gloves, undoes the belt of her red coat. Her shoes are high, he sees, and her legs are bare. "I heard your wife died." She stuffs the gloves into her pocket.

"You must be pretty hard of hearing." Ted tries to sit up. "She died a long time ago, love."

She shrugs the coat off. The dress is black velvet with a deep V neckline. He has to force himself to keep his eyes on her face. "But you're still wearing a wedding ring," she says.

He glances down at his hand, sees the new bruise that has seeped out around the needle of the morphine pump they inserted this morning. Is he just imagining it, or is the ring looser on his finger?

She whooshes herself up on the windowsill, her elbow brushing against the flowers his daughter brought yesterday, or was it the day before? "Avalanche roses." She picks up a fallen petal, puts it into the palm of one hand, presses her nose to her palm for a moment. "My favorites."

"What are you doing here?" he asks her again.

She shrugs. "I was just, you know, in the area." She looks around, the pale arch of one eyebrow rising as she takes in the tangle of wires that sprout from beneath the bedcovers, the metal drip stand, the oxygen tank. "More to the point, what are *you* doing here?" Her eyes arrive back on his face. She shakes her head. "You don't look too good."

"You look . . ." He tries to find a word that can contain it all. The treacle and chestnut of her hair. The creamy triangle of skin above the velvet neckline of her dress. The sheen on her long pale legs. The word that swims to the surface of his consciousness is "ravishing." But instead he says, ". . . just the same."

Three sudden stabs of pain pass through his chest cavity like laser beams. He gasps and presses the pump. The morphine bails the pain out of him as if it is water and his body is a sinking boat. After half a minute, he can breathe normally again.

"How bad is it?" she asks softly.

"How bad is it when the love of your life walks in looking like sex on legs and you're wearing a hospital gown your ass is falling out of that has little ribbon ties up the back?" he replies. "Pretty bad."

He catches the shadow of a smile as she turns to look out the window. Behind her he can see the blurry green haze of the golf course. A minute ago, this was his idea of torture. To know that it was only a hundred yards away. The springy, rain-drenched grass, the buffeting wind, the line of sight from the sixth hole down past the elms to the velvety green. But the real torture is to have to lie here, trussed up like a turkey, tethered to the bed by the catheter and the oxygen line and the drip, too weak to stretch a hand across and touch her. He finds the pump button with his thumb and presses again.

She turns back at the bleep, lifts a hand to her mouth, nibbles the skin at the side of her thumb. "Anything I can do?"

"Yeah," he says. "Come to bed."

"You and your one-track mind," she says. Then, to his amazement, she slides down off the windowsill and walks over to him. She kicks off her shoes and clears a space between the lines and the tubes and lies down beside him, propped up on one elbow, her face just inches from his.

He can see the curve of her breast beneath the velvet. Her bare left arm with the wishbone scar left by the metal pin that held her wrist together where she broke it. "Your breath smells like a hundred-year-old turnip," she says.

"It tastes like one too."

"Let's see." She presses her warm, soft, wet mouth against his dry, cracked lips for a long time. "It's not so bad," she says softly. Then she whispers, "*Te dua*."

He knows it means "I love you," but is it Turkish, or Armenian or Albanian?

A Spanish "*Te quiero*" is all he can dredge up in reply. He lets his head drop and presses his face into her neck. He can feel her warmth, the buzz of her blood beneath her skin, but he can't find her scent. The hospital smell is too overpowering.

He lets her name rise up his throat and come into his mouth. How long is it since he has said it out loud? Three syllables. "Mar-ga-ret."

When he opens his eyes again, she's gone and so are the roses. There is a vase of anemones on the windowsill now. Purples and whites and dark pinks. His daughter is sitting in the uncomfortable orange plastic chair by the bed, reading a book.

"Lara, what happened to the roses?" His voice is a croak.

"I changed them on Tuesday when I was in with Phil, remember?"

Desperation. He tries to sit up. What day is it now? How long since Margaret was here?

"Dad?" Lara looks alarmed. "Will I call a nurse? Do you need something?"

His body concertinas back down onto the pillows but doesn't fall into place right. It feels like a piece of origami that has been folded badly along the wrong creases. "Just some water!" he croaks.

She holds the glass, the rim cool and hard against his trembling mouth.

His beautiful daughter has lavender-colored circles beneath her sherry-brown eyes and they are his fault. The poor child has been running around looking after him for how long? Weeks? Months? But his daughter is not a child, he realizes with a sudden jolt. She is two years older than Margaret.

"You should go home now," he tells her. "Get some rest."

She pulls her chair closer. "Dad, I only just got here. I want to spend some time with you."

She holds the hand without the cannula in it and tells him about her day, a tangle of words from which he tries to unpick meaning. A woman who hugged her when she delivered a bouquet of flowers. A man who wanted her to tie a five-thousand-euro engagement ring around the stem of a white rose. A couple who were getting married in June but who wanted daffodils and tulips for their wedding.

There is silence, and he finds a question to slip into it and fill it. "How's the garden?"

"It's good. It's been hot so I'm watering it every day. I'll do some weeding at the weekend."

"Let Michael do it," he says.

"He's . . ." Her thumb running backward and forward over the gold band on her finger for a few seconds—he sees it. "He's busy. I can do it myself."

Something is wrong with what she's saying. A thought catches, tugs at his brain, a fish on the line, but then pain roars through him and it takes all his strength to keep it out of his face, and when it is gone, it has taken the thought with it.

A nurse with red hair and breath that smells of cigarettes tucks a towel under his chin, squirts shaving foam onto her palm, rubs lather on his face.

She has already washed him and helped him into the new pajamas he asked Phil to bring. He wants to look good when Margaret comes again. He feels an ache beneath the ache in his chest: she will come again, won't she?

The nurse holds his head gently to steady it while she shaves his chin. He can feel kindness in the tips of her fingers. Cancer has given him a hypersensitivity to compassion in other people.

He remembers the consultant who gave him the news after the first tests. He had been putting up with the cough for months. He had only gone for the scan to please Lara. The man, a boy really, only a few years older than Phil, was nervous. He wanted to look away, who wouldn't? But instead he held eye contact, kept his gaze on Ted's eyes, like a hand steadying his shoulder, while he explained that the prognosis was not good.

Ted thanked him, then left the hospital and drove to Bullock Harbour. It was a stormy day in early April, the sea heaving under a sky of fast-moving gray clouds. Seagulls rode the wind above the tossing waves. The smaller boats with their scuffed and peeling hulls had been pulled out of the water. A few lads were fishing off the end of the jetty. The air smelled of rotting fish and tar. Ted closed his eyes and took huge lungfuls of it. How could he be dying? He had never felt so alive in his life.

If he was lucky, he might get to see Rory McIlroy give the U.S. Open another shot in June. Might. Possibly. But he almost certainly wouldn't see Dublin qualify for the All-Ireland in August.

He would have liked to see Leonard Cohen again, he thought, to watch the white stars of his little *Magnolia stellata* bloom one last time, to be there when—if—his bloody son ever found a girl he wanted to be with for more than a fortnight, to see his daughter holding a son or a daughter of her own.

The nurse holds up a mirror. His cheeks are sunken and his forehead seems to extend to the crown of his head, where a few pathetic wisps of hair still cling. His collarbone protrudes through his mottled skin like a coat hanger. He starts to laugh, though he's not supposed to. Laughing makes him breathless. Margaret was right. He looks awful. He looks like Gollum.

The morphine pump chirps and the pain liquefies. He remembers the sun on his neck on a beltingly hot Sunday morning. Walking hand in hand with Margaret down Sir John Rogerson's Quay. The eggy smell of the river at low tide as they crossed the bridge. How old was she then? Twenty-one? Twenty-two? She had wanted to go to Bray, to the sea, that morning, but so had half of Dublin.

The train was still on the platform at Tara Street but the doors were closed. When Margaret went up to the office to ask about the next one, the stationmaster took one look at her and added an extra carriage to the train. That's how beautiful she was. Is.

She is thirty-eight and he is seventy-one. How is this supposed to work? A summer shower outside the window. Beyond the clang and rattle of the approaching lunch trolley outside his door, he can hear the drops whisper against the glass. He imagines breaking out of this overheated room, pulling out the wires and the tubes, striding along the corridor, taking the stairs in twos and walking out into the parking lot, turning his face up so a curtain of cool rain closes over his face.

When he opens his eyes, Margaret is back floating at the corner of his vision near the window, looking at a framed photograph of Lara and Phil.

"You were snoring," she says.

A short, round woman in a blue overall that looks about to pop pokes her head around the door. "Knock! Knock!"

Ted wants her to go, wants to be alone with Margaret, but he knows he has to play this stupid game. "Who's there?"

"Boo."

"Boo who?"

"Cheer up!" The woman grins. "It's corned beef and cabbage today!"

He shakes his head. The door closes. Margaret sits on the end of the bed giving him a quizzical look. Drops of rain sparkle in her hair. She is wearing the same red coat. "Aren't you hungry?"

His appetite dwindled away the last few weeks before he came into the hospital. The morphine killed the last of it. Now he remembers a salad he shared with her at a beachside restaurant in Italy. He can almost taste the feathery green spears of rocket, the juicy pink shreds of Parma ham, the two ripe figs halved, the salty Parmesan shavings. He can see the cracked blue Formica table, the cheap, battered cutlery, the sooty red wine in the chipped tumblers. He can hear the music of Italian being spoken all around them.

Margaret leans over and picks up the photograph. The children, taken a few Christmases ago. Lara in an elegant green dress with her hair up in a bun, smiling her serene smile. Phil in his bike leathers with reindeer antlers planted on his rumpled black hair, his chin tilted back, caught in mid-laugh.

"Tell me about them," Margaret says.

"Lara's the sorted one. She's been with Michael for ten years now, married for eight. She runs a flower shop."

"A flower shop? I thought she was a graphic designer."

"She was"—he feels his throat tighten with sadness—"but she lost a baby. He died when she was six months pregnant." He has to swallow before he can say his name. "Ryan."

"She was going to call him Ryan?" Margaret's eyes widen.

He has to look away. "I thought she'd never recover, to be honest. But the shop has been great for her. All those people and all those flowers." Lara always loved flowers. Was always at his elbow in the garden, soaking up the Latin names for plants like a thirsty plant herself. "It's that little place on Camden Street, you can't miss it. It's painted bloody pink. Blossom & Grow."

"That rings a bell." Margaret smiles down at the photograph for a long moment. "She's lovely," she says.

Lara's dark hair is as long as it was when she was a little girl, long enough to sit on. She still has the bony-shouldered gymnast's body she had back then and the same watchful kindness in her dark eyes. Only her hands show her age, the skin dry and flaking from so much time in cold water, her fingers permanently nicked from thorns.

"What about him?" Margaret touches the glass over Phil's face with a fingertip.

"Don't talk to me about that fella. I put him through college. You know what he did with his degree? Pulled a bloody rickshaw. He's a motorbike courier now. With an IQ of a hundred and forty-five."

"He looks happy."

Phil was born happy. A C-section. He was pulled out of his mother's belly like a rabbit out of a hat. The first thing he did was pee all over the pompous obstetrician, and when the nurse handed him to his father to hold, he was smiling. Ted half expected him to wink.

"Is he married too?" Margaret asks.

"Are you joking?" Ted snorts. "He's had a string of girlfriends. It was like bloody Miss World at home till he moved out. A herd of leggy beauties trampling up and down the stairs, but he won't settle. He's twenty-bloody-seven. I don't know what he's waiting for."

Margaret puts the photograph back and swings her legs up onto the bed. She moves the oxygen tube out of the way and tucks her head into the space between his chin and his shoulder. "Don't you?" she asks.

And suddenly, he does. This is what his son is waiting for, the feeling of fitting perfectly against another person, like the parts of a two-piece jigsaw puzzle.

He turns his face so he can press his lips against the crown of her head. "*Miluji tě,*" he whispers.

"*Miluji tě* too!" She rubs her nose against a patch of stubble on his Adam's apple. "You missed a bit. But I like the aftershave."

"It's for you."

"What's for me, Dad?"

He opens his mouth and pain slams into his chest like a juggernaut. He claws for the morphine pump, and by the time he can breathe again, he is too worn out to speak.

"Look." Lara holds a bunch of small flowers close to his face. His cheek touches the damp velvet of something that smells of the garden and rain. Pansies. The name comes from a French verb. To something, he thinks, but to what?

Margaret used to press pansies. He'd pick up a book, years after she'd gone, and the wafer of a dried flower would slip out and slice open the scar she'd left like a scalpel. He feels for the pump again.

"Dad?" He hears his daughter's voice from a long way off. She sounds frightened.

"Gone to sleep again," his son says teasingly. "Lazy bugger!" His voice softens. "But you look like you haven't slept for a week. Come on. Let me buy you a hospital canteen-achino, a.k.a. the world's worst coffee. We'll let him rest and come back later."

Do what your brother says, Ted thinks. Lara puts her hand over his and he squeezes her fingers. Something is wrong with her hand—what is it? He can't quite figure it out and is losing his train of thought, then suddenly it comes back and he knows. His daughter is not wearing her wedding ring. Maybe she took it off to wash her hands, he thinks. But no. He remembers her telling him she had it resized so it wouldn't slip off in water. She never takes it off.

He tries to remember the last time he saw his son-in-law, his mind stumbling back through the fog of days and weeks. It's June now, isn't it? Or is it still May? It must have been April, because he was still having chemo. Could it really be that long ago?

Lara was working so Michael drove him to the hospital for his appointment and he decided to have the conversation, the one that he, who had never been afraid to call a spade a spade, had been tiptoeing around for five years. Even then, when time was running out and the drugs had about as much chance of winning the battle against the cancer as Watford had of beating Chelsea, he found himself putting it off till he was settled into the leather armchair in the crowded day ward with the catheter leaking poison into his arm.

His son-in-law was hovering beside him. He was a hoverer, Michael. Always trying to slip into the background. "I'll go and get you a paper."

"Wait!" Ted said, too quickly, too sharply. "There's something I have to ask you." Michael looked uneasy. He was shy to the point of reclusive, a man who'd be happier digging over your entire garden than having a conversation with you.

"Man to man"—Ted lowered his voice—"is there a problem with you and Lara?"

Michael's eyes almost popped out of his head. "A problem? No! What do you mean, a problem?" He said it the way you might say, "Well, of course there is, any fool can see that."

"I mean that if you two can't have children, you know, the normal way, well, there are, you know, other options. IVF. Surrogacy. Adoption." Suddenly it felt good to be talking about a new life here surrounded by all the bald heads and gray faces, the lives hanging as precariously as the trembling silver drops in the IV bag over Ted's own bald head.

"No, there's no physical problem"—his son-in-law flushed—"as such." He was twitching like a mackerel on the end of a line but Ted could not let him off the hook: this was too important.

"Good. I'm glad to hear it. Look, I know the two of you will never get over losing Ryan, but that shouldn't stop you trying for another baby. Life is short, Michael, and time is moving on."

Michael's phone rang and a nurse came over to tell him to take his call outside. He mumbled something and hurried, well, fled really, out into the corridor. Ted watched the door swing behind him and it crossed his mind, like a flash, that there was a problem, a real problem between Michael and Lara. Something that had nothing to do with losing Ryan or having another baby.

His life is like a leaf caught in the bare branches of his bones. Pain is trying to shake it free but he can't let it. He can't die, not now, not if Lara's marriage is in trouble. He has to hang on somehow to look after her.

Margaret is there again, a red blur that won't settle. Why is she wearing that coat? It's summer outside and it must be nearly eighty degrees in here. He puts off pressing the pump despite the pain, waits till he can squeeze the room into focus. She is flicking through the crooked line of Get Well cards on the windowsill.

"There's an untapped market out there for Get Worse cards," she says drily. "Stuff the Hallmark crap. Say it like it really is."

Something stinks. His nose traces the stench to a bedpan covered with a sheet of paper towel on the metal trolley by the sink. A nurse was called away earlier and forgot to come back for it. The smell of shit and the shame of it are too much.

Margaret turns when the pump beeps. "You should be careful with that stuff."

"Jesus Christ! Give me a break, will you? I've got inoperable lung cancer. I've got secondaries in parts of my body I didn't know existed until a few months ago. And my daughter's marriage might be on the rocks."

"A wise man told me once"—her eyes are mocking beneath her fringe—"that if you get into bed with self-pity, you're the one who ends up getting screwed."

"Fucked." His voice is sharp. "I said fucked, not screwed. And I'm not sorry for myself. I'm sorry for Lara."

He was wrong before. Phil is the sorted one, not Lara. A mother dying at any age is difficult for a girl, but he can't think of a worse time then twelve years old, when she needs her mother most. He did his best. He turned away from his own grief and poured his love and support into her. He was her protector till Michael came along, and now she might need him again.

"I can't die," he says quietly.

"Oh come on!" Margaret laughs softly. "She'll survive without you. That's what children are designed to do, you know."

He wants to storm out of the room the way he used to back when they rowed, because they did row sometimes. But he doesn't even have the strength to put his hands over his ears to shut out what she says next.

"Get over yourself." She shakes her head. "You're going to be pushing up the daisies pretty soon. Wallowing in self-pity and pickling yourself in morphine isn't going to change that."

"Get out!" He tries to shout but his voice comes out as a faint whisper. "What are you even doing here?"

"You tell me." She walks to the door, tall and slender and beautiful and alive. So alive that it hurts to look at her and he has to find the pump, press it with his thumb.

He hears her voice as he drifts away on the sea of morphine; she is mocking him. "Aren't you going to say 'I love you' in Swahili or Urdu, Ted?" A pause. "Aren't you going to say good-bye?"

He never could say it, not while Margaret was dying, not even after she was dead. He tried. He stayed in the small room where she had spent the last four weeks of her life. He sat beside her until it got dark outside, until her hand was stiff and cold as a windowpane on a frosty morning. From time to time one of the hospital staff came along and tried to reason with him, but he would not be separated from his wife. The lights in the ward went off and still he sat there. He told her he loved her over and over, in Dutch and Danish and Polish and French and Thai. But he couldn't say good-bye.

Margaret was buried on the tenth of January in the red coat he had bought her for Christmas, the one she would have loved and had never got to wear. He wanted her to be warm in the afterlife, which he knew made absolutely no sense. There were other things that made no sense. He kept on buying her flowers. That first Friday after the funeral, he drove into town and walked down from St. Stephen's Green to the stall on Grafton Street. He only meant to look, but before he could stop himself, he had bought a bunch of white roses.

He drove across the city to the graveyard. He wanted to rip the petals off and scatter them on the ugly mound of dirt. No. He wanted to claw through the dirt and climb in beside her. But he had to make a choice right then, before it was too late. Grief for his wife or love for his children? Which was it going to be? The living or the dead? He started the engine. He drove home. He gave the roses to Lara. He chose love.

"Your wife's a lucky bird," the old man who ran the stall used to say, handing over a bunch of roses or gerbera or freesias. Ted didn't have the heart to tell him that his wife had not been lucky and the flowers were his way of trying to heal his daughter.

The morphine is still humming through him but the pump has gone, he guesses because he is too weak to press it. The IV is gone too. This is a kind of euthanasia, though that is not what they call it. He is dying, like a forgotten plant might on a windowsill, of dehydration. Everything is closing and fading, the edges blurring. His legs, which haven't moved for weeks, are now restless; his hand, free of the IV line, shoots out and knocks the photograph off the bedside table. He dreams of bringing a frosted glass of wine to his lips, a tumbler of cold water, but he would settle for a drop licked from the tap over the basin.

Someone moistens his puckered lips with a cotton swab and he swims through the whirling darkness up to the surface. A gurney squeals outside the door and he hears himself moan over the boom of his heart, then he hears his son's voice.

"Dad, it's okay. I'm here."

"Lara," he manages to say through his parched mouth.

"She'll be in later."

He concentrates his whole being into the three words. "Michael. Splitting up."

"She told you he left?"

No, Ted thinks, you just did, you Muppet. He opens his eyes, or maybe he just imagines that he does. Because there, instead of his grown-up son, is the five-year-old Phil in yellow Peter Rabbit pajamas, with Rory, the grubby stuffed lion he used to carry everywhere, tucked under his arm. Ted used to have to wash Rory in the middle of the night, then tumble dry him and put him back in bed beside Phil before he woke up.

Phil stands on tiptoe to put the cotton swab into a dish on the table and takes Ted's hand. He is not smiling. His dark eyes are serious beneath his jagged fringe. "Listen to me, Dad," the child Phil says in Phil's adult voice. "You don't have to worry. I'll look after her, I promise."

Margaret is wearing a hospital gown. She lifts the ends and does a twirl. He sees a flash of her bare bum in the gaps between the ties at the back as she spins.

He can't move. Can't speak now. But his mind, for once, is clear. She's not here, he tells himself. I'm just imagining her.

She cocks one eyebrow and marches over to the bed. Taking his hand, she slides it up under the cotton gown and presses it against her belly. "Are you imagining this?" The tips of his numb fingertips brush inch by inch along the raised seam of a Caesarean scar.

Why did you have to die of a stroke? he thinks when she is lying next to him. Do you have any idea how often I've had to hear that word? *Diff'rent Strokes*. Golf strokes. The backstroke. Stroke of genius. Strokestown.

"I'm so sorry," she sighs theatrically. "I should have died of something much more exotic. Like trypanosomiasis or Chediak-Higashi syndrome." There's a pause. "Yes," she says, "I can hear it when you laugh inside."

He laughs again in his mind when he is telling her about five-year-old Phil's solemn promise to look after Lara.

She shrugs. "What's so funny? He's been doing it for years."

The penny drops. He thinks of Phil, at two, in the months after Margaret was gone, plodding up the stairs one at a time to hammer on the locked door of his sister's bedroom.

"Kitoons!" he'd demand. "Kitoons!" and he wouldn't budge till Lara had dried her tears and come out and brought him downstairs to watch *Scooby Doo* or *ThunderCats*.

He remembers Phil as a teenager standing thigh-deep beside him in some river for whole afternoons, handing the rod to him when he got a bite because the sight of the hook caught in the mouth of a trout made him woozy.

Phil last summer, traipsing around the golf course in his head-to-foot bike leathers, insisting on playing eighteen holes though he couldn't care less about his handicap. It was just an excuse to spend time with his dad.

All those years when Ted and Lara thought they were looking after Phil, Phil was looking after them.

Do you remember how much Lara wanted us to have another baby? he thinks. Jesus! All those wishes on rainbows and bloody stars! Do you remember how hard we had to try to grant them come true?

Margaret laughs, a ripple that washes over him like cool water. "Oh yes," she says. "We had fun trying, though, didn't we?"

And he does not have many moments left, but he would give all of them to be back in their creaky divan bed on one of those Saturday mornings when they tried. The door closed, the curtains drawn, their daughter safely planted in front of a video downstairs. He would, he thinks, give anything, everything, to be thirty-eight again and making love to his wife.

"Shut up," Margaret says, "or you'll make me cry."

What was the name of the imaginary baby Lara had? he thinks. The one who slept in her top drawer till she was ten? Daisy? Poppy?

"Lily," Margaret says.

She disappeared overnight, he thinks, when Phil came along.

"She'll be back," Margaret says lightly. "Lily. She's just waiting for the right moment."

Like you, he thinks.

"Like me."

Margaret is still there when it gets light and the nurse comes to open the curtains. The nurse straightens his pillows and wraps a blood pressure cuff around his limp arm and clips a thermometer to his ear. She taps his arm gently until she finds a vein and slides a needle in, and the morphine fog rolls in, but still Margaret stays and the dark behind his eyes blooms with velvety pansies.

Where does it come from? he thinks. The word "pansy"? I can't remember.

"It comes from the French verb *'penser,'*" Margaret says. "To think."

Margaret, are you really here? Or am I just imagining you? There is a long pause. Margaret?

"Does it matter?" she whispers.

"He said Mum's name," Lara says. "At four o'clock. He tried to sit up and he said 'Margaret.'"

"Jesus," Phil says softly. "He's still in there." His voice is thick with tears. "He's a fighter."

Ted hears the sleeve of his son's leather jacket creak as he puts his arms around his sister. They are both crying. He wants to cry too, but there is no water left in his body.

Love doesn't break your heart, he thinks, but dying crushes it. Flattens it with an iron fist until every last drop of love has been squeezed out.

"Remember my nicknames for them?" Margaret whispers.

"Blossom" for Lara, because she was delicate and pretty as a cherry flower. "Grow" for Phil, who was like a beanstalk.

I read somewhere, he thinks, that your life flashing before your eyes is just a medical phenomenon. That when your organs start to shut down, your brain just cycles through everything that's ever happened, looking for something it knows might save you.

"Save you for what?" Margaret asks. "Haven't you had enough of this, Ted? Aren't you ready to go yet?"

She has a point.

The flashes come not in a rush but slowly, like the fireworks they saw once on a long-ago holiday in France. They bloom, like flowers, in the velvety darkness.

Fragments Ted had forgotten. Lara, at seven, swinging upside down from monkey bars in St. Stephen's Green, her hair so long it swept the ground. Coming downstairs one morning to find Phil, about four, sitting in a shaft of sunlight, his spoon of cereal on hold halfway to his mouth while he sang "Twinkle, Twinkle, Little Star" to himself.

A deserted beach they found on their honeymoon in Crete, after a long, hot, dusty trek down a steep gorge. Margaret yelping with delight when they finally saw the glittering mirage of the sea ahead of them. Tearing off her boots, her socks, her shorts and knickers, her T-shirt and bra and running naked over the hot sand to dive into the water.

"Come on!" she yelled.

Ted looked around. There were some goats perched on the steep red cliff watching them, but they were the only people on the vast stretch of rock-scattered shingle. They were Adam and Eve and it was the beginning of their marriage, the beginning of the world.

His son has gone. Gone to the canteen for a bottle of water. Gone forever. Ted heard the door swing closed as he left.

His daughter is sitting by the bed holding his hand. She thinks they are alone. Behind the dark of his eyelids he looks into Margaret's face. She has been swimming. Her hair is wet; there is a speck of sand between two eyelashes.

I don't know how to do this, he thinks.

"You don't have to do anything," she says. "Just follow me."

He summons the final glimmer of his life force and squeezes Lara's hand one last time. He feels her fingers curl around his and her say, from a long way off. "*Ti amo*, Dad."

He holds her voice in his ear so that he won't forget it, then he lets go of her hand and follows his wife into the sea.

DELPHINIUM

Comfort and Healing.

The old lady was wearing zip-up sheepskin booties and what looked suspiciously like a real fur coat. In June. She sighed and turned the card carousel again. It squealed like chalk on a blackboard. Ciara winced and closed her eyes. When she opened them again, she had lost her place in the online order form. How many peonies for next Saturday's wedding? She flicked back through the order book, looking for her scribbled notes. The carousel squealed again.

"Can I help you?" Ciara said rudely. In her defense, it was the third time she had asked.

"Speak up!" The woman pointed at the hearing aid that protruded from one ear.

"Can I help you?" Ciara shouted.

"No! I'm waiting for the other girl, the dark-haired one."

Nobody over the age of twelve years old could still be called a girl. "The other *woman*," Ciara said pointedly, "is not here."

"I'll wait."

"She's not coming in today."

"Oh." The woman looked annoyed. "Is she sick?"

Ciara shook her head and gazed at the jumble of tick-boxes on her screen. Zinnias: color, quantity, degree of opening. She was tired of customers asking questions she couldn't answer. Tired of being reminded a dozen times a day that she was no substitute for her boss. Ciara was good with bouquets and boutonnieres and corporate arrangements but was bad with people. She didn't have Lara's uncanny ability to hear all the things they didn't say as well as the things they did, and to somehow translate their unspoken feelings into flower arrangements.

The old woman stopped turning the carousel and tapped the back of Ciara's screen. "Is she on holiday then?"

"No." Ciara closed the laptop, almost grateful to this annoying woman for saving her from the weekly order. Lara could get it done in half an hour, but Ciara had been tinkering with it all day. Adding and subtracting flowers, dithering over colors, changing the quantities. She hadn't conditioned this morning's flowers or checked last night's orders, and the water in the buckets hadn't been changed since the day before yesterday.

"Look," she said, "I'm a trained florist. If you just tell me what you want I'll—"

"What I want," the woman said petulantly, "is to know when the other *girl* is coming back."

Ciara wanted to know too. Lara had thrown herself into her work after her dad was diagnosed with cancer in April. She had plowed on after Michael had left her. She had worked through the awful weeks of her father's illness—helping customers, taking orders, making deliveries. She had insisted on doing all the flowers for a wedding the week her poor dad had died, but she hadn't come back to the shop since the funeral. Not once, and it had now been six weeks. Ciara and Phil were trying to keep everything going, but Blossom & Grow was falling to pieces without her.

"What flower are you today?" Lara's dad used to ask her those first years after her mother was gone. Trying, without prying, to see how she was doing. Sometimes she was a thistle, prickly and defensive. Sometimes a forget-me-not, tiny and blue and invisible. Today she was a dicentra, a heart-shaped red flower drooping on a bowed stem. Raw, exposed, turning itself inside out.

At night she dreamed of her father standing beside her as she watched his coffin going into the ground. Of Michael passing her in the street without knowing her. Then of endlessly losing them both and trying to find them. But waking up to reality was worse. It always took Lara a few seconds to figure out what she was doing sleeping in her father's house, in his room. Then it hit her. Her father was gone. Her marriage was over.

The first shadow had fallen the Monday after she had held the baby in Holles Street. Her dad had a bad cough since Christmas and she had been nagging him to go and have a checkup. Eventually, after a lot of grumbling, he had given in and his GP sent him to the hospital for tests. Lara had been worried enough to put off asking Michael about trying to get pregnant, but not too worried. Her dad had been overdoing it, she thought; he probably just needed a week in bed.

The week after Saint Patrick's Day, he arrived at the shop one evening and asked her to go for dinner. She should have known when he took her to Milano that something was wrong. He liked the cozy snugs of old-fashioned bars and the hushed luxury of expensive restaurants. This was a bright, noisy pizza place with an open kitchen where chefs spun wheels of dough in the air like jugglers.

Her dad barely touched his food. He sipped one Peroni and sat watching her eat her dough balls and salad, then pressed her to have cheesecake.

"Better bring two spoons." She smiled up at the waiter. "He'll end up eating most of mine."

But her dad shook his head when she held her plate out to him. She put her spoon down and stared at him. She had never known him to refuse dessert before. "What's wrong?"

He reached across the table and took her hand. Whatever it was, it was bad. Her dad was the most loving man she knew, but he did not do public displays of affection.

"I got the results back from the hospital, that's all."

Her heart gave a sickening lurch. This was why he'd brought her here, to this clattery, public place, she thought. So that neither of them could get upset.

"No tears." His voice was steady but his blue eyes were pleading with her. "Or I'll do a runner and leave you with the bill, okay?"

"Okay."

His fingers tightened around hers. "It's cancer."

"Cancer," she repeated, as if it was a foreign word she didn't understand.

"Metastatic small cell lung cancer to be exact. A big name for a couple of little tumors."

Behind him, a table of women were laughing and clinking glasses. It seemed odd and awful to Lara that anyone could laugh at a moment like this.

"Oh, Dad," she whispered. "Is it bad?"

"Well, it's stage four, so I suppose it could be better." He was keeping his voice light. He was trying not to upset her, putting her first, the way he always did.

Fear hurtled through her like a freight train, pulling carriages full of terrifying possibilities behind it. Her strong, steady, invincible dad suffering, frightened, vulnerable, even dying. She dug the nails of her free hand into her palm.

"What's the prognosis?" How did she even know that word? she wondered. How was she managing to sound so calm?

"Well, it's straightforward, at least." Her dad's dark eyes slid away toward the kitchen, where a chef was pulling a pizza out of an oven with a long-handled shovel. "It's inoperable. Chemotherapy is an option but I'm not too keen on the idea. I've googled it and the chances of success at this stage are not that great."

"Dad!" Her voice came out too loudly and one of the women at the next table turned to look at her. "Don't do that! The Internet is full of misinformation and worst-case scenarios. What about getting a second opinion?"

He stared down at their hands. His broad and tanned and bunched with veins, hers long and pale, red at the knuckles, the nails short and peeling.

"You know there are no mistakes," he said softly, "only lessons, and some of them are hard ones. And you know me: I'm strong as an ox. But when my time does come"—he swallowed a mouthful of his beer and wiped his mouth and looked into her eyes—"well, let's just say that I'm not going to rage against the dying of the light."

"Listen," she said. "Those doctors don't know you, Dad, they don't know how bullheaded you are."

He tried to look offended, but he had the ghost of a smile. "Me?"

"You're the most stubborn person I know. If anyone can beat cancer, then you can. But you have to promise you'll do the chemo. Please? For me if not for yourself."

He rubbed his gray hair with the flat of his hand until it stood up like cotton candy. "If I was half as stubborn as you say I am, I'd say no."

His eyes locked with hers, and the fear and the sadness that neither of them could give voice to passed between them; and Lara felt love, like a tight fist, clench around her heart. "But you know me too well, Lara. I'd go to Timbuk-bloody-tu for chemo if you wanted me to."

When someone came into the shop, Lara could almost always intuit before they even spoke what feeling they wanted to express. Knew without having to think what flowers to pick to give it voice. But her intuition had not worked when Ryan was dying inside her, or when the cancer was growing in her dad's chest.

"I should have known," she told Michael that night, sitting up beside him in bed, her arms wrapped around her knees, her eyes raw from crying. "Why didn't I know that something was wrong?"

"You did know," he said. "You're the one who made him go to get the tests, remember?"

"But I should have made him go *sooner*."

"Don't be so hard on yourself, Lara," Michael said sadly. "You can't know everything."

At the end of April, after two cycles of chemotherapy, the shadows were gathering. Her dad was going into the hospital for another three-day battery of tests that would reveal whether the cancer had spread.

Lara took the morning off work to drive him in. That April day seemed almost painfully beautiful. Cherry blossom in drifts in the gardens of the redbrick houses of her dad's street in Ranelagh. Heavy green canopies of spring chestnut leaves along Shrewsbury Road. She rolled down the windows so her dad could breathe in the scent of the chestnut blossom. Fear, like a fishbone, stuck in the back of her throat. What if this was the last spring he would ever see?

As they waited for the traffic lights to change so they could turn in to the hospital grounds, her dad turned to look at her and she saw, in the bright spring sunlight, how much the last four weeks had changed him. The skin on his face was too loose for the bones. The white baseball cap he wore at a jaunty angle didn't hide his threadbare eyebrows. The too-bright yellow golf jumper bagged across his thin chest.

"Lara, I need you to do me a favor."

"Anything, Dad."

He exhaled slowly. "Will you think about trying for another baby?"

This was what he wanted—something for her, not for him! He had spent a lifetime putting her and Phil first and he was still doing it, even now.

She had to swallow the lump in her throat before she could answer.

"I have been thinking about it already," she said quietly. Since the day she'd held the newborn baby at the hospital, she thought about it all the time, but she had been too caught up in her dad's illness to do more than think. "I'll talk to Michael this weekend," she said. "I promise."

"Good! Great!" Her dad started to laugh. "Jesus! If I'd known I could get my way like this, I'd have gotten cancer years ago."

"Dad! That's not funny!" But secretly Lara was glad that her dad was laughing, as the lights changed and she turned the car onto the long avenue that led up to the hospital.

"This time next year," she said, "you could be driving me to the maternity hospital."

"I could!" he said, turning away quickly so that she couldn't see his face. "Couldn't I?"

Lara had asked Ciara to open the shop on Saturday and Phil had promised to call into the hospital. She left Michael sleeping and went downstairs to make breakfast. She couldn't remember the last time she'd taken a Saturday morning off to spend with him.

Looking back, it seemed like all they talked about the first three years of their marriage was getting pregnant. And after they lost the baby, it was as if they had run out of things to say.

They still made love, occasionally, but from the very start, the desire for a child had been so strong that it overshadowed their desire for one another. When it was gone, what was left behind felt halfhearted and hollow.

They had put up a wall between them, Lara could see that now. Whatever happened, this morning's conversation would bring them closer.

She put the coffee on to brew, then opened the back door and stepped outside in the flimsy silk nightdress she had not worn since her honeymoon. The small pergola that Michael had built was covered in loops of jasmine, and Lara's flower beds were blazing with color. Blowsy white peonies, dusky purple irises with golden stripes, pale orange poppies with sooty centers. The first tea roses of the year were budding. Elinas, pink petals tipped with crimson, and the ivory Jeanne Moreaus that smelled faintly of lemons. Lara wanted to pick one and put it on the breakfast tray, but Michael hated cut flowers.

She went back inside and began to set the tray. Her mother's blue Venetian glass dish filled with raspberries. Orange juice in a white jug. A honey pot with a wooden dipper.

Sunshine streamed in through the window, warming the terracotta tiles beneath her bare feet. She could not have cut flowers in the house so she had pictures of them instead. Two huge framed Georgia O'Keeffe poppy prints. An apron with a pattern of climbing roses. A wooden clock that Phil had given her with a pendulum in the shape of a red rose.

She broke eggs into a bowl. The second one had a double yolk. If they weren't pregnant within six months, she had decided, they'd try IVF. That would mean a chance of twins. She thought about the havoc, the challenge of juggling two babies and a full-time business, and could not imagine anything lovelier.

She melted butter in a copper pan and cut slices from a crusty loaf. She dipped them in the egg, drizzled them with maple syrup and dropped them into the sizzling butter.

She had craved white bread when she was carrying Ryan, the yeastier the better. She remembered Michael driving to the all-night petrol station at 2 a.m. to buy her yesterday's baguette. Bringing it to her in bed spread thickly with butter.

For the first time in five years, she let herself imagine being pregnant again—the surge of life in her body, the thrill of it. Then she allowed herself to imagine the thing she had not been able to think about since Ryan died. Holding a healthy newborn baby in her arms. A small head tucked beneath her chin, the beat of a tiny heart against her ribs.

"Lara!" She opened her eyes and saw Michael standing in the doorway. She flushed.

"You're up!" he said. He was wearing jeans, an old check shirt, scuffed Caterpillar boots. Lara felt a flutter of desire for him, a winter creature waking up from a long hibernation.

"And you're dressed!" She smiled at him. "I was going to bring you breakfast in bed."

"Oh." He looked surprised.

She could still feel the baby she'd imagined against her heart. She was smiling as she walked over and put her arms around him. Her heart began to race.

He blinked down at her warily.

"I've been thinking," she said softly, "that I'd like us to try for another baby."

She had expected his face to light up, but it clouded over.

"I know we've left it late, but I thought we could give it six months, then if nothing happens we could think about IVF. I can take the money out of the shop."

He wouldn't meet her eyes. "I can't do this to you."

"You're not doing anything to me. It's my own decision." She wished he would look at her. "Look, I fell apart after Ryan, but I promise I'll be okay whatever happens this time. And this is our last chance. I don't think I could stand it if we don't at least try."

He pulled away from her and she saw that the color had drained from his face. He looked as if he might be about to pass out.

She pulled out a chair. "Don't move! I'll get you some water."

He sank into the chair and took the glass she handed him, but he did not drink from it. She crouched down beside him, the nightdress pooling on the tiles around her, and looked up at him.

"I'm sorry, I didn't mean to spring this on you. I've been thinking about it for months. Dad's illness"—she shook her head—"it's kind of put things in perspective for me." She fiddled with a button on Michael's cuff. "I'm not sure whether he's going to get better, and when I drove him to the hospital, he asked me to try again."

"He asked me too." Michael stared down at the glass. "A few weeks ago. I should have told you then." He gave her an anguished look.

"Told me what?" Her heart slowed down to a sickening thud. She hoped he wasn't going to say that it was too late, that they were too old to think about being parents.

"It's not working, Lara," Michael said in a whisper. "This. You and me."

"I know." She put one hand against his cheek. "I just realized that this morning. We've drifted apart, Michael. We shouldn't have let it happen, but we can change that . . ."

"We can't." He shook his head sadly. "I can't."

She stared at him, trying to understand. "What do you mean?"

"I'm sorry!" he said, almost to himself.

"For what?"

He closed his eyes and took a long, shuddering breath. "Lara"—his voice was so faint that she had to lean forward to hear him—"I'm gay."

She wondered for a moment if she was still asleep upstairs. If the whole morning had been a dream that she was about to wake up from. Then the kitchen filled with an earsplitting shriek. For a shocked second she thought the noise was coming from her, then she realized it was the smoke alarm.

She stood up and went to the cooker, turned off the gas and covered the smoking pan with a lid. When she turned around, Michael was on his feet following her, but she shook her head and he stopped where he was. They stood looking at one another across the small kitchen through the wall of noise that shook the air between them.

Michael's face began to crumple as he sat again. She had never seen him cry, not even when they lost Ryan. His lips were moving but she couldn't hear what he was saying, then suddenly the alarm stopped.

"I don't want to hurt you, but I can't stand the lies and the deceit anymore."

"I don't understand," she whispered. "If you're gay, why did you marry me?"

"Because I love you. Because you are the most beautiful, kind person I've ever met. And because I wasn't sure that I *was* gay, not completely.

And I didn't want to be. All I wanted was to be with you. For us to have a life together, a family."

His words flew around her, like shards of something solid that had been blown apart and could not be put back together again.

His eyes were brimming with tears. "We tried so hard for those three years and it just didn't happen. I knew I had to tell you, but then you got pregnant. After Ryan died, I couldn't walk away from you. You were so lost. And when you walked out of Green Sea to start the flower shop, I was afraid it would all come crashing down around you. I had to stay, I had to look after you."

Lara wrapped her arms around her chest as if she could hold on to the baby she had imagined a few minutes ago. "We could still try. And if it happened, we could stay together, bring a child up together as friends."

"There's something else, Lara." Michael put his hand over his eyes as if he couldn't bear to look at her. "Someone else."

Even as she waited for him to speak, she knew who it was.

"It's Glen." Glen, who had befriended Lara, brought her croissants and coffee, complained that there were no eligible men in Dublin.

"Nothing has happened between us—I swear I would never betray you like that—but it's made me realize that I can't give you what you need."

It came back, then, what Michael had kept saying after Ryan had died. That it had happened for a reason. Now Lara knew what that reason was. Michael had never wanted Ryan in the first place, not really. Having a child might have stopped him from leaving her. She turned away. "I have to go."

"Where?"

"To the hospital. To the shop. I don't know. I'll pack some things."

"If one of us is moving out, it should be me!" Michael stood up.

"No!" She could not bear to be left in the house they had poured so much love into. It was like their marriage, a beautiful, carefully constructed lie.

Somehow she managed to climb the stairs to the bedroom. She pulled off the nightdress and hauled on a long jersey skirt, a T-shirt, a cardigan, socks, her leather boots. She filled a carry-on case. Michael was waiting in the hall when she came downstairs. He made as if to put his arms around her, but she shook her head and he stepped back.

"Where will you go?" His face was chalky, his eyes were red-rimmed.

"I'll go to Dad's. He'll be in the hospital till Tuesday."

But her dad didn't come out of the hospital on Tuesday. The cancer had spread. He had less than a month to live.

Lara pushed Michael out of her mind. She spent every hour she could at the hospital and all the hours she couldn't at Blossom & Grow, using work like a drug to manage the pain. Phil came to stay with her at their dad's house, both of them sleeping in their old childhood bedrooms, making a circle of their father's life, the end like the beginning.

She had never told her dad that her marriage was over. She had kept her wedding ring in her purse and slipped it on when she walked from the parking lot into the hospital.

"You have to tell him," Phil said one evening when they were sitting in the coffee shop with cups of vending-machine mushroom soup in front of them. Lara was pressing little crescent moon shapes into the lip of her plastic cup with her thumbnail.

"He thinks we're trying for another baby," she said quietly. "If I tell him the truth, it'll break his heart."

Phil reached across, moved her cup, took her hand and pressed it between his the way she'd taught him when he was small; made what they used to call a "hand sandwich." "You have to tell him anyway. Before it's too late."

"I'll think about it," she said.

But it was already too late. By then, their dad was slipping in and out of something that was darker, deeper than sleep.

So Lara told him lies instead. She told him she'd been mowing the lawn and weeding the beds but that she'd leave the pruning for him to do when he got better. She told him that Michael was as excited about trying for another baby as she was.

She read him the P. G. Wodehouse stories he'd read to her when she was a little girl, pages he had turned over thirty years ago. When he seemed too far gone to hear her, she held his hand and told him that she loved him in every language she could think of.

She held his hand all day that last day, pressed pansies between their palms as if she could keep him there, tethered to the world with her fingers and her flowers.

Ciara was cashing up when Phil came into Blossom & Grow. Her head was bent over the book, her blonde fringe falling into her eyes.

"Hi," he said as he tucked his leather gauntlets under his arm and took off his helmet.

"Sssh!" She held up one hand. "I'm adding something up."

Ciara could add two figures together a dozen times and get thirteen different answers, so Phil stopped where he was, halfway between the door and the counter. He glanced around, waiting for her to finish. Buckets jumbled together without any eye for color. A fine layer of dust on the leaves of the orchids. Two bulbs blown in the low chandelier. Not a single lantern lit.

He had a feeling that even if they spent the whole evening sweeping and cleaning and rearranging, the shop would still look like shit. He wouldn't dream of saying it out loud, but it was as if Blossom & Grow was a living thing that could not survive without his sister.

Ciara threw down her pen. "I can't get this right. Can you give it a go?"

"Having a good day?" he asked drily.

"Fabulous," Ciara snorted. "I managed to piss off the wildflower man. A woman who rang up to order a sixty-euro bouquet canceled when she found that Lara wasn't here to make it up. Oh! And I made a little girl cry."

"How did you do that?"

"The way I upset most of the regulars." Ciara rolled her heavily mascaraed eyes. "By not being your sister. It was that little red-haired girl, Zoe, who comes in Saturdays with her dad. I forgot to put out the vase of free flowers this morning. I tried to give her a bloody African daisy but she didn't want it. Apparently Lara lets her pick her own. She practically drowned in her own tears."

"She'll get over it." Phil put his helmet on the counter.

"Maybe by the time she's twenty. I managed to do the wedding flowers, though. They're in the cold room, and those incredibly fiddly boutonnieres are in the—" Her hand flew to her mouth. "Shit! I put a punnet of cherries in the fridge this morning." She dashed out to the small kitchen with Phil on her heels, but it was too late.

The ethylene from the fruit had already spoiled the edges of the petals on the roses. A hundred euros' worth of flowers ruined. "Sorry," Ciara sighed. "My bad. I'll stay late and make them up again."

"Do we have enough roses?"

"We do, but only because I ordered them twice by mistake." Ciara plucked at her sleeve. She looked as if she might be going to cry. "I can't seem to do anything right."

"Why don't you do these at home?" Phil threw the ruined boutonnieres in the bin. "Have a bit of R and R. A glass of wine with your husband."

"Really?" Her face brightened. "It's Mort's only night off from the bar. I could put them together while we watch a movie." She clumped off upstairs in her high shoes to collect wire and scissors, and Phil went back out into the shop and looked at the order book.

Ciara had stapled the till receipts to the edge of today's page. He didn't have to add them up to see that sales were way down. It was there in the blank lines where phone and email orders should have been listed. Walk-ins and corporate work were keeping the shop going, but two hotels had canceled their regular arrangements since Lara had stopped coming in. He had told Ciara to cut back on stock, but still, looking around, he saw that they would be throwing out far too much again this week.

Ciara reappeared carrying a cardboard box of roses and rolls of wire and ribbon. She had put on lipstick that was an even brighter pink then her cycle helmet. She nodded at the book. "How does it look?"

"Not too bad," he said, trying to keep the worry out of his voice.

"Phil, we're going have to get someone in if Lara doesn't come back soon."

"I know."

"Do you think she will come back?"

"Course she will." He closed the book, hoping that saying it might make it true. He had promised his dad that he'd look after her, but it wasn't easy.

Ciara switched off the chandelier and they started for the door.

"Oh my God!" she hissed, gripping his arm. "It's him."

Phil looked past the tall heads of the lilies in the window and saw the owner of the Camden Deli across the street. He was locking the door. He darted a quick, nervous look over his shoulder and hurried away.

"Little shit!" Ciara said with venom. "He saw your bike and he's sneaking off in case he bumps into you. It's me he should be afraid of. If I wouldn't miss Mort so much, I'd quite happily do ten years for the pleasure of killing him."

"Funny how we always want to hurt the accomplice," Phil sighed, "instead of the betrayer."

"Oh don't worry, I'd kill Michael too." Ciara's eyes glinted in the dark. "How could he do it to her? Marry her knowing he was gay. Waste the best years of her life, then drop that bomb on her the week she found out your dad was dying?"

Phil shook his head. His first reaction had been anger too. He had never been in a fight, not even a schoolyard scrap, but Lara had had to physically stop him getting on his bike and going to confront his brother-in-law. But watching his father die day by day had swept all his rage away. Then grief had tumbled him like a wave, and when he got to his feet again, all he felt was pity. Michael had wasted the best years of his own life too . . .

The street was bright after the cool darkness of the shop. Summer heat rose from the pavement. The air smelled of cut grass, exhaust fumes and pizza. Crowds of drinkers were spilling out of the pub on the corner. Boys in wetsuits were strolling past on their way from swimming in the canal.

"I don't know," Ciara said, still looking across at the café. "If the sweetest, most beautiful, most generous woman on the planet can be dumped for another person, then what hope is there for anyone?" She shivered suddenly, despite the warmth of the sun on her back. It could never happen to me and Mort, she thought. Could it?

Phil held the cardboard box while she unlocked her bike. "Did you suspect anything?" she said, turning to him suddenly. "Did you have any idea that anything was wrong between them?"

"No," Phil said, and he meant it. But after she had cycled away, as he was climbing onto the motorbike, he realized that that wasn't true. Not quite. His parents had been the real thing, he knew that. He had no clear memory of seeing them together, but he could remember what their togetherness had felt like. Lara and Michael had never had anything like that.

"So, what are you thinking?" Lara's therapist, Leo, asked.

Lara stared at the gray rug with the abstract black pattern on the floor and listened to the sound of a washing machine running in another room. This was their fourth session. Lara had cried all the way through the first two when she talked about her dad's death, but when

Leo moved on to the breakup of her marriage, the tears had dried up and so had the words.

She was thinking that there must have been signs with Michael, things that any other woman would have seen. That she was stupid and blind and useless. She shook her head.

"No pressure," Leo said. "Take your time." He looked at the woman in the armchair opposite him. She was wearing a skirt with the hem coming down and a shapeless jumper. Her long dark hair, flecked with gray, was unwashed. Her eyes were wide and glassy. She looked shell-shocked and he didn't blame her. When her husband had redrawn the boundaries of his life, he had redrawn the boundaries of her life too.

"You think you're the only person this has happened to?" he asked. She looked at him, met his eye for the first time in the half hour since she'd arrived. "In the States, there are two million gay or bi men and women married to straight people. I know that right now you feel like you're alone, but you're not. Other people have come through this and so will you." Her dark eyes were skeptical. "You've lost your father, you've lost your husband. You're in shock. You're questioning the nature of reality. But time will change your perspective. You know, someday you might even be able to forgive Michael."

Lara stared at her scuffed boots. It wasn't Michael she needed to forgive; it was herself. For not seeing the truth. For not realizing sooner that he wanted out. For not being brave enough to bring up the subject of having another child after Ryan died. For wasting the years when it might have been possible with someone else. How could she forgive herself for that?

Michael had written to her. There were three letters on the table in the hall in her dad's house, jumbled in with free newspapers and flyers for window cleaners. But reading the letters was one more of the things that Lara could not imagine ever doing. Like sleeping more than three hours straight. Dealing with the sympathy and curiosity of her friends. Going back to work. Facing her customers.

Seeing Phil would have been on that list too, but even though he'd moved back into his own place, he still came over to the house every few days. He brought her groceries she didn't want, cooked her meals she couldn't eat. Insisted, like Leo just had, that she would get through this. Everyone seemed clear about that.

Lara left Leo's with an armful of photocopied sheets. Mood logs to keep, a daily journal to fill out, a list of affirmations to repeat last thing at night and first thing in the morning. She dumped them into a recycling bin by the People's Park in Dún Laoghaire, then stood on the curb of the busy road, without the faintest idea of where to go or what to do next. What was it Leo had said? She was questioning the nature of reality. Well, it was about time, she thought bitterly. She should have grabbed reality by the throat and interrogated it years ago.

Terrible things happened. They could be happening again right now. She had a vivid, terrifying premonition that Phil was going to have a crash. That at this very moment his bike was skidding under the wheels of a juggernaut on the M50. What was the point of loving anyone, she thought, if it was only going to be taken away? Leo had asked her if she had any suicidal thoughts, and she had answered, truthfully, that she hadn't. But now she imagined closing her eyes and stepping out into the road and—

She heard her dad's voice behind her, or thought she did. "Jesus, Lara! Watch where you're going, would you?"

She whipped around, half expecting to see his ghost, but instead she saw Frank, her boss from Green Sea.

He grabbed her arm. "I thought you were going to walk out into the traffic." The cars had stopped and he steered her across the road.

"Where are we going?" she asked.

"I'm taking you to lunch."

"I'm not hungry."

"Well, I am. You can keep me company."

McDonald's was where they'd always gone on the way home from meetings in Naas. They'd pull over at the drive-in on Kylemore

Road and sit in Frank's monstrous Lexus and eat burgers and chips from greasy paper bags, rewarding themselves for getting another piece of decent design over the line.

Lara took a seat at a table by the window with her back to the lunchtime crowd. Knots of office workers and little clusters of mums with preschool babies. Elderly people making a single paper cup of coffee last an hour.

Frank queued at the counter and came back to the table, and when she saw the tray loaded with food, Lara suddenly felt ravenous. They sat in silence, opening paper cartons, ripping open salt and ketchup packets, poking straws into their supersized cardboard cups of Coke. Lara hoped the silence would last. That she could eat and leave without Frank asking her a single question.

He took a gulp of Coke. "So how are you doing?"

She lifted her shoulders and dropped them in an attempt at a shrug. She put two French fries in her mouth and took a bite of her burger so she wouldn't have to speak.

"You must miss him so much."

She stopped chewing. Did he mean her dad or Michael? Did everybody know about Michael now?

"He was an amazing guy, your dad," Frank said, ducking his head to slurp a mouthful of Coke through his straw. "If I can be half the father he was, I'll be doing well."

"How are the girls?" Frank was divorced with two daughters, eight and ten.

"They're going through a bit of a hating-their-old-man phase. But you don't appreciate your parents till they're gone, do you? I certainly didn't. You think of orphans as if they're all little kids from Dickens." He shook his head. "But here we both are, forty-year-old orphans. Except that you have Michael." Lara bent her head so he would not see her face. "I seem destined to become one of those sad old blokes you see eating on their own. Which is the reason why I kidnapped you and dragged you here. Well, one of the reasons."

It was a mystery to Lara, to everyone at Green Sea, that Frank was still single years after his divorce. He was in his early forties now, with a dusting of gray in his blonde hair, carrying a few extra pounds since she'd seen him last. But he was handsome and funny and kind.

He balled up the wrapper from his burger and wiped his hands on a napkin. "I called into Blossom & Grow and talked to what's-her-name, the blonde girl with the raccoon eyes."

"Ciara," Lara said. "They're kohl-rimmed."

"She said you were taking some time out."

Lara poked a fry into a congealing pool of ketchup. "The thing is, I don't know," she said carefully, "if I want to go back at all. I don't know if I can cope with all those people." A flower shop, as Ciara often said, was an emotional revolving door and you never knew what would come through next—love, sadness, guilt, joy. Lara could barely cope with her own feelings. The thought of trying to cope with someone else's was too much to bear.

"What will you do?" Frank asked. "If you don't go back?"

"I don't know."

He let her off the hook. Changed the subject, told her anecdotes about clients, tidbits of scandal from the incestuous design world. Drank her Coke as well as his own.

He had told her once, when he was drunk at an awards ceremony, that she was the most beautiful woman in the room. Maybe, she thought suddenly, crazily, she should have had an affair. If she had been more experienced, she would have known that everything wasn't right with Michael.

"I miss you, Lara," Frank said, then added quickly, "We all do. Green Sea hasn't created a decent corporate identity since you left. If you decide not to carry on with the shop, we'd take you back in a heartbeat."

Go back to design? Lara stared at him.

"Think about it? Will you?"

She nodded. "Okay."

Outside the sky had opened up, high clouds, patches of blue, a stiff breeze coming from the direction of the sea.

"Thanks," Lara said. "For making me have lunch. I was hungry. I just didn't know it."

"My pleasure." He looked at her for a long moment, then leaned over and kissed her quickly on both cheeks. She felt his stubble graze her ear, caught the familiar scent of his aftershave.

"Look both ways this time," he said as she turned to cross the road. "Every time. Promise?"

She nodded. He stood where he was and watched her walking away. She took the narrow road that led to the seafront; the wind lifted her hair, making dark scribbles with it in the air.

And as he watched her go, the warm glow that had spread through Frank's chest in McDonald's began to fade, and by the time she turned the corner, it had gone.

Phil had persuaded his boss to slot him in for the 6 a.m. to 2 p.m. shift so he could spend the afternoons doing deliveries for Blossom & Grow. On Friday morning, he was on his way back from a drop-off in Arklow when the phone in the breast pocket of his leather jacket began to buzz like an angry wasp. He ignored it till the Enniskerry turnoff, then pulled over, kicked down the stand and parked the bike.

"Ciara, I'm on the road."

"It's an emergency." She sounded brittle. "Funeral flowers for one of the regulars. Her son."

"How old?"

"Twelve or thirteen," Ciara said in a bright, hard voice.

"Cancer?"

"A heart condition."

Phil stared unseeing at the litter on the hard shoulder, the beer cans and crisp packets, the sodden newspapers, the discarded teat from a baby's bottle. It was hard enough when your seventy-year-old father died; how would it feel to lose your twelve-year-old kid?

"His mother," Ciara was saying, "the regular, she wants a wreath, a really complicated one, and she wants Lara to do it. She's coming into the shop in an hour. Will you tell Lara that it's Karina?"

She should never have let Phil talk her into this, Lara thought, clinging to her brother's back as the bike ducked and dived between cars on the Ranelagh Road. Fear expanded in her diaphragm like an inflating balloon, but it wasn't Phil's driving that scared her; it was the thought of seeing Blossom & Grow. She tightened her arms around her brother's waist, trying to signal to him to stop the bike, but he didn't notice, or pretended not to. Five minutes later, they were pulling over outside the shop.

She climbed off the bike, pulled off her helmet and looked up at the tall pink building, the fronds of ivy she had painted so carefully, the pale green logo with pink type she had spent weeks perfecting. She felt as if she was looking at a ghost.

It wasn't just the thought of the customers that had kept her away for the last six weeks. She blamed herself for not knowing about her dad's illness and her husband's unhappiness, but she blamed Blossom & Grow too.

The shop had soaked up all her attention and her energy. It had blocked her from feeling the raw pain of losing Ryan, but it had blinded her to the truth of what was going on around her too. And if it weren't for Blossom & Grow, Michael would not have met Glen.

If she turned and looked across the street, she would see the tasteful gray sign above the Camden Deli. She might even see Glen watching her through the window. Maybe Michael was in there too. Maybe they were both looking out at her, pitying her for being such a fool. Why had she let her brother talk her into this? She wanted to ask him to take her home again, but he was already at the door of the shop.

"Come on, Lara," he said, turning to look at her over his shoulder. "We can't keep this poor woman waiting."

Karina was a tiny, elegant, dark-haired woman in her fifties, the owner of a French bistro on Wexford Street. She had been one of Blossom & Grow's first customers. Lara had been nervous and needy back then, so desperate to get her business that she had offered a weekly order of table and reception flowers for only a fraction more than cost price. When she called in with the second delivery, Karina had poured her a cup of coffee and steered her into a chair.

"First rule of business," she had said. "Don't undervalue your product." She had asked her for the wholesale price of the flowers and then insisted on paying a 60 percent markup. She had been a friend and a business mentor to Lara during those first years when she was finding her feet.

Karina had always wanted a child, and when she was in her late thirties and still single, she had a baby with the help of a Californian fertility clinic and a sperm donor she nicknamed "Odin." He was a Viking god, she told Lara, this stranger who had fathered her child. A perfect specimen of manhood according to the information the clinic had given her. Six foot five and blonde, with 20/20 vision. A triathlon winner with a doctorate in engineering.

But Damian had somehow missed his father's genetic longboat. He was small-boned and dark and sallow-skinned, like his mother. He was also dyslexic and, Karina complained, allergic to any activity that involved fresh air. But Lara was sure there wasn't a boy anywhere on the planet who was more loved.

Karina was already in the shop, sitting in the wrought-iron chair under the shelf of orchids, staring into her lap. The anguish in her face was so raw that Lara forgot her own panic. She nodded at Ciara and Phil and they disappeared into the kitchen. She turned and put up the "Closed" sign on the door, then walked over and put her arms around her.

"I don't have the words to tell you how sorry I am," she said softly. Karina pressed her lip between her teeth. Minutes passed before

she could speak. "Everything happened so fast." She inhaled quickly
in three short, sharp breaths. "On Monday morning he said he had a
pain in his back. I thought he was making it up—he had rugby camp,
and you know how much he hates rugby—but I was working and I
made him go." She bent her head and rubbed her forehead hard with
her fingertips. "I should have taken him to the doctor." Her eyes darted
wildly around the shop. "How did I not know that something terrible
was wrong?"

Lara remembered her father's diagnosis. Just because you loved
someone, it didn't mean you could know everything, she thought.

"I got home at seven"—Karina's voice was robotic—"and I was
exhausted and he was still complaining about his back, so I gave him
paracetamol and a plate of lasagna and I plonked him in front of the
TV. All I wanted to do was have a glass of wine and get into the bath.
So that's what I did. At about eight, he knocked on the door, and I
was annoyed. I told him to wait five minutes, to give me a bit of peace."
She made a fist and pushed her knuckles against her mouth. "But he
started to cry. He hasn't cried since he was six or seven, so I knew
something was wrong then. But by the time I came out of the bathroom, he had collapsed. He could hardly breathe and he couldn't speak.
He lost consciousness just before the ambulance came. He died on the
way to the hospital. They tried to bring him back. They did everything
they could, but . . ."

She doubled over; it was a minute before she could speak again.
"When we were still waiting for the paramedics, when he was lying
on the landing, he was staring into my eyes. He was trying to tell me
something, Lara, but he couldn't, and now I'll never know what it was."

Lara's father, too, had looked into her eyes just before he died. He
had been slipping in and out of consciousness for days, but he came
back to be with her, and it felt as if he was with her again now. "Damian
was telling you that he loved you," she wanted to tell Karina, without
knowing where these words came from. "He was saying good-bye."

"It was his heart," Karina said. "They don't know for sure yet but they think he had a tear or a rupture. How is that possible? He wasn't even thirteen. His birthday is on Thursday. He wanted a guitar."

She wiped her eyes with the back of her hand and fumbled in her bag for her phone and showed Lara a photograph of a blue acoustic guitar.

"This is the one he wanted. Can you make it for me, Lara, in flowers?"

"Of course," Lara said, without even thinking. "Is there anything else I can do?"

Karina clenched her jaw. "Can you make me cry? Everyone around me is crying. My bloody parents, who didn't even want me to have Damian. The customers at the restaurant. The fucking undertaker had tears in his eyes this morning." She made a sound that was almost a laugh. A short, sharp bark. "But I can't!" She shook her head hard. "What's wrong with me? Why can't I cry?"

After Karina had gone, Lara stood at the door and remembered the last time she'd seen Damian. He had been in the shop at the beginning of the summer, his inky black hair shaved into a buzz cut, his wrists covered in friendship bracelets. He had been bored, fidgeting with his phone while his mother had dithered between snapdragons and fox-gloves. How was it possible that a boy who had everything to live for would go home to his mother's house in a coffin tomorrow morning?

Tomorrow morning! A wave of panic hit Lara. She had promised Karina that she would deliver the guitar wreath first thing. How was she going to do that? What had she been thinking? She wasn't ready to come back to work. She might never be ready.

She reached for the phone. She'd call all the florists she knew in Dublin. Get someone else to take the job on. She began to scroll frantically through her contacts. Appassionata, Gingko, the Garden. Then she stopped, remembering the look in Karina's eyes. She could pass any other job over to someone else, but not this one. She pulled her hair into a bun at the back of her neck and rummaged in the clutter on the counter for a pen to pin it into place.

She wasn't even sure where to begin. Most of her customers wanted simple, elegant arrangements. She had made a few frame wreaths at her training course in London six years ago, but nothing this elaborate. There might be a supplier out there who stocked a guitar-shaped wire frame, but if there was, it was too late to order one now. And the guitar had to be blue. It was going to take a hundred flowers at least, maybe even two hundred. She looked around at the rows of buckets. There was nothing blue in stock except for some anemones that looked as if they were going over.

She picked a card off the carousel and turned it over. Then she pulled the pen out of her bun and began to make a list.

"I'm going," Phil whispered to Ciara, "before she changes her mind."

Ciara peered at the card over his shoulder. Lara's handwriting, chaotic at its best, was almost illegible. *Hydrangeas. Vanda orchids, royal blue. Blue Star delphiniums. Cornflowers.*

"You're never going to manage that on the bike," she whispered back. "You'd better take the van!" She took the keys from a hook by the till and tossed them to him. "Try the wholesalers in Dún Laoghaire. They're expensive but they usually have a lot of stock. You might be lucky."

Phil tucked the card into the pocket of his leather jacket. "Don't let her leave, okay?"

They both looked up at the ceiling toward the workroom. They'd left Lara sitting at her worktable, her chair facing the wall instead of the window, staring into space.

Lara listened to their lowered voices, to the jingle of the temple bells as Phil left the shop, to the sounds of a few customers coming and going, to Ciara's footsteps walking back and forth as she served them.

For a long time she studied the photograph that she had emailed herself from Karina's phone. The blue acoustic guitar that Damian had set his heart on. Then she reached for a pencil and one of the drawing pads she used to plan wedding arrangements and began to sketch.

By the time Phil came back up to the workroom, she was re-creating her drawing in three dimensions, using wire.

"Ciara's conditioning the flowers. I brought you a muffin and a coffee," he said. She looked up at him quickly, and then down at the takeaway cup, afraid she was going to see the gray Camden Deli logo.

"Starbucks," he said gently.

"Thank you." She bent her head over her construction. "Could you check if there's any more of this eighteen-millimeter wire in the drawer? It should be next to the ribbon rolls."

For a moment there she sounded almost like her old self, Phil thought. "Sure," he said, turning away so she wouldn't see the relief on his face.

Phil and Ciara wanted to stay after the shop had closed but Lara sent them home. She couldn't bear being around other people right now. The way they treated her, as if she was breakable, reminded her of how broken she was.

She thought about Frank's offer as she worked, imagining the ordered hush of her top-floor office at Green Sea. The door closed, the only sound the click of her mouse as she tinkered with typefaces. Whole days slipping by without having to talk to another person.

She stared at the five buckets that Ciara had lined up on the floor beside the workbench—a carpet of two hundred and fifty flowers. Blue after blue after blue. She might not miss the shop if she went back to design, she thought, but she would miss the beauty of the flowers.

She went downstairs to find what she needed. Her neat store cupboard was unrecognizable. She stared into the chaos, feeling as if she was looking into a mirror. One of the low-hanging bulbs had blown. Flattened delivery boxes that should have gone out with the recycling weeks ago were shoved onto the deep shelves that had been built to hold rows of clean jam jars. Unstable stacks of teetering vases stood here and there on the floor. They clinked and jingled as she stepped over them to get to the blocks of Oasis.

What would happen to Blossom & Grow if she didn't come back? she wondered, as she stood in the kitchen by the two huge shallow plastic basins, waiting for the feather-light foam to soak. As if in answer to her question, an odor of decay seeped through the doorway from the darkened shop.

Senescence, she thought. A beautiful word for what happened to all living things as they progressed toward death. Petals fading, leaves falling, stems beginning to rot. It happened to some cut flowers fast— gerbera and irises and brassica—but it happened to all of them in the end, and now it was happening to Blossom & Grow. Lara's job had been to keep it nourished for five years, but now it was beginning to die.

She sloshed the water from the basins into the sink and carried the heavy, dripping Oasis upstairs. She set it on the workbench, then found her scalpel and began to cut the foam to fit the frame. She slotted it into place in sections, carefully, then smoothed it down with the palm of her hand and beveled the edges with a sharp knife. She cut thick blue ribbon to length and pinned it along the exposed edges. Then she set to work on the flowers and foliage. Carefully clipping the dark green heather she would use for the fretboard. Searching through the vases for flowers that were open to just the right degree, then cutting each stem on a diagonal to exactly one and a half inches long.

It was after midnight by the time she began to insert the flowers. Slotting them in one by one at a downward angle so there would be no gaps in the dense tapestry of blue. Dusty hydrangeas pale as robins' eggs. Delphiniums iridescent as butterfly wings. Cornflowers the hazy blue of the summer skies above the grave where the dead boy would be buried.

Lara's mother had chosen her own grave because it had a view of the sea. She had been buried there on a bitterly cold January day the year Lara turned thirteen. Lara remembered looking up and away from the horrible open mouth of the grave, at the gray sweep of the bay, the black silhouettes of the Wicklow hills on the horizon. What did the view matter, she had thought, when her mother was not alive to see it?

Her dad never brought Phil and Lara back to the graveyard. He had buried some of her mother's things beneath a honeysuckle in the garden. A worn leather glove, a birthday card that she had written for each of them. The last photograph of the four of them together.

There was a wisdom to what he had done; Lara saw it now. As the memory of her mother faded, the honeysuckle grew stronger. When Lara stood beneath it in summer, when it was in full bloom, her mother's sweetness seemed to live on in the scent of the flowers.

Her dad had always called her "your mother," but in those last few weeks before he died, when he was dying, he had started saying her name. Margaret. He had said it with longing and surprise and sometimes with annoyance, as if she was in the room with him. Her name had been his last word. And hearing it was what made it possible for Lara to let him go. The thought that maybe, after so many years apart, her mother and father were finally together again.

They had buried her dad on a beautiful summer's day, six weeks ago. Sunshine pulling sequins and glitter from the sea, the hills dreamy and purple and green in the distance.

"I hate this bloody place as much as Dad did," Phil had whispered, putting his arms around Lara. She buried her face in his shoulder and closed her eyes so she did not have to look at her father's coffin, or the headstone with her mother and her son's names on it. Two people she loved who had never met but who shared a name. Margaret Ryan and Ryan Gray.

When the time came to take the baby away so that they could bury him, Lara could not let him go. At the time the funeral was supposed to start, she was still sitting on the edge of the bed in the spare bedroom in her dressing gown, cradling Ryan's small body in her arms.

The IKEA flat-packs for the cot and the changing table were piled up on the stripped floorboards. The room smelled of fresh paint and of the roses from her father's garden. He had cut every single one and brought them over in a saucepan, but they were not enough to hide the sweet, cloying smell of death.

Michael stood at the door. He hadn't slept in days and his eyes were red-rimmed. He was wearing his wedding suit and carrying a black dress she did not recognize over his arm. She could hear voices downstairs. "Lara, you have to let him go now," he said. "It's time."

"Please, don't make me."

In the end, her dad and her brother came and sat one on either side of her. Phil held her hand, her dad held her head, leaned his temple against hers.

"You don't have to go anywhere," he said quietly.

"People are waiting," Lara whispered.

"What do they matter?" her dad said fiercely. He touched Ryan's cheek with the tip of his finger. His voice cracked. "Nobody's going to take him from you again until you're ready to let him go."

"What if I'm never ready?"

"Then we'll stay here with you. Right, Philip?"

Her brother squeezed her hand. "Right."

Time passed. The sun rounded the corner of the house and poured in through the window. A sharp-edged rectangle of light moved slowly across the floor and climbed into Lara's lap, then fell over her arms. And she saw that there was nothing she could do for her baby now except bury him. She closed her eyes and nodded. She still did not know which one of them had taken Ryan from her arms, her brother or her father.

It rained at the graveyard that day. The view her mother had loved so much dissolved behind a wall of water. Lara leaned on Michael's arm while they lowered the little white casket into the ground. Her father put his hand on her shoulder. "You don't ever have to come back to this place," he said. "You're not leaving him here. You're taking him with you in your heart."

* * *

He had been right, she thought, as she reached for another delphinium to slot into the frame. She had given Ryan up but she had never let him go. Her arms remembered his exact weight: two hundred and forty-one grams. The weight of a jug of water, a Kindle, a pot of African violets.

The street beneath the window of the workroom rang with loud voices and laughter as the nightclubs began to close and people poured out looking for taxis. After that, there were a few hours of quiet. Through the haze of her concentration Lara half heard an occasional sound. The clatter of a lorry delivering crates to the pub on the corner, the distant wail of a siren, the swish of a taxi driving past, too fast, on the way to the stand on St. Stephen's Green.

It was getting light again as she unwound the silver ribbon for the guitar strings. She cut it into lengths and pinned them into place. Most nights now she lay awake thinking about all the years she'd been married, running them back and forth in her mind, trying to find a clue she had missed. But tonight, she had not thought about Michael at all. She wondered whether he was asleep in their old bedroom, or whether he had moved to wherever Glen lived. She hoped that wherever he was, he was happy. There wasn't any point to both of them being sad.

The wreath was so big she had to carry it in both arms. She left it on the counter in the shop while she cleared a space in the cluttered cold room, then she closed the door and checked the time. It was 6 a.m. Too late to go back to her father's house, too early to deliver the wreath. She didn't feel tired, so she rolled up her sleeves, went back into the shop and began to go through the buckets of flowers, sorting out the living from the dead.

Phil had taken the keys to the van home, so at nine o'clock in the morning Lara hailed a taxi on the corner of Montague Lane.

"Dear God," the driver said softly when he saw her loading the guitar-shaped wreath into the back. He didn't speak for the whole journey, and when she tried to pay the fare, he shook his head. "Sorry for your trouble."

"Oh no," she tried to explain. "It's someone else's trouble."

"We all have troubles, love," he said.

Karina answered the door. As she took the wreath from Lara's arms, she began, finally, to cry, tears falling into the delphinium bells.

"Do you want to see him?" she asked through her tears.

"I'd love to."

Lara followed her down the hall, past a mountain bike leaning against the wall. There was a baseball cap on a coat hook. A pair of scuffed trainers kicked off and left by a shoe rack.

Karina led her into the living room. A flat-screen TV on one wall, bookcases against another. A bureau with a clutter of framed pictures. A window looking out onto a neat lawn with a trampoline in the middle of it. The coffin was in the center of the carpet on a folding stand. Karina tried to prop the guitar against it, but it slid sideways. "Damn it!" she said through her tears.

"Let me." Lara bent down quickly and, pulling scissors and a roll of wire out of the pocket of her raincoat, secured it to the stand. Then she stood beside Karina and looked down at the boy lying between the fussy satin ruffles. He looked as if he had just climbed in for a rest. He was wearing jeans and a blue Superdry T-shirt and the same tangle of friendship bracelets Lara remembered.

He had so nearly become a man. The ghost of his future self was there in the hands that were too big for his arms, the hardening jawline below his childish mouth, the thickening eyebrows above his closed eyes.

We want to protect ourselves from the pain of death, she thought, but we can't. And even if we could, would we choose to? Would Karina have decided never to have a child if she'd known this was going to happen? Would Lara herself have passed up on those blissful months that she carried Ryan if she had known she was going to lose him?

* * *

The exhaustion she had kept at bay caught up with Lara after she left Karina's house and followed the maze of redbrick streets that led to the canal. The banks were blooming with tall bulrushes. The world was turned upside down in the mirror of the water. Swans floating over trees that seemed to be rooted in the sky. Her own world had been turned upside down. But fathers die, marriages end. Her loss was nothing compared to Karina's.

She walked on as far as Charlemont Bridge, then she stopped and waited for her feet to tell her which way to go. She wanted to go home, but the house she had lived in with Michael was not her home now and her father's house had stopped feeling like home when he had died.

The shop was her real home, she realized. It always had been. It had comforted her last night, when she thought she was beyond comfort. It had helped her to comfort Karina. And it needed her now the way she had needed it once. So she turned and crossed the bridge and started walking back toward Blossom & Grow.

WISTERIA

An Open Heart.

Ben sends flowers on my birthday. Beth, my art director, picks them up from reception and carries them in to me like a sacrificial offering. She lurks behind me, fussing over them, crackling the cellophane, while I finish writing captions. It's deadline day and the magazine is due to go to press in two hours.

"Wedding Belles," my fingers clatter on the keys. "All White on the Night." I am dying to slip in a "Bridal Wave" or a "Frilly Cow," but weddings are a serious business.

"Twenty-eight roses! One for every year," Beth says in that wistful voice that some women reserve for flowers and babies and people who die young and tragically. "How lucky are you?"

Everyone passing my cubicle interrupts me to give me tips on flower care. Maggie, the receptionist, tells me to pierce the top of the stems to help draw water up. Tony, the editorial assistant, advises me to mash the ends with a wine bottle. Ruth, our boss, orders me to plunge the roses up to their necks in cold water. A man I've never met dressed in head-to-foot motorbike leathers offers to go out and buy them a Sprite.

"Citric acid travels up the stems quicker than water." His voice is muffled by his enormous motorcycle helmet.

"Right." He doesn't look like a person who knows one end of a flower from the other. I take the padded envelope he's holding, but his gloved hand stays where it is.

"Phil." He looks at me expectantly; his deep-set brown-black eyes are all that's visible through the flipped-up visor on his helmet.

"Fill what?" I frown. I've kind of had it with floral advice at this point.

"Phil Kiely. I'm the new courier."

"Right." I realize that he's waiting for me to shake his hand, so I do. The worn fingertips of his gloves remind me of the rough pads of Pat's paws. I start to swivel back to my desk, then I remember my manners. "I'm Katy."

When I can finally take a break, I call Ben to thank him.

He says, "Beautiful flowers for a beautiful lady," in a very convincing Italian accent.

"You do realize that the older I get, the more this is going to cost you?" I say.

He switches back to his normal voice. "I plan to leave you before it gets too expensive. Before you get to three figures, definitely. So you'd better enjoy the flowers while you can."

"I will."

But I won't, not really. I don't trust roses. They're like those fainting goats you see on YouTube. If you look at a rose sideways, it'll just keel over. I should know. I've seen them do it on dozens of bridal shoots. I'd much prefer lisianthus or anemones. But Ben has been giving me red roses on my birthday every year for seven years. It's a bit late to tell him that now.

Ben has invited my mother and my sister over for a birthday dinner and they are in the kitchen drinking wine when I get home. Mia is an accountant, but she's the one who looks as if she has the funky job. Tonight, her long blonde hair is loose and she's wearing a jade-green silk halter-neck dress that leaves her shoulder blades bare. I briefly consider changing out of my boring gray office dress, but what's the point? I'll still look more like an accountant than she does.

My mother is Mia's fainter echo, her older, silvery twin. Both of them are tall and slender and blonde. I have missed out on their Viking genes. I can thank my father for my height (short), my build (solid) and my curly dark hair (uncontrollable). But I've never had the chance.

Everyone kisses me and wishes me happy birthday, and Pat, my old greyhound, wags at me from his basket. He's too arthritic to leap around when I get home the way he used to, but his tail hammers an impressive drum solo on the creaky wicker.

My mother finds a vase for the roses and Ben produces a bottle of pink champagne from the fridge. Pat is gun-shy, so any loud noise terrifies him. I bend down, put my face next to his and cover his ears with my hands so he doesn't hear the cork pop.

In the dark tent my hair makes around us, he is all eye-shine and whisker-tickle. Whatever time of year it is, Pat always smells of autumn. Damp leaves and bonfire smoke. He sniffs behind one of my ears and licks my nose thoughtfully. His muzzle is gray and the tips of his black eyelashes are white. When anyone asks how old he is, I say he's ten, though it's fourteen years since I found him.

"If that dog was a man," Mia says to Ben, "you'd be in serious shit."

"Tell me about it," Ben sighs.

The kitchen smells of garam masala and chocolate. My favorite Fionn Regan CD is playing. The table is laid with a white cloth and there's a brightly wrapped pile of presents on my chair. It wasn't always like this. Until Ben came along, Mia and I walked on eggshells on birthdays, waiting for our mother to remember that our father wasn't there for yet another important family event.

On my tenth birthday, I came home from school to find her sitting at the kitchen table with a compact, drawing her eyebrows on with a kohl pencil. She had decided to gas herself and turned on the oven. After ten minutes, nothing had happened, so she lit a match to see if the gas was working. A sheet of flame scorched her eyebrows away.

Mia and I joke about it now, but back then I used to take my mother's shoelaces out of her runners at night because I'd read that prisoners sometimes used them to hang themselves.

After dinner we drink Frangelico and eat amaretti, lighting the tissue paper wrappers and letting them rise in columns of trembling ash while we make our wishes.

Mia wishes for a man. Not one of the ones who fall at her feet on a weekly basis. *The* man. My mother says that's like a turkey wishing for Christmas.

"Hey, I'm a man!" Ben pretends to be offended.

My mother ruffles his hair and says, "You're different." Then she wishes for her wisteria to blossom. It's been seven years since she planted it and she hasn't had a single flower.

Ben wishes that this will be the year when he finishes his screenplay so he can sell it to Hollywood and give up his job at the library. I wish that Pat was immortal.

While Mia and I are clearing the table, Ben goes out into the garden and closes the back door. My mother darts an accusatory little glance at me.

"Relax," I say. "I told you he's given up. He's just out there having a cigarette."

Ben and my mother have only ever had one row, and they have had it about a hundred times. It's the one about legalizing marijuana. I have had too many rows with him about smoking pot to count.

He has always said the same thing. That a joint is a piece of punctuation after a day at work, a full stop that allows him to start a new sentence. That it helps him to write. But the truth is that most nights he hardly writes at all. I'm not sure what he even does in the tiny box room that he uses as an office. I gave up asking long ago.

And a month ago, I gave up waiting for him to grow out of getting high and I asked him to stop and he said he would. If I'd known it would be that easy, I would have asked him years ago.

I spoon coffee into the French press and watch my mother out of the corner of my eye. She is picking at the tape on a prettily wrapped parcel with a perfectly lacquered fingernail and watching the back door.

Ben is my boyfriend, but he is the man in my mother and my sister's lives too. The tap-fixer, the plug-wirer, the tire-changer, the map-reader.

"He's one of the good guys," Mum said once. "He'll never leave you in the lurch the way your father left me."

I hate talking about my father, so I did what I always do when she brings him up. I changed the subject. "What is a lurch?" I asked her. "I've always wondered."

My mother's present for me is a framed picture of the two of us on my first birthday. A crooked orange washing line cuts the photograph into two uneven triangles. My mother is holding me by the hand. She's wearing denim dungarees and her blonde hair is in Krystle Carrington flicks.

I am bald, wearing a white onesie and stretching my free hand out toward the camera, toward the father I don't remember.

Mia gives me a book called *The Dog Whisperer*. On the flyleaf she has written: *Takes one to know one!*

"Are you calling me a dog?" I throw my napkin at her.

"Well, you can be a bit of a bitch!" she laughs.

"Cow!"

"Girls!" our mother says. "Language." When we were small, she was so tense that sometimes she communicated in single words for days.

Ben's present is an oval silver locket on a fine chain. I snap the catch and it hinges open. On one side there is a tiny photograph of Ben in the black fedora I gave him last Christmas. It's a serious hat, but he's wearing it with a goofy grin.

On the other side is my favorite picture of Pat. The one where Ben caught him winking. People who don't believe that dogs wink are the same ones who think that babies only smile because they have wind.

"That's so sweet!" I get up and walk around the table so Ben can fasten the locket around my neck.

"You're so sweet," he says, pulling me down into his lap. His eyes are slightly glassy. His breath has a sour, musky tang.

"Have you been smoking pot?" I whisper.

"No! I swear! I just had a roll-up." He nibbles my ear.

"Not in front of the children," Mia groans, putting her hands over her eyes. And I think how little my little sister knows about me.

My mother comes and stands beside me at the sink while I'm washing up the china plates that are too delicate to go into the dishwasher. I can hear Mia and Ben crashing around the living room. She is teaching him to salsa to the Gipsy Kings.

I hand my mother a soapy plate to dry, but she stares down at it instead. "I was probably washing Mia's nappies on *my* twenty-eighth birthday," she says. This doesn't sound like a question, but it is.

I nod at the plate. "Are you going to stand there till that dries itself?"

"Leave all that, birthday girl," Ben says after my mother and Mia have gone. "Come to bed."

"Are you sure?" I ask carefully. He takes my hand and twirls me around the kitchen, humming "Bamboleo."

Pat lifts his head and looks at us wistfully. In his day, he used to love to join in any kind of horseplay.

"Sure I'm sure," Ben says.

But by the time I have brushed my teeth and undressed, he is already asleep, his face half covered by his tangle of red-brown hair, one pale arm thrown across my pillow as if he is frozen in a salsa spin.

I sit on the edge of the bed and stare at his arm. I know the scatter of his freckles by heart. But I'm not sure I know *him* anymore. Or maybe I just know him too well.

I peel off the cream lace slip I put on in the bathroom and pull on the sweater that Ben has thrown on the floor, and then I go back out to the kitchen. I dry the plates and put them away carefully. I empty the dishwasher. I load the washing machine with the linen cloth and napkins. I scrub Pat's food bowl and his water dish. I find some Sprite and pour a few capfuls into the vase with Ben's roses. I rearrange the order of the three framed watercolors of Sandymount Strand and then change them back again. I clean out the fridge. I tidy the saucepan drawer. Then, when there is nothing else left to do, I open the back door and go out into the garden.

Pat heaves himself up stiffly and follows me, walking on the tips of his toes. He puts his head on one side to watch me rummaging in the tall blue glazed plant pot by the back door. But he doesn't stay around to watch me picking out the tiny cardboard cylinders that Ben has stuck into the soil around the base of the camellia.

"I'm confused." Mia doesn't sound confused. She sounds grumpy, but I can't tell if that's because I've woken her up in the middle of the night or because I'm having trouble explaining why I called in the first place.

"What's this about?" She yawns.

"It's me and Ben," I whisper. I'm sitting in the yellow armchair by the window with my toes tucked under the sleeping dog. The floor around me is strewn with the petals I have pulled off every single one of Ben's roses. The stalks have been planted upside down in the bin.

"It's four in the morning, Katy. If you've had a row, go back to bed and make up."

"We didn't have a row." I bite my lip.

"Then what's the matter?"

I close my eyes, as if saying it in the dark will make it easier. "We haven't, you know, been getting on"—I take a breath—"in the bedroom. For a while."

"How long is a while?" She sounds wide awake now.

I press my thumbs into the sockets of my eyes. Soft fireworks of color blossom in the darkness beneath my eyelids as I do the math. The last time was New Year's Eve. That's six months ago. The time before that was Ben's birthday last year. "I don't keep count," I say.

"Have you had your hormones checked? Are you taking vitamin B?"

"It's not me." I hesitate. "It's Ben. He just doesn't want to anymore."

Mia snorts. "Come on, Katy! Ben is crazy about you. He couldn't keep his hands off you tonight!"

When she was small, my sister used to cut the corners off jigsaw pieces to make them fit.

She starts telling me a story about a couple who put a bean in a jar every time they make love the first year they get together, then take a bean out every time they make love for the rest of their lives. I think the point is that they will never empty the jar.

But as I listen to my sister, I am lining Ben's tiny cardboard roaches up in neat rows along the windowsill. There are twenty-nine.

"I woke up and you weren't there." Ben touches my shoulder.

I don't look up from the magazine I'm pretending to read. "I couldn't sleep."

His hair is all over the place and he's wearing a gray dressing gown over blue pajama bottoms and a faded T-shirt that says: *I'm not perfect but parts of me are outstanding*. His eyes have a wary look. He puts a finger under my chin and tilts it so that I have to look at him.

I jerk my head away.

Ben looks down at the rose petals. "I'll get you more roses," he says. He takes a strand of my hair and winds it round and round his finger. "I'm sorry about last night."

"It's not about last night."

I see his eyes drop to the windowsill, to the row of tiny cardboard cylinders. "What's all this?"

"You said you stopped."

He blinks fast and I imagine the cogs in his brain trying to turn. "I haven't stopped completely," he says finally, "but I've cut right down. Come on, don't you think you're overreacting? One little joint a day is not the end of the world, you know."

But the thing is, I don't. I pull my knees up to my ribs. Beneath them I picture my heart like a power station. I imagine Ben and me walking around it, turning out the lights, one by one.

Ben is slumped in his chair, his head in his hands. It's the middle of the afternoon and he is still wearing his dressing gown. He has tried to talk me round. He has tried to kiss me. He has brewed coffee that neither of us has drunk. He has thrown his silver-foil-wrapped stash and his cigarette papers down the waste disposal and sworn that he'll never smoke again.

Pat has watched it all from his basket, his head low, his ears swiveling like antennae, his raisin-colored eyes darting from one of us to the other.

"If you loved me, you wouldn't want to change me!" Ben says tiredly, through his fingers.

"I don't want to change you. But we can't be together like this." My voice is hoarse from talking and crying. "We need a break. Take time. Take three months. Write. Try and straighten your head out. Decide if you want us to be together—"

"Of course I want us to be together! We're soul mates!" Ben's face is angry, but his chin is trembling.

"We're flatmates, Ben," I say.

"Fine!" He stands up. "I'll go, if that's what you want. But you can forget the terms and conditions, Katy. I don't do ultimata."

I watch him storm back to the bedroom and I wonder where I will ever find another man who knows the plural of "ultimatum."

On Monday, at work, I try to act like a person who has not spent the last thirty-six hours in a state of sleepless panic. When Maggie asks how my birthday was, I tell her it was lovely. Then Tony wants to know what Ben gave me and I mutter, "A locket." His eyes go straight to my empty throat and I babble something unconvincing about having it resized.

At lunchtime, I wait for everyone to finish eating, then I sneak out to get a sandwich. While I'm queuing to pay, "Someone Like You" comes on the radio. I have to get out of there fast. I manage not to cry until I reach the door of the office. I make it as far as the lift, but when I get in, I can't stop myself. Tears are pouring down my face as the doors close, then they open again and the courier steps in.

He nods and we stand side by side in silence and wait for the doors to close again. He unzips the pocket of his biker's jacket and passes me a clean tissue. He gets out at the next floor without saying a word.

Ben moves in with his friend Diane, who has always been a little bit in love with him. We agree not to communicate at all for three months. It's the first time we have been apart for more than a few days since college. I feel as if I have had some obscure but crucial organ removed. One I didn't know I had and now apparently can't live without, like my thymus or my spleen.

Neither of us is sure that Pat will live through to the end of our break, so on Sunday evenings I go out and Ben calls around to the flat. Coming home is the worst part, finding Ben gone but the lights still on. The cushions on the sofa piled up where he must have sat. The remote control on the floor by Pat's basket, a John Steinbeck novel facedown on the coffee table, a scrunched-up tortilla chip bag and an empty bottle of red wine in the recycling bin. I sniff the air for dope smoke and I check the camellia pot. Old habits die hard.

On the third Sunday, when I'm getting into bed, I find my cream silk slip, Ben's favorite, balled up beneath the pillow. I look at the empty space where he must have been lying an hour ago and I realize with a sickening jolt that we might never share this bed again.

I bury my face in the pillow, trying to find a trace of the musky cinnamon of his cologne. Pat is watching me from the door, his head cocked, his velvety forehead a concertina of concern.

Mia tries to make me do an audit of my relationship. She might not look like an accountant, but in her heart that's what she is.

"You're overreacting about this dope thing," she says. "Half the people I know take Ecstasy. You need to put this in perspective." She hands me a sheet of paper.

"Draw a line down the middle," she says. "Write down why you love Ben on one side. And what this breakup is all about on the other."

She puts a pen between my fingers and I stare at it. I imagine what I'll write. On the left: *I never really had a family before I found Ben.* On the right: *I can't have a family with Ben.*

"It's not that simple." I put the pen down. "It's not as simple as just drawing a line."

Mia's blue eyes widen and she nibbles the inside of her cheek the way she used to when she was small. "Come on, Katy," she says. "What can be so bad? Seriously?"

I wonder why all the things that really hurt us are hidden away. I never talk to my mother about the time she tried to gas herself. Or the fact that, as far as I know, there has been nobody in her life since my father left.

I've never asked Mia why all her relationships crash and burn after only a few weeks. Why a girl who can work out the tax liability on a six-figure salary without a calculator has never learned the knack of counting on other people.

I've never told her that Ben stays up watching late-night films most evenings, pretending to take notes on three-act structure. That when he finally comes to bed, we lie back-to-back, like strangers, pretending this is some kind of normal.

My mother hasn't seen Ben for weeks and she's getting suspicious. Mia and I talk about the best way to break the news. For as long as I can remember, we have been managing my mother together, swapping notes on her emotional form, as if she is a highly strung thoroughbred horse.

Mia thinks I should tell her face-to-face, but in the end I chicken out and call her instead. "It's not a big deal," I say. "Ben and I have a few things to work out. We're just taking a break."

If she was a different kind of mother, she might make sympathetic noises. But the only noises she makes are hysterical ones. It takes me a full fifteen minutes to talk her down.

At work, I throw myself into puff pieces about "Perfect Party Favors" and "Maid of Honor Etiquette" and "Inspiring Centerpieces." What Ben scornfully calls "the whole nine yards."

I sort through picture files of Tiffany engagement rings and Giuseppe Zanotti sandals and I try not to picture myself alone at thirty and forty. Always the bridal magazine editor, never the bride.

I haven't kissed anyone except Ben since I was at college. The only other person who has seen me naked in the last seven years is my doctor.

I read somewhere that you should never have your hair cut when you're going through a crisis. I ignore this advice. The hairdresser, who has a shaved head, holds a frizzy foot-long curl under his nose like a Salvador Dalí moustache and says, "Are you ready to rock and roll?"

"Absolutely!" I keep my head bent over a copy of *OK!*, but out of the corner of my eye I glimpse drifts of my dark curls piling up around the chrome wheels of my chair.

"Don't say anything," I warn everybody when I step out of the lift. I make for my cubicle, head down, trying to shut out the collective intake of breath.

"I like it." Tony follows me into my tiny office. "It takes years off you."

"You're right." I run my fingers through my shorn hair. "I used to look like a twenty-eight-year-old woman; now I look like a twelve-year-old boy."

Phil the courier appears and hands me a padded envelope. "You look like Joan of Arc."

"Jo Novark?" Tony says when he's gone. "Is that a guy or a girl?"

"My point exactly." I'm angry at myself for letting the hairdresser massacre me; I take it out on the envelope. "What is it with that bloody courier anyway? Every time I look up, he's hovering around in those stupid leather pants."

Tony arches an eyebrow. "I think he looks pretty good in them."

"I'm a pescatarian. I don't approve of leather pants."

"Steady on, Katy," Tony says. "Nobody's asking you to eat them."

At some point my mother came up with the idea of having a remembrance mass for our father every year, though as far as we know, our father is alive and well and living in a suburb of Glasgow called Shettleston. Mia and I hate having to go, but boycotting it is not an option.

"Let us pray for the souls of the departed," the priest booms. He begins to read a long list of the deceased. When he gets to "David Hughes," Mia rolls her eyes.

"He left," my mother hisses. "That's departing."

My father departed when I was three. I have no memory of him at all, but I still have a father-shaped space in my heart. I look into it now, as the priest drones on, and I wonder if my father is out there somewhere with a Katy-shaped space in his heart.

I try to call his face up from the framed photograph my mother keeps in the bottom drawer of her bedside table, but it is Ben's face I see.

It's been six weeks since *he* departed, and I'm not sure if I can take another six weeks of limbo. I wonder how my mother managed to get through all the weeks and months after my father went. For the first time ever, I think how hard that must have been for her.

After the mass, we have lunch in Roly's Bistro in Ballsbridge. Mia goes to the bathroom and my mother and I are left alone.

"I hope you know what you're doing, Katherine." She has put her glasses on to read the menu. Her pale hair is carefully blow-dried and her makeup is beautifully applied, but her blue eyes look faded and lined behind the thick lenses. She leans across the table and strokes my bare arm. Alarm bells go off in my head. When Mum is affectionate, she usually has an agenda.

"Ben is a good man," she says dramatically, sounding like a character witness in a court case. "And he's completely devoted to you. What more do you want?"

The truth starts to come loose like a wobbly tooth. Children, I think. I want children. But you have to have sex to have children. Quite a lot of it, apparently. I shake my head.

"Well, I hope you know what you're doing." Mum sits back against the banquette, her back ramrod straight, her mouth set in a hard line. "Because there's nothing worse than being alone. I should know."

You weren't alone, I think. You had us.

I found Pat the day my mother took it into her head to depart too. She had found out that my father was living with a woman in Glasgow, that they had a child together. She stayed up all night drinking the brandy that was meant to go into the Christmas cake. The next morning, when I got up, she was packing a bag.

I lurked on the landing sucking the end of my dressing gown belt and watching her stuffing neatly folded clothes into a suitcase, throwing cosmetics and jewelry and shoes in on top.

"Are you going away for long?"

She wouldn't look at me. "As long as it takes to find your father and have it out with him. We're his family." She snapped the case shut. "He can't just walk away from us like that." It was eleven years since he'd gone.

Mia was crying in our bedroom. It was the kind of crying that's meant to be heard, but my mother was in her own world and she couldn't hear it. I thought about crying too. Sometimes feeling sorry for us became bigger than feeling sorry for herself. But I was too old to act like a baby. I was fourteen but in dog years that's one hundred and twenty-four, which is about what I felt.

"I'll be back in a few days," Mum said, stuffing her hands into the arms of her best coat. Her words were fuzzy at the edges. "Don't tell anyone I'm gone. You'll be okay, Katherine. Look after Mia. There's food in the fridge and money in the tin."

After the door slammed and the taxi had driven away, I picked up all the dresses and skirts that had been thrown around the floor and hung them up in the wardrobe. I folded the nightdresses and sweaters and put them back into their drawers. Then I took a twenty-pound note out of the Coleman's mustard tin my mother kept hidden in the freezer and told Mia I'd take her to Penney's in the shopping center. Shopping always cheered her up.

She saw the dog first. He was cowering on the concrete division in the middle of the Blackrock bypass. He was still a puppy, his paws way too big for his body. He was so thin that every rib showed through his black and tan fur. His bony back legs were covered in sores. My mother had taught us to be wary of all dogs, especially strange ones. But when I grabbed hold of the frayed rope someone had tied around his neck, he lifted his head and his long mouse-tail began to whip against my legs. He wasn't strange at all. He was just a friend I hadn't met yet.

I held my hand up like a lollipop lady and hauled Mia and the dog across two lanes of traffic.

"You said we were going *shopping*!" Mia whined.

"Sssh! Pat the dog!" I pulled the belt off my coat so I could use it as a leash.

My mother came home in our uncle Desmond's car just before it got dark. Desmond carried her suitcase into the house, avoiding our eyes, and she followed him, looking smaller than herself.

Mia ran straight into her arms and I got up slowly and stood still while she hugged me. Her hot, wet tears plopped onto my scalp like Chinese water torture.

I felt her stiffen when she saw the puppy curled up on the bed of towels I'd made for him under the stairs.

"What's that?"

"It's Pat," Mia said. "Pat the dog. Katy wants to keep him."

"I *am* keeping him," I corrected her.

"Really?" Mum's voice hardened. "Who says?"

"What's the harm?" Uncle Desmond said, jingling his keys, eager to be on his way. "If he makes the girls happy."

My mother and I locked eyes for a long moment. I stared her down until I saw the shame swim up into her eyes. And I didn't look away again until I saw the flash of surrender.

Every time I think I am adjusting to being on my own, something happens. Something that reminds me how much I relied on Ben.

A fuse blows, and when I go outside to the fuse box in my night-dress, the door slams closed and I have to force the bathroom window to get back in. I wake up at five in the morning thinking how easy it would be for a burglar to force that window. I pull on a dress and a huge black spider runs over my shoulder. I drink too much wine and fall asleep in the bath and wake up when the water is cold. I drop a heavy saucepan on my foot and I don't even say "ouch." There doesn't seem to be much point "ouching" when there's nobody listening.

Something strange happens. Mia, who has never even been in like, falls in love with a performance artist called Ronan. I know that it's serious when she tells me, with a straight face, that his current "piece" involves dressing in a tree costume and standing around in Mount Merrion Woods.

Mia invites my mother and me over for dinner to meet him. I can't remember the last time any man except Ben set foot in Mia's flat.

Ronan is tall and shy, and when I see the way he and Mia look at one another, I feel dizzy and light-headed with longing for Ben. I feel jealous.

"I liked him," my mother says as she is driving me home. "Do you think he liked me?"

"I'm sure he did," I say. But what I'm thinking is, it shouldn't matter whether he likes you or not. What matters is that he likes Mia.

We pull up outside my flat and my mother looks up at the dark window and sighs. "Don't you just dread going back to an empty house?"

Something else strange happens. Flowers start appearing on my desk. It begins with a bunch of bright red gerbera in a coffee mug. A few days later, there's a frothy pink peony in a water glass. Then a leggy blue agapanthus in a jam jar.

There's no note from Ben, but the flowers are a good sign, and the following Sunday there's another one. He leaves a piece of paper folded into an origami bird on my pillow. I sit on the bed and unfold it.

I've been thinking about your ultimatum, it says. *Meet me for lunch tomorrow. The new tapas place on Baggot Street.*

I arrive too early. The restaurant has oxblood-red walls and blown-up black-and-white prints of bulls and matadors. The red leather booths are full of businessmen in twos and threes, eating *patatas bravas* and ordering cerveza with a lisp.

There's a bowl of green olives on the table. Each one has a tiny red tongue of red pepper peeking out of it. I can't stand olives—the vinegary smell of them makes me queasy—but I'm so nervous that I eat them all. The waitress brings another bowl.

I smell Ben's aftershave a moment before I feel his hand on my shoulder. He slides into the seat opposite me. He is clean-shaven and clear-eyed and he looks nervous. He hands the dish of olives to the waitress, who has reappeared with menus.

"My girl—" he begins, then catches himself. "My *friend* hates these."

The waitress eyes the little pile of olive stones by my glass but she takes the bowl away.

"You cut your hair," Ben says sadly, when she's gone.

"I did."

"You look like Anne Hathaway."

"Not Joan of Arc?"

"You're trying to look like a martyr?"

"No." Meeting his eyes feels weird so I pretend to study the menu. "How's the library?"

He shrugs. "Quiet."

We talk in clumsy fits and starts about work and Mia and Ronan and Pat and my father's anniversary mass. We talk about the trip we took to Spain last summer. The smell of orange blossom in the streets of Seville. The convent bakery we found in Vejer de la Frontera. The stray beach dogs we fed every day in Conil.

We don't talk about us until we have finished our coffee and Ben has paid the bill. Then he drains his wineglass and looks me straight in the eye for the first time since he sat down. "I've been seeing someone."

His words hit me in the stomach like a tire iron. The undergrowthy taste of the olives comes back up into my mouth.

"I mean I've been seeing a counselor," Ben corrects himself. "Well, I've seen him once for a kind of assessment thing, but I've got another appointment."

He rubs his temples with his fingers. "Look, I know things haven't been great. I can see that now. I'm sorry. I think I've been anesthetizing myself for the last few years, you know?"

Anesthetizing himself against what? I think. Me? Us? The unfinished screenplay?

"I've cut it out," he continues. "The dope. Completely this time. I'm writing again. I feel good, Katy."

He reaches across the table and takes my hand. It twitches, unused to his touch. "I want us to have it all." He squeezes my fingers. "Marriage, kids. The whole nine yards."

I want the whole nine yards too. It's what I've always wanted. But I have to know that he's doing this for *him* as well as me.

"Look," I say, "I don't want you to rush into this. I need you to be sure."

Ben takes his hand away and folds his arms. "I am sure! I want to come home."

"We said we'd live apart for three months. There's only two weeks to go. That gives you time to see your counselor again."

He rolls his eyes. Then he leans forward and plants his elbows on the table. "Two weeks. Then I can come back? No ifs or buts. For good? Yes?"

"Yes," I say. "And, Ben, thank you for the flowers."

He nods curtly. "You're welcome."

The next morning, there's a freckled saffron-colored lily in a clay pot beside my in-tray. I water it every day and it releases a sweet fragrance that makes my tiny office smell like a church. I say a little prayer that Ben means what he said.

On Friday, Ruth pops her head around the door as I'm shutting my computer down. "The florist for Monday's shoot has stomach flu so I've booked a new place called Blossom & Grow." She hands me a pink card with an ivy leaf logo. "Can you pop over on Sunday afternoon to make sure they're on top of everything?"

I turn the card over to read the address. There's a line on the back that says: *Every flower is a little bit of summer.*

I spend most of the weekend cleaning the flat, polishing the dining table Ben and I made from a carved Balinese temple door we found in a junk shop. Dusting the IKEA chandeliers we spent days assembling. Ironing the bed linens that have been piling up in the washing basket. I tug the cover on over the goose-feather duvet and tell myself and Pat that in a week and one day, Ben will be back.

At about four, I put on shorts and a T-shirt and walk into town. I was worried that I might walk past Blossom & Grow, but it stands out like a flower between the gray and red buildings on Camden Street. The tall, narrow front is painted pale pink and there's a mural of ivy trailing up the wall. There's a "Closed" sign on the door, but when I knock, the owner comes and lets me in.

The shop is cool and dark. There are lanterns and candles flickering among the pails of flowers. The owner, whose name is Lara, is exactly the kind of woman you'd expect to find running a florist's. Tall and slight and graceful, with a yoga body and black hair with glints of silver shot through it. She looks like a woman from a W. B. Yeats poem, beautiful and sad.

I follow her into a storeroom at the back of the shop and catch my breath when I see the bouquets she has made for the shoot. I've seen a lot of wedding flowers, but nothing like these.

There are soft apricot roses with dusty-blue delphiniums, creamy-white peonies with miniature pink alliums. Waxy green orchids with deep purple irises.

A phone rings in the shop and she excuses herself and goes back outside to answer it. I bend down and pick up a pretty tumble of glossy green ivy and pale purple bells on slender stems.

The flowers have a delicate scent, something elusive between hyacinth and freesia. I close my eyes and breathe it in, then I get that hair-on-the-back-of-the-neck feeling and I know that somebody is watching me.

I snap my eyes open. Phil, the office courier, is standing in the doorway. It must be nearly eighty degrees outside, but he's wearing his biker leathers and managing, somehow, to look cool.

"Did Ruth book you to pick up these flowers?" I sound ruder than I mean to, but there's no way I'm going to let these delicate arrangements go for a ride on a motorbike.

"Nobody booked me." He folds his arms across his chest. "Lara asked me to give her a hand. I was supposed to be driving to Hook Head today but she made me an offer I couldn't refuse."

I want to fold my arms too, but I'm still holding the bouquet so I can't. I realize that I'd presumed that Phil had a crush on me and I feel like an idiot. Lara is in her forties, probably ten years older than Phil, but I can see them together. She's one of those women, like my sister and my mother, who will still be beautiful when she's ninety.

I, on the other hand, was beautiful for about fifteen minutes when I was seventeen, when almost everyone is beautiful. If I make a marathon effort, I can still manage pretty. But not, obviously, when I'm wearing a faded Primark T-shirt and a pair of ratty cutoff shorts.

"So how long have you two been . . ." I juggle the options. "Together?"

"Oh, let's see. I've known Lara for what?" Phil counts the long fingers on his left hand with the index finger of his right. "It must be about thirty years now."

I stare at him, confused.

"She's my sister," he says. "The offer I can't refuse is dinner. She's had a tough couple of months and this will give me a chance to hang out with her. Plus, when she bothers to cook, her food is nearly as good as her flowers." He smiles. "You thought she was my girlfriend?"

"No!" I start to babble, trying to cover up my embarrassment. "I knew right away that you were related." I didn't, but I should have.

"You look exactly like her." It's true. He has the same polished conker-colored hair as his sister, the same dark-brown eyes, the same easy grace. "Except," I say, "that you're a man."

"I wasn't sure you'd noticed," he says drily.

And suddenly it's all I do notice. The inverted triangle of his broad chest, the thick broken black line of his eyebrows, the sooty five-o'clock shadow around his mouth.

I can hear Lara in the shop, winding up her call. The sound of her voice makes the silence in the tiny room thicken till I feel I can actually taste it at the back of my throat.

I remember what Mia said about the first time she met Ronan. She said: "You could have cut the air between us with a butter knife."

I'm still looking at Phil's mouth and neither of us seems to be moving, but the distance between us is contracting. I feel myself tipping toward him, my weight shifting forward till my toes are pressing against the rubber bumpers of my sneakers.

What am I doing? But I know exactly what I'm doing. I'm going to kiss him.

Then I see a shadow behind his shoulder and I take a step back.

"Lara, I was just wondering," I say quickly, my voice sounding croaky, "what these little purple bells are." I hold up the flowers.

Phil moves aside to let her come into the room.

"That's wisteria," she says. "Isn't it lovely?"

"Really?" I hand Phil the bouquet and he bends down to put the flowers back in their pail. His jacket stretches over his broad shoulders like a second skin. "My mother has wisteria in her garden," I say, "but it refuses to bloom."

Lara twists her hair into a rope and anchors it with a pen. "How long has she had it?"

Ben planted it for her a month after we met.

"Seven years," I say.

Longer than my mother spent with my father, I think. A quarter of my life.

"Well, seven years is make-or-break time," Lara says. "You could try pruning the roots. Sometimes the shock will trigger bud-set. But if it hasn't bloomed by now, it probably never will. You'd be better off digging it up and starting all over again."

I feel too unsettled to go to a film and I know that Ben will be at the flat until eight, visiting Pat, so I walk all the way to Irishtown, to Mia's house.

"Stay for dinner!" she says, and I follow her down the hall, into the kitchen. She's wearing a backless black dress and heels and making a complicated seafood dish from a recipe she found on the Internet.

"It's fuck-me food." She winks, gouging the bone out of a cuttlefish with a bread knife. She starts to use the same knife to massacre some mange-tout and I wince and hope it's not going to be poison-me food too.

I haven't seen her since my lunch with Ben and she wants to know all about it.

"Yay!" she whoops when I get to the bit about the whole nine yards. "You're going to get married!"

"Not necessarily," I say. "We haven't really—"

But she doesn't want to hear this. She grins and gives me a spontaneous hug. "Ben's going to be my brother-in-law! For a while there I thought we were going to lose him. Jesus! He hasn't even met Ronan yet. Hey!" She leans back and lifts my chin with a hand that smells of fish and Marc Jacobs Daisy. "What's wrong with you? This is what you wanted? Isn't it?"

What's wrong with me is that I keep thinking about the moment in the shop when I almost kissed Phil. I push it to the back of my mind and nod. "Of course it is."

Ronan comes in looking exhausted. Mia jumps into his arms, and after he puts her down, she picks a few leaves out of his hair and they examine one another with delight. His hands are painted green. "You have green fingers!" she says.

"And you have fish fingers." He kisses her fingertips.

"Health and safety!" I say, but they don't break their gaze for a long moment, and when they do, Mia blows her hair out of her eyes and grins at me. She reminds me of her little-girl self and every trace of jealousy I felt before dissolves.

The cuttlefish tastes like damp, chewy suede, but Ronan valiantly clears his plate.

"Here, I'll eat yours," he whispers, when Mia is in the kitchen opening more wine. "It'll hurt her feelings if there are leftovers!" He swaps plates and posts a forkful of limp mange-tout that Mia has turned into mange pas.

I don't want to run into Ben, not until I have erased the moment with Phil in the flower shop from my mind, so I hang on at Mia's for as long as I can. I hang on until it's obvious that Mia and Ronan are about to tear one another's clothes off whether I leave or not.

When I get home, the flat is in darkness and Pat is fast asleep in his basket. I light a candle and run a bath. I pull my clothes off and get into the scalding water and I lie there trying to think about Ben, trying to imagine the whole nine yards.

But I can't. Instead I imagine what would have happened if Lara hadn't come back into the storeroom. I imagine the kiss that didn't happen. I imagine it in great detail. I imagine unzipping Phil's jacket and the crackle of static as I pull my T-shirt over my hair. I imagine lying down among the buckets of flowers with the cold tiled floor under my bare back and the heat of Phil's skin under my hands.

Then I imagine how Ben would feel if he knew what I was imagining and I make myself stop.

After the water has cooled, I get out and put on my dressing gown and go into the kitchen to make some chamomile tea and I realize that something is different. Something is wrong.

It's Pat. He's too quiet and too still. I turn on the light. His head is lying at a strange angle, his tongue lolling out to the side from his half-open mouth.

I dash over and pull his head onto my lap. He doesn't open his eyes so I lift one eyelid gently with my finger and see a little crescent of bloodshot white. I put my ear close to his snout. He is breathing, but only just.

I run back into the bathroom to get my phone so I can call the emergency vet. I crouch by Pat's basket while I am put on hold. When I've given my name and address, I hang up. I'm about to call Ben when I feel something hard caught under my heel. It's a ball of half-chewed silver foil. There are still a few hard brown grains trapped in the folds—all that remains of Ben's stash.

"Did he eat any cigarettes?" the vet asks, when he comes. "Or was it just the hash?" He is not even trying to hide the fact that he thinks I am a lowlife.

"I'm not sure." I have left half a dozen messages for Ben, but he hasn't called me back. "Is he going to be okay?"

"Well, if he'd eaten tobacco, he'd probably be dead by now. And if he is okay, it's no thanks to you." I nod, my face burning. "If it's just hash, he'll probably sleep it off."

Pat sleeps all through the night and into Monday morning. The phone starts ringing at eight and it keeps ringing every five minutes until nine. It's Ben finally calling me back, but by now I'm too angry to talk to him.

At eleven, the doorbell rings and I get ready to read Ben the riot act, but it's my mother standing on the steps. It's pathetic how grateful I am to see her.

When she comes in, Pat lifts his head and opens his eyes and gives her a hungover look, and I almost cheer.

"I was just passing, I'm on the way to the hairdresser for a blow-dry. I have a brunch." Her pale blue eyes take in my bathrobe, my bare feet, my anxious face. "I called the office but they said you hadn't come in. Are you sick?"

"I've been up all night." I wrap my arms around myself. "I had to get the vet for Pat."

"Why?"

"He wasn't well." Tears come into my eyes. "I thought it might be the end."

Mum goes over and crouches down on the floor beside Pat's basket. She's wearing a green velvet jacket, and she hates getting dog hair on her clothes, but she takes hold of Pat's face. She has always tolerated Pat, but I don't think I've ever actually seen her touching him before. He's drooling slightly onto her sleeve, but she doesn't seem to care.

"Now listen to me!" she says to him sternly. "You're part of this family. You have to stick around!"

Pat gazes at her dreamily. Then he licks her hand.

"Did you see that?" She smiles up at me. "I think he likes me. I knew he'd come around in the end."

And I wonder if my father has left a space in my mother's heart too. A space she's tried to fill with approval. Mine, Mia's, Ben's, Ronan's. Even Pat's.

"I'd better go." She stands up.

"Who are you having brunch with?" I ask her at the door.

"Someone I met at bridge," she says. And from the way she says "someone," I know she means a man.

She never dated anyone while I was living with Ben. She didn't need to, and neither did Mia. I realize with a jolt that now that Ben has gone, both of them have moved on.

I call Ruth to tell her that I'm too sick to come into work and that Beth will have to art-direct the shoot. Then I switch off my phone and boil up some mince that was lurking at the back of the freezer.

Pat's bloodshot eyes widen as the smell fills the kitchen, and I'm so happy that he's alive that I sing all the songs I can think of, adding in dog-related lyrics.

I'm belting out a pretty awful version of "I'm going to fall from the stars, right into your paws" when the bell rings again.

I have been rehearsing what I will say to Ben, but when I look through the spyhole, he's not there. Instead I see a stem of wisteria held up in a big leather-gloved hand. I open the door warily.

"I heard you were sick," Phil says, "so I decided to deliver this by hand." He takes his helmet off and there is his mouth again. It's just as I remembered it.

"It was you!" I say slowly. "Not Ben! You've been leaving all those flowers on my desk."

"Who's Ben?" Phil hands me the wisteria.

And somewhere in the dark power station of my heart, a light goes on, the kind you leave burning to stop a child being frightened of the dark, and I take a deep breath and open the door and let Phil in.

FIR

Friendship and Acceptance.

Forty-nine pairs of eyes are looking up at Mia. The one pair that is closed belongs to a guy who is snoozing in the front row. He has unkempt brown hair and an unruly beard and he's wearing a duffle coat with the toggles done up wrong. If Mia wasn't in a room full of artists, it might cross her mind that he is a homeless person who has wandered in off the street, but all the artists have a carefully disheveled look.

"You're here because you're broke," she announces dramatically, looking around at their rabbit-in-the-headlights faces. "And I am here to fix you."

She ignores the few groans at the pun. She has delivered this financial planning talk to dozens of self-employed groups, app designers and day-care managers, B and B owners and dog groomers. She could do it in her sleep, although, she thinks as the man in the front row lets out a small snore, this is the first time she has had to do it in someone else's.

She fires up her PowerPoint and runs through the basics of budgeting and credit control. The sleeping man snores softly when she is talking about double-entry bookkeeping until the woman beside him digs him in the ribs with her elbow. He blinks and rakes his beard vigorously with his fingers, then his head drops down onto the bulging plastic bag he is using as a pillow and he drifts off again.

During the coffee break, when Carlo, the seminar organizer, is shepherding Mia from group to group, one tanned hand planted proprietorially in the small of her back, the man wakes up and wanders over to the refreshments table. She watches him from the other side of the room as he posts whole triangles of sandwich into his mouth. When she was very small, she convinced herself that her father hadn't abandoned them. That he was lost. Out there somewhere, cold and hungry, trying to find his way home. Sometimes, if she turned the pity around and around in her heart enough, it almost felt like love. Later it turned out that her father wasn't lost at all. That he had found his way home— just to a different home in a different country with, in time, a different family.

She excuses herself and goes to the ladies' to touch up her makeup. On her way back, she stops at the refreshment table to get a cup of coffee. Up close, the man in the duffle coat is younger than he looked from a distance, late twenties at the most. The beard is awful and his coat looks as if it has been dragged through a hedge backward. There are dried leaves stuck to both sleeves. But his teeth, sinking into yet another sandwich, are white and even and he smells strongly and pleasantly of Acqua di Parma cologne. He has a dramatic face. Long and thin and sallow-skinned, full of unexpected angles. A prominent chin. Hollow cheeks. Jutting brow bones that overhang his deep-set eyes. He's not handsome in a highly polished way, like Carlo, but he might scrub up well, Mia thinks.

"Do you have plans for all of these?" she asks drily, pointing at the last few sandwiches on the tray. "Or can I take one?"

"Help yourself!" He hands her a cardboard plate. "They're free. Part of this whole financial seminar thing. I didn't catch the first half. I was out cold."

"Really?" Mia says. "The speaker must have been pretty boring."

"I needed the sleep. I was working all night."

Mia picks up a cucumber sandwich and takes a bite. "What do you do?"

"I'm a conceptual artist."

"As opposed to a real one?"

"It's a tough job but someone has to do it. Conceptual art allows us to interrogate our ideas of what art is in the first place." His face takes on a look of almost religious fervor as he warms to his subject. Somewhere between "execution is a perfunctory affair" and "the idea becomes the machine" Mia stops listening and watches his face instead. All his features become involved when he talks. His eyebrows, his forehead, even the tips of his ears, which appear and disappear through the tangle of his hair. He reminds her of the predator from a game she and Katy used to play when they were small: "What Time Is It, Mr. Wolf?"

"Well, thank you for the lecture." She puts down her plate and her half-eaten sandwich. "It's a shame you missed mine earlier."

"Was it any good?"

"Extremely."

"That's a pity. I'm pretty awful with money. I don't suppose you'd give me a one-to-one?"

"Pardon?" Mia says just as Carlo appears at her elbow. Ten minutes ago she had been thinking about giving Carlo her phone number, but now she can't remember why.

"Mia, I need you," he says in his strange half-Irish, half-Italian accent. "I have a sculptor with a question about the artists' tax exemption scheme."

"I'll just be a minute," she says and he pouts and marches back across the room like a sulky child.

"He's got a thing for you," the wolf in the duffle coat says.

She pretends to be surprised.

He looks her up and down, from the top of her perfectly blow-dried blonde hair to the toes of her Kurt Geiger sandals. "I'm sure he's not the only one. You're exceptionally pretty," he says bluntly, "and you know it."

Mia blushes for the first time since Miss O'Connor in Senior

Infants caught her stealing Wendy Williams's felt-tipped markers. She wants to snap back a one-liner but she's lost for words, unexpectedly marooned on an awkward little island of silence with this strange, really strange man.

"Ronan," he says, without taking his eyes off her.

"Mia."

Behind those eyes, which are the color of wet gravel, she has the sense of an animal looking out at her. And as if in answer, an animal of her own, one that has been lurking in the neatly pruned maze of her heart, pads out and looks straight back at him.

A smile tugs at the corners of her mouth but she won't give in to it. "I could give you a printout of my PowerPoint presentation," she says, all business.

Ronan looks puzzled, as if he thinks a PowerPoint might be something electrical. He sighs. "I don't think a printout will save me. I'm so crap with money that I'm about to spend my last tenner—a tenner I should be saving for my share of the gas bill—to buy a girl a drink."

"That's too bad." Mia feels oddly flat now. "I mean the bit about your lack of fiscal acumen, not about the girl."

"Say that again." He breathes out all five syllables of "fiscal acumen."

"I think," Mia says pointedly, "that the girl you're buying a drink for would probably prefer if I didn't."

"The thing is . . ." He picks up the plastic bag from the floor by his feet. It seems to be full of leaves. "I haven't asked her if she'd like to have a drink with me. Not yet."

"Ah." The smile is back and this time Mia doesn't bother fighting it.

"So?" He raises his eyebrows. "Would you?"

She is supposed to stay till the end of the seminar to take part in a panel discussion, and then go for dinner with the other speakers. "I can't. Maybe some other time?"

"The possibility of me ever having a spare ten euros to spend again is pretty unlikely, but I'm usually in the Palace Bar on Fridays between four and five."

Guys ask Mia out all the time. Clients at the accountancy firm where she is a partner. Strangers at petrol stations. Assistants in shops. Why is she still single? people always ask. People who think that being picky is a bad thing.

She knows what she wants in a man and she's happy to wait for as long as it takes. On her checklist are, in no particular order: tall, broad shoulders, nice eyes, and hands that are bigger than hers. (It's amazing how many tall men have little hands.) Ambition, modesty, wit, patience and financial independence.

The problem is that on the few occasions when she has found a man who ticks every box, there hasn't been a spark.

"I've had iceberg lettuces that have lasted longer than most of your relationships," her sister's boyfriend, now perhaps ex-boyfriend, Ben, once teased her. "You're going to be one of those sad old cat-ladies unless you stop ticking all those boxes and start thinking outside of them."

Running along the slippery cobbles of Temple Bar in heels at a quarter past five the following Friday is further outside of the box than Mia had planned to venture. She is half hoping that Ronan won't be there, but he is sitting at the bar, nursing a half-pint of Guinness, scribbling in a notebook.

He points at a small pile of change on the counter. "I can't buy you a drink," he says, "but I can get you a packet of delicious ready-salted peanuts."

"Dry-roasted." Mia slides onto the stool beside him. She has a rule about never letting a man pay for anything on a first date, but this, she reminds herself, is not a date.

Mia has other rules about first dates. Keep her mouth shut is one.

Let him do all the work. It's strange the things men will say to fill a
long pause, and quite off-putting too. Most guys have talked themselves
out of a second date within five minutes, but tonight she finds herself
having the kind of random conversation that students are supposed to
have at three in the morning but that she never did.

At about eight, Ronan suddenly remembers that he has to meet his
best mate, and they part hurriedly. Mia gives him her number. He is
obviously not boyfriend material, she thinks, but she might have a fling
with him. She will decide later, when he calls.

When he doesn't, she replays in her mind all the things she seems
to have confided—breaking her first-date rules—and wonders which
one put him off. Was it her first memory—collecting insects in a jam
jar because her mother had said that life would be easier if they had an
"ant" they could count on? Or her desert island luxury—a calculator,
so she can keep count of the calorific content of coconuts? Or her
phobia—watching kissing scenes in movies? It was probably the calculator or the kissing, she decides. There is only one way to find out,
and that's to go back to the Palace, but she has no intention of ever
doing that. The most important rule Mia has about dating is never look
keen.

The following Friday, Ronan glances up and catches her eye in the
gilt-framed mirror behind the glittering optics. The bar is full but he
has draped his duffle coat over the empty stool beside him.

She looks at his profile as he orders their drinks. There could, she
thinks, be a nest inside that beard. Why then is she wondering what
it would feel like against her face? This can't be happening, she thinks.
When the pub closes, he walks her to a taxi stand and says good-bye
and she is too exhausted from all the sexual tension to care.

Mia has always been looking for that elusive spark but never thought
to look for it in a rowdy bar that smells of beer and anoraks, but since
that is where it has shown up, the following Friday so does she. There
is less talking this time, more drinking, more meaningful staring,
longer pauses. There are "whats?" and "nothings!" between them that

would not be out of place at a teenage disco. She feels as though she is being wound up like an old-fashioned watch, one slow turn at a time. It's noisy, and Ronan has to lean over to shout into her ear, and finally she can't wait any longer. She turns her face quickly, intending just to brush his lips with hers, but instead her chin connects with his nose and he jolts back and knocks his glass over. Guinness pours over the counter in a creamy wave. It rains down into the lap of her favorite Karen Millen dress.

"Sorry!" Ronan reaches for a napkin from the bar but Mia has had enough. She grabs a fistful of his shirt and drags him to her. She doesn't care about the scratchy beard or her ruined dress or the man on the next stool who is nudging his friend and gaping at her. All she knows is that if they don't kiss now, she will explode.

Mia owns a neat two-bedroom apartment in Irishtown. She has a walk-in wardrobe. She drives a Volkswagen Golf. She has a pension plan, private health insurance and an investment portfolio. On dating websites she lists her interests as working out and eating out.

Ronan shares a dilapidated house with three other artists on a street Mia wouldn't cross without a personal alarm. He rides a bicycle—not one of those hipster bikes with long handlebars and a white saddle; a scratched and dented BMX held together with duct tape. He has never been inside a gym and most of his eating out involves takeaway cartons.

They have nothing in common. But after that glass-toppling, earth-shattering kiss, that does not matter to either of them. Ronan works best at night. He stays late in his small studio in Temple Bar and texts Mia when he is on his way over, often at two or three in the morning. She gets up, puts on her makeup, brushes her teeth and swaps her pajamas for something sexy.

He approaches her the way he approached the sandwiches the day she met him—methodically and with a ravenous appetite. In between bouts of devouring they lie in Mia's antique sleigh bed, talking about what Mia used to cynically call "life, the universe and everything."

"Do you think," she asks him one night, "that we're one of those opposites-attract couples, like chalk and cheese?"

He props himself up and frowns, which for him involves a full facial workout. His forehead furrows. The comic-book caterpillars of his dark eyebrows inch along a bit then down over his eyes. "Chalk and cheese are way too similar. We're more like"—he tugs at his beard—"chalk and skis. Squawk and fleas."

"Pork and knees." She grins.

"Forks and antifreeze." He rubs his chin against her shoulder, his beard prickly on her skin. She already has half a dozen friction burns. She wonders if it's too soon to start dropping hints about him shaving it off.

"You know, I've never kissed anyone with a beard before," she says.

"How about after?" He growls like a bear and rolls her across the bed till her head is dangling over the edge, the tips of her hair brushing the floor. And she wonders why she never put growling on her checklist.

Mia meets Katy for lunch at the Fern House in Avoca in Kilmacanogue. "You're having dessert!" Mia says before they've even ordered. "We're going to have to fatten you up!"

"Says the size-eight minx to the size-twelve heifer." Her sister rolls her eyes.

"You're not a heifer. You're a classic hourglass shape and skinny doesn't suit you, Katy!" Mia scrutinizes her face. It looks pinched and pale. "Single doesn't suit you either."

Katy has instigated some kind of crazy three-month break from her long-term boyfriend, Ben. It's a bad idea and Mia needs to talk her out of it. Ben is practically a member of their small family and she doesn't want to lose him, but she can't say this so she is planning to restrict herself to sympathy followed by advice. Take. Him. Back.

"Don't start, Mia!" Katy holds up a hand. "I don't want to talk about me and Ben. You lured me here to tell me about this new man, remember?"

"Okay, but you have to eat. We'll both have the risotto," Mia tells the waitress. She usually has the superfood salad but all the sex has speeded up her metabolism. She pushes the basket of bread across the table.

Katy sighs but takes a piece of brown bread. She is used to Mia's orders. She has been taking them for years.

"Okay!" Mia begins. "His name is Ronan. Ronan Slattery. He's twenty-seven. Very tall. Brown hair. Kind of craggy. Fit in that kind of 'I never go to the gym but I eat a lot of lentils' way. Huge beard, but that's only temporary." Mia's inner auditor has opened a mental spreadsheet with "Ronan" in the box titled "Project name."

"Is he in finance?" Katy begins to butter the bread fast.

"No. He used to lecture at the art college but now he's a conceptual artist."

Her sister stops buttering, knife suspended in the air, to stare at her. She shakes her head. "Lentils, possibly. A beard, maybe. But an artist?" She says "artist" as if she is saying "porcupine" or "wildebeest."

"I love art!"

"You do?" Katy says. "I mean, do you?"

"I had that poster by Van Gogh on my bedroom wall for years, remember?"

"It was Magritte and it was mine. You only put it up after the ceiling leaked and that weird patch appeared on your wall."

"What I know about the art world could fit on a pinhead and what Ronan knows about finance could fit on a . . ." Mia tries to think of something much smaller than a pinhead and can't. "Another smaller pinhead. But we're amazing together. You'll see when you meet him.

Come to dinner on Saturday. Bring—" She is about to say "Ben" but manages to change it, at the last minute, to "Mum."

"Introduce him to Mum?" Katy's eyes widen. "Are you sure?"

Mia wants to say "Of course not," but she finds herself nodding instead. "Why not?" She is so loved up that not even her mother could spoil it. She covers her mouth with the back of her hand to try to hide her Cheshire Cat smile. "I'm sorry!"

"For what?"

"For being so happy when you're so miserable."

"Mia, I don't need you to be unhappy just because I am." The waitress puts down their bowls. Katy pokes at the pearly rice grains with her fork. "Stop worrying about me. I'll figure things out."

But it's not just her sister that Mia is worried about. It's herself. For nearly eight years, Ben has been the fourth leg on the three-legged stool of their family. The much-needed dollop of testosterone in their estrogen soup. They are all much nicer women when he is there. Their mother, Angela, might go back over the edge without a man around to fix her dripping taps and bleed her leaking radiators and tell her she looks young enough to be their sister. Somehow Mia can't see Ronan doing any of those things.

The dinner is an unexpected success. Katy and Ronan hit it off right away. Ronan is polite to Angela but he doesn't let her monopolize him the way Ben did, and to Mia and Katy's amazement, she doesn't throw an attention-grabbing hissy fit. Maybe, Mia thinks, she's finally ready to relinquish her role as drama queen. But Angela can't resist turning the situation toward herself the way a compass automatically finds true north.

"I've never seen you so happy," she says when she calls the next morning. Mia is sitting in the window seat of her kitchen on Ronan's lap while he tears at a baguette with his teeth and reads *The Brothers Karamazov*.

"No, that's not true," she corrects herself. "You were a very sunny baby. I used to put you out in the garden in your pram and you'd lie there all day, chuckling to yourself."

"Did I?" Mia remembers herself as a whiny child, perpetually trying to enlist the sympathy of adults. She used to scrape the thin skin on her shins with the pointy plastic hand of a particular Sindy doll till it turned red, on the off chance that Angela might kiss it better. Sometimes the only way to get her mother to stop crying was to cry herself.

"You changed, of course," her mother sighs. Ronan brandishes the baguette and Mia takes a bite, then closes her eyes. She knows what comes next.

"Everything changed," Angela says, with the telltale tremble in her voice, "after your father left us."

Mia waits for the familiar doom-laden cloud of her mother's martyrdom to descend upon her, followed by the forked lightning of the remark she will make in order to shrug it off. But instead her mother's tragic tone sparks a fit of the giggles.

"Are you laughing?" Her mother sounds appalled.

"No!" Mia splutters. "Something went down the wrong way."

Maybe, she thinks after she hangs up, that was a Freudian slip. After her father left, all of them had gone the wrong way. Her mother toward despair, Katy toward sensitivity, Mia as far away from her own heart as she could get.

Forget diaries, Mia thinks. You can learn pretty much everything you need to know about a person from their credit card statement. A payment to an iffy website? An expensive lunch followed by an extravagant purchase in the lingerie department of Brown Thomas? A significant payment to an optometrist who just happens to do Botox shots on the side? Everyone has something to hide.

But Ronan doesn't have a credit card. He pays his rent and his bills in cash. As far as Mia can tell, he gets by on fresh air, surviving on measly community grants and arts bursaries and trickles of corporate sponsorship. He shops at German supermarkets. His house is furnished with things other people have thrown away.

It's the kind of place where terrorists would live in an HBO series. The living room is painted black, with a huge, lurid abstract oil painting instead of a flat-screen TV. The communal kitchen is not painted at all. The cooker is connected up to a gas cylinder with an orange rubber hose, the table is made from a Georgian door covered in a sheet of glass and surrounded by office chairs sprayed Day-Glo colors. There are half a dozen battered suitcases piled into one corner.

"Is someone moving in or out?" Mia asks, brushing plaster dust off a chair before she sits on it in her new Kooples trouser suit. This is her first sleepover at Ronan's place. Till now, they've always spent the nights at her apartment.

"Nobody's going anywhere." Ronan is poking around in the fridge. "The suitcases contain Hilary's past." He emerges, triumphant, with a saucepan. "They're part of an installation on psychological baggage. You're going to love Hilary. Everyone does."

"He's your best mate, right?" Mia asks.

"He is a she." Ronan takes the lid off the saucepan and peers in. "Yes, she probably is my best mate. We go back a long way."

Mia pictures a woman like the ones who showed up her seminar. Dungarees and home-dyed hair, Dr. Martens, too much makeup or none at all.

Ronan holds out the saucepan. "Lentil and carrot soup. I made it on Friday but it just keeps getting better."

Mia shakes her head. It is Wednesday.

Ronan's room looks as if it has been recently burgled by impatient, clumsy, tree-dwelling thieves. The floor is littered with books and cardboard boxes and bags of leaves and twigs and bundles of wood that somehow relate to Ronan's project. The radiator is still attached to the water pipes but not to the wall. A couple of hundred coat hangers are piled to head height in one corner. It's only weeks later that Mia finally realizes they have been sculpted into something; exactly what is not clear, but it is probably art.

They sit on Ronan's lumpy futon with his ancient, cracked MacBook overheating while he takes her on a virtual tour of his artist heroes. A Korean who covered a ten-story building in brightly colored doors. A Belgian who lived in a giant bird's nest attached to a tower in Rotterdam. His favorite pieces are by a Scottish artist who spent weeks building enormous, intricate snow spirals and icicle stars in the Canadian Arctic and then left them to melt.

They are beautiful but she doesn't get it. Who is going to see them in the bloody Arctic? What's the point of going to all that trouble to end up with a pile of slush? Why didn't the artist make the sculptures in plastic so he could hang them in a gallery where someone might buy them?

"How is this monetized?" she says.

"Monetized?" Ronan looks up from the screen.

"How do people buy this guy's work?"

"They don't buy it," he says. "They collect it in their heads."

"But it's so impermanent."

"Correct. The whole point is impermanence," Ronan laughs. "The snow is a metaphor. Everything melts away to nothingness eventually."

This thought scares Mia. She pushes the laptop away and pulls Ronan down beside her before this can melt away to nothingness too.

After Ronan has gone to sleep, Mia wraps herself in a sheet and picks her way through the piles of clutter to the door. She tiptoes down the uncarpeted wooden stairs to the landing, and she has her hand on the tarnished brass knob of the bathroom door when it is flung open from inside. The girl backlit in the doorway in the harsh bathroom light has delicate features and cropped inky black hair and very white skin. White except for the tattoos. The name "Donal O'Driscoll" is scrawled across her left breast. Mia can see this because the girl is completely naked.

"I'm sorry." Mia backs away and a splinter of wood catches in her bare heel.

"I'm Hilary." The girl lounges in the doorway, eyeing her coolly. There are other names Mia can't read scribbled on the undersides of her arms—they look like signatures. "What are you sorry for? That racket you and Ro made earlier?" She shrugs. "I was working. I just put my headphones on." She steps out of the way. "All yours," she says.

She walks slowly, deliberately slowly, Mia thinks, up the stairs. She pads past the open door of Ronan's room, then disappears into the room next door.

Mia soaks her foot in the grimy bathroom sink and has a go at the splinter with a pair of tweezers that has been left to rust on the window-sill. She is clumsy and ends up breaking it in two. What kind of woman wanders naked around a house that she shares with three men? Not the kind of woman Mia wants to be best mates with her boyfriend.

"Mia keeps smiling for no reason," her irritating assistant Dermot says at a work do a few weeks later. "Either she has a boyfriend or she's been brainwashed by a religious cult." He calls her the Ice Queen, Mia knows, behind her back. "So which is it?" he asks her.

"The former," Mia says. There is a moment of confusion while her half-cut colleagues try to work out what that means.

They badger her for details but Mia has had a lot of practice at stonewalling and she gives nothing away, and soon everyone at work loses interest, except Dermot, who thereafter never misses an oppor-tunity to ask her about her "mystery man."

In every other relationship Mia has maintained a mental spreadsheet of outgoings and incomings. Actual and emotional. But with Ronan, that's like trying to herd mice. On paper, she is the one with all the outgoings. Restaurants, movies, taxis. But she is the one who wants to go out in the first place. Ronan would prefer to spend an evening with a bottle of cold wine in Mia's claw-footed bath. His idea of Sunday brunch is taking a flask and sandwiches to a sculpture garden. He would prefer to walk, not take a taxi, whether it's raining or not.

He never buys her flowers or chocolates but he gives her other things. A copy of a poetry book she loved at school that he tracks down in a secondhand bookshop. A heart-shaped ivy leaf he staples to her pillow. A gray pebble with a white seam of marble that makes a perfect "M."

Ronan is right—everyone loves Hilary. Eamon and Andrew, his housemates, all of his arty friends, even the notoriously bad-tempered barman at Cassidy's. The only person who doesn't fall under the spell of her glittering eyes and her smoky voice and her carefully cultivated feline languor is Mia. She finds Hilary pretentious and stylized and it's hard to love someone who thinks they own your boyfriend.

Everything Hilary says to Ronan seems designed to exclude her. She starts intense conversations about artists Mia has never of. She brings up exhibitions they've seen together. She makes little in-jokes about people Mia has never met—lecturers from art college, characters she and Ronan met the summers they backpacked around Greece and Croatia. It was bad enough finding out that Ronan is best mates with a woman who strolls around naked. It's worse listening to her finishing his sentences.

Mia tries to avoid Hilary as much as she can, but she can't avoid her completely, because every time Ronan passes a Dumpster, he feels compelled to hoist himself up into it and rummage around to find something for her psychological baggage project. A detached steering wheel or a broken clock or an empty paint tin. Usually Mia tries to avoid skips too, but Ronan spots one as they are hurrying along Grantham Street on their way to a movie.

"Hang on!" He sprints back and climbs into it. After a moment, he reappears with a broken vacuum cleaner in his arms.

"Put that back!" Mia plants her hands on her hips. "We are not taking it to the cinema."

"You don't understand!" He lowers it carefully to the pavement by the hosepipe and gazes down at it in rapture. "This is a genuine 1970s Electrolux. Hilary's dad used to work for them. This will definitely have to go in the piece." He turns and disappears again.

"Ronan! Get back down here or I'll walk away."

"Hi, Mia!" She turns to see Dermot from her office. He's wearing jogging pants and a T-shirt, but he looks immaculate, as if he has just stepped out of a taxi around the corner and jogged the last few yards. "Who were you shouting at?" He looks up and down the street.

Ronan doesn't care who sees him rummaging in a skip, but Mia cares, on his behalf and on her own.

"I was on the phone," she says. Dermot looks at her empty hand. "On my headset." He looks at her head, where no set exists.

"Wait till you see this!" Ronan swings himself down off the skip and then hauls down a filthy wooden contraption with a long flex and puts it on the pavement. He has cobwebs in his beard and his jeans are filthy, but he is so excited that he doesn't even notice Dermot, who is staring at him openmouthed.

"Ronan," Mia says tightly, "this is Dermot, who works with me." The two men shake hands.

"I work *for* you really," Dermot corrects her, "don't I?"

"I can't hang around quibbling about prepositions," Mia says imperiously. "We're late for the cinema."

"Well"—Dermot smirks—"it's nice to finally meet Mia's mystery man!" He wipes the dust Ronan has left on his hand on his sweatpants. "I've got to run." He jogs away.

Mia wants to kick herself for caring what Dermot thinks but she kicks the wooden contraption that Ronan has dumped beside her instead. "What is this?"

"A trouser press," Ronan says, in the tone most men save for when they're saying "a Lamborghini." He rubs the dust off the top of it with his sleeve. "Did I ever tell you that me and Hilary once made a toasted cheese sandwich in one of these in our room when we were working in that fancy hotel in Antiparos?"

He didn't. He didn't mention that he and Hilary had shared a room either.

All summer Mia turns down invitations from her friends. Dinner parties, cocktail evenings, engagement drinks, a wedding in a country hotel in Laois. She doesn't want to expose Ronan to their scrutiny. Not yet.

"What kind of artist is he again?" her friend Caroline keeps asking. She is in charge of investments for one of the country's leading pension funds, but she can't seem to place the word "conceptual."

He's the kind kind, Mia wants to say. When she gets period pains in a tapas bar, he disappears to the pound shop next door and returns with a hot-water bottle, which he persuades the waiter to fill. He listens to her sardonic little anecdotes about how unhinged her mother was when she was growing up but doesn't laugh at her polished punch lines. Instead he says, "That must have been tough, how did you and your sister cope?"

In August, one of Mia's clients, a property developer who lost everything in the recession, drives all the way from Dublin to Clare and then over a cliff into the Atlantic. Ronan insists on going to the funeral with Mia. He puts his arm around her in the church, and afterward he walks up to the man's sons and shakes their hands and says he's sorry for their trouble. When Mia starts to cry on the way home, he makes her pull over and he holds her while she sobs. He seems to know, without her telling him, that she is crying not just for her client, but for her own father too.

But kindness does not pay Ronan's bills. When Mia counts the number of hours he has already spent on his current project and divides it by the pitiful arts grant he is getting, she realizes that he is earning about a quarter of the minimum wage. Mia has had her future mapped out since she was a student, but it is quite possible that Ronan will still be living like a student when he is forty.

So the next Saturday, on the way home from Cassidy's, after she has spent an hour listening to a bunch of his mates having a collective moan about cuts in arts funding, she says, casually, "Maybe you should think about building your own brand, like Damien Hirst."

"I don't"—Ronan frowns—"like Damien Hirst. All shock, no trousers."

Mia doesn't like him either. What sort of a person wakes up in the morning and decides to saw a cow in half or pickle a shark? But he is a conceptual artist and he is successful. That proves it can be done.

"Okay," she says, "but a bit of profile building might help you to get funding. I could set up a Facebook page for you. You could tweet about your work in progress."

"Mia, I'm too busy working to give a running commentary on what I'm doing."

"What about if I talk to my clients about corporate sponsorship?" she says. "It's tax-deductible, so you'd be doing them a favor."

"I can't see corporates going for my work." Ronan sounds doubtful. "Maybe Hilary's. Her installations are easier to put in an office foyer. You should suggest that to her."

The only thing Mia wants to suggest to Hilary is that she talk less and wear more. "Ronan, these cuts in funding are not good news, and with my accountant's hat on, I think you need to be thinking about a plan B. I suppose you could go back to lecturing."

"If I ever need a shortcut to destroying my soul, maybe." He shudders. "What's all this about?" He stops beneath a street lamp and looks down at her. "Oh, hang on, it's coming back to me, the very first thing I heard you say." He grins. "What was it? I'm broke and you're going to fix me."

Mia jabs him in the chest with her finger. "You told me you'd slept through my talk!"

"I was awake for the most important bit." He bends down and nuzzles her clavicle. "The money shot! Now, let me take that accountant's hat off . . ." He tries to lift an imaginary hat off Mia's head but she pulls away.

"I'm supposed to be interested when you talk about art, but you have no interest in what I do, what I'm good at."

"Mia, wait! Listen!"

"Why should I?" She hails a cab and climbs into it. "You don't!"

She is in bed, with the lights out, telling herself that she hates him, when the doorbell rings. When she opens the door, he picks her up and carries her back upstairs, and soon it turns out she doesn't hate him that much after all.

There is a box shoved into a corner of Ronan's room, between a bookcase and the wall. When he is downstairs making coffee, Mia tiptoes over, opens it and finds dozens of spiral-bound sketchbooks. She flicks through one. It's filled with drawings, two or three on every page—proper portraits. A study of a teenage boy hugging a football. An old man sleeping on a bench. A tough-looking woman smoking a cigarette.

Ronan can draw, really draw! If he can do this, she thinks, looking over her shoulder at his latest artistic endeavor—a body suit made from stitched-together leaves—why on earth is he doing that?

"Out of milk again!" he calls from the bottom of the stairs. "I'll go and get some." It's a ten-minute walk to the nearest Centra, so Mia takes her time as she turns the pages of the other sketchbooks, stopping to examine faces she recognizes. Ronan's housemates captured washing dishes at the sink, asleep on a sofa, playing cards. Two of his male housemates anyway. There isn't a single drawing of Hilary. Mia checks again, and this time she notices that a handful of pages have been torn from each sketchbook. Ronan must have thrown them away, she thinks, or deliberately hidden them.

She can't ask him if he's slept with Hilary, not straight out, but she desperately wants to know, so she starts by asking him how many women he has slept with. They are playing chess. Mia has just put Ronan's black king—represented today by her MAC lipstick, because the real king is missing—into check.

"That's a pretty weird question." His gray eyes drop in temperature, wet gravel to stone. Then he shrugs and takes the top off the lipstick and draws the number thirteen on his palm. He looks down at the board. "Your turn."

She doesn't have to think about it, but she pretends to, hoping to make him just a little bit jealous but also wondering how he'll react. "I've slept with—"

"I don't want to know," he says firmly. He nods at the board. "I meant it's your turn to make a move."

Nothing Mia owns is too short or too tight or too clingy, but she has always known how to draw attention to herself without appearing to try. She can flick through a clothes rail and pick out a color that will switch on her white-blonde hair like a lightbulb, a dress with a scooped neckline that will give her the neck of a Degas ballerina. If she rates her attractiveness against other women in a room, which she does, automatically, she is always in the top 10 percent; all right, 5 percent. But she has no idea how to measure herself against Hilary, who plays by different rules. Wears tiny camisoles over shapeless tweed skirts. Baggy jumpers with cutoff denim shorts. And then there are the tattoos.

"Is there a unifying principle to your body adornment?" Eamon's girlfriend asks one night in Cassidy's. Roughly translated this means "Tell us about your tats." If Mia had a euro for every time Ronan's mates used incomprehensible jargon like "context of futility" or "postmodern discourse," she would be richer than Bono. It turns out that Hilary did not just get very drunk and wander into a tattoo parlor, like a normal person. Instead she has turned her own body into a performance space. "People are works of art," she explains, "shaped by everyone who matters to them." So she has asked everybody important in her life to sign her skin and then turned the signatures into permanent markings.

Where is Ronan's name? Mia wonders. A few days later, when Hilary climbs onto a stool to open the kitchen window, she sees it, "Ronan Slattery," scrawled across her dusty right instep.

It could have been worse. It could have been on her inside thigh or on her bum, but still Mia's inner auditor decides to add Hilary in permanent marker to the list of "Things That Will Have to Go," right up there after "Beard."

Mia wants to fly Ronan to Rome for his birthday. "It's too much," he says, meaning the expense, not the eternal city.

"I can afford it, and I'd get to go too."

"You don't need me to go," he points out. "You could bring your sister."

A month ago, when Katy was still miserable about Ben, she might have come. But Ben, so much a part of Mia's history, is now actual history and her sister is seeing someone called Phil.

So instead of dining by candlelight in Trastevere on Ronan's birthday, Mia finds herself drinking beer and eating chicken wings in Rathmines with all his arty mates. And as if that isn't bad enough, Ronan is more impressed with Hilary's present—a piece of paper that says he has sponsored a tree—than hers—a brown cashmere jumper from Harvey Nichols and a set of expensive oil pastels.

By the time they pile out onto the street to go to a nightclub, everyone, including Mia, is drunk. They are too broke to pay for taxis to Leeson Street, so they walk up along the canal. It's cold and clear and the full moon is a silver balloon tangled in the reflections of the reeds. It should be a romantic walk but Ronan's mates ruin it, chasing one another along the grassy banks like overgrown children, which, Mia thinks spitefully through a haze of beer and bitterness, is what they are. Grow up! she wants to yell at them. Get a real job! Stop endlessly discussing the meaning of life and start living it.

The oil pastels are still in their box a week later. "Aren't you going to even try these?" Mia asks, hurt.

Ronan is sitting on the side of the futon, one sneaker off, one sneaker on. He has just pulled a T-shirt over his head and his hair is sticking out, a messy halo of static. "Probably not," he says, after a long pause. "I don't really draw."

"But I saw your sketches," she says before she can stop herself. "They're amazing!" He stares at her. "I was . . ." She clutches for a word that sounds prettier than "snooping." "I was curious."

"I see." Ronan frowns. "Well, those notebooks are pretty old. I moved on from figurative work a long time ago."

"It seems a shame not to use all that talent. You wouldn't have to stop doing your conceptual stuff but you could always do some portraits on the side. Commissions, you know, to earn a bit of money."

"I could." Ronan looks at her levelly. "But I don't want to. I'm curious too, Mia." His eyebrows disappear into his fringe. "Were you looking for something in particular? Because if there's anything you need to know about me, you can just ask."

She can't ask if he was ever in love with Hilary. If he might still be. That would make her sound weak, and weakness, she believes, brings out the worst in men. So instead she decides that it's time to take action.

"If you could change one thing about me, what would it be?"

"Why would I want to change anything about you?" He runs a thumb along her wrist, following the line of blue vein beneath the skin.

"Because you're human! Come on. There must be something!"

It doesn't matter what he says. All that matters is that he asks the question back so she can say "that beard" or "this house."

"You know what? There is one thing I would change about you." Ronan looks so serious that she feels scared, then she sees the softness in his gray eyes. "I'd change your childhood. Your father taking off. Your mother going crazy like that. I'd change it so you had a happier beginning."

"How can I get Ronan to give me flowers?" Mia asks Katy.

"Ask him. Say, 'Ronan, I'm a woman, I desire flowers, buy some for me.'"

Mia gives her sister a withering look.

"Did you ask Phil to bring you those?" There is a vase of bright orange Asiatic lilies on Katy's table. A bud vase with a single white rose on the mantelpiece. A spray of pink orchids in a water glass on the windowsill.

Katy laughs. "Phil's sister owns a flower shop on Camden Street. He's in and out of there every other day."

Maybe that's what she should do, Mia decides. Bring Ronan to a florist's. Make him think buying flowers is his idea, like getting rid of the beard. The beard is gone. It was easy in the end. She told him that kissing him was giving her a rash, and the next time she met him he had shaved it off. He looks kind of strange without it, a bit exposed. Not quite himself, but definitely better. It will just take getting used to.

Hilary's work is being exhibited as part of a group show in a gallery on Merrion Row. If, Mia thinks, you could call a dozen suitcases full of random objects surrounded by piles of junk "work."

Ronan drags her to the opening night. She stands beside him, reading Hilary's artist's statement over his shoulder.

Title: *I Am a Sad Case.*

The idiosyncratic selection of luggage items coupled with their random organization forms a galaxy of densities implying an idiomatic syntax of organic fluctuation.

Materials: Found objects.

Mostly found, Mia thinks, by Ronan when he and Mia were in hurry to get somewhere.

Hilary is looking nervous. She's wearing lace-up Dr. Martens with a green satin prom dress. There are dark green patches of sweat under the arms, Mia notes. Ronan has told Mia that it's a given that Hilary's installation won't sell, but that it needs a good reception from certain key critics to secure her funding.

She shoots Mia a jittery look now and plucks at Ronan's sleeve. "Shit," she whispers, nodding at a knot of journalists who have just arrived. "The wolves are gathering."

Ronan pulls her in for a hug, then ducks his head down so he can butt her forehead with his.

"You rock!" he says.

"Yeah, but what if I fucking don't?" she whispers.

He sways her from side to side. "You're rocking now."

They look at one another as if they are the only two people in the room. The sip of wine in Mia's mouth turns to vinegar.

Mia is chopping organic peppers and zucchini, which she is about to make into something inedible, when she sees Ronan pick up the card she left on her kitchen windowsill. It's an invitation to the office client Christmas dinner, a black-tie event in a gentlemen's club on St. Stephen's Green. "Plus one?" He grins. "That's me, right, the positive digit?"

Ronan doesn't have black tie; Ronan doesn't own a tie.

"I wasn't going to ask you." Mia tries to sound casual. "It's just work, no big deal, and most people won't be bringing partners anyway."

Ronan flicks the gilt edge of the creamy card with his thumbnail. "Okay." Mia tries not to hear the unexpected catch of disappointment in his voice.

No big deal. Her own voice comes back to mock her as she scours the Dundrum shopping center for the perfect cocktail dress. Tries on every pair of shoes she owns, then every pair of Katy's. Lies in a reclining chair in a beauty salon while a Lithuanian girl with icy fingertips glues extensions onto her eyelashes, one by one.

She is the only person at the dinner who hasn't brought a partner, but she is doing Ronan a favor, she tells herself, as she stands clutching her champagne flute, listening to the dreary talk about golf handicaps and the latest European financial reforms. Ronan has nothing in common with the people she works with. They are like—she feels a wave of mortification as the words come into her mind—chalk and cheese.

She wants to grab her coat and get a cab to Ronan's house, but instead she takes her seat in the oak-paneled dining room and pulls a cracker with the chief operating officer of an IT recruitment firm, and then lets him unfold a white tissue paper crown and place it clumsily on her head.

She dances with her boss. She brushes off a clumsy pass from Dermot. She comforts Orlagh, a partner in her fifties, who is crying her heart out in the ladies'. It is nearly midnight by the time she escapes. There is a long queue at the taxi stand. Carriages are lined up at the railings of St. Stephen's Green, the drivers with blankets in their laps, the horses' breath coming in smoky little clouds. Mia is tempted to take one, but she is just too sensible. She joins the queue at the taxi rank and waits her turn.

When she gets to Ronan's, music is blaring from the living room. Through it she hears voices and laughter. Ronan is wearing antlers made from two Christmas tree branches. Hilary seems to be wearing only a pair of odd socks and the brown cashmere jumper that Mia gave Ronan for his birthday. They are decorating an eight-foot tree. There's a half-empty bottle of tequila on the table, surrounded by abandoned lemon halves.

"No! Don't come in yet!" Ronan jumps up and propels her back out into the drafty hallway. He is very drunk.

"What's going on?" Mia sounds like the jealous girlfriend, or worse, the nagging wife.

He puts his hands over her eyes and they stand there, Ronan swaying, Mia seething, until Hilary yells, "Ready!"

Ronan steers Mia back into the living room just in time to see Hilary squatting on the floor, flashing her knickers, to light the last of dozens of tiny candles that are attached to the tree. The ends of the branches are sparkling with what look like real icicles. It is beautiful, Mia thinks, through the scald of jealousy she feels.

"We made the icicles in the freezer using Hilary's condoms," Ronan explains.

"At least I got some use out of them!" Hilary nudges him and they both giggle.

"Is it safe?" Mia snaps, wanting to cut through their camaraderie. "With all those flames?"

"Sssh!" Ronan says. "Don't ruin it!"

They stand together watching the tree until the last little flame dies away, then Hilary starts pulling the spent candles out of the holders and pushing new ones in.

"I thought you disapproved of Christmas trees?" Mia says to Ronan. She asked him to go shopping for one the previous week and he refused, saying they were bad for the environment.

"It's not a Christmas tree!" Ronan and Hilary say together.

"It's a pagan tree!" Hilary adds pompously.

"We liberated it," Ronan adds, "from a skip on the South Circular Road."

"Then we bought every birthday candle in Tesco!"

"And most of the lemons." Ronan reaches for the tequila bottle. "Time for another slammer. You want one?" He squints at Mia.

She shakes her head. "I think I'll just go up to bed." She waits for him to say he'll come too.

"Okay." He tips salt onto the back of his hand. "See you later."

When she wakes up, it is 7 a.m. and Ronan's half of the futon is empty. She dresses quickly and tiptoes downstairs, shivering. The house is in darkness. There are pools of water under the Christmas tree where the icicles have melted. The tequila bottle is lying on its side, empty. She creeps from room to room but there's no sign of Ronan and no sign of Hilary. She stands outside Hilary's room for a long time, biting her lip, asking herself whether this is something she wants to see or something she has to see. Then she wraps her fingers around the cold brass doorknob and in one swift movement opens the door.

The room is empty. The ironwork bed is made up with a carefully folded gray crocheted throw. There is a desk with ordered piles of papers. A corkboard with dozens of postcards pinned neatly to it in lines. An IKEA rail half full of clothes organized by color. Hilary's installation—the suitcases and junk that were carefully arranged in the gallery—is heaped in one corner.

One of the cases is open and a pile of loose drawings has spilled out. The drawings that are missing from Ronan's sketchbooks! Mia glances over her shoulder, then tiptoes across and kneels down to look at them. Thirty or forty pen and pencil sketches. She rifles through them, her heart pounding, looking for the naked portraits she is sure must be here. But the sketches she finds are just like the ones of Ronan's other housemates. Hilary asleep with her head resting on her arms. With a toothbrush tucked into her cheek. Doing a yoga shoulder stand.

"What are you doing?" Mia looks up to see Hilary at the door, still wearing Ronan's cashmere sweater, her hands wrapped around a steaming mug.

Mia drops the pages and stands up quickly. "I was just looking for Ronan."

"In my room?" Hilary says scornfully. "He's gone for a cycle to burn off the hangover. He left you a note."

"Oh." Mia bends down and shuffles the sketches together, trying to construct some sort of exit that might possibly contain a shred of dignity.

"Why don't you take them?" Hilary says calmly as she puts her coffee down on the desk and walks over. "They're Ronan's. I only borrowed them for my exhibition." She flicks the suitcase lid open with a movement of her bare foot. Her toenails are painted blue. "It's all in there, Mia. All our personal baggage. Every postcard he ever wrote me. Every picture we ever took."

"I'm sorry—" Mia begins.

"For what, exactly?" Hilary interrupts her. "For going through my things? For ignoring me? For yawning whenever I'm talking to Ro? For sticking your tongue down his throat so he can't answer when I ask him a question? We're best friends. For the record, that's all we are. We have ten years of history"—Hilary gives the suitcase a vicious kick—"but I don't fit into your perfect little picture. I bet you can't wait to get rid of me, like you got rid of his beard."

Mia starts for the door but Hilary cuts her off.

"What else is on your list of improvements, Mia? What exactly will Ronan have to do before he's good enough for you to bring him to your office party?"

Mia is shaking with anger but she can't get past Hilary, not without pushing her out of the way. "How dare you!"

"No!" Hilary shakes her head sadly. "How dare *you*! Ro is the nicest guy you will ever meet and you're trying to change him. And he'll let you because he's crazy about you. But if you keep changing him, he won't be the person you fell in love with." She walks to the door and holds it open. "You think I'm the big threat to you and Ro. But I'm not. You are."

"Hilary has to move out," Ronan tells Mia on a Sunday afternoon in January, when they are walking on the pier in Dún Laoghaire.

Mia turns away to look at the crumpled gray sheet of the sea so he won't see the look of relief on her face. "Really?"

She hasn't seen Hilary since the scene in her room, and she hasn't told Ronan what happened.

"I feel so bad for her." Ronan digs his hands farther into the pockets of his duffle coat. "Her show tanked. The bursary that was supposed to take her through to the summer has fallen through. She's paid rent up until the middle of February, but after that she's out on the street."

"Not literally out on the street," Mia says. "Surely?"

Ronan sighs. "She might be better off, to be honest. She'll have to move back in with her parents."

"I'm sure she'll be fine." Mia links his arm, noticing how worn his sleeve is, wishing he'd wear the North Face down jacket she bought him for Christmas. "Hilary strikes me as pretty tough."

"It's all an act." Ronan shakes his head. "The last time she lived with her folks, she got depressed, ended up trying to kill herself."

A splinter of pity catches at Mia's heart. Her inner auditor takes out a pair of tweezers and prepares to extract it. Hilary is not her problem, not anymore.

"I'm surprised you haven't considered art," Mia says to James Delaney. He is her least favorite client by some margin. The cocky twenty-five-year-old CEO of an app design company that has made two million euros' profit in the first two years of trading. "It's very tax efficient."

James, who is leaning back in his chair pouring a can of Red Bull down his throat, sits forward. "How efficient?"

"Let's see." Mia leaves a long pause to whet his appetite. "You can claim a wear-and-tear allowance at twelve and a half percent, so you'll recover your purchase price in about five years, by which time the art you've bought could have tripled in value."

His handsome face is neutral but his eyes have narrowed slightly, which she knows is his tell.

"I don't want cows and clouds in a gilt frame," he says.

"What about an installation?" Mia says, as if this has just occurred to her. "Something edgy, playful and provocative."

"Sounds like you," he says, though he is very publicly engaged to a TV presenter.

"Like your brand." Mia smiles. "I know of an artist who has a piece that would be perfect for your foyer. I'll ping you the details. But listen," she says, "you can't mention that it was me who hooked you up."

The flower section in the supermarket has taken over half of the fruit and veg aisle. "What's with the garden center in here?" Ronan stares at the massed bouquets of roses. "Where have they hidden the eggplants?"

"It's Valentine's Day next week." Mia has been wondering when he will notice.

"Or"—Ronan frowns—"as I call it, Hallmark Day. I could throttle the person who decided to turn love into a branded retailing op-portunity."

Mia's heart sinks. Everyone at work knows she has a boyfriend. She is going to look like a pity case if she doesn't get a single red rose. She hatches a plan.

The next morning, when they are walking into town from her place, she overshoots the turn for St. Stephen's Green and leads him along Camden Street. Ronan doesn't even notice. He is talking excitedly about Hilary. About the phone call she had out of the blue from some hotshot businessman who wants to buy her personal baggage installation. She was supposed to be moving out in two weeks. If this comes through, she can stay.

"I wonder how this Jack Donegan guy got hold of her details," he is saying as they get closer to Blossom & Grow.

"Yeah," Mia says innocently.

"Hey, I love this place!" Ronan puts his hands on his hips and looks up at the tall pale pink building. "That trompe l'oeil"—he points at the painted-on ivy—"is amazing."

Mia takes his arm and steps closer to the window, which is full of white tissue paper hearts.

"Can we take a quick look inside?" Ronan says.

"Really?"

"Well, I know I said I don't do the whole flower thing, but I was thinking . . ."

She smiles. Getting him to buy her flowers is going to be even easier than getting him to lose the beard.

"It would be nice to get Hilary a plant, you know, to celebrate her news."

Mia gapes at him. The fact that she is Hilary's secret benefactor does not change the fact that Hilary is a thundering bitch. But she is Ronan's best mate. And something she said that morning when she caught Mia snooping in her room has stuck in her mind.

If you keep changing him, he won't be the person you fell in love with.

"After you," she says. And she follows him into Blossom & Grow.

At four o'clock on Valentine's Day, Mia is at her desk attempting a complex tax calculation when her phone rings. "Delivery for you," the receptionist says. "It's a cardboard box," she adds quickly, with a trace of pity, in case Mia might be holding out for a dozen red roses.

The box is very heavy. Mia lumps it back to her office and dumps it on her desk. She is opening the cardboard flaps when Dermot puts his head around the door.

"Are those the files from DTL?" he asks.

Mia is staring into the box. There's a sheet of red tissue paper on top, and beneath it, packed tightly together, are twelve bags of flour. Plain. Self-raising. Rice. Corn. Rye. Buckwheat. Potato . . .

There's a page from a spiral-bound notebook tucked between the spelt and the whole wheat. It has been torn, roughly, into the shape of a heart and signed with a small "r."

"Jesus." Dermot comes over and stares into the box. "What the hell is this?"

"No idea." Somehow Mia manages to keep a straight face as she looks down at a dozen Valentine's Day flours.

CARNATION

Disappointment and Refusal.

Lara's therapist, Leo, made her list every single thing she had to do every day. Literally everything. *Get up, have a shower, eat breakfast, go to work, drive home, make dinner, go to bed.*

If she found herself frozen at her worktable, without the energy to reach into a bucket and pick out a flower, or sitting outside her dad's house, where she lived now, unable to get out of the car, she was supposed to take the list out of her bag and simply do the next thing written on it.

Each line on the list, Leo had explained, was another stepping-stone across the torrent of grief that she had been trying to get over since her marriage ended and her father died.

She felt the sadness rise as she unlocked the door of Blossom & Grow on a damp, dark late-October morning, so she fished around in her bag until she found her list. Her heart plummeted when she read what was written at the top. She let her eye skip farther down the page, then got to work.

- *Check that both delivery boxes have arrived.*
- *Plug in seven strings of fairy lights.*
- *Light candles for the lanterns.*
- *Sweep up last night's debris!*
- *Trim any dead leaves off the bay trees and set them up on either side of the door.*

When all this was done, she locked the door again, found a Stanley knife and cut the tape on the smaller of the two delivery boxes. There were three buckets inside and each one held bunches of blooms, tightly wrapped in paper. She opened them and ticked the flowers off on another list, the one she had written in the order book. White and purple veronica. *Alchemilla mollis*. Salvia Picante. Green hypricum. Purple dahlias.

She cut a half inch off each stem, pulled the lower leaves off and plunged the stems into clean water, then left them to rehydrate while she moved on to the second box.

It was packed to the brim with crimson velvet—seventy Black Magic roses. She unwrapped them carefully but not quite carefully enough. She felt a sharp hook tear at the pad of her thumb and a little bead of blood ran down along her wrist.

Why did roses have to have thorns? she asked herself for the millionth time.

It is 7 a.m. on a wet autumn morning but the atmosphere in the kitchen of the one-bedroom apartment on the third floor of Block A, Beacon Court, is wintry.

Jennifer Kelly, in a pink fleece dressing gown with dried baby spit on the lapel, is looking out of the window so she doesn't have to look at her husband's face.

"Oh no," Jack says again, staring at the cufflinks in the little red leather box. A silver "X" for one sleeve, an "O" for the other. A kiss and a hug. This is how they still sign their texts, though kissing and hugging have been in short supply since Ava came along.

"If you don't like them," Jennifer says huffily, "I can take them back!"

"I didn't know we were doing presents."

"Are we doing cards?" she asks, looking pointedly at the unopened envelope propped against his cereal bowl. "Because I can't bring that one back, I've already signed it."

"I was going to give you yours tonight."

"Well, don't bother." The kitchen is so small she doesn't even have to turn around completely to reach out and dump her bowl and coffee cup into the sink. The clatter wakes Ava on the other side of the paper-thin wall and she begins to wail.

"That's all I need," Jennifer says, under her breath.

Jack looks at her, then looks at the door, unsure of what to do. When Jennifer does not move, he sighs, puts his glasses on and hurries into the baby's room. She can hear him walking slowly backward and forward in the bedroom, talking to Ava in the low, soothing tone of voice he used to use when Jennifer was upset.

Does it never occur to him that she still needs soothing too? Ava has developed silent reflux, which means she has to be fed every hour. Jennifer can't remember the last time she slept through the night.

When Jack comes back, he has his coat on. "She's gone back to sleep. You probably have half an hour. Why don't you have a shower? Look"—he comes over and puts his arms around her and holds her tight—"can we start again?"

"I don't know," she begins. "I just feel we're not on the same page anymore, not even the same book, and I—"

"I'm sorry." He is trying to catch sight of his watch over her shoulder. "I meant can we start again when I get back. I'm already late for my train."

She shrugs him off. "Well, don't let me keep you!" She turns away.

"I'll make it up to you," he says. "I promise."

She shakes her head and squirts washing-up liquid into the sink and turns on the tap. After a moment she hears him go out into the hall. The front door opens then closes with a loud click. Ava begins to wail again.

Jennifer goes into the bedroom and picks the baby up. Ava smells of Woolite and breast milk and a trace of Jack's aftershave where he must have pressed his chin against her cheek. The musk and bergamot scent, which used to make Jennifer weak at the knees, catches in her throat now. "He'd better not try to make it up to me with a bunch of petrol-station flowers," she says loudly over the baby's protesting squawks.

Across the courtyard in the penthouse flat of Block D, Jenny Kelly, in an embroidered red kimono that skims her toned thighs, is flinging bottles of aftershave into a bulging black plastic bag that already contains James's Xbox, his iPad and his precious Nespresso with water still sloshing around inside it. Is there room for his books? James is not a big reader. She retrieves *Who Moved My Cheese?*, then *Blink*, and she has *The Presentation Secrets of Steve Jobs* in her hand when her mobile chimes. Her self-respect has no intention of answering it, but her free hand has other ideas.

"Jenny, I'm so sorry I missed your calls last night. My phone died and I was working late. I'd left my charger back at the hotel."

"You were working late!" She sounds unconvinced, James thinks. Somewhere between "significant doubts" and "incredibly suspicious." "How late exactly?"

"I don't know." He yawns. "Half twelve or one."

"Well, that's funny"—she doesn't sound amused—"because according to Mark Zuckerberg, you were in a club called Madame JoJo's at a quarter past midnight with your arm around someone called Annelise."

Fucking Internet, James thinks, ignoring the irony that he earns a considerable living from it. It's impossible to do anything, *anything*, without broadcasting your every activity as it happens to the world and its wife (or in this case, his fiancée).

"Yeah," he says, trying to sound casual. "A whole bunch of us headed over after we finished the pitch rehearsal. They were all gagging for a drink. I only went along to pay for the first round, then I came straight back to the hotel." *With Annelise*, he does not add, *who is asleep on the other side of the closed bathroom door.*

"The hotel where, presumably," Jenny grunts as if she is lifting something heavy, "you were happily reunited with your phone charger. So why didn't you call me then?"

"I didn't want to wake you. Listen, I'd better go. I'm out on the street trying to catch a cab." He opens the bathroom window so the traffic noise from the Tottenham Court Road will filter in to support his story. "The presentation is in half an hour." "I'll call you the minute I get out. Okay?"

Jenny twists off the antique diamond engagement ring that he gave her on the Ponte Vecchio and drops that into the bag on top of *The Seven Habits of Highly Successful People*. "Don't bother."

She tucks the phone under her ear and drags the bag past the double-height plate-glass windows and out into the hall.

"Look," James says soothingly, "I should have called you, no matter how late it was. I'm sorry. I haven't been looking after you. I've been distracted."

He hears something that sounds like a snort of amusement from the other end of the phone.

"That's one way of putting it." Jenny slides open one of the white doors on the floor-to-ceiling storage cupboard and hauls out a bag of golf clubs.

James winces. "What are you doing?" he asks. "What's all that crashing around?"

His head is still booming from the music in the club and blurry from the line of coke Annelise cut after they finished the vodka in the minibar. But the meeting isn't till 9 a.m. A couple of espressos will soon sort him out.

"I'm packing up your stuff," Jenny says coldly. "You can pick it up when you get in from the airport."

Suddenly his head clears and he realizes just how much trouble he's in. "Jennifer?" He always defaults to her full name when he wants her to know he is being sincere. "Don't you think you're overreacting just a little bit? I'm sorry from the bottom of my heart if I upset you, but—"

"Hey?" Annelise taps on the door. "Open up! I need to pee!"

James turns on the shower. "It's lashing rain here. I've got to go. We can sort this out later. You know I love you, and if you don't, I'll prove it. I'll—" He realizes the line has gone dead.

Jenny stares at the wallpaper on her phone. A photograph taken two years ago, when he was still a software coder working eighty hours a week trying get his app design company off the ground.

She'd met him a few months before, in an Indian restaurant on George's Street. "Don't look now, but a seriously cute guy drinking a mango lassi is checking you out," her friend Liz said. Jenny had seen him on the other side of the restaurant, looking at her over the rim of his glass, giving her what her brother called "the hairy eye."

She had forgotten all about him by the time they left. Suzanne had hailed a cab for herself and Jenny was walking down Merrion Row to catch the Dart when she heard running footsteps behind her. Her hand closed around the Mace spray in her pocket and she swung around, and there he was, holding out a dozen carnations.

"Did you just steal those?" She blinked at them. "From the restaurant?"

"I borrowed them." His voice was gravelly and self-assured. *I like me*, it seemed to say. *I think you'll like me too.* "But I don't think they'll welcome me back at that restaurant in a hurry."

"That's a shame," she said. "It's the best Indian in Dublin."

"You've obviously never been to Vermilion." He handed her the carnations. The guard leaves, like little green hoods, had slipped down off their red heads. They smelled of cloves. "We'll have to do something about that."

The phone buzzes suddenly in Jenny's hand. It's the journalist who is coming to interview her at two this afternoon. Hair and makeup girl has come down with flu. Can you do your own? Also can photographer come at 1 to get the snaps out of the way?

Great. Jenny gives the golf clubs a quick kick as she passes. This is all she needs.

The interview is a promo for the new travel show she's fronting. They're going to ask about James. If she tells the truth, it'll be all over the paper on Sunday. But maybe that's a good thing, she thinks. At least if she goes public, James won't be able to change her mind.

The envelope had been in the bottom of Lara's bag and at the top of her list for four days now, but there always seemed to be something more urgent on her list. *Clean out the cold room. Feed the succulents. Design a window for Halloween. Answer the phone.*

The shop didn't open for another hour, but it might be urgent. She took the call. "Blossom & Grow?"

"I was just about to give up!" It was a man's voice. He didn't sound, Lara thought, like the kind of man who gave up that easily.

"We don't open till nine."

"I'll be in a meeting at nine and it'll be too late. Look, you're the third florist I've tried. This is an emergency. My future marriage is going down in flames and you may be the only person who can save it."

"How can I say no to that?" Lara opened the order book. "What do you need?"

"An urgent delivery to Jenny, no, make it *Jennifer* Kelly, Penthouse, Block D, Beacon Court. Can you do it right away?"

Ciara wasn't coming in until eleven. "I could do it around eleven thirty if that's any use."

"It'll have to do. Okay, we need to get all the big guns out here. How many red roses do you have?"

Lara looked at the four buckets of roses she had just finished conditioning. "How many do you need?"

"Twenty—no, make it fifty. Are they definitely all red?"

"I'm pretty sure all the red roses are red today"—she smiled—"but that's a lot of roses."

"Well, between you and me," he said meaningfully, "I'm in a lot of trouble."

"Oh." Her smile faded. She didn't want to know what kind of trouble required two hundred euros' worth of roses to put right. She just hoped that Jennifer Kelly had a lot of vases and a very forgiving nature. She found a pen to take down the message.

She was picking out the fifty best Black Magics when she heard a frantic tapping. She looked up and saw a man wearing glasses peering in the window. He waved frantically at her.

"I'm really sorry," he said when she opened the door. "I know you're not actually open until nine, but I have to be at my desk at eight forty-five and I've just ruined my wife's day and it's our fourth anniversary. Do you think I could . . ." He waved his hand tentatively in the direction of the shop. His nails were bitten down to the quick.

"Of course," she said. "Come in."

He headed straight for the pink carnations. Lara didn't usually stock them. These were an over-order for a seventies-themed party. They were meant to be ironic, like the little cocktail sticks with cubed cheese and pineapple that had been served as canapés.

"Can I take six of these?" The man pointed at them. "No, what the hell! Make it a dozen. Could you deliver them today?"

"Would just before lunch be okay?"

"Better than okay." He checked his watch. "Could you put a message in? I know what I want to say but I don't have time to write a card." Lara copied down the message, the name and the address.

It was only after he'd paid her and dashed away that the coincidence hit her. Two women with identical names who lived in the same apartment complex getting "sorry" bouquets on the same morning from desperate husbands?

Michael was writing to say sorry. That was what her therapist kept telling her. Lara had been seeing Leo once a week since her father died. He was tiny and gray-haired, with a Boston accent. He wore terrible T-shirts with therapist-y slogans like *Be Unafraid, Be Very Unafraid* and *The Mind Is a Darkroom Where Negatives Develop*, but despite that he was wise and gentle and incredibly kind.

She had given him all of Michael's letters to read because she still couldn't face reading them herself and it didn't seem right to throw them out. He had handed the last one back to her on Friday. "This one is different," he'd said. "I'd like you to read it yourself. You know I wouldn't ask you to if I didn't think you were able." She did know. Leo and the shop had been her lifelines. Lara had marked off the months since the summer with the hours she spent at her therapy sessions and the flowers she held in her hands.

Agapanthus and peonies in June. Scented stock and sweet peas in July. Sunflowers and sweet William in August. By the time September's oriental lilies and ornamental cabbages appeared, she wasn't hiding upstairs in the workroom anymore. She was spending more time in the shop, answering the phone, dealing with the customers. One Sunday she spent the afternoon at an allotment belonging to a friend of Ciara's, picking lamb's ear and dusty miller and veronica for a wedding, and didn't think about Michael once, but she kept remembering a Patrick Kavanagh poem she'd learned at school, the one about how every old man he saw reminded him of his father.

Her dad would have approved of the carnations, she thought, as she chose the stems from the bucket. He had wooed her mother with carnations long before they fell out of fashion. Twelve didn't look like enough, so she filled them out a little with silver dollar eucalyptus leaves, and wrapped them in layers of pink and purple tissue paper.

Then she got to work on the huge bunch of roses. By the time she was finished, the bundle of stems was almost too thick to hold, and she had to tape four sheets of tissue and cellophane together for the wrapping.

The bouquet was magnificent, but it looked more like an arrangement for a luxury hotel reception than a gift for a person. Beside it, the small, inexpensive bunch of carnations looked sweet and heartfelt.

How many miles has she walked this morning? Jennifer wonders, as she trudges back and forth across the IKEA rug in the apartment's doll's-house-sized living room. She was too miserable to get dressed and wrestle with the stroller but now she wishes she had gone out for some fresh air because Ava won't go down. Her eyes are glassy with tiredness but every time she starts to drop off (please, please, please, Jennifer wills her to sleep), her hands clutch at the air and she wakes herself up with a heartbreaking cry.

"It's okay!" Jennifer croons but Ava knows that it isn't. The baby can pick up on the slightest change in her mood and she feels Jennifer's upset as if they are still part of one body.

Jennifer pulls her phone out of the pocket of her dressing gown, but there are no missed calls, no messages from Jack. She remembers their first proper fight. A stupid argument about whether global warming was a real threat to the planet, as she believed, or, as Jack kept stubbornly insisting, a sideshow to distract the West from Third World poverty.

The next morning when she got to the bank call center in Tallaght where she worked, there was a huge bouquet of white lilies on her desk. They lasted for a week and every time she looked at them she felt happy. And nothing, not the fear that she might soon lose her job or the angry callers who seemed to hold her solely responsible for the collapse of the entire Irish banking system, could spoil her happiness.

There have been other fights since the wedding. Occasional flare-ups about important things, like whether they could afford to buy the flat and whether she should take redundancy and have a baby. But since Ava came along, the fights seem to be about things that don't really matter. Who used the last of the low-fat milk? Who left the heating on? Who put the bin bags in the wrong drawer? And somehow these tiny, pointless niggles feel like bigger issues than global warming or world poverty ever did.

The only flowers Jack has given her in the last year were a bunch he brought home after he'd forgotten to book the babysitter and they had to miss out on a friend's birthday dinner. Awful yellow and orange chrysanthemums wrapped in plastic with the Maxol price tag still stuck on. It was hard, looking at them, not to remember the lilies and compare their lives now to the happiness they'd had back at the start.

The baby seems to be settling at last. Jennifer walks to the door and back to the window. She sees her own ghost floating in the glass and stops short. Who is that? she thinks. She still hasn't lost her baby weight and the unflattering dressing gown is pulled tight around the bulge of her stomach. Her hair is lank and her roots are growing out. Who could blame Jack, she thinks bitterly, for not loving her as much as he used to?

She looks through her reflection across the courtyard and up to the penthouse apartment in the block opposite. A woman of her own age is sitting in front of the huge arched window putting on makeup. Her blonde hair ripples down the back of her tiny red silk dressing gown that does not, Jennifer guesses, have dried breast milk stiffening in patches on the front. For a moment she feels as if she would give anything—her husband, even the baby in her arms—to be that other woman for a day.

Jenny dips the individual lashes in a blob of glue, tilts her head back, narrows her eyes and drops the lashes one by one onto her own. Her phone buzzes again and she squints at the screen. A text from James. Sent you a little something to say a big sorry, it says. Some colossal floral monstrosity this way comes, she thinks grimly. But it's not going to work this time.

The lash glue is making her eye stream. As she reaches for a tissue, she sees a silhouette in the window of an apartment across the way. A woman, probably not much older than she is, cradling a baby in her arms. A picture of domestic contentment. Madonna and child. Before she can stop herself, she is crying, really crying. That was supposed to be me, she thinks.

And for a moment she is ready to forgive James. Then she remembers the Facebook picture. James with his arm thrown around the bare shoulders of the tall, dark-haired girl. Something that might have been innocent but then again might not. It didn't matter, because by now Jenny couldn't tell anymore.

"I was just a penniless coder when we got together," James said in his most recent interview. "Jenny was this superstar TV presenter. Totally out of my league. I made a complete idiot of myself to get her." But it was that idiot Jenny wanted to have children with, she thought, not this one in the Facebook photo.

"Wow!" Ciara leaned her bike against the counter and stared at the enormous bunch of roses. "What did the guy do? Kill someone?"

"Possibly." Lara was struggling to get her arms around the bouquet.

"Here! Let me give you a hand."

"No, you stay here. If you could get the flowers for the Fitzgerald wedding started while I'm out, that would be great."

"Did you read the letter?"

"Not yet." Lara gasped under the weight of the roses. "Hand me those carnations, will you? And my keys?"

She began to edge carefully across the floor, hidden by the flowers.

Ciara went ahead of her and held the door open. "You have to read the letter, Lara. It's hanging over you like the sword of . . . whoever's sword hangs over you waiting to drop."

"Damocles," Lara grunted.

"Yeah, him. The swearier cousin of Hercules."

Lara looked over the roses at the shuttered front of the Camden Deli across the street. A sudden gust of wind rattled the "For Sale" board that hung outside and tore at the cellophane on the bouquet. Lara dropped her car keys as she tried to hold on to the flowers. As she bent down sideways, trying to scoop them up, her bag slipped off her shoulder, scattering its contents into the gutter. She glimpsed her phone facedown in a puddle, her purse upside down, half open, and then, out of the corner of her eye, she saw a tiny flash of gold rolling away. Her wedding ring! She let the bouquets fall from her arms and made a dive for it just as it disappeared into a drain.

She fell to her knees. The ring, glittering in the darkness below, had landed on a pipe, but as she pushed her fingers through the grate to try to reach it, it fell into the water.

Just when you think you have lost everything, she thought, there is always one more thing to lose.

"It's only a ring, Lara." That's what her dad would say. She forced herself to stand up and wiped the grit off her knees. She wasn't the first person to have her heart broken, or the last. Look at her dad, who had lost the love of his life when he was younger than Lara was now. Look at poor Ciara, who had been dumped by the husband she adored.

She bent down to examine the bouquets. The cards had been knocked off and the heads of two of the roses had been snapped. If she went back to replace them, the deliveries would be late, but there were so many, two would hardly be missed. She'd slide the stems out and made a mental note to refund the difference to the customer's credit card.

She steered the flowers into the van and bent down to pick up her things and stuff them back into her bag. As she stood up to go, she saw it. The envelope was a few feet away, by the wheel of a car, the edge of it lifting slightly in the wind. Lara held her breath, willing it to blow away, but it stubbornly stayed put. She picked it up, sighed and shoved it back into her bag too.

The woman in the dressing gown who opened the door of Apartment 22A Beacon Court looked utterly miserable. The baby in her arms was wailing like an ambulance siren. Lara had to lean to one side to see around the bouquet of roses. "I hope I didn't wake her when I rang the buzzer."

"No, she was—" The woman stopped and blinked at the flowers, as if she thought they might be a hallucination. The baby, sensing the change in the atmosphere, suddenly fell silent.

"Are those," the woman whispered, "for me?"

Lara smiled at her over the baby's head. "They're pretty heavy and you have your hands full. Why don't I put them in water for you?"

"They won't fit in the sink." The woman stood to one side to let her in. "You'd better put them in the bath."

Lara put the bouquet carefully in the tub and ran in some cold water. "Give them a few minutes before you put them into vases," she said.

The woman was smiling, jiggling the baby on her hip. "Thank you. I'm just a bit lost for words here. Neither of us has ever seen so many flowers in our lives."

"Well, enjoy them! Both of you."

The woman beamed. "Thank you, we will." All the sadness was gone from her eyes. They were shining with happiness. Lara saw this small miracle happen every day but she never got tired of it. Words had to pass through the head but flowers, she thought as she waited for the lift to come, went straight to the heart.

The whole flat is filling up with the sweet scent of the roses. Jennifer puts the baby down, then goes back and sits on the edge of the bath. She opens the tiny white envelope and slips the card out. *Sorry! X O, J.*

She reaches out a finger and counts their velvety heads. There are forty-eight. One, she smiles as she realizes, for every month of the four years that she and Jack have been married.

Jenny is bagging up James's clothes when the doorbell rings. She freezes. The journalist is early and now she will have to explain why the flat is littered with bulging black sacks. But when she opens the door, it's not the journalist standing out in the corridor. It's a tall, thin woman with long dark hair holding a tiny bouquet of flowers.

"Delivery for Jennifer Kelly?"

That old trick of James's, Jenny thinks, using her full name to try to get around her. "Yes, I'm Jennifer Kelly, but I don't want—" She stops as it hits her, the sharp-sweet scent of cloves. She hasn't smelled carnations since that first night when James chased her down the street with the table decorations he'd stolen from the Indian restaurant.

"Oh!" She claps her hand over her mouth. "I think I'm going to blub!"

"That's okay." The delivery woman smiles. "That's allowed. It's pretty much expected."

She pulls out a tissue and hands it over. Jenny dabs her eyes. "Not when you're wearing a full set of stick-on lashes. I was expecting flowers, I just wasn't expecting"—she takes the carnations the woman holds out to her—"*these*."

She stands in the hall after the door has closed and counts the carnations. There are exactly twelve of them, like there were that first night. She opens the little cream envelope, hoping that it won't say something glib that will ruin this perfect gesture. But James has kept it simple. *Sorry!* the card says. *XoXo, J.*

"I lost my wedding ring," Lara told Ciara when she got back to the shop.

"I gave mine to that homeless woman who sits beside the bank machine on Baggot Street," Ciara said bitterly. "Poor cow. I hope she has better luck with it than I did."

They went upstairs to check the wedding flowers. Ciara had almost finished the centerpieces. Lara would come in early next morning to do the bouquet.

The creamy millefeuille roses had arrived from Holland yesterday and been left in the warm kitchen, where they were opening like tulle ballerina skirts. The pale pink peonies were in the coolest corner of the shop downstairs so they wouldn't go over. The wildflower man would be in at 6 a.m. to deliver the cornflowers and foxgloves. Every flower in the bouquet had a special meaning for the bride. She had known exactly what she wanted, Lara remembered, and had turned up at the shop with her own color swatches and mood boards and Pinterest links.

Ciara went back to work while Lara went downstairs and put the kettle on. As she waited for it to boil, she slipped her hand into her bag and took out the envelope. It was dog-eared and damp from where it had fallen on the road. The American postmark was blurred. Her name—her maiden name—in Michael's small, neat handwriting was smudged. Lara Kiely. She was so used to seeing Lara Grey that it looked strange to her. That's who I am now, she thought. That's who I've always been.

She was about to open the envelope, when the phone in the shop began to ring. "Are you trying to ruin my life?" a voice said when she picked up.

"Sorry?"

"This is James Delaney. I rang first thing this morning. I ordered two hundred euros' worth of red roses."

"Yes," Lara said, placing his voice. "I just delivered them."

"Really? Then why did my fiancée just text me a picture of a scabby bunch of carnations?"

"I don't know—" Lara began. Then she stopped, because suddenly she did know. The cards had fallen off the bouquets. She must have clipped them back on to the wrong ones then delivered the flowers to the wrong addresses. "I'm so sorry."

"Screw sorry! I've just stepped out of a meeting to call you. I'm going back in again now and the fifty red roses I ordered and paid for had better be delivered by the time I get out."

Lara swallowed. "I don't have fifty roses left. I could deliver them tomorrow or I could refund your money right away."

"I want a full refund anyway," he said. "And I don't care where you get the roses, but they'd better be in my fiancée's grateful hands exactly one hour from now. Is that clear?"

When she heard what the man had said to Lara, Ciara wanted to call him back and tell him where to shove his roses. She wanted to take the envelope out of Lara's bag and tear it into a hundred pieces. She wanted to ring Lara's therapist and tell him to get his finger out because even now, half the time, Lara seemed to be drowning not waving, clinging to the wreckage of her past life when she should be swimming to save herself.

There were a lot of things she wanted to do, but in the end she settled for making a pot of mint tea, sticking on Lyric FM and trying to talk Lara into calling around to the woman who had been given the roses by mistake to get them back. But of course Lara wouldn't hear of doing that, so Ciara got on her bike and did a mercy dash to three local florists to beg, steal and borrow every Black Magic rose they had in stock.

When Jenny opened the door again, all she could see were roses. Dozens and dozens of them crowded together in a massive bouquet that appeared to have grown legs. Then a head leaned around the side of the cellophane. It was the same delivery woman who had brought the carnations.

"Oh, hello!" Jenny smiled at her. They'd only met for a minute earlier, but it had turned out to be a very important minute, the one before she had decided to retrieve her engagement ring from the bottom of the bin bag. "Are you lost?"

"No. I've made a terrible mistake. I got two deliveries confused. The carnations I brought here earlier were for someone else. This is the bouquet your fiancé actually ordered." She held out the roses.

Jenny stared at them. James hadn't sent her carnations to show her that he was still the guy who had chased her down the street. That guy didn't exist anymore.

"Tell him I don't want it!" she said.

"Please," the delivery woman said. "This is all my fault, not his."

"But something is his fault." Jenny looked into the woman's eyes—they were brown, almond-shaped, honest. "Nobody sends that many roses unless they've done something really bad, do they?"

The florist opened her mouth as if she was going to contradict her, then closed it again and shook her head slowly. "No," she said.

"Ciara," Lara said when her assistant picked up the phone, "would you mind locking the shop up today? It's been a pretty emotional day. I'm too worn out to come back."

"No problem. Oh," Ciara said, "a guy just came in. Glasses, kind of frazzled-looking? He said you delivered forty-eight roses to his wife by mistake."

"Was he upset?"

"He was walking on air. He said thank you about a million times. Apparently you might just have saved his marriage."

"I think I've just broken up someone else's," Lara sighed. "I can't seem to do anything right today."

"That other guy sounds like a right bollox!" Ciara said, after Lara had told her what had happened. "And that girl dodged a bullet. You might have gotten the address wrong but the flowers got it right. They always do. Now you go straight home"—she took a beat—"and read the bloody letter. Get it over with and move on."

When Lara got home, she took the letter out of her bag before she even took her coat off. She stood at the kitchen window, looking out at her dad's overgrown garden. It was where she had seen Michael for the very first time. Her father had hired him to landscape the garden and to clear a line of pines that were casting long shadows over his wildflower borders.

Lara had stood in this exact spot and watched them plan it out. Her dad, in his mid-fifties then, still dark and striking, striding back and forth in his crisp three-piece suit, talking nonstop, while Michael, tall and silent, in browns and greens that made him seem part of the earth and the leaves, followed a few steps behind.

She tore the envelope open, pulled the letter out and began to read.

Dear Lara,

I hope this letter finds you well, as happy as you can be with everything that has happened. And I hope that it won't come as a shock to you that, if you have no objection, I would like to file for a divorce.

I want to marry Glen—as you've probably guessed. But I want you to be free, Lara, to find someone else, to have all the love and happiness you deserve.

Lara remembered the day Michael had proposed, in a Victorian glasshouse in Kew Gardens in London. It was November outside but the air was tropical beneath the lush canopy of palm trees.

Lara had thought that marriage would be like that glasshouse. A place that let in the light and kept the cold out, where trust and love could be planted and flourish protected from the outside world.

She looked back down at the letter.

I think about you often and always with love and regret for the pain I caused you. And I think about something I said to you after Ryan died, something that I realize now must have sounded cold and hurtful.

When I said that Ryan had died for a reason, the reason was that I was being punished for lying, for hiding the truth about myself. I deserved it, but you, Lara, you had done nothing wrong, yet you were being punished too.

Of all the things I am sorry for, I am sorriest for that.

Love,
Michael

There were tears of sadness in Lara's eyes as she folded the letter, but there were tears of forgiveness too. She propped it up on the windowsill and looked out.

Her dad would be brokenhearted if he could see what had become of his garden. There were two smashed panes in the greenhouse. The trellis for the honeysuckle had buckled. The flower beds were choked with weeds and fallen leaves. The grass was a foot high, flattened by the wheels of the bins that Lara dragged in and out whenever she remembered.

She imagined how it would look if her dad was still alive. The green velvet of the lawn trimmed, the flower beds covered in a blanket of wood chippings. The roses pruned. The water feature he'd been planning before he died, sitting on the circle of white gravel. The garden had been, for him, what the flower shop was for her. "There is no hurt that a garden spade won't heal," he used to say.

His gloves were still on the hook by the back door. When she slipped her hands into them, she had the strongest sense that she was touching his hands. As if this was something they were going to do together. She unlocked the back door and stepped outside.

It was dark by the time she was finished, but the lawn was cut and the greenhouse was sparkling and she had dumped six wheelbarrows of rotting leaves onto the compost heap. And she knew now where her dad would have put the water feature.

Not on the gravel at all, but beneath the winter-flowering cherry he had had planted the year her mother died. It came into flower in December, just in time for her anniversary. Tiny, fragile pink blossoms that smelled of summer.

Maybe Lara would put in the water feature herself. A slab of Wicklow granite. Her dad would like that. He had proposed to her mother by the river in the place they had named her after. Driven her to Laragh for a walk by the waterfall, with a ring in his pocket and the trunk of his car filled with flowers.

She was standing at the sink, scrubbing the earth from under her nails, when she heard her dad say her name. He didn't sound ghostly at all. He sounded alive and quite impatient. "Are you going to leave those flowers in the trunk all night or what?"

She suddenly remembered them, the forty-eight red roses she had forgotten to bring in. They'd never survive a night without water.

She dried her hands and went out to get them. Back in the house, she found scissors and cut the twine that held the stems together. The roses seemed to sigh with relief when they were released. She put a plastic bucket into the sink, and as it filled with water, she looked at the envelope propped against the window.

Leo was always saying that no matter how bad things were, she had choices. She had a choice now. She could go on asking herself why roses had thorns or she could be thankful that thorns had roses.

She turned off the tap and went upstairs. The spare room was still full of unpacked boxes she'd brought with her after she split up from Michael. She searched until she found the one she was looking for. Inside, wrapped in newspapers, were all of her mother's vases. She carried them downstairs and washed them carefully one by one. The green glass amphora, the heavy Waterford crystal, the red and white Lalique.

Then she filled every vase with roses and every room in the house with beautiful flowers.

DAFFODIL

Survival and New Beginnings.

The snow was back. It had started falling at four o'clock, and by the time Phil pulled the bike into the loading bay outside Blossom & Grow, Camden Street looked like a peaceful scene from a Christmas card. Inside the shop, though, Lara and Ciara were furiously busy making festive wreaths. He had only dropped in, as he did every few days, to check on his sister, but as soon as he stepped inside, he found himself helping out. Washing a bag of ivy, then cutting short sprigs from stems of boxwood and cypress that had been soaking all day. He stood between the two women at the counter and watched them twist the greenery expertly onto wire frames, handing them sprigs of rosemary and cinnamon sticks when they needed them.

It was late when they were finally finished, and Ciara left, anxious to get home before the blizzard that Met Eireann was cheerfully predicting. Lara put the kettle on and time seemed to stand still as the two of them sat at the counter drinking their tea, watching the cars glide past like baby deer on ice. A few guys in hoodies had stationed themselves at the corner with a stack of rubber mats and were throwing them down in the slush to help drivers get traction, refusing the offers of money that were thrust at them through open windows. People got grumpier when it rained, Phil thought, but there was something about snow that brought out the best in everyone.

Lara used the pretext of the icy road conditions to have a go at him about giving up being a courier, or at least getting off the bike and starting a courier business of his own with the money their dad had left him. He'd heard the lecture many times before but he pretended to be taking it in.

"You're not listening to me, are you?" Lara said.

He shrugged. "I'm listening to what you're saying between the words."

"Which is?"

"The usual. I'm twenty-nine. You want me to put my toys away. Get my shit together. And"—he drained his cup—"you love me."

"I do," she admitted, "but I'll be the only one who loves you in ten years when you're heading for forty and losing your hair and stuck in a job that means you have to dress like a teenage hell-raiser." She took their cups out to the kitchen, and when she came back into the shop she was wearing a long, elegant black coat with a shawl collar and a pair of green Wellingtons that looked several sizes too big.

"If only I had your fashion sense." He grinned, winding the cashmere scarf Katy had given him around his face.

"The boots are Michael's." Lara looked down at them.

"Maybe it will do you good to walk a mile in them," Phil said. "He's moved on; maybe you will too."

"I can hear what you're saying between the lines too . . ." She shook her head. "But I'm not going to meet someone else, Phil. That's not going to happen."

He got it. It would be hard for her to trust someone again after the way her marriage had ended. But the idea of his lovely sister on her own for the rest of her life? He was supposed to be looking after her; he couldn't let that happen.

"Give it time before you say that," he said. "Give it a year."

"You're starting to sound like Leo!"

"There are thirty-one million seconds in a year," he said. "A lot can happen in thirty-one million seconds."

"Maybe," she said. She went around snuffing out the small candles in the lanterns, switching off the fairy lights, until the shop was in darkness.

Maybe he'd buy her a session with a psychic, he thought. She believed in that kind of thing. If someone with a crystal ball told her she'd meet someone, it would give her something to live for apart from her customers and her flowers.

He peered into a bucket on a shelf near the door as they were leaving. Long green spears with tightly closed heads. "Daffodils," he said through a mouthful of scarf, "in December? I think that's what's technically called 'a blooming miracle.'"

"It's not the only miracle. You and Katy have been together for three and a half months now. That's a Phil Kiely record, isn't it?"

He pulled his helmet over his head and flipped down the visor. Four months on Saturday, he thought.

She flipped the visor back up again and stared at him. "You're serious about this girl, aren't you?"

"You know me," he said lightly. "Like Dad used to say, I'm never serious about anything."

Lara bent down and picked up a handful of daffodil stems. "Here." She unzipped his leather jacket and tucked the daffodils inside, then zipped it up again. "Maybe the warmth of your heart will open them up by the time you give them to her."

"Hey!" Phil felt a cold, damp patch against his rib cage where the stems were dripping into his T-shirt.

Lara fished her keys out of her bag and locked up the shop, and they stepped out into a blinding whirl of snowflakes. She gathered her long rope of hair and tucked it under the collar of her long black coat, which was already covered with white flakes, so that it looked like ermine in reverse. "Don't say anything!" she said as she took a fake fur hat out of her pocket and pulled it on. "Someone left it behind in the shop last year. It's the only one I have."

"From the neck up," Phil said, "you look like you've stepped out of a Russian novel."

"Really?" He saw her eyes flick to the boarded-up front of the Camden Deli. "Are you sure you don't mean a bad late-night drama on E4?"

He handed her his heavy leather gauntlets and unlocked the padlock on the chain of the bike.

"Is it wise to take that thing out on these roads?" She turned her gloved hand up and watched a few flakes land on it. "I get a bad feeling sometimes."

Phil laughed. "Nothing's going to happen to me, trust me. I lead a charmed life."

"It better not." She handed back his gauntlets. "Because you are now officially my sole next of kin." She planted her gloved hands on either side of his helmet and locked eyes with him. "Be careful out there, okay?"

"Okay!" He watched her walk away, her tall, slender figure erased in a few moments by the blur of what was fast becoming a blizzard.

He looked up at the sky, the glimpses he could see of it between the dizzying wheels of snowflakes. The heavy gray clouds were so low now they seemed to be pegged to the rooftops. They had already dumped several tons of snow on the city and, Phil guessed, there was more where that had come from. A flash of goose bumps ran across his shoulder blades, quick as a lizard up a wall, leaving him with a feeling that something bad was going to happen. He thought about locking the bike up again, walking to Katy's. But that would take him the best part of an hour, and he wanted to see her now.

His sister had told him once that after a couple of years in the shop, she had started to see people as flowers. In that case, he thought, brushing the thick fur of snow off the saddle and the handlebars, Katy was a Solanum Glasnevin, like the one Lara had given his dad a few summers ago. One minute it was a small, innocent shoot, a handful of leaves, a few tiny purple star-shaped blossoms with asterisks of white at the center. The next it had taken over the entire bottom half of the garden, covering the ugly redbrick wall with a heavy tapestry of flowers and sending armies of vigorous shoots up the branches of the rowan tree. His dad had fought a losing battle with it; in the end, he just gave in. It was one dangerous plant, that Solanum, and Katy was one dangerous woman.

The first time he'd seen her, she was bent over her computer at her desk in the bridal magazine where she worked. Her back might as well have had a sign on it that said "Do Not Disturb." Her shoulders were hunched, her fingers were clacking away on her keyboard. Even her hair, which had been long back then—a wild tangle of dark curls that fell past her shoulders—looked busy.

The ostentatious bouquet of roses on her desk was obviously from a boyfriend. Walk away, Phil had told himself. Just put the envelope down and walk away. But whoever had sent her those roses had gotten it wrong. They were too stiff, too formal for someone with hair like that. And there was something about the shape of her back that made him want to see her face. So he said something about giving the roses Sprite, just to make her turn around.

She was gorgeous. Olive-gold skin, a strong, straight nose, quizzical eyebrows above wide-spaced green eyes that glittered with intelligence and, at that moment, irritation. He had gone out with scores of girls, but there was nothing girlish about her. She was all woman. Damn right he had pursued her. Boyfriend or not. He had to after he'd seen that face. She had taken root in him that day, and now she seemed to be everywhere in his life.

Sometimes, when he was between jobs, hanging around the newsagent on Leeson Street with all the other couriers, waiting for his radio to crackle into life, he tried to think of a single thing he didn't want to do with Katy. Getting stuck in a lift? That sounded kind of sexy now that he thought of it so definitely. A package holiday in some awful concrete, beer-swilling, "Y Viva España" resort? Ah, yeah. A joint bank account? Pushing it a bit, but nearly worth doing just to see her name printed next to his. Buying a burial plot, like people used to do back in the day? A bit ghoulish, but what the hell. All right, that was getting too soppy.

He bumped the bike down off the pavement into a gutter full of slush and climbed on. He was going to have to prune his feelings for Katy back a bit, he thought, if he didn't want to meet the same fate as his dad's wall. Careful, Phil, he told himself. He edged out gingerly onto the road through clouds of exhaust and flurries of snow, then threaded the bike through the static line of cars, alert for the slightest hint of a wheel about to slide away, glimpsing frustrated faces, white knuckles clutching steering wheels, behind the furious whap-whap of windscreen wipers.

His dad had given him his first bike when he was sixteen. "Philip, I will kill you if you hurt a hair on your body with this!" he'd said, handing over the keys to the secondhand Yamaha 50. But from the moment he'd first sat on the bike, Phil had never, for a moment, been afraid. He had felt as if it was a missing piece of his own body, a two-wheeled bionic limb that made him invincible. The CX500 was his fifth bike in twelve years.

Phil had gone to college, but only to please his father. He had pulled a rickshaw for the long hot summer after he got his arts degree. Blown the money he earned on a month in Thailand. He came back fully intending to do the MA his dad wanted him to do, but the thought of another two years at university was stifling. Instead, he'd walked into a job at Zip Couriers. He still couldn't believe that someone actually paid him to ride a bike. It might not have great career prospects, but it beat years of essays and tutorials or clocking in and out of an IT company, like his two best mates, or giving eight hours a day to a faceless insurance company like his father had before he retired.

"What do you deliver?" people wanted to know, girls usually. Half the time he didn't know and he didn't care. Theater tickets, legal documents, blood samples, photographic prints—stuff. It wasn't about the contents of the padded envelopes in his courier bag. It was about freedom. Waking up not knowing which part of Dublin his job would take him to that day. Ailesbury Road and Shrewsbury Road, lined with nineteenth-century mansions that housed the embassies. The treacherous cobbled laneways around the Coombe Hospital. The endless sprawls of new apartment complexes that had taken root in the fields at the foot of the Dublin mountains where his Dad used to take him and Lara on Sunday picnics.

Weather never stopped him. He knew all the tricks. In a storm, he'd stick one leg out to the side, relax his muscles, use it like a sail to pull the bike into a straight line. Riding in snow like this was fine if you made ultra-gentle touches on the brakes, clutch, steering and throttle. Stayed slow and smooth and alert.

But this evening his mind was racing ahead of the bike. Crossing the intersection at Baggot Street before he'd reached it, flying down Serpentine Avenue, through the roundabout, taking a right onto Seafort Avenue, pulling over in front of the iron railings outside Katy's house. Climbing the steps to the green door with its panels of stained glass and its brass knocker in the shape of a hand of Fatima that Katy said warded off bad luck. Knocking, though he had his own key. Wanting to be standing on the frozen steps when the door opened so he could feel the warmth from the hallway pour out onto him. So he could see the light on Katy's face when she opened the door. And pull her warm body into him, curve by curve by curve.

He should have known, he *did* know, that bridges freeze before roads. When his front tire hit the patch of ice on Portobello Bridge, the bike jerked sharply to the right, then glided, horribly graceful and weightless, toward the center line of the road.

He hit the clutch. Freewheeling was a risky maneuver. But not as risky as smashing into the huge black 4×4 that was heading for him. His skin beneath his leathers prickled with sweat as he began to skid. He felt the cold patch on his T-shirt where the daffodils had leaked their sap. He heard a woman on the pavement screaming the moment before the 4×4 swerved and the bike slid to a stop, two inches from its bumper, and he looked up into her eyes and saw, through the falling snow, how close a call it had been. Heard over the pounding of his own heart the shouts of the man who had jumped out of the 4×4.

"You fucking idiot! You could have been killed!"

Katy didn't answer the door. Phil's hand trembled as he tried to fit the key into the lock. His legs shook as he walked along the hallway, trailing slush from his boots on the candy-striped runner, calling her name, though he already knew from the darkness in every room that the flat was empty. He pulled off his gloves and checked his phone. No buses. No taxis. No, I don't want a lift on that death trap you call a bike. I'll be there as soon as I can! XXX.

He paced back and forth, afraid to stop moving, trying to pull himself together. Past the sink and the cooker and the kitchen island, past the empty fireplace and the gilt-framed mirror, past the shelves of books and the three unframed watercolors of the sea and the framed picture of Katy and her sister, one blonde, one dark, as different as day and night. Past the rectangle of lighter paint by the light switch where the framed picture of Katy and her ex-boyfriend used to be.

"You fucking idiot!" he whispered, echoing the angry driver of the 4×4. "You could have been fucking killed!"

He hadn't hung around to talk to the driver. He just climbed onto his bike and took off as fast as he could in a cloud of his own exhaust fumes. Idiotically fast in the snow, as if by accelerating hard he could get away from what had nearly happened. And as long as he was riding fast, his head tucked back into his neck, his eyes straining to see through the snowflakes that flew at his visor, he could outrun it. But the fear had caught up with him the moment he stopped. His head was light. His chest was tight. His tongue bitter with the aftertaste his heart had left when it jumped into his mouth on the bridge.

On his sixth lap of the room, Phil realized that he was being watched. He hadn't noticed Katy's dog curled up in his basket. Pat was a greyhound—literally a *gray* hound. His coat was mottled silver. His long mousy snout was dappled with gray. His whiskers were white. He was old, really old, but Katy had persuaded herself that he was immortal.

His head was resting on the wicker rim of the basket but his molasses-brown eyes followed Phil as he marched back and forth, and the two or three wiry silver hairs that counted as his eyebrows twitched with concern. As Phil passed by again, Pat tried to get up. He managed to get two creaky front legs and one back leg into upright positions, wobbled for a moment, then collapsed down again with a deep sigh.

"No, Pat! I'm okay!" But it was too late. The dog was already trying to rise again. This time he managed to get the fourth leg involved. He tottered unsteadily out of his basket and blundered toward Phil with a queasy and embarrassed look, slipping and sliding, unable to find a grip on the polished wooden floor.

"Shit!" Phil said. Pat looked at him for a moment quizzically, then sighed and sat obediently and clumsily just where he was by the sofa. Then, like a drunk letting go of a bar, he slid down onto the floor in a tangle of limbs. He looked up at Phil, surprised and, for some reason, wagged his tail.

Phil went over and bent down. A long, wet, mobile nose poked into his visor and Phil realized that he was still wearing his helmet. He tugged the strap open, pulled it off, felt the relief of cool air on his overheated scalp and took a few deep breaths. He unzipped his jacket and the spears of the daffodils scattered around Pat, who sniffed them with interest.

"Come on, let's get you back into your basket." Phil knelt and slipped his hands under the dog to lift him up, but Pat looked so mortified that he changed his mind and slid down onto the floor beside the dog instead. "You know what? Why don't we just rest here for a minute."

He ran his shaking hands along the dog's side. He could feel every rib through the short, smooth fur. He pinched a tuft of it between his thumb and forefinger. "I came this close to being killed," he said to the dog. "This close to never seeing Katy again."

The dog let out a shuddering sigh, as if he understood.

Phil took one of Pat's paws in one hand and covered it with the other. When he was five or six he had decided that he was too old to have his hand held, so his sister had come up with the idea of making "hand sandwiches." A way of comforting him without making a big deal of it. She had found so many ways to mother him, to make up for all the mothering he had missed out on.

By the time he heard Katy's key in the door, Phil's heart rate had slowed and his breathing was back to normal. "Let's not tell her what happened," he whispered to the dog and to himself. "We'd only freak her out." When she opened the door, he was sitting on the sofa with the daffodils in his hand and Pat at his feet.

"Look at this!" Katy grinned. "A bromance! You should have lit a fire, Phil, you look frozen." Her cream beret and coat were dusted with snowflakes. The ends of her hair were damp. The tip of her nose was pink. She looked too good to be true.

"Come here!" Phil ordered her. "Warm me up."

"I'll do my best, but I had to walk all the way from Mount Street. It's crazy out there. Are those daffodils?" she asked, amazed. "In December?"

She kicked off her shoes, crossed the room and knelt down and patted Pat, then Phil pulled her up into his lap and kissed her.

He pulled off her beret and buried his face in her hair. The brush with death had heightened every sense. His nerve endings fizzed as they undressed one another, their lips locked, her fingertips freezing on his warm skin. He had escaped; he was alive. Every moment felt like a miracle.

Afterward, Katy pulled her coat back on like a dressing gown and lit the fire and put the daffodils into a vase. Phil wrapped himself in the rug and hopped through their scattered clothes to the fridge to cobble together a supper out of what he could find. A few slices of Parma ham, half a jar of olives, a couple of bagels and a lump of stale lemon drizzle cake that went, mostly, to Pat. They ate it all hungrily and naked, then, suddenly craving wine, they pulled on their clothes to go to the wine shop.

Katy wanted to take Pat, so Phil got him togged up in the weird dog coat she had bought him on the Internet. A black waterproof with red fleece lining that made him look like a canine Dracula. To Phil's relief, as much as Pat's, Katy did not even try to put on the blue nylon and Velcro dog boots she'd bought to stop him sliding on the wooden floors. So far, she hadn't managed to get more than three on at the same time.

Phil carried Pat down the steps and put him down on the path outside the gate. The sky was clear now. The blizzard had packed up and left town, leaving behind a pristine white carpet crusted with ice crystals rolled out along Seafort Avenue. Pat lifted his long snout and sniffed the air coming in from the sea.

"Do you think he'd make it to the sea wall?" Katy looked hopeful. Phil doubted it. Since he'd come on the scene, the farthest the dog had been was the end of the street. But Pat's tail was high and his nose was pointing toward Wales. He trotted off slowly, slightly sideways to stop himself slipping on the snow.

Phil and Katy followed him. The air was so frigid that it almost hurt to breathe. They wrapped their arms around one another and thought of all the Christmas cracker jokes they could remember to distract themselves from the cold. What do you get when you cross a snowman with a vampire? Frostbite. What do you call people who are afraid of Santa Claus? Claustrophobic. Why did Santa go into therapy? Because he suffered from low elf-esteem.

They had to stop twice so Phil could pick the ice out from between the pads of Pat's paws, and by the time they got to the sea road, all three of them were shivering, but it was worth it for the view. The beach looked like a glass of Guinness, the sand a wide band of white, the water beyond it a deep velvet black. The sky glittered with stars.

Pat stopped to sniff delicately at every gatepost. Phil guessed this was just an excuse to catch his breath. He peed twice, defiantly, managing somehow to balance on the slippery path on three creaky legs. Phil wanted to give him a high five. Maybe he was immortal. Maybe Katy was right.

They left Pat sitting patiently outside the wine shop and went inside, gasping with relief when the warm air in the shop hit them. They were at the till when they heard the yelp. High and sharp and startling, like glass shattering. Katy was at the door in a heartbeat, Phil right behind her. They arrived outside in time to see the cyclist picking herself up off the road, a girl of about twenty with a streak of blood running from her hand onto the fluorescent yellow sleeve of her jacket.

She looked around, stunned.

"Are you okay?" Phil said.

"I'm fine, it's only a graze. But there was a dog," she said, as if unable to believe it. "He looked like he was wearing a cape. He sort of tottered out in front of me. I swerved but I caught him with the front wheel." She looked around. "Where did he go?"

"Pat!" Katy called out, standing out in the road. "Pat?"

The three of them searched for a few minutes before Phil found the dog cowering beneath a white van. They tried to coax him out but he wouldn't budge. He was panting, and his eyes in the beam of Phil's iPhone torch blazed with fright.

"I don't think he can get up," Phil said, and before he could stop her, Katy was first on her knees, then lying flat in the snow, wriggling underneath the van. Phil had a sickening flashback to the moment when the bike almost slid under the 4×4. "Come back." He crouched down. "Let me do that!"

But she had already squirmed under the chassis and reached Pat. "Get me something to put him on," she said, her voice muffled. He stood up and ran to the wine shop and came back with a flattened cardboard box. He passed it to her, and she somehow managed to maneuver Pat gently onto it and slide him out.

He whimpered when Phil picked him up, box and all, but then lay still as they retraced their steps to the house where the cyclist told them a retired vet lived. The lights were off, but Katy hammered on the door and after a minute he came out, a man in his late sixties in a plaid dressing gown who led them past a living room, where a coal fire blazed, into a small, tidy kitchen. He found a towel to spread on the table and Phil laid the dog gently on it.

"Is he a biter?" the vet said, over his shoulder.

Katy shook her head. Beneath the ceiling spots, her face was whiter than her coat. She held Phil's hand while the retired vet examined the dog, and squeezed it so hard every time Pat whimpered that he had to clench his jaw.

"The back hind leg is badly sprained, maybe broken." The vet washed his hands at the kitchen sink. "But it's hard to tell without an X-ray."

Katy still kept tight hold of Phil's hand. She hooked the fingers of her other hand under Pat's leather collar. "I can take him to my own vet in the morning."

The man sighed and retied the belt of his dressing gown carefully. "How old?"

Katy swallowed. "I don't know," she said evasively. "He was a stray when I found him. I think he might be fourteen."

The vet raised one bushy gray eyebrow. "More like fifteen or sixteen." He bent down till he was nose to nose with Pat. "You, my man, should be in the *Guinness Book of Records*." Pat's tail tapped twice on the kitchen table as if he was agreeing.

"And you, my dear"—he turned to Katy—"have to decide whether you want to put this poor old fellow through a surgery he probably won't survive. Or to do the kindest thing, which might be to let him go."

"I can't have him put down." Katy rubbed the velvety tip of one of Pat's ears between her fingers. "I can't do that to him."

They were back at home on the sofa, the fire dying, the dishes from their impromptu supper still on the coffee table. Phil had found a bottle of sherry that Katy used for making soup and forced her to drink a glass.

The dog was sedated after the Valium the vet had given him. The thin whip of his tail was tucked between his legs, and his back left leg had an awkward twist that didn't look good.

"But I don't want him to be in pain." Katy put a hand over her mouth. "What am I going to do?"

"You're going to get out of those wet clothes and have a shower." Phil hauled her to her feet and unbuttoned her coat. It was soaked from where she'd lain down in the snow under the van.

He walked her to the bathroom and turned on the shower. He put a towel on the radiator, then went into the bedroom and turned on her electric blanket. Pat gave a few little yelps of pain as he was carried down the hall, but he looked around, surprised and faintly pleased, when Phil put him carefully on the bed. And his ears pricked up to listen to the sound of Katy's voice from the bathroom, calling out a thank-you to Phil for the warm towel.

The dog's eyes had seemed to be dimming, like two faraway torch beams moving farther away into the night. But for a few seconds they seemed to brighten, sharpen, intensify. He looked straight at Phil as if trying to communicate something.

"You love her, don't you?" Phil said softly. The dog blinked and then closed his eyes. "Me too."

"Phil, I'm so sorry," Katy whispered at about five in the morning. They were whispering so as not to disturb Pat, who was sleeping fitfully between them. "You must think I'm incredibly stupid to be getting so upset over a dog when it's only been a few months since your dad's been gone."

"No, I don't think you're stupid. Love is love, Katy, and loss is loss. And I'm not so sure Dad's really gone. Lara thinks he's still around."

He swallowed, knew he risked sounding crazy, then went ahead anyway. "Maybe she's right. Sometimes, in the queue in the Spar, or traffic, waiting for the lights to change—I get the feeling that he's standing there with me."

"Do you ever feel your mother around?"

"I don't know." Phil's mother had died when he was two. He didn't remember her as a person, only as a collection of sensations. Light and warmth and ease. He thought of her sometimes when he caught the flare of sunlight bouncing off the wing mirror of a car ahead of him in traffic, or felt summer sunshine on the back of his neck. Once in Hua Hin, a butterfly had landed on his arm, the spots on its wings the exact blue of her eyes in the photographs, and for a few seconds he had the strongest sensation that she was with him, that she had made this trip back into the world just so they could spend that one moment together.

There were things beyond understanding. Anyone who even watched a couple of hours of the Discovery Channel knew that. What compelled eels to cross the Atlantic from the Sargasso Sea to spawn in Irish rivers where they'd been born? Or birds to cross whole continents, following precise lines that no scientist could identify, to land in the same trees every year?

He remembered those long summer nights the year he'd pulled the rickshaw. Hauling stupefied drunks from St. Stephen's Green back to their apartments up in Christchurch and Clanbrassil Street. He'd had the strangest feeling back then that he was running somewhere, that there was a point to it all, a destination, he just didn't know it yet.

He lay beside Katy, stroking her hair while she stroked the dog. Long, gentle sweeps along his knobbly spine, from the top of his head to the bump where his tail began.

"Even if Pat makes it through the night, I have to let him go"—her voice was full of tears—"don't I?"

The dog's breaths were so far apart that Phil thought the next one might be his last. He remembered his father's last few minutes, when his own selfish need to hold on to his dad had been burned away by pity and by love. All he'd wanted was for his dad to be free of pain, to be released from the husk of the body that lay on the bed. He put his hand on the dog's rib cage and felt a faint, faraway flutter.

"Even if Pat does go, he won't go far, Katy."

"What do you mean?"

"I think he loves you too much to leave you."

"Maybe he'll come back and haunt the cheese compartment in the fridge. That's his idea of heaven." She gave a shaky laugh that turned into a sob. She pressed her face against the dog's neck, then looked up at Phil. Her eyes were wild. She looked awful, he thought, and she looked beautiful.

"What will I do without him? Before he came along, I felt as if I was on my own. No matter how bad things were, with Mum and then with Ben, he was always there. If I let him go, I'll be on my own again."

"You won't be on your own," Phil whispered. "I'm not going anywhere. I'm here to stay."

And suddenly he was sliding sideways, like the bike had, letting the weight of his body pull him over the edge of the bed, onto the floor. It was outside of his control. He couldn't have resisted the gravity of his heart even if he wanted to.

He propped himself up on one knee and looked up at Katy. For a long moment she didn't understand, then she put her hand to her mouth.

"You're kidding me!" Her eyes widened above her fingers. "Here? Now? No!"

"Why not?" he said.

"We've only known one another for four months—"

"On Saturday," they both said together.

"I think it's what Pat wants," Phil said. "I think it's what he was asking me to do earlier."

"In that case, in any case, yes! I'll marry you!" She was crying through her laughter or laughing through her tears. It didn't matter which. What mattered was that this was where he had been running all those nights when he'd been pulling the rickshaw. He'd been running here to this room and this woman—he'd been running home.

He must have fallen asleep, because when he woke up, the lamp was on and Katy was sitting up in bed, one hand on Pat's ribs.

"Is he . . ."

Katy nodded. Then she pointed to the vase on the bedside table. The daffodils had opened. Every single spear had blossomed into a yellow trumpet.

"But he's not gone far."

MOTH ORCHID

Childlike Innocence.

Noah sits on the wall and watches the traffic inch past. The January cold seeps through his thin school trousers and into his bones. The wind slices the tips of his ears like a scalpel. He has to force his jaws together to stop his teeth from rattling.

Five. Eleven. Seventeen minutes. Why is Sharon always late? He doesn't want to look too anxious when she eventually turns up so he pretends to be fascinated by the people in the passing cars.

In all that time, only two people look back at him. A baby in a booster seat who gives him a dreamy smile, and an old woman who frowns and hits central locking. He hears the telltale "thunk" as she passes and he sees himself through her eyes. A youth, loitering on the street, up to no good.

It's been snowing on and off since the start of December. It starts again now. The first raggedy-edged snowflake flutters past, then changes direction abruptly and comes at him with purpose, as if it has been sent spiraling through the atmosphere specifically to find him. It lands, a feathery little guided missile, on his cheekbone. When he puts his fingers up to brush it off, they come away wet.

More flakes begin to fall. Noah should take the hood of his anorak out and pull it over his head but he'd rather turn into Frosty the Snowman out here than risk looking uncool to her. He kicks his heels back against the wall to deaden the ache of the cold, careful not to knock over the brown paper bag on the ground in front of him. He hopes the plant doesn't freeze to death before he can give it to her.

He pictures her face when she opens the bag and sees it. A whole load of dark purple flowers stuck onto a tiny bendy stem like a bunch of butterflies about to fly off. Exposed roots like knobbly toes climbing over the rim of the plastic pot as if the whole thing is planning to get out and do a runner first chance it gets. It's a moth orchid. When the bloke in the shop told him the name of it, Noah thought at first he said "mother kid." Weird.

He didn't even know what an orchid was until half an hour ago. His plan was to get her something from the Tesco Express next to school, but that was before he'd had the wake-up call. There was always a gang of fifth and sixth years hanging around in there after school. Prowling the aisles looking for girls from Teresa's, trying to shoplift crisps and stuff under the watchful eyes of the security bloke.

There was no way he'd get a bunch of flowers to the till without being seen. He got enough grief for being different as it was. The last thing he needed on top of it all was some smart-ass whipping his phone out and posting a photo of him with a bloody bouquet. #NoahCasey #PrinceOfGaylords.

So Tesco was a no-go. Instead he walked all the way into town, along Sandford Road into Ranelagh and out the other side. He passed a couple of flower shops along the way. He was going to nip inside, he really was, but they were brightly lit places with big windows, meaning anybody might see him in there, so he walked on, his eyes stinging with the cold, excitement and fear twitching in his stomach like two fish snagged on the same hook.

He stopped on Charlemont Bridge to look at the canal. There was a huge swan on the frozen water, slithering around, flapping its wings, trying to break through the ice. It didn't seem to understand that there was no way back. Noah knew that feeling.

He walked the length of Camden Street, then went back and stood on the other side of the road looking at this flower shop—Blossom &

Grow. It was completely and utterly pink except for a whole lot of real-looking leaves painted up the front and around the windows. It was the girliest building he'd ever seen in his entire life and normally there would be no way he'd go in there, but he only had a few minutes left before he was supposed to meet her. It had been hard enough to get her to agree to meet him at all. If he chickened out now, he'd hate himself for it later.

He tried to slip in quietly but wind chimes tinkled and jangled as soon as he pushed the door open. It was pretty dark inside except for a load of candles and Christmas lights and a little glass light over the counter. It was like church.

"Christ, close that door, will you? It's brass monkeys out there," a deep voice said. Noah had thought only women worked in flower shops, but the voice belonged to a bloke with messy black hair who was wearing head-to-foot motorbike leathers, complete with gloves. He was leaning on the other side of a wooden counter with his head bent over a book.

Noah shut the door and stood looking around while his eyes tried to adjust to the dark. He'd thought the shop would stink like a perfume counter but the air smelled fresh and good. He took a deep breath and felt the tight band of worry around his rib cage loosen a bit. Then he saw them—the flowers. They weren't in neat bunches tied with ribbons; they were in big metal buckets on the floor and on shelves surrounding him. There were about a million of them and all of them looked expensive. He had exactly twelve euros thirty-two cents to spend. Thirteen fifty if he walked the two miles back to Milltown instead of getting the bus. He should have gone to Tesco. At least things there had price stickers and buy-one-get-one-free.

"Fair play!"

Noah looked around. "What?"

"I wouldn't have been caught dead in a flower shop when I was your age." The bloke put the book down and crossed his arms. "Definitely not one painted bright pink."

"How come you ended up working in a flower shop if you wouldn't be caught dead in one?"

"I'm helping my sister out. She's gone to see a medium."

"A medium what?"

The man laughed as if Noah had made a joke. "It's a long story. Back to you. You must really like her."

"Who?"

"The girl. I presume it is a girl you want to buy flowers for."

Noah shrugged.

"Does she like you back?"

Noah tried to look blank but he felt the blood rush to his face.

"Ah!" The bloke frowned. "So maybe she likes someone else."

His face felt like it was about to burst into flames.

"I'll take that as a yes." The bloke sighed and shook his head. "I've been there, mate. What's your name?"

They told you not to talk to strangers, didn't they? But his mother never had. There were strangers hanging around the flat all the time when he was small. Blokes who left the toilet bowl full of dark, foaming piss and used his *Monsters, Inc.* toothbrush and finished his Coco Pops. Once, one of them had just walked off with his Nintendo DS. Sometimes they stuck around for a while and Noah was supposed to talk to them. Answer the same stupid questions. How old was he? What class was he in? What team did he support? When his mum wasn't listening he'd tell them lies. Most of the time they weren't going to be around long enough to catch him out. But his nervousness now made him blurt his real name out.

"Noah."

"I'm Phil. Take a long look at me, Noah. I'm a good-looking guy, but I'm no Brad Pitt, am I?"

Oh great, Noah thought, it was turning weird. This was all he needed. He balled his fists inside the pockets of his anorak. He'd been looking after himself since way back.

The bloke didn't notice that Noah was giving him evils. He dug around in his leather jacket and took out a battered iPhone and held it up.

"Now," he said, "take a look at this." He pointed at the screen-saver with a scuffed leather-clad finger. "This is my fiancée. Beautiful, right?"

Noah wasn't sure where this was going, but it was better than where he'd thought it might. The woman on the screen had short, mad-looking dark hair and she was smiling. She was all right but the bloke obviously thought he'd won the EuroMillions, so he gave a sort of nod.

"Now, she liked someone else when I first met her." Phil smiled down at the picture. "She had a boyfriend. She didn't want to know me. But I got her to change her mind and you know what helped win her over? Flowers." He shoved the phone back into his pocket and waved his arm. "You think this is just a flower shop, don't you?"

Noah calculated the distance to the door behind him, ready to run.

"But it's not. It's an armory. And those"—he pointed at the buckets of flowers—"are your weapons. Inside these four walls, four *pink* walls—I know, my sister's idea, not mine—you've got everything you need to win that girl over. And you know what they say? All's fair in love and war."

They're wrong, Noah thinks. Nothing is fair. It's been twenty-five minutes now and the snow is getting heavier and there's still no sign of her. He swings his foot back and gives the wall one final kick, feeling the sharp points of the pebble dash bite into the back of his shoe. And that's when he sees her making her way through the traffic between two cars, her red down coat swinging open, her head bare.

"Hey!" He is waving before he can help it, his face lit up with a big cheesy smile.

"Jesus!" She scoots up on to the wall beside him, avoiding his eyes, saying nothing about being late. "It's like the fucking Arctic, isn't it? All we need are the penguins."

Penguins don't live in the Arctic. They live at the South Pole, Noah thinks. But it doesn't matter. Her voice turns the key in a locked door inside him. He has to sit on his hands to stop himself from reaching out and touching the sleeve of her coat.

"Yeah." He starts swinging his foot again, trying to get his cool back. He pretends to be watching a bloke walking a boxer dog on the other side of the road, taking little secret sips of her out of the corner of his eye, though all he can see is her profile. The arch of one dark eyebrow, the small dip above her top lip, the tangle of frizzy blonde hair with its little crown of melting snowflakes.

She shivers and pulls her coat around her, still not looking at him. The zip is broken and the coat falls open again. Beneath it she's wearing a striped red and black top and a very short black skirt. Her tights are thin and black and the toes of her tan ankle boots are so wet they've turned dark brown. "It's fucking freezing."

"It's minus two," Noah says. "But the real feel is minus eight." His foster dad gave him his old iPhone 3 when he got a new one. It has a weather app. He wants to show it to her, tell her about the dew point and the humidity and the wind speed, but he doesn't want to look as if he is showing off.

She tips her head back and looks up at the snow, which is falling steadily now. "We must be out of our minds," she says to the sky, "sitting out here like this."

"I'm not that cold." Noah, chilled to the bone, stifles a shiver. "Do you want my anorak?"

She shakes her head. "No. I have to get going in a sec."

"But you just got here." The whine in his voice—why did he have to say that?—pushes one of her buttons.

"Yeah, well"—he hears her voice harden—"I shouldn't be here at all, should I? You know you're not allowed to just call me like that. That's the rule." She is looking at him now.

He has never seen eyes quite like hers. Blue on the outer rim of the iris floating into green farther in. When he's not with her and he imagines her eyes, they are full of warmth and love, but today they are empty, her pupils narrowed to pinpoints. He can't look into them when they are like that, so he stares down at the brown paper bag at his feet.

"This can't go on, okay?" she says.

There is a dusting of snow on the top of the bag. He nods. He wants it to stop too, but for different reasons.

"You need to choose your ammunition carefully!" the bloke in the shop said. "Is she tall or short?"

"She's tiny." She used to tower over him but he caught up with her when he was fourteen, then passed her by.

"Petite—so no giant thistles or birds-of-paradise, then." The bloke, Phil, began dragging buckets of flowers around. "Fair or dark?"

"Fair."

"Is she predictable, does what she says she will?"

Noah shook his head.

"Okay! Let's lose the roses. Give me a hand, will you? Not those, they're anemones." Water sloshed out of one of the buckets onto Noah's feet as he pulled it into the corner.

"Now we're getting somewhere."

"Look, I probably don't even have enough money for—" Noah began.

"Don't think about money." The bloke stood back from the dozen or so buckets that were left. "Just pick the one that feels right.

Noah looked down at the flowers. The pale pink pointy ones with a bunch of little bells. The big red ones with the trumpets. Some rude-looking ones with one big yellow finger sticking up.

Nothing.

Then he looked up and saw it on the shelf above the bloke's head. She used to have a dress the same color as the purple one. He pointed at it.

"The moth orchid?"

"Is that what it's called? A mother kid?"

"Moth orchid," the bloke said again.

"How much is it?" Noah held his breath while the bloke checked the price on a list and looked at him.

"How much do you have on you?"

"Thirteen euros fifty cents."

"Funny," the bloke said, "that's exactly what it costs."

She pulls a packet of Silk Cut Blue out of her pocket and holds her hands up as if she is surrendering. Her blue nail varnish is chipped. There is a number scrawled in pen on the palm. "Okay, okay, I was supposed to give up. You're not going to kill me, are you?"

If this was a computer game, Noah could press a key now and go into bullet time. Jump up, spin around, stop her from lighting the cigarette, freeze the flake that is about to land on her shoulder, stare into her open palm until he found himself in there, somewhere between the lines.

But she is already fiddling with her lighter. "I'm too young to die."

He will be sixteen in ten days. He wants her to mention this, to reassure him that she remembers, but she doesn't.

Instead she leans back and looks at the sky again, letting the smoke curl up into the air. Her phone rings. Her ringtone is "The Only Girl in the World." She pulls it out of her bag and clamps it to her ear. Noah can hear the voice on the other end. Deep. Male. Baz. She was supposed to give him up too.

"I'm on my way, babes," she says and her eyes sweep the street, one way and then the other, sliding right past Noah.

"No, don't! Wait for me! Hang on," she says softly. "I'll only be five minutes."

She hangs up, then stands up.

"Got to go, No," she says, tossing the cigarette.

He stands too. His left leg is dead and he feels it give way, makes a grab for her hand.

"Don't!" she says sharply, but she doesn't push him away and for a moment they are standing holding hands in the snow. His hand is bigger than hers now; he wonders when that happened.

He wants somebody to see them like this. A witness to make this moment real. That woman who frowned at him from the car. The man with the boxer dog. The bloke from the shop. But rush hour is over now. The street is empty except for the two of them.

She pulls her hand away and quick as a flash he bends down and picks up the paper bag by the handles and gives it to her.

She looks into the bag. "What's this?"

"It's a moth orchid."

"A moth orchid!" She stares at it for a long moment. She likes it, he thinks, and a warm buzz fizzes from his heart down to his frozen feet. Then she looks up at him. "What's it for?"

"It's for my birthday."

"*Your* birthday."

"Next week."

He waits for her to get it, then when she still doesn't, he prompts her. "You said I could come and live with you again when I was sixteen."

She puts the bag down on the wall, takes out her cigarettes. Lights another one. "Sure, but the thing is, now is not a good time, okay?"

Noah blinks at her in disbelief. He has been in a tunnel for two years. Four foster homes. This has been his light.

"I had to move someone into the flat. To help with the rent."

She gets rent allowance. "Baz?" He spits the name out. "You're with him again!"

"Jesus! Give me a break, No, he's just a friend."

Who sleeps in her bed and takes her money, Noah thinks, and gives her drugs.

"Look, when I get everything sorted, then you can come back, I promise. Come here." She puts her arms around him, all affectionate now, and pulls him in for a hug. He can smell the smoke and honey of her breath. "By the summer, definitely," she says, "I swear!"

He pretends to be busy pulling his hood out of his backpack so he doesn't have to watch her cross the road, hurry past the line of shuttered shops and turn the corner.

When he looks up, he realizes that she has forgotten the bag with the orchid in it. He thinks about going after her but doesn't. Instead he picks it up and hugs it to his chest, not caring that he is crushing the delicate purple flowers. All that is left of her now is the two ragged lines of her footprints that lead away from him. He stands for a minute and watches them as they begin to fill up with snow.

ROSE

Passion and Grief.

Every single woman Ciara knew was going to see a psychic of some kind. Single as in unattached. Psychic as in phony.

"You have to see this clairvoyant," her new flatmate, Suzanne, said as she picked her way around the packing boxes and parked herself on the end of Ciara's bed. She was starry-eyed with excitement. Ciara looked up from the book she had only been half reading.

"She says I'm going to meet a tall, athletic man." Suzanne kicked off her shoes and curled up, settling in for a long chat. "Do you think that's clairvoyant-speak for a six-pack and a great ass?"

"It's hard to say." Ciara tried to sound neutral.

The stars in Suzanne's eyes dimmed a little. "You're being cynical."

"I'm being skeptical," Ciara said. "There's a difference."

"I don't need someone with a crystal ball," she told Lara, "to tell me that *my* future contains an ass. All I have to do is look at my past."

"Go easy on yourself, Ciara," Lara said softly. "It's early days."

It was the eve of Valentine's Day, and they were working late in Blossom & Grow. The shop was outdoors-cold and heady with the scent of hundreds of roses and stargazers and freesias. Lara was sitting cross-legged on the floor in a soft gray woolen dress hand-tying bouquets of Holland roses with meter-long stems and perfect crimson heads. The light picked out silver threads in her waist-length black hair. She had tucked a white lily behind one ear. She looked, Ciara thought, like an Indian queen on a carpet of flowers.

Ciara was slouched on a stool at the counter. Her blonde highlights were growing out and her dark roots were growing in but she couldn't be bothered doing anything about it. Her hair was pulled back into a ponytail with a rubber band and her post-breakup uniform of black sweatshirt matched her frame of mind. She had a pen pinched between her numb finger and thumb and she was writing sappy message after sappy message and checking each one against the order book.

All these idiots out there genuinely believed that their love was unique, she thought, slipping another creamy card into its Lilliputian envelope. But the world was hopping with "Honeybunnies" and "Stud-muffins," "Secret Admirers" and "Devoted Husbands." *Supposedly* Devoted Husbands.

"I went to see a medium after Christmas." Lara was ringletting an ivory ribbon with the blade of her scissors. "Phil gave me a present of a session with her."

"Phil sent you to a fortune-teller? Did she tell you that you have a very gullible brother?"

Lara smiled. "No. She said I was a healer, but she probably says that to everyone."

It wouldn't be true of everyone, Ciara thought, despite herself. "Did she tell you anything useful? Like the winning lotto numbers? Or where the key to the petty cash box has gone?"

Lara looked down at the flowers. "No. But she said I haven't met my soul mate yet. Apparently he's still out there somewhere."

If he was out there, Ciara thought, he might as well get used to it. It was ten months since Lara had found out that her husband was gay and she was still in reeling from the shock of it. She wasn't bitter about the end of her marriage—unlike Ciara, who felt as sour as a rotting brassica—but she was adamant that she was through with re-lationships, which was a shame, because Lara spent ten hours a day making other people happy. If anyone deserved to be happy, she did. She deserved a little happiness herself.

"So who do you think it is? Your soul mate?" Ciara flapped a card in the air to dry the ink. "That wildflower man who's always coming on to you? That guy Frank you used to work with who just keeps happening to pass by?"

"I know, soul mates! It's ridiculous, right? But . . ." Lara paused, the ribbon in one hand, a rose in the other. "The weird thing was, she knew things."

Ciara bent her head over the book so Lara wouldn't see her eye-roll. "What kind of *things*?"

"Well, that both of my parents were dead." Not exactly rocket science, Ciara thought, when Lara was forty-one. "And that I'm going to put a water feature in the garden in Dad's memory. She said he had a message for me."

"What was it?" Lara's father had been a straight talker. Ciara hoped the message had been: "Don't believe anything this con artist says."

Lara started to laugh, and at the same time a tear slid down her cheek and dropped on the rose. "'That builder you got a quote from is a cowboy.' Which is exactly the kind of thing he'd say. Do you believe in, you know"—she waved the rose—"spirits?"

"Absolutely not." But a contradictory trail of goose bumps tiptoed up Ciara's spine as she said it. When she was six, her sister, Alice, had moved out of their bedroom and her granny Rose moved in on a cloud of Coty L'Aimant, Elnett hairspray and cigarette smoke. She was in Dublin to do "tests." Ciara had hoped they weren't math tests, which were her least favorite kind.

Her grandmother stayed up late every night reading, sitting up in the bottom bunk wearing one of her many pastel chiffon nighties. Every morning, the cut-glass ashtray on the bedside table was full of John Player Blue cigarette butts with lipstick-smeared filter tips.

Ciara was fascinated by her grandmother's library books. The covers had lurid pictures of women with cascading hair and wasp waists wearing nurse's uniforms or swimsuits or ball gowns. They had titles like *Sudden Surrender* and *Passion's Promise* and *Moonlight Mystique*.

"What's a mist-i-queue?" Ciara had once asked, hanging over the top bunk like a bat and reading the word upside down. Blood fizzed and popped in the roots of her hair like space dust.

Granny Rose inhaled deeply on her cigarette. "It's what makes men want to . . ." She took a puff of her cigarette and pressed her lips together. "To give you flowers."

Ciara hooked her bare toes under the bars of the bunk and swung down a little lower. "How do you get it?"

Her grandmother squinted up at her through a haze of shifting smoke. "You're born with it. But you lose it if you ever let your husband see you in curlers."

Ciara had found out about her grandfather by eavesdropping, which she knew was wrong but was always interesting. "Did Grandad see you in curlers?" she asked. "Is that why he ran away with the little shopgirl?"

When her grandmother laughed, no proper laughing sound came out; just a chorus of wheezes, squeaks and faraway whistles that gathered into a rattling cough.

"That's the first thing I'll ask him"—she gasped when she caught her breath—"if I ever see the SOB again."

"What's an SOB?" The upside-down-ness was starting to make Ciara's head feel weird.

Granny Rose tilted her chin and exhaled a smoke ring for Ciara to pop with her finger. "I hope you never find out."

Her grandmother spoke to Ciara as if she was a proper person and not "the baby." She was always available for hugs, unlike Ciara's mother, who was permanently late for something. She didn't think sleeping with a teddy bear was stupid, like Ciara's sister, Alice, did. She produced an endless supply of Cadbury's Tiffin from her handbag and she didn't make Ciara brush her teeth after she ate it. Her own teeth grinned out from a glass of water on the bedside table, like the Cheshire Cat's ghostly smile.

All in all, it was a very satisfactory arrangement, but unfortunately it didn't last. One afternoon when Ciara was at choir practice, a girl from sixth class came in and whispered importantly to Sister Barnabas. The nun told all the other girls to sing "Greensleeves" and took Ciara out into the corridor.

Twenty-five years later, every time Ciara was put on hold and heard the tinny strains of that song, she remembered the day that Granny Rose died.

"She's in heaven, pet." Sister Barnabas had tried to unstick Ciara's hair from her tear-stained face. "Now she can watch over you always."

Ciara grew up imagining the ghost of her grandmother watching over her, which was fine unless she was doing something embarrassing. Peeing. Picking her spots. Stealing Alice's sequined Whistles dress to wear to the Trinity ball. Doing that clumsy little dance that was supposed to look sexy before she took the dress off and got into bed with Barry Quinn.

Sometimes her grandmother was joined by other ghosts. Mr. Duncan from across the road. The Caseys' puppy, Grin, who had been squashed by Mr. Casey's Volvo. River Phoenix. Audrey Hepburn. John Lennon. It could get quite crowded in Ciara's bathroom sometimes.

"Promise me you'll never, ever take hallucinogenic drugs," Mort had said when she'd told him about her spectral voyeurs. They were about to get married, and every time he made love to her, some old, hurt part of her past healed and a dried-up scab of truth came loose.

"Cross my heart and hope to die."

Her head was pillowed on the hard cage of his ribs. The tip of her ear had pins and needles, but she still had trouble believing that this man's heart belonged to her. Mort shuffled down until his long-lashed green eyes were level with hers. He was already tanned, though they'd only been in Bali for three days. The ceiling fan that stirred the soupy tropical air was lifting the ends of his blonde hair.

"Promise me one other thing." He kissed her lightly on the nose. "If you do die, promise you won't come back and haunt me when I'm taking a leak."

* * *

"Just think," Lara said, tying the last ribbon on the last bouquet. "Tomorrow morning, women all over the world will wake up to a hundred and ninety-eight million roses."

All Ciara could think about was whether one of those women would be waking up next to Mort. She began to line the bouquets up for Phil, who was coming in at six to start the deliveries. When she was finished, they looked like a cellophane army waiting to launch a surprise attack.

She washed her hands under hot water, trying to get some feeling back into her frozen fingertips. "Are you sure you don't need me tomorrow?" she asked, shrugging on her coat.

"I'm absolutely sure. I know it's going to be tough." Lara sighed, then handed her a dozen red roses tied with a red bow.

"Come on, boss," Ciara said, trying to sound hard-bitten. "You're giving me a day off on the busiest day of the year. You don't have to give me flowers as well."

Lara hugged her carefully so as not to squash the bouquet. "I just wish there was more I could do."

Nobody could have been kinder than Lara had been, Ciara thought, turning down a lift, turning up the collar on her coat and setting off along Camden Street. She had helped Ciara move her stuff out with the van. Lent her the money for a deposit for an apartment. Listened to her catalogue her pain, even though it must have brought up painful memories of her own.

A moon she couldn't see was silvering the few shreds of cloud in the clear February sky. Her eyes automatically picked out the constellations Mort had given her from the glittering geometry overhead.

Orion. Cassiopeia. The Pleiades. Pegasus. Leo. One for each birthday and each wedding anniversary she'd spent with him. Now she wished that he'd given her something less permanent. She couldn't exactly stuff bits of the universe into refuse sacks and give them away to Oxfam.

"What's wrong, Mort?" she'd asked him that day last August. He had been avoiding her eyes for weeks. They were sitting in the car in Killiney. His wetsuit was drying on the bonnet in the sunshine. His hair was still damp. He smelled of the sea.

She expected him to say that he was homesick, or bored. That he wanted to quit working at the bar. That they needed to plan another trip. He was always restless when they came back from holiday.

"It's not that anything is wrong," he had said carefully. "It's just that this doesn't feel right anymore."

Ciara stared down at her bare, faintly tanned knees. Mort had kissed her behind her knees in Sicily. He had kissed her everywhere, but absently, as if he was thinking about doing something else.

She looked up. "We can get the rightness back. That's what being married is all about."

He sat perfectly still, but his eyes were moving, scribbling a message that she didn't want to decode. She stared back down at her knees. They looked, suddenly, like babies' heads. Mort had wanted a child, but Ciara had wanted to wait. Afraid, in some tucked-away pocket of self-doubt, that if she lost her body, he might love her less. Now she wished that she *was* pregnant, because if she was, he wouldn't leave.

"Mort," she said. "Is there somebody else?"

He shook his head. "But there would be someone else at some point. And I don't think you could deal with that, do you?"

She'd thought, after Michael had left Lara, that nothing could be as bad as being left by a man for another man, but she'd been wrong. Being left for a woman who hadn't even come along yet? That was worse.

The moonlight had papered over all the cracks on the facade of the shabby Georgian terraced house that Ciara had moved into last September. It looked reassuringly solid from the outside, like a proper home, but it wasn't the kind of place that anybody stayed in for very long. It was a shabby mansion full of temporary lives. The huge, drafty rooms had been subdivided into odd-shaped flats with incongruously high sash windows and chipped plaster ceiling roses.

Ciara stopped at the bottom of the granite steps that led up to the front door and shoved the roses into the green bin. It was nearly three in the morning, but all the lights were on in the basement flat where Mrs. Costello, the eighty-eight-year-old widow who owned the house, still lived. She took the bouquet out of the bin and went lightly down the steps and left it on her worn doormat. As she climbed the steps again, she heard Mrs. Costello singing to Princess, her ancient, battle-scarred cat. One of these days they were both going to join Ciara's ghostly pee-watch.

The next morning, when Ciara got up, Suzanne was kneeling in the shower stall dressed in a pair of silver hot pants and a pink T-shirt that said: *I may not have free will but I have free won't.*

Suzanne liked to dress up when she cleaned the flat. "It's impossible to feel like a drudge when you're wearing a tiara," she'd explained to Ciara the week she moved in.

Ciara flipped the loo lid down and sat watching Suzanne scrubbing the grotty grouting between the tiles with an electric toothbrush.

"Is someone coming over?" She had been planning to turn on the TV and stay on the sofa all day. Possibly all weekend.

"My parents will be here in an hour," Suzanne said over her shoulder. "Dad wanted to take Mum for lunch, but she wasn't up to it so I said I'd cook."

Suzanne's mother was terrified of spaces, open and enclosed, and eating in public, and meeting strangers, and dirt.

"You aren't planning on staying in, are you?" Suzanne looked worried. "I thought you'd be going into the shop as it's, you know"—she waved a rubber-gloved hand—"V-Day."

"I am," Ciara lied. "I just slept late." The thought of having to go out into the world made her feel queasy. What would she do? Where would she go?

"Oh, I forgot to tell you, some flowers arrived. They're a little weird. And that's 'little' with a capital 'L.'"

It was the bouquet of roses that Ciara had left outside the basement flat, but each rose stem was now just three inches long.

"Mrs. C found them outside her door," Suzanne explained. "She didn't have a vase big enough for them so she did some surgery. Then she thought maybe they were actually for one of us, so she brought them up. She thoughtfully taped the stems back on but they just fell off again."

Suzanne peeled off her rubber gloves and made a coffee in the mocha pot that Ciara and Mort had bought at a street market in Palermo two weeks before they split up. Mort had thrown away one of his favorite sweatshirts so he could squash the pot into his carry-on. It hadn't even been unpacked from its box when she moved out.

"Let's have our coffee outside," Suzanne said. "Everything smells of bleach in here." She went to get their coats while Ciara brushed the cobwebs off the rusty garden chairs. Then they sat in the watery February sunshine, warming their hands on their cups.

Suzanne had been busy. The leaves had been swept up and the various clapped-out bicycles belonging to the students who lived upstairs had been tidied into a corner. The higgledy-piggledy plant pots that didn't really belong to anybody had been regimented into a neat row along the wall.

"I don't know why I did that," Suzanne said. "My mother won't even come out here. Sometimes I think I'm CDO."

"What's that?"

"It's OCD arranged in the correct alphabetical order. Holy Mother of God!" She jumped up. "The erotic poetry kit!" She hurried back into the kitchen and began to pluck explicit magnetic words off the fridge door.

"You've forgotten 'erotic pleasure,'" Ciara pointed out as she came inside with the cups.

"I will have," Suzanne sighed, "unless Mr. Athletic comes along soon."

Ciara heard the distant whisper of Mrs. Costello's slippers. There was a long pause, then the basement door opened just a crack. Through it Ciara could see a sliver of pale face and a bright slash of unevenly applied lipstick.

"It's me, Mrs. Costello. Ciara. From upstairs," she began. "I brought back the roses. They were actually for you—" The door closed again before she could finish.

She trudged back up the basement steps and dumped the roses on the passenger seat of her car. She switched on the engine, then turned the heating on full and sat there until Suzanne's parents arrived.

She watched them get out of their huge 4×4. Suzanne's mother was clinging to her husband's arm, scanning the street as if she was expecting a predator, a mountain lion or an eagle, to swoop in and snatch her.

In the photograph that Suzanne kept on her dressing table, her parents were young and glamorous, captured in black-and-white, kissing in a cloud of confetti. Ciara wouldn't have recognized them from that picture. She wondered if they recognized themselves.

She and Mort had been married beneath an arch of white hibiscus and frangipani flowers by a petite Balinese woman wearing a navy micromini business suit, the kind that sassy paralegals wore in TV dramas.

"*Could* you take this woman to be your awfully wedded wife?" the woman had asked Mort, and he'd grinned at Ciara and said, "I could."

In their wedding picture, Ciara was standing under the arch, barefoot, her newly highlighted hair loose, her floaty white Ghost wedding dress damp up to the waist where it had trailed in the water when Mort carried her into the sea. She was smiling straight up at her husband and he was smiling past the camera at the Swedish girls in ice-cream-colored sarongs who had acted as their witnesses.

Ciara pulled away from the curb before Suzanne opened the door to her parents. She drove into town, circled St. Stephen's Green twice and then took the coast road back out again. She slowed down as she passed the small town house in Sandymount where she had lived with Mort, where he still lived. There were flowers in the window.

She drove to Killiney and parked by the beach shelter where Mort had proposed to her. The heart with *Ciara, will you marry me?* that he had spray-painted on the whitewashed wall three years ago had disappeared beneath layers of new graffiti. *Macker is a knacker. Foxrock girls are dykes. Fight apathy! Or don't.*

They hadn't meant to get married on Valentine's Day. It just happened. When they arrived in Bali, they'd applied for a license, but it had taken ten days instead of a week. Ciara had lost track of time. It all merged into one exotic blur. Mornings in a double hammock watching scarlet and purple butterflies hovering over them like floating flowers. Afternoons exploring temples with lotus-choked ponds and offerings laid out under wheels of incense smoke. Nights eating under the stars watching distant electrical storms flaring on the horizon and counting fireflies as they walked home along Monkey Forest Road to make love.

It seemed like a delicious slice of destiny when their photocopied wedding certificate was dated February 14, as if the universe was rubber-stamping their love. As if the universe, Ciara thought now, gave a crap.

She started the car again and drove past the pier where Mort had first kissed her and the cinema where they'd seen their first film and the Indian restaurant where they'd had their first fight. It was boarded up now. Teenage boys in low-rise baggy jeans and baseball caps were hanging out in the doorway, passing a beer can between them. Somewhere between meeting Mort and breaking up with him, Ireland had started to look like another country.

She parked opposite Finnegan's. It was a proper old-fashioned pub with nicotine-stained ceilings and cracked leatherette stools and chipped Formica tables with folded beer mats wedged under the wonky legs.

She switched off the engine and watched the narrow street dissolve as the windscreen misted over with drizzle. Nearly four years ago she'd walked into the soupy gloom of Finnegan's out of the dazzling light of a June afternoon. She had been wearing a summer dress and flowery flip-flops and carrying a summer arrangement addressed to someone called Peggy.

A couple of old men were sitting at the polished mahogany bar, their heads raised like withered sunflowers toward the TV. The volume was on low and Ciara could hear the faraway rattle and click of snooker balls and the soft "ooohs" of the studio audience.

The guy standing behind the bar polishing a glass wasn't old; he was heart-stoppingly beautiful. He looked as if he had slipped through a hole in a Calvin Klein ad and landed in a grungy Dublin local. In three lazy blinks he took Ciara in. Her mouth, her light summer dress, her bare legs.

"For me?" He nodded at the flowers.

"Not unless your name is Peggy," Ciara said, trying to put him in his place.

"I'm Mort." He sounded Australian but he was, it turned out, from New Zealand. "And you are?"

"Double-parked," Ciara said, "looking for Peggy, remember?" But she heard the waver in her voice and so did he.

"Well, leave the car when you come back later," he said, taking the flowers, "so you can have a drink."

She sat in the cooling car, gripping the steering wheel as if it was a lifebelt. Every atom in her body was telling her to open the door and cross the busy road and walk into Finnegan's and tell David Mortimer that she could cope with anything if they were still together.

She closed her eyes and begged Granny Rose and River Phoenix, John Lennon and Audrey Hepburn for a sign. When she opened her eyes again, she saw it in the one lit window above the pub. A wonky hand-lettered card that said: *Psychic.*

She was expecting a woman in a traily dress, but the psychic was a man in his sixties with porcupine spikes of silver hair and stubble like iron filings. He was hunched over a two-bar electric fire popping a piece of Nicorette from a blister pack. His lined face lit up when he saw her.

"I'm sorry, wrong door." Ciara backed away.

"No such thing." He popped the gum into his mouth. "Take a pew."

He wheeled himself over on an unsteady swivel chair. The thought of Mort mere feet away below her in the bar hit Ciara behind the knees. She sank down onto the arm of the grubby sofa. "So"—the psychic worked his gum—"what can I do for you?"

"Nothing. I just came in to ask about prices. For a friend."

"You'd be amazed how many people say that." He scooted a little closer and took her hands before she could stop him. He squinted down at her palms for a full minute.

"You've been through a dark time, but it's coming to an end. It's like you're in a tunnel, but you're walking toward the light."

Ciara wasn't sure what she'd been expecting, but this was just too trite. She pulled her hands away.

"That's all you see? A tunnel and some light?"

"Yeah. Oh, hang on!" The psychic chewed his gum and gazed over her left shoulder intently, as if he was scanning an invisible queue. "Your grandmother is here now."

"What about Mort?" Ciara asked him slyly, laying a trap, willing him to fall into it, face first. "Is Mort here too?"

His dark eyes darted around the room. "Nope. Nobody answering to that name, I'm afraid."

"Great, what do I owe you?" Ciara rummaged in her purse for her wallet.

"You don't have a cigarette in there, do you?" The psychic looked sheepish.

"You're the psychic," she snapped. "You tell me."

"Sssh!" He was looking over her shoulder again. "Your grandmother has a message for you. She says that you know where to find Mort, but you should leave him alone because he's . . ."

Ciara's heart was caught inside her rib cage, a trapped hamster on a wheel. "Because he's *what*?"

The psychic frowned. "She's fading. She's saying something about three letters. She says you'll understand."

Ciara snorted. Granny Rose had never even written her *one* letter. She stood up. She was at the door when he called after her. "Do the letters 'S,' 'O' and 'B' mean anything to you?"

It was only four o'clock, but the sky was already folding itself away for the evening, exhausted. Grubby clouds were banked above the high granite walls of the graveyard.

There were flower sellers at the gate. Early daffodils and forced tulips blazed in aluminum buckets.

A line of wet black cars was snaking between the high gray pillars. Ciara followed the slow procession along the narrow gravel road that wound between the grassy avenues.

There were fresh wreaths and bunches of flowers laid out on the graves, and here and there, heart-shaped balloons on sticks had been stuck into the damp earth.

She dimly remembered that the grave was close to a stand of winter-flowering cherry trees. When she found it, the small granite cross and the rectangle of grass were covered in leaves. She used her scarf to brush them away, her breath coming in little puffs, like smoke.

She snapped the rubber band off the butchered roses and fanned them out over the rectangle of grass, roughly where she thought her grandmother's heart must be. She lifted her face and tried to make a smoke ring with a puff of breath, but it vanished into the air.

The first stars were already appearing. Ciara picked one that was caught in the branches of the cherry tree and gave it to herself for her third and last wedding anniversary. Then she put her head down and walked quickly through the gathering darkness to the gate, out of the tunnel and into the light.

AMARYLLIS

Beauty and Enlightenment.

She'd have to go to a proper florist, Becca thought. She picked the one on Camden Street with all the ivy painted up the outside. She told Josh that it was the beanstalk from the fairy tale and he gaped up at it, his hands planted on the hips of his Spider-Man costume, hoping he'd see Jack appear on the roof. Maybe that was a mistake, she thought as she pushed the door open. He was going to be gutted when he saw that it was just an ordinary shop. That was the problem with making stuff up—Santa, God, Debra the Invisible Zebra who knew when little boys were only pretending to brush their teeth: sooner or later Josh was going to catch her out. But inside, the shop wasn't ordinary at all. It was like something out of one of Josh's storybooks. A little cave full of flowers and candles and fairy lights. Tiny bells tinkled above their heads as the door closed.

"Whoa!" Josh gazed around in amazement. "We have to tell Dad about this!"

Becca gritted her teeth and fished her phone out of her bag and handed it over. That was the other problem with making stuff up—once you started telling a lie, it was hard to stop.

"Hello!" she called out. Silence, except for some posh piano music coming from hidden speakers. "Is there anyone here?"

Please, she thought, don't let the assistant be some patronizing cow and don't let the flowers cost a fortune. She had already blown thirty euros on a Moon in My Room for Darcy, seventy on the dress and shoes she was wearing and fifteen on a bottle of wine that she had thought was champagne. And by the time she realized it was only Prosecco, she had already paid and was too embarrassed to ask for her money back.

"Sorry." A tall, dark-haired woman was standing in the doorway at the back of the shop with a stack of vases in her arms. "I was upstairs, didn't hear the door. Can I help you?"

The florist was old, forty maybe, but her hair was even longer than Becca's. It hung over one shoulder in a loose plait tied at the end with a piece of twine. She looked posh, Becca decided, but not snotty. She seemed kind of familiar.

"Is Prosecco okay?" Becca blurted. "To bring to an afternoon party? Kind of a swanky one?"

"It's perfect," the florist said firmly. "Luxurious but casual."

"Really?" Becca bit her lip. "It's going to be all the parents from my son's school and I don't want to screw it up." She lowered her voice so that Josh wouldn't hear. "I thought the whole schoolyard popularity contest ended when I left school; now here I am all over again, wanting the popular girls to like me so my son can have friends. Do you have kids?" She saw the quick flash of pain in the dark eyes. A memory surfaced at the back of her mind, then slid out of view again. "Oh! I'm sorry, I didn't mean to . . ."

"No! It's fine." The florist put down the vases and folded her arms across her green apron. "I don't have kids but I can imagine the pressure. I'm sure they'll like you." She rummaged in the cubbyholes of the counter for a cloth. "But if my dad was here, he'd say, 'It's not other people's job to like you, it's yours.'"

"I like that," Becca said. She tucked it away in the back of her mind, where she kept all the little bits of wisdom she wanted to pass on to Josh. "Is it okay to just look around?"

"Absolutely." The florist began to polish the vases. "Take your time."

Becca walked over to the rows of buckets. There were a dozen kinds of roses. Four different types of lilies. And pails full of beautiful, exotic flowers she had never seen before. Everything looked kind of expensive.

"I've only got about fifteen euros," she said uncertainly. "Is that enough for something that looks nice?"

"It's plenty! Do you want a hand?" The florist came out from behind the counter. "Right, let's see!" She looked not at the buckets but at Becca, and after a few seconds, she nodded. "I don't know if it's just that gorgeous red dress"—she went over to a bucket of mixed flowers, fished one out—"but you remind me of one of these."

Becca looked at the tall, straight green stem topped with three red trumpets. "What it is?"

"It's an amaryllis. It comes from a Greek word, I can't remember which one, but it means radiant and sparkling."

Josh had been off in a corner, but now he was tugging at Becca's sleeve. "Hey!" the florist said. "Superman, I didn't see you there!"

"I'm not Superman," he sighed. "I'm Spider-Man. I'm just not wearing my mask yet." He handed the phone back to Becca. Dad, his message said, were inside a bees talk!!!!!! It is orsome. Xoxo Josh. She pressed send for him and straightaway the phone gave a little ping.

Josh stood on his tiptoes trying to read the screen. "What does he say?"

Becca held the phone out of his reach and pretended to read. "'Wow! That's so cool. If you find Jack inside the beanstalk, tell him I have that euro he lent me. X D.'"

"Dad knows Jack?" Josh's eyes widened. "That means he *exists*."

Becca slipped the phone back into her bag. She held out the tall red flower for his approval. "For Darcy's mum—what do you think?"

"Why is Dad always in America?" Josh picked at the little nylon cobwebs under the arms of his costume.

"Why is the man in the moon in the moon?" Becca asked.

He frowned. "You're not supposed to answer a question with a question."

The florist came to her rescue. "I have some more of those amaryllis upstairs. And I think I have some beanstalk seeds up there too but I might need a hand to find them."

"I have a hand," Josh told her. "I have two hands."

The nicest thing about working in a flower shop, Becca thought, listening to their footsteps in the room above her, must be the smell. The office cleaning work she'd done after Josh was born had always left her hands smelling of bleach. Now, even when she wasn't in the nail salon, the sharp odors of glue and gel hardening under the heat lamp seemed to cling to her clothes and hair. It would be heaven to spend your days working in a place that smelled of roses and trees and damp clay, like a garden after the rain.

Josh came dashing down the stairs, one cupped hand full of tiny brown seeds. He counted them while the florist wrapped the amaryllis.

"They're sunflower seeds," she whispered to Becca. "Plant them in a bit of soil in an eggbox to get them started. With any luck, they should grow to about six feet tall."

The house was enormous. A dozen silver helium balloons were tied to the wrought-iron railings. Beyond them, on a manicured lawn, a sheet of matching silver water poured noiselessly over a gleaming steel sculpture the size of a motorbike.

"What's that?" Josh peered through the railings.

"It's art." Becca imagined sneaking back in the dead of night and plonking her mum's garden gnomes around it. Throwing in a couple of ceramic fishing frogs just to scare the natives.

She took Josh's hand and they went up the sweep of granite steps to the white front door. From behind it came the sound of people talking, glasses clinking, laughter.

"Your hand is wetting," Josh complained, wiping his own palm on the leg of his red pants.

"Tell you what," Becca said, taking a deep breath, "why don't we count to twenty before we knock?"

Josh's eyes, denim blue, fringed with eyelashes that were so long they looked fake, narrowed with scorn. "Counting to twenty is for babies."

"Not if you do it in French." Becca hadn't learned French in secondary school but they taught it to six-year-olds at St. Bartholomew's. That was just how they rolled over here on the Southside.

"Ooon, duh," Josh said carefully, as if the words were inching unsteadily along the tightrope of his tongue, "twah . . ."

Becca tweaked the hem of her dress down again. The nude slip kept riding up under the red lace. She took the not-really-champagne bottle out of the plastic Smyths Toys bag, tucked it under her arm and held the tall red flowers out in front of her like a shield.

Josh was still counting, saying something that sounded like "cat-whores."

Her mam had told her that if she ever got pregnant, she would have to move out. When Becca said she was keeping the baby, Mam had come home with a bunch of official forms—children's allowance, rent allowance, that sort of thing. "If you're doing this, you're on your own."

It was just another of her tactics to scare Becca into having an abortion, but it had the opposite effect. Becca had given up school and moved into a bedsit above a chemist's shop ten minutes on the bus from her mam's house, and had stayed there until Josh was four.

The estate had a bad enough reputation when she was a kid but the recession had pushed it over the edge. Gangs of boys hung around the corner of her street in the middle of the day drinking, shouting, lobbing their empties at passing cars. The guards were afraid to go into the flats by the roundabout, and then a drug dealer had been shot in the chip shop four doors up from the bedsit. That was when Becca had cracked.

Her mam, who had been dead set against her having Josh, then adamant that Ferndale was no place to bring up a child, had thrown one of her fits when Becca told her they were moving away. "You can't just pull the poor kid up by the roots and drag him to the other side of the city," she had said. But by then Becca would have taken her son to Mars to get him away from Ferndale.

After she'd shouted herself hoarse, her mam had changed tack. "I thought you said you wouldn't touch that man's money?"

"I won't touch it. I'm not going to spend a cent of it on myself." The money was going to pay for Josh's school fees. She had been very clear about that. "Donnybrook is only six miles away, it's not Outer Mongolia. You can come and visit."

"Right," her mother had said sarcastically, "I'll apply for a passport. He'll be a fish out of water once he crosses the Liffey, Rebecca. I'm warning you."

Her mam had been wrong about Josh, though. In his first week at Bart's he'd made a dozen or so friends. Sage and India—they had names like that here—and Arlo and Milo. It was Becca who was having trouble fitting in. And she had to fit in. If she wanted Josh to be part of this world, she had to be part of it too.

It had taken forever to get this invitation. Weeks of hanging around after Josh went through the quaint arched wooden door, of waiting for one of the other mums to include her in the called-out invitations to coffee mornings and Pilates classes and book clubs. She got an occasional "Hi!" from a couple of them, but most of them looked straight through her as if she was invisible.

She definitely wasn't invisible to the handful of dads who showed up to do the school run. She'd caught them checking her out, sneaking little glances over the shoulders of the kids who were kissing them good-bye.

One of them, a short guy old enough to be her dad, kept smiling at her. He drove a massive BMW but he dressed (at his age!) like one of the deadbeat kids back in Ferndale. Baggy jeans and outsize sweatshirt and trainers so brightly colored they could be seen from space.

Last week he'd been parked at the gate checking his emails and had rolled his window down when she passed, asking her if she needed a lift. She had her headphones on and kept walking, pretending not to hear him.

"Deese-nuff. Vont!" Josh looked at her. "That's twenty in French, Mum."

Becca lifted the heavy knocker. Head up, she told herself. Sparkle.

The door was opened by a beaming Asian woman of about thirty in a black dress. A friend of Karen's, Becca guessed.

"Welcome," she said, making it sound like two words.

"Hi," Becca said, trying not to let her jaw drop. About twenty people were standing around sipping wine and chatting in a black-and-white-tiled hallway that was bigger than her mam's entire house. What looked like a hundred white roses cascaded from a huge urn on an ornate marble hallstand. An aquarium ran the length of one entire wall. A girl in a bumblebee costume and a boy dressed as a pirate had their noses pressed up against the glass. Josh ducked under Becca's arm and ran to join them.

"Sorry! That was Josh," Becca said, "and I'm Becca." People in Ferndale didn't kiss one another, but the St. Bart's mums air-kissed one another at least twice a day. She leaned forward to kiss the Asian women, then stopped when she saw her look of horror.

"We're invited," she stammered, holding out the flowers and the present as if they were proof, forgetting the bottle that was tucked under her arm. It dropped and exploded, scattering shards of glass and splattering Becca and the Asian woman with wine. The chatter in the hall stopped abruptly, as if a switch had been flipped.

"Oh God," Becca gasped. "I'm so sorry!"

"It's okay, madam," the Asian woman said smoothly.

Madam? Suddenly Becca saw that the black dress was uniform. Flustered, she handed over the flowers and the present, still in its yellow plastic bag. The woman put them on the hallstand beside the roses.

A second girl in an identical dress appeared with a dustpan and brush and began to sweep up the glass. Becca bent down to help her.

"Don't worry about that." It was Karen. Anytime Becca had seen her before, she'd been wearing killer heels and business suits, but today she was dressed down in skinny jeans and ballet flats, a white T-shirt with a deep slash neck showing off her bony shoulders. "I'm so glad you could make it."

She held out her hand.

"I'd better not." Becca held her own hand up. Prosecco dripped from her elbow. "I brought you some wine but it's ended up all over your floor. I'm so sorry."

"And over your dress. Do you need to change? You can borrow something if you'd like."

Becca imagined trying to squeeze her curvy size-twelve body into one of Karen's tiny size-six dresses. "No, but could I use the loo to clean up?"

"Of course."

Becca followed Karen out of the hall, past the open door of a huge, busy kitchen with one high glass wall.

"What an amazing house!"

"Oh, it's not a house, it's an albatross," Karen sighed. "If I even start to think how deep in negative equity we are, I'll expire." She turned left into a glassed-in corridor then right into a smaller hall and opened the door to a vast white-tiled bathroom. "I've got some baby wipes in here somewhere." She walked over to a double sink and bent down to search drawers and cupboards. "I hope your dress is okay," she said over her shoulder.

Becca caught sight of herself in the mirror. She had a horrible feeling that it wasn't. The children at St. Bart's had a uniform. Gray wool trousers for the boys, gray pleated skirts for the girls. A white shirt with a red knitted tie. A navy blazer with the school crest on the pocket. A black wool cap with a gray silk lining. The mothers had their uniforms too. Becca had studied them carefully. Skinny jeans with shearling waistcoats and UGG boots or tiny flowery dresses with outsize cardigans and ankle boots. Yoga pants and tees in ice-cream colors with down gilets, slinky black running gear with two-hundred-euro Nikes. Cashmere coats, expensive suits, heels.

She had tried hard to blend in on her limited budget, not wanting to let Josh down. She ditched her gel nails and wore stick-ons. She tinted the highlights out of her long brown hair and wore it loose. She got rid of the ten-euro eternity ring that she'd bought in River Island before she moved here. These women, she guessed, could tell a real diamond from a fake a hundred feet away.

"Here you go." Karen handed her the wipes.

Becca began to dab at the splashes of wine that had soaked through the material to the inside layer of her lace dress. When she'd tried it on, she'd thought the dress was kind of Kate Middleton. Now, with her overdone makeup, she realized she looked more like Katie Price. Her eyes met Karen's in the mirror. "I didn't realize everyone would be so casual. I should have just worn my jeans. This is a bit low-cut, isn't it?"

"Maybe a little, but"—Karen dabbed on some lip balm—"you know what Nora Ephron says?"

"No." Becca didn't know who Nora Ephron was.

"You should put on a bikini when you're twenty-two and you shouldn't take it off till you're thirty-four."

Becca sighed. "I should put mine on next year, then."

"And I should take mine off." Karen shook her head. "God, you're only twenty-one?" She fluffed up her thin blonde hair and looked at herself regretfully. "I felt old. Now I feel positively ancient."

"Well, you don't look it," Becca said. Though if she was truthful—and she felt bad for thinking this way—Karen did have a kind of pinched look and a couple of frown lines under her fringe that made her look more like forty.

She had met Karen because it was raining. The heavens had opened as Becca ran up the long driveway to collect Josh. He was excited about a story he'd written and he wanted to show it to her before he put his coat on. Appropriately, it was about heaven. *Heaven is washing TV with my mum*, he'd written. *There are dogs in heaven. Heaven is when my dad techs me to say good night.*

She fought a pang of guilt as she tucked Josh's damp copybook back into his bag. She took his hand, and as they turned around, she saw a girl with long white-blonde hair spilling from beneath her hood hovering uncertainly at the bottom of the steps.

"That's Darcy!" Josh said in a loud stage whisper. "She's adopted and she has a seahorse."

The three of them were sheltering under a dripping chestnut tree when the black SUV roared up and a frazzled woman in her work uniform climbed out. Becca caught a flash of red from the soles of her shoes. "Did you wait with her? That's so kind. Thank you. My husband was supposed to pick her up but he's gone AWOL. Sorry, I'm Karen."

"Becca."

Karen was belting Darcy into the backseat when she turned to look over her shoulder at Becca. "Are you waiting for Josh's mum to pick you up?"

"I'm his mum," Becca said.

"Oh God!" Karen's light blue eyes widened. "We all thought you were the nanny."

She had got the clothes right, Becca thought, so it must have been her accent that had given her away.

There was a long, awkward pause. The rain was really coming down. "Well, get in," Karen said. "I'll drop you home."

Karen slipped her phone headset on as she accelerated back down the drive. "Sorry, I have to take this," she said. Becca tuned out her work call and lay back against the padded headrest, listening to Darcy telling Josh about seahorses. They mated for life, apparently, and swam with their tails linked together. The male seahorse had the babies. And it sounded to Becca that sea creatures the size of her thumb made a better job of relationships than most people did, herself included.

"This is us," she said on Sandford Road.

Karen pulled over outside the neat redbrick town house swathed in Virginia creeper. "It's lovely," she said, a little hesitantly.

Becca and Josh didn't actually live in the house but in the two-roomed granny flat around the side. The rent had been eight hundred euros a month, but the owner had come down to six hundred when Becca offered to do her shopping and cleaning and keep the garden tidy. The shopping was the easiest part. Miss Swanson was in her seventies and seemed to survive almost entirely on cigarettes and anti-inflammatories. She only used one bedroom so the cleaning wasn't too bad, but Becca still vacuumed the entire house twice a week, washed the windows, mopped the floors and sorted out the little pile of laundry. She ended up dropping in every other evening. Josh sat up at the table with his markers and his coloring books and they'd talk while Becca gave Miss Swanson a manicure or set her hair with heated rollers. The old lady was lonely, and it wasn't as if Becca had anything better to do.

The flat had been in a right state when Becca moved in. She had scrubbed burned-in grease off the cooker and stripped the wallpaper and painted the walls white. Josh had the bedroom and Becca slept on the sofa bed in the living room. She was up first and last so it was easier that way. Sleepovers were going to be a problem in the future, but she could cross that bridge when she came to it. She had already crossed plenty of bridges to get here, and burned a few of them too.

Her mam was keeping her distance. Becca went back home every week but so far Mam hadn't come to visit them. She was hoping that Becca would crack without her and move back Northside. And without Miss Swanson to keep her company, Becca might have. She was lonely too.

The night that Karen gave them a lift, as Becca was edging the hot tip of the iron into the pleats in one of Miss Swanson's old-fashioned cotton nighties, she heard Josh saying his prayers. Thanking Allah and Jesus and Buddha for oven chips and Iron Man and for the invitation to Darcy's party, which meant that he would get to meet her seahorse.

And Becca, who didn't believe in any gods, threw a little thank-you prayer out there too. Because the party was for adults as well as kids, and after six weeks of waiting, the door to the tight little world she'd moved into had finally opened.

There wasn't much that Becca could do about the dress, but, after Karen had gone, she used a baby wipe to scrub off most of her makeup. She was peeling off her stick-on lashes when there was a sharp rap on the door.

"Open up!" A male voice. "It's an emergency. I have a broken nose!"

Shit! She stuffed the baby wipes, packet and all, into her bag and ran to the door.

A tall man in a clown suit was leaning on the doorjamb, dangling a squashed red plastic nose from a piece of elastic. He was wearing white face paint. A wide red mouth that stretched all the way to his ears. Black quotation-mark eyebrows that shot up his receding hairline when he saw Becca.

"You didn't tell me you'd invited the Kardashians," he said and she saw that he wasn't on his own.

"Hi!" His friend was wearing normal clothes. If it was normal for a man in his thirties to dress like a teenage skateboarder. He smiled at Becca. "Remember me?" And she did. It was Mr. BMW from the school gates.

"It's all yours," she said.

"Now that," she heard the clown say as she walked away, "is my kind of *fancy* dress."

It was sunny in the garden but the air was still cold. All the women were clustered around the heaters in the marquee that extended out of the back of the house. The men had ventured down onto the middle tier of the long, sloping lawn where a chef was basting a whole hog on a spit. Beyond them, the children were swarming all over a huge bouncy castle. Becca could just make out Josh, one of at least five Spider-Men in among a blur of bouncing pirates, robots and princesses. A waitress offered her a glass of real champagne and she stood on her own, holding it nervously, her arms folded, trying not to look conspicuous, before she spotted Karen through the crowd.

"Glenda, Emma, Alannah. This is Becky, mother of the adorable Josh."

"It's actually . . ." She wanted to correct Karen but didn't. "Nice to finally meet you."

Emma—who was dark and pretty—was the only one who smiled. "I'm India's mum."

"I'm old enough to be *his* mum." Alannah turned to ogle a passing waiter. "Do you think he'd mind?"

"Ignore Alannah." Emma rolled her eyes. "We're having a serious conversation about Pilates for kids."

"It's ridiculous!" This must be Glenda. She had a feathery cap of dark red hair and a gray jersey dress that showed off her perfectly toned body.

"I know." Becca jumped right in. "Kids don't need exercise classes. I mean, they never sit still, do they? Josh runs rings around me in the park."

"Oops." Alannah raised her glass to hide a little smile.

"I meant," Glenda said, "that it's ridiculous that St. Bart's won't offer classes. I teach Pilates. It's a wonderful practice for children. Juvenile obesity is an epidemic, you know."

"Yes," Becca backtracked. "Of course it is."

A roar of laughter rose with a plume of smoke from the spit.

"Men and barbecues!" Alannah sighed. "It's all fun and games till they start battling it out to decide who's Lord of the Wings." She looked over her shoulder. "Which of those Neanderthals is yours?"

"None of them," Becca said. She had rehearsed this. "Josh's father is not in the picture."

What do Northsiders use for protection when having sex? Bus shelters.

What's the difference between a Northsider and Batman? Batman can go into a shop without robbin'.

What do you call a Northsider in a suit? The defendant.

Becca had thought the whole Northside/Southside thing was just a joke till the winter she was sixteen, when she got a weekend job in a shop in a Southside shopping mall.

"You'll need an interpreter," her friend Jasmine said. "They won't understand your accent south of the Liffey."

But it wasn't the river that divided north from south, Becca soon realized. It was an attitude. The teenagers who came into Shoe Locker acted as if they owned the world and she was only there to keep them happy.

The day she met Gavin, she had been running to and from the stockroom getting endless pairs of trainers for a fourteen-year-old girl in a Juicy Couture tracksuit who had barely even looked at her.

When she came out after searching everywhere for the last four pairs, the girl was wandering off, leaving behind a jumble of shoes strewn all around the floor.

"Hey," a guy in a white Hollister sweatshirt yelled after her.

The girl turned and her fake-tanned face lit up when she saw him. He was over six feet tall. Blonde hair stood up in random spikes around his freckled face as if he'd been electrocuted. He was ridiculously hot.

"You forgot something!" he said.

"What?" She flicked her ironed blonde hair and batted her fake eyelashes.

"Your manners." He picked up one of the trainers and pretended to throw it at her. "You're supposed to say thanks."

"It's her job."

"Lovely." He turned to Becca but she wasn't buying it. He was just going to be another flavor of arrogant; give him five minutes and he'd find a way to humiliate her.

She went back to the storeroom and put away the trainers the girl hadn't bothered to try on. When she got back, he was sitting on the padded bench, sorting the other pairs out and putting them back into their boxes.

"You don't have to do that!"

"I want to."

"Well, you don't always get what you want," she said. "Actually, around here," she muttered, "you probably do."

"You're not from around here then?"

"Widda naxent like dis?" She exaggerated it, flattening out the vowels, dropping the *h*'s. "Whadda yew tink?"

He scratched his chin. "I think you've just put those trainers into the wrong box and accents don't matter as much as people think."

"Yeah?" She pushed the bulging lid down, trying to squash the reluctant Reeboks into the Adidas box. "Well, you would say that, wouldn't you? I've had it up to here with stuck-up Southsiders."

"Look," he said. "I apologize for our Tango-skinned friend, but you can't write off half the population of Dublin because of a stereotype."

"Why not?" Becca loaded her arms up with boxes. "She did."

"See you," he called after her as he left.

"Not if I see you first."

That same Saturday night he was waiting for her when she came out of the shop after it closed, sitting in the deserted mall like a benched footballer, his legs apart, his blonde head bent, his hands clasped between his knees.

"I was wondering if you'd like to do something?"

"Like what?" she said. "Rob a car?"

He grinned. "Never break the law till the second date. It's kind of a rule of mine. I'm Gavin."

"Date?" Where she came from, people shifted and snogged and shagged. They didn't date.

She walked away, the sound of her footsteps rattling around her in the empty mall like gunfire. "Nice idea, but we have nothing in common."

"Come on." He caught up with her at the door. "I just want to hang out with you. Is that a crime?"

She slowed down and they walked out into the piazza. It was

raining, and the skating rink was almost empty. The ice, lit from beneath, glowed the blue of a butterfly wing.

"You want to try?"

"I don't know how," she said, biting her lip.

"Come on. I'll teach you."

"Hey!" Gavin tottered at the edge, clinging hard to the railings as she swooped past. "You knew how to do this all along."

"Try to keep up, Southside boy." Her laughter trailed in little foggy puffs behind her as she gathered speed, and the Christmas lights on the shopfronts around the rink dissolved into a jeweled blur.

"Well, that was embarrassing," Gavin said afterward when they were at a window table in the Thai restaurant that overlooked the piazza. "Any other Olympic-level skills you haven't mentioned that I should know about? Pole vaulting? Snake charming?"

"Lots of Poles Northside, not so many snakes." She peeled the paper off her chopsticks.

"Never used chopsticks before, but I think I'll be just brilliant at it." Gavin stabbed a wonton and held it up. She shook her head and laughed.

"Okay." He twisted a strand of noodle around one chopstick like spaghetti. "How's this?"

"You need to hold both of them at the same time."

"Like this?" He deftly picked out a single grain of rice.

"Hey!" Becca said. "You knew how to do this—"

"All along. You see. We have more in common than you think."

But did they? Becca wondered. Living on the other side of a river didn't make you better than someone else, but it made you different. Gavin's parents, she learned, were lawyers who lived in a big house in Donnybrook somewhere. Her mam was an office cleaner. Her dad was on disability. They lived in a two-up two-down on an estate that had more cars stuck up on blocks in the front gardens than flowers.

He asked her about her friends, offered a couple of times to give her a crossbar ride home on his bike. But Becca felt sick at the thought of him seeing the house, let alone sitting in their tiny living room being too polite to her mam and dad. Squirmed when she imagined how nice he'd be to Jasmine, who'd fancy him but would still be laughing at him behind his back.

She didn't want to go back to his house either and feel out of place. Didn't want to hang out with his mates worrying about her accent. She'd seen them around the mall—rucks of raucous rugby player types who wolf-whistled when they passed her on the opposite escalator.

So they spent almost all their time in no-man's-land. Wrapped around one another in the doorway next to the Cath Kidston shop at the shadowy end of the piazza. In the shelter with the broken light trying to stretch out the last few moments before her bus arrived. They kissed through entire movies at the mall cinema. Love scenes and car chases and shoot-outs and once to the screechy soundtrack of an opera beamed in live from Italy.

Becca had kissed other boys before but it had always felt like a battle of wills, as if she was being pushed over a line she didn't want to cross, but this was different. Every week, they edged closer to the line and just about pulled back. Part of her was scared to cross it but part of her couldn't wait.

Gavin was going skiing with his parents at Christmas. "Three weeks." He leaned his chin against the top of her head. "How am I supposed to get through three weeks without you?" They were in a corner of the emptying cinema foyer, putting off the moment when they had to go back out into the world.

Three weeks was nearly as long as they had been together. It was long enough to lose him. He'd meet someone in France or realize that he didn't want to be with someone like her. Even if he didn't, even if they made it through Christmas, what was going to happen in the New Year? Her job at the mall was ending after the sales.

"Tell them you don't want to go," she said.

"I can't." He tucked his hands into the back pockets of her jeans.

"But they're leaving a day before me," he said. "You could come and stay. We'd have the place to ourselves."

Just looking at the huge redbrick house behind the high hedge made Becca feel small. She had the sense that it was looking down at her and that if Gavin's parents had been there, they would be looking down at her too.

"Come on," Gavin said, leading her down some steps to a basement door. She felt as if she was shrinking when she stepped into the kitchen. It occupied the whole basement area of the house. There was an enormous Christmas tree at one end and at the other a wall of framed pictures that Becca tried not to look at. Snapshots of Gavin's *real* life. Teenage boys and girls in black tie and evening dresses. Family dinners in posh restaurants. Tanned faces, white teeth, swimming pools.

They sat like tongue-tied children at the huge dining table, picking at a lukewarm Thai takeaway with forks, then they swapped Christmas presents. She gave him the Nike Zooms she had spent too much money on, even with her staff discount. He handed her two small packages wrapped in tissue paper. A silver bracelet with two charms and a red T-shirt with a screen print of white chopsticks. Becca pulled it on over her top. Gavin took it off again on the way upstairs to his room.

Afterward, he ran her a bath and found a hair grip that must have been his mother's so she could pile her long hair up. She got under the water quickly and shuffled down till her body was hidden by the bubbles, awkward suddenly, though a few minutes before she'd been anything but.

Gavin sat on the floor in a gray dressing gown, one finger making slow circles in the water. He lifted her arm out of the bath and wiped foam off the bracelet. "The charms are supposed to remind you of something."

She stared at the tiny silver trainer and the miniature ice skate, then looked up at him. "I don't think I'm going to forget this."

He reached into the dressing gown pocket and then held out his hand. On his palm was a third charm, a claw-footed bath the size of her fingernail.

"Just in case."

The dad dressed as a clown twisted balloons into swords and crowns. Two of the others had an air battle with giant remote-control balloon goldfish. Josh watched them the way he always watched other children's fathers, with a mixture of envy, curiosity and awe.

After Darcy had blown out the candles on her mermaid cake, the kids invaded the bouncy castle again while the grown-ups, in twos and threes, wandered back up to the house. Becca was turning to follow them when a tiny figure in a pink tutu ran up the grassy slope, stopped abruptly and vomited at her feet. It was Darcy.

"I've got sick on my fairy dress." She hiccuped.

And my shoes, Becca thought. They were ruined. "Just as well"—she opened her bag, pulled out the packet and started cleaning Darcy's dress—"that I brought my magic wipes!"

"I've been looking for you." It was him again, Mr. BMW, coming toward her.

Becca glared at him but he walked straight past her and held his arms out to Darcy, who toppled into them and clung to him like a wallaby. So this was Karen's husband, Becca realized.

"Oooh!" He winced. "Something smells bad."

"It's my sick." Darcy looked down at her dress, then pointed a sparkly pink-nail-varnished finger imperiously at Becca. "But it's going to be okay. She has magic wipes!"

"Right," he sighed, "let's get you out of public view and get you cleaned up."

He carried Darcy behind a box hedge and they worked on the skirt together, on their knees, scrubbing at the scratchy pink net till most of the damage was gone, leaving a damp patch.

"Kids," Becca heard the clown dad shouting, "come on! Gather round for the goodie bags."

Darcy's eyes opened wide and she smiled at Becca, then squirmed away from them and ran back out into the garden.

They began to stand up. "You've just cleaned vomit off my ungrateful child." Mr. BMW took her hand and helped her up. "And I don't even know your name."

"Becca."

"I'm Gary. Nice to finally meet you." He bent forward to kiss her on the cheek just as she turned, and their mouths collided briefly. She pulled away instantly.

"Wait!" he said. "Don't move."

"But . . ." Becca felt embarrassed and anxious.

He put a hand on her shoulder to stop her getting away. "Darcy got you!" He leaned over, picked up a strand of her hair at the root and zipped his fingers along the length of it.

"Ugh!" He shook his hand. "How come kids' puke always has carrots in it, when it's near impossible to get them to eat them? Is there something about a child's digestive system that magically transforms sugar and E numbers into vegetables?"

They both started to laugh, but just then, out of the corner of her eye, Becca thought she saw someone watching them through the gap in the hedge and realized how they might look to others—alone, out of view, standing close together. Had someone seen that stupid kiss, Gary touching her hair, the two of them laughing?

"Wait!" she called, but by the time she'd scrambled past Gary back onto the lawn, Karen (why did it have to be her of all people?) was already some way away and didn't look back.

"Oh no," Gary sighed from beside her. "I'd better go sort this out."

He'd explain, Becca thought, as she rushed back to the house trying to find somewhere to wash her hands. Karen would understand. The

glass corridor that should have led to the bathroom took her instead
to a shallow flight of gray-carpeted stairs. She hesitated, caught a whiff
of Darcy's vomit, then took off her shoes and hurried upstairs up—a
house this big probably had half a dozen bathrooms she could use.

She heard the voices just before she got to the top and saw the two
women standing at a closed door, their heads bent, listening intently.

"Karen, let us in, please." Glenda tapped on the door with her ring,
the diamond on it the size of a piece of popcorn.

"Why is she so upset?" Emma whispered. "What happened?"

"That slut in the red dress happened!"

Becca froze, unable to go forward, too scared to go back downstairs.

"*Josh's fader is noh in de pitcher.*" Glenda's malicious impersonation
of her accent was horribly accurate. "Well, she obviously doesn't intend
to be on her own for long. Karen just got a charming *pitcher* of her
trying to get off with Gary behind the bushes in the garden."

The children were sitting in a circle around the clown dad, who was
handing out bags festooned with ribbons, pink for the girls, blue for
the boys.

"Josh!" Becca grabbed his arm. "It's time to go home."

"In a minute," he said reasonably.

"Now!" She hauled him to his feet, making the other kids turn and
stare.

"Wait! I haven't had my goodie bag!" He dug his heels in as she
dragged him up the garden. "Mum! You! Have! To! Wait!"

Emotional stress, a change in routine, not eating properly, tiredness.
There were lots of reasons for a period to be late. Becca had googled
them. But by New Year's Eve, she was frantic. She sneaked out of work
on her coffee break and bought a test at Boots, loading her basket
up with other things—shampoo, a sparkly nail varnish, a fake tan

mitt—so nobody in the queue would notice it. She hid it at the bottom of her bag, then transferred it to the hot press, stuffing it under an old pile of towels at the very back. Every night, after her mam and dad had switched their light out, she took it out. She locked herself in the bathroom. Sat on the edge of the bath, her heart thumping so loudly she was scared her parents would hear it through the paper-thin walls. She held the box in her hands, turned it over, read the instructions until she knew them word for word, but she didn't tear the cellophane. She didn't need to; it wasn't going to happen, it couldn't be true.

The day Gavin got back was her last day at Shoe Locker. He wanted to go a movie but she told him to meet her at the Thai place after work instead.

His eyes were on the door when she walked in, his grin too bright, his eyes too blue in his newly tanned face. He stood, and reached out to hug her, but she slipped past and slid onto the bench opposite him without a greeting.

"What's wrong?"

"I have something to tell you."

"Are you . . ." The grin faded. "Is this where you break up with me?"

She stared out at the bare and chilly piazza. All the Christmas lights had been taken down. There was a circle of yellowy grass where the ice rink had been.

"I don't understand," he said when she told him. "We only did it once."

"Twice," Becca said miserably. "And you didn't use anything the second time."

"The bath." He touched the tiny silver charm on her bracelet. "I remember." He looked up at her. He was supposed to be angry. He was supposed to ask her how she could have been so stupid, if it was even his, if this had been her plan all along, if she wanted money for it; to tell her she was on her own. All the things that men said on TV and in films. But instead he was beaming at her.

"Oh no! Don't even go there!" she said fiercely. "I can't have this baby."

"Why not?"

Because, she wanted to say, when you go to college you'll be surrounded by hundreds of middle-class girls who'll fancy you and will
be prettier, more interesting and funnier than me—girls your mates
and your family will approve of and who'll fit into your life the way
someone like me and some kid never will. And, she thought, you'll
hate me for that. But instead she said, "Gav, you're eighteen, I'm sixteen.
We're supposed to have our whole lives ahead of us."

"What are we going to do with our lives that's more important than
making another person?" he said, which completely floored her. He
was dead right, she knew, but he was also so wrong.

"Gavin, you don't get it. For starters, my mam will kick me out. I
won't have anywhere to live."

"I'll talk to my folks. They'll be cool with this, Becca. You can move
in and I'll do my exams in June." She could see him working it all out
like he was organizing a skiing trip or something. "Then I'll take a year
out, get a job and we'll have a place of our own by the time the baby
comes."

"You make it all sound so easy," she said with tears in her eyes.

"That's because it is!"

"Your world might be like that"—she shook her head—"but the
real world isn't."

Josh began to cry, loud, shouty sobs of protest, as Becca hauled him
past groups of bemused and disapproving parents. She snatched him up;
he squirmed to try to get free but she clung to him and carried him
through the marquee and into the kitchen.

"Did he fall?" a concerned woman in a cream dress asked her.

"He's fine!" Becca kept her head down as she hurried through the
hall in her bare feet, carrying her shrieking son.

On the marble table by the door, beneath the huge vase of roses,
she saw the amaryllis flowers she had brought still lying there wrapped
in their cellophane, as if they weren't worth bothering about. The sight

of them abandoned there without water sparked her anger into a blaze. She snatched them up and turned to the waiter who was passing by.

"Can you get that, please?" she said abruptly, and nodded at the door.

"I. Want. To. Go. Back!" Josh roared as she carried him down the granite steps, past the sculpture, out through the gate and onto the street.

"You can't always go back." She deposited him on the pavement outside the iron railings.

"I. Hate. You!" Josh glared up at her.

"Tough." She rubbed her arms, which ached from his weight. "Because I'm all you've got."

"I've got Dad!" he said.

Her heart was pounding against her ribs. "No," she said softly, "you don't."

It was all a lie. The dad she had invented for Josh who had lived with them when Josh was very little and who loved him more than anything but had gone to America to do an important job and would come back someday.

The whole story was like a beanstalk—a make-believe ladder to let him escape into the clouds from the harsh truth that existed below.

Becca had only seen Gavin twice again. The first time was when she came home from school and found him sitting between his parents on the brown leather sofa in her mam's tiny living room. He stared up at her helplessly.

The whole thing felt so surreal that all she could think was how horrible she must look to him in her brown school uniform.

"Rebecca!" The armchair was empty but her mother was standing, her lips white with anger, to stay calm for the sake of Mr. and Mrs. Summers. "Tell me this isn't happening."

Fergus Summers, a small, dark-haired man, looked mortified and cleared his throat a lot but never said a word. Becca's mam and Rita Summers did all the talking. She was tall and blonde and wore an expensive cream mac that she didn't take off and a determined expression that said that she didn't know how her son had gotten involved in all of this—meaning Becca, her mother, the house, the cheap leather sofa—but that she was here, behind enemy lines, to get him out.

None of it seemed real. It was as if they were discussing what to do about someone else they all vaguely knew—a neighbor from hell, a dodgy relative, someone that nobody liked. She kept trying to find Gavin's eyes but he was staring at the floor, not at her.

They were all reasonable people, Rita Summers said calmly, but they had found themselves in a difficult situation. There was a lot at stake. She was sure they could find a compromise that suited everybody. But she wanted to make a few things clear. Becca found herself nodding.

Gavin was being sent to boarding school to do his Leaving Cert— nobody looked at Gavin when she said this. If Gavin and Becca still wanted to be *involved* (she said the word as if it tasted of mold) after that, his parents would not stand in the way. But in the meantime, there was to be no contact whatsoever—no phone calls, no text messages, no meetings.

"This is just a cooling-off period," Rita continued, becoming a bit more legal-sounding, "but Gavin is not evading his responsibilities. We are willing to help with any reasonable expenses Rebecca might incur in resolving this issue."

"Meaning," Becca's mam said, "if she has an abortion?"

"I didn't use that word," Rita Summers said quickly. "Abortion is illegal in this country, but it's up to Rebecca." She looked at Becca for the first time. Her expression, like her voice, was neutral and anger showed in her eyes. Becca felt herself shrinking under her gaze. "If that's what she wants, well . . ."

"It's not what either of us wants—" Gavin began.

"Gavin!" His mother cut across him. "Do not go back on your word. We've talked and we all agreed this was the only way forward."

Becca stared at Gavin and saw a deep flush creep up his neck.

"I'm sorry!" he mouthed.

The last time Becca saw Gavin was outside the Mace across from her school, holding his bike in the rain. His gray uniform was even worse than hers, which she found oddly comforting, and his hair was plastered to his head.

"Jesus! State of him!" Jasmine snickered.

"Yeah!" Becca said. "Tosser." She took Jasmine's arm and pulled her toward the bus stop.

"Did you get my texts?" he called across at her. Becca had blocked his number. If he had agreed to no contact, that was fine with her.

Gavin kept pace with them but on the other side of the street. "Please, I need to talk to you."

"Do you know him?" Jasmine asked her.

"No!" Becca saw the bus turning onto Kylemore Road. She pulled her hood up, picked up speed and tried to lose him.

"Wait!"

Jasmine looked over her shoulder. "He's following us. You do know him, don't you?"

"No!"

"Becca!" He was wheeling the bike across the road through the traffic. "Becca!" he shouted above the car horns.

"Then how does he know your name?" Jasmine grabbed her sleeve. "What the fuck is going on, Becs?"

"Nothing!"

The bus pulled level with them. "You get it!" Becca pushed Jasmine forward. "I've got something to do."

She waited till the doors had closed, then wheeled around to face Gavin.

"What are you doing here? I don't want to talk to you ever again."

"I'm sorry about the day in your house. My mother freaked out. You saw what she's like. Look, I have to go to boarding school. I don't have any choice. But I'll be finished before the baby is born. She can't stop us being together then."

"There isn't going to be a baby. I'm going to get rid of it, okay? My mam is going to book the flights to England."

"You don't mean that!"

"It's over Gavin—o-v-e-r. What do I have to do to get it into that big, thick Southside head of yours?"

"Becca, please, listen." He tried to take her arm but she pushed him away.

"Go away!"

"Okay!" He lifted his arms like a prisoner surrendering. Trickles of rain were running under the sleeves of his blazer. There were tears in his eyes and she had to look away because if she didn't she was afraid that she would start to cry too.

"I'll go," he said, "but I'll call you. Please, don't do anything about the baby until I call you. I love you, Becca. We can make this work, I swear!"

She looked back once. He was cycling away through the teeming rain, his head down, his back wheel churning up water as he turned onto Kylemore Road. Then he was gone.

Gavin's bicycle was hit by a car that lost control on Arran Quay. The driver, a man with Alzheimer's who should not have been driving at all, survived. His wife died a week later, but Gavin was dead before the ambulance arrived.

Becca's mam had been sympathetic at first but then she had taken the hard line, as she always did. It wasn't her fault really; it was just the way she was. She told Becca that having the baby would just heap tragedy on top of tragedy. That she was being selfish. That a sixteen-year-old had nothing to teach a child about the world.

What she didn't tell Becca was that the first time she held her son, her heart, still full of grief for Gavin, would burst open like a piñata and all the sweetness that had been concentrated into the few short weeks that she had been with him would pour out.

It was true that she hadn't a clue how to look after a baby, but she was a fast learner. She knew before he opened his mouth to cry whether he needed feeding or changing or burping. She could hear a change in his breathing from her deepest sleep.

"You're on your own if you do this," her mother had warned her. But she was wrong. Because once Becca had Josh, she was never on her own again.

When Josh was six months old, Becca got a letter sent on from her home address. It was just like her mam to forward a letter instead of calling around with it. It was from Gavin's father. She couldn't imagine his mother had had anything to do with writing it. Gavin's grandparents had left him money, he said, and they wanted it to go to his son for his education. There were no strings attached. There would be a place available at Gavin's old school when he was four. He would love Becca to take it up in memory of their son but he'd understand if she didn't feel that was right. The letter ended with an apology. The day they'd met must have been upsetting for her, especially in the light of what had happened afterward, but people said and did rash things in the heat of the moment. Maybe she would bring her son to visit his grandparents sometime?

Becca had decided to swallow her anger and take him up on the money but not on the invitation. Rita Summers had wanted no contact between Becca and her son. She did not deserve to see her grandson.

Josh walked three steps behind Becca all the way along Herbert Park, grizzling, but when they got to Morehampton Road, he stopped at the curb and took her hand.

"I'm sorry," she said as they crossed over.

"The goodie bag had a lighty-up yo-yo," he said sadly. "And a mini Frisbee. And a Mr. Potato Head with different kinds of eyes."

She crouched down when they got to the other side so that they were eye to eye. "I meant that I'm sorry about your dad."

"You told me lies." He stared at the ground.

"They weren't all lies, Josh. Your dad didn't meet you but he did love you. He was so excited when I told him you were going to be born and he went to your school just like I told you."

"But where did he live if he didn't live in America?" Josh looked up at her.

"Near here," she said. "I'll show you sometime."

"I want to see now."

"What about your beanstalk seeds? Don't you want to go home and plant them?"

"I don't believe in beanstalks anymore," he said, biting his lip.

Becca hadn't walked down Marlborough Road again since the night she went home with Gavin.

"Is it this house?" Josh kept asking, all the way down the road, until she began to regret ever mentioning it. "Is it this one? Is it this one?"

"It's this one," she said softly when they finally got there. Just looking up at the redbrick facade gave her that shrinking feeling she'd had the first time she'd seen it, as if the house was looking down at her and whoever was inside it would look down at her too. "This is where your dad lived and this is where you were made."

"Wow!" Josh gazed at the house beyond the tall hedge. "It's a big house for just one person, big enough for a giant."

"He didn't live there on his own," Becca said. "His mum and dad lived there too."

"Do they still live there?"

"I think so."

"Then why don't they come and see us?" He frowned.

"I don't think they're home." She pulled him away before his eagle eyes spotted the light on in the basement window.

Josh walked beside her, unusually quiet, trying to figure all this new information out. Becca could almost hear the cogs turning in his head. Gavin and his mother must have walked along this road, she thought, when he was a little boy.

Now Rita Summers walked along Arran Quay every week to visit the spot where her son had died. Becca had seen her once, from the bus, tying a bouquet of white lilies to the lamppost and she had looked away . . . She hated that place and she hated Rita Summers, but still, she was grateful that Gavin wasn't forgotten. That somebody still brought him flowers.

She wondered if anyone gave Gavin's mother flowers. She looked down at the bouquet in her hand. She remembered the way Rita Summers had looked at her the day she first came to the house. Becca hadn't felt like an amaryllis that day; she had felt like an unsightly weed that somehow managed to intrude into the perfectly manicured garden of Rita Summers's life.

Nobody had a perfect life, not for very long. Not Rita Summers, not the lovely woman from the flower shop. Becca knew now where she'd seen her before. It was at the hospital the night she'd gone into labor with Josh. She'd glimpsed her through a gap in the curtain, the woman in the next cubicle whose baby had died.

Her heart went out to her now, and in the same moment, it went out to Rita Summers. Gavin was eighteen when he died, but he had been Rita Summers's baby once.

And Josh was part of his grandparents' story and they were part of his, no matter what they thought of her. What was it the florist's dad used to say? "It's not other people's job to like you. It's yours."

She took her son's hand and they turned around and began walking back the way they'd come.

PEONY

Blossoming Attraction.

The tiny chapel was like a white shell—hollow inside and arched and echoey. Lara would have tried out the acoustics, thrown out a "We Three Kings" or an "I Will Survive," if she had been on her own.

He had come in just after she had, and taken a seat on the last bench on the right. She memorized his appearance, just in case something bad happened and she had to describe him to the police. Late twenties. Medium height. Curly red-brown hair. Freckled arms. Jeans and gray T-shirt.

But nothing happened. He just sat there for the next half an hour. She could feel his eyes on her back as she looped swags of hydrangea and larkspur around the ends of the pews, fixing them in place with pale-green silk ribbon the color of river water.

When she had finished the last one, she gathered her things from the red-carpeted step at the altar and hurried down the aisle. Katy's bouquet was relaxing in a pail in the trunk of her car, but she had left the buttonholes till the last minute because camellias were temperamental.

His head was bent as she passed, his hands clasped loosely between his legs. He looked so dejected that she stopped at the door, took a breath and backed up, hoping she wasn't going to regret this. "Are you okay?"

His dark gray eyes were a surprise in his pale face. "I'm dandy. That's just a saying. It's not actually my name . . ."

Lara hesitated, primed to make a run for it if necessary. He didn't look threatening, but you never knew. He had probably just come in here for some peace and quiet. But it wasn't going to be quiet for long. The wedding was due to start in an hour and a half. As if he read her mind, he tilted his head back and whistled a few bars of the Wedding March.

The high, sweet, clear sound bounced around the dome above the altar and echoed back from between the arches.

Their eyes met as the last silver note died away.

"Wow!" he said. "I had the feeling the acoustics in here would be amazing."

She smiled. "So did I!"

"I'm Ben."

Lara shifted two rolls of wire under her arm so he could shake her hand. To her surprise, a little flicker of attraction feathered the back of her neck. He might be dangerous after all.

"Lara." She took her hand back quickly.

He stood up, and as they walked out through the arched doorway into the heat of the day, Lara had a sudden, unexpected flashback to her own wedding day.

The warmth of the sun on her bare arms that day too, as she and Michael came out of the church. The flickering cloud of confetti. The blur of smiling faces. The feeling that all she wanted was to be on her own with Michael. In the limousine, he'd ducked his head and she had picked tiny flecks of green and pink and silver paper out of his fair hair while her mind expanded around the two lovely syllables she had just acquired. *Husband.*

But she had been relieved to let it go in the end. Almost grateful when the divorce papers she had been dreading had arrived four weeks ago. She had no use for that word anymore; she could pass it on without a second thought to the girl who was about to marry her brother.

Ben walked beside her as she crossed the wooden footbridge to the parking lot. The taut lines of brightly colored bunting that she had made on her mother's ancient sewing machine snapped over their heads. The only car outside the gate was her pink van, customized with the Blossom & Grow logo and the line *Every flower is a little bit of summer*.

"This may be a pretty wild guess"—Ben patted the roof of the van—"but are you a florist?"

"Either that or a car thief," Lara said. Where had that come from? she wondered. Was she *flirting*?

Whatever she was doing, it got a smile. A small one that nearly reached his light brown eyes. Lara dumped her stuff in the back of the van, closed the door and walked around to the driver's side.

He drummed his fingers on the roof. She wondered if he was going to ask her for a lift. She was only going a couple of hundred yards to the B and B where Phil and Katy were staying.

"I suppose you're off to do another wedding."

"Not today. My little brother's getting married here in . . ." She glanced at his wrist and he held it up so she could read his watch. "God, eighty minutes. I really have to go."

His pale eyebrows disappeared up under his tangled fringe. "You're kidding me. You're the groom's *sister*?"

She nodded. "I'm Lara."

He folded his arms and tucked his hands into his armpits. "I'm Ben. I used to go out with the bride."

Stop! Lara told herself, trying to blow-dry her two-foot-long hair with the asthmatic hotel dryer. Ben was probably still in love with Katy, and even if he wasn't, he was way too young for her. So why did thinking about him make her feel carbonated, as if she was hooked up to an IV of Coke?

Katy, who edited a bridal magazine, was determined not to be a bridezilla. The invitations had been sent by email. There wasn't a whiff of a hen party. There were no bridesmaids. The reception was going to be a picnic in Glendalough and the cake was three tiers of cheese.

Katy had, she'd told Lara, no intention of looking like "a pavlova in a car crash." She wore a simple pale green cocktail dress and carried the bouquet of flowers Lara had made. Purple and white fritillaries, dusty-pink foxgloves, wisteria that fell from her hands like pale blue rain.

The ceremony was simple. A humanist minister said a few words, Katy and Phil read their vows, then everyone clapped and cheered and spilled outside into the sunshine.

Katy's sister, Mia, and her boyfriend, Ronan, came around with trays of Manhattans and mojitos in children's party paper cups.

Phil came over and hugged Lara.

"I was pretty sure you'd show in your bike gear," she laughed, pinching the sleeve on his dark suit.

"Yeah, well, Katy vetoed the leathers. She hates that bike nearly as much as you do."

She looked up into his face, remembering how small he'd once been. Amazed that her little brother was married, and yet not amazed at all. She had known, this time last year, when he asked her to hold the ladder while he climbed into the beech tree to cut down a spray of wisteria for Katy, that this was where he was heading.

"I wish Dad was here," Phil said, a flicker of sadness moving like a quick cloud across his dark eyes.

"Maybe he is." Lara smiled.

"You think he's looking down, don't you?" Phil teased her. "From the great golf course in the sky?"

Lara thought he might be. And she hoped that her mother, who had never set foot on a golf course in her life, was up there looking down too.

She was hanging back at the edge of the small crowd, planning to make a quick getaway if she saw Ben heading for her, when Mia drifted over looking like a goddess in a gold sheath dress. She filled Lara's Winnie-the-Pooh cup from a pitcher.

"Uh-uh." She shook her head. "No wall-florists allowed!" She took Lara's arm. "Let's find a gorgeous man for you to talk to."

And Lara, who hadn't wanted to talk to a man in over a year, unless she was making a bouquet for his wife or his girlfriend, realized with a shock that a tiny part of her was hoping that Mia would lead her to Ben. The rest of her was horrified. She had thought she was done with all of that.

"Don't give yourself a hard time for being attracted to someone," Leo said. "There's no real reason why you can't fall in love and have a healthy relationship."

He was right. There was no real reason, but there was the baby, the one that Lara had imagined in her arms that morning in the kitchen when she was getting ready to tell Michael that they should try again.

She had let her husband and her marriage go, but some part of her was frozen in time, standing in that sunny kitchen holding that imaginary baby in her arms.

She had spent the last year of therapy trying to find a way to move on from that moment and now she had given up. But Leo hadn't. No matter what she started talking to him about, this was where they always ended up.

"How about we do a thought record," he said now, "about this man you met at your brother's wedding."

Lara's heart sank. Leo opened a leather folder and pulled out a preprinted sheet divided into columns. He uncapped his fat black lacquered Montblanc pen. His hand hovered over the first column.

Had Ben noticed her hands? Lara wondered. They spent so much time in cold water that they were prematurely old, and pretty soon the rest of her would catch up. Sometimes she wished it would hurry. The place between the bright garden of her twenties and the no-man's-land of forty-one. Except that it wasn't a no-man's-land anymore. Not since she'd seen Ben in the church.

"Okay," Leo began, "let's start with facts!"

Lara listed them. "I met him at my brother's wedding, well, before it. He wasn't actually at the wedding. He wasn't invited. He's at least ten years younger than me, maybe more. He's my sister-in-law's ex-boyfriend. Which is incredibly awkward and embarrassing and—"

"Hang on!" Leo was still writing. "We're coming to feelings." He moved on to the next column. "Okay, naming emotions is the first step to creating new thought patterns. So, is there anything you want to add to 'awkward' and 'embarrassed'?"

There was. "Vulnerable," "afraid," "humiliated" and "ancient."

"Ancient is not really a feeling," Leo pointed out, "but I'll let you have it."

He listed her automatic thoughts in the third column and circled the hot thought: "I'll never meet anyone else. I'll always be on my own." Then he made her find evidence to support it.

Lara had never been a girlie girl. She had grown up in a masculine house with no mother to model herself on. Her marriage had been a test that she had failed.

She had already been over all of this with Leo, so she dredged up a headline she'd read in a magazine in the waiting room. "A woman of forty has more chance of being kicked to death by a mule than of meeting someone."

"A mule?" Leo looked up and frowned. "Like a shoe?"

"Like a donkey."

His smile was quick and followed by a look she had grown to know and dread. "Let's find some evidence that does *not* support the thought that you will always be on your own."

They sat for a long time in silence. In the next room, Leo's wife, Hope, was talking on the phone.

"What's the problem, Lara?" Leo asked.

"It's always the same problem," she said quietly.

"I know, and you know what you have to do. You have to close your eyes and imagine you're back in that kitchen, just before Michael came in."

"Please don't!" she said. "I can't."

"And you have to talk to that baby you wanted so badly. You have to tell her that someday, not today, but soon, you're going to let her go."

When Phil came back from their honeymoon in Marrakesh, Lara hardly recognized him. He turned up at seven in the morning in Katy's car, wearing khaki chinos and a blue linen shirt. It was the first time Lara had seen him without a biker jacket since he was sixteen. She was just back from the flower market and she sent him inside to make coffee while she unloaded the van.

She was stacking boxes by the door when she heard him in the kitchen talking to Ciara.

"Three days into the honeymoon, guess who calls? Katy's ex. Looking for Lara's number."

"Your girlfriend's ex wants to go out with your sister?" Ciara gasped. "That's a bit Jeremy Kyle."

She was right, Lara thought. She went back out onto the street, waiting for her personal tsunami of self-pity to roll up, but for once, it failed to show. Instead, she found herself standing on the pavement smiling at the grim-faced pedestrians who flowed around her, hurrying to work. Ben wanted her number. He wanted to see her again.

After she had unpacked the flowers, Phil hung around and helped her with the orders. He chatted about the wedding and the honeymoon, but he didn't mention Ben's call. He wasn't going to tell her, she realized, and she didn't blame him. And part of her was disappointed and part of her was relieved.

When the half-dozen bouquets for the morning delivery were made up, they settled on either side of the counter under the glow of the chandelier to write the cards. Phil read the messages from the order book. Lara wrote them down carefully on tiny cream cards.

"'You do to me what spring does to cherry trees,'" he read. "'Get well soon.' 'Good-bye, best beloved friend.' Will you come to dinner on Sunday?"

She looked up. "Is that a message?"

"No." He closed the book. "It's an invitation. Katy wants your advice about fixing up the garden."

Phil wasn't the only one who looked different, Lara thought. The honeymoon had changed Katy too. Her dark curls had grown out, her skin was tanned an olive gold. She had blossomed.

She put the sweet peas that Lara brought into a pink jug on the mantelpiece. The tiny blossoms exhaled a breath of sherbet and rain.

"Phil's out getting wine and I'm at a tricky bit of my Moroccan chicken!" Katy went over to the cooker. "Grab a chair. I'll only be a minute."

Lara sat on a stool and took off her coat. A year ago, when Katy had come into the shop to pick up bouquets for a shoot, she had been a stranger. Now she was practically a sister. It was so weird and so wonderful. She looked around the cluttered room. At the overflowing bookcases, at the Balinese temple door that had been covered in a sheet of glass and made into a table, at the framed watercolors of Sandymount Strand.

Ben had lived here. He had eaten at this table with Katy and slept with her in the bedroom down the hall. She tried to picture him watching the tiny TV or reading in the velvet armchair by the window, the sunshine picking out the red in his hair. She looked into the oval mirror above the mantelpiece where he must have seen his reflection thousands of times. But all she saw was herself. The steely glints of gray in her own hair, the starbursts of lines at the corners of her eyes. Even if Katy and Ben had not been involved, she was too old for all this.

Mia arrived alone. "Ronan can't come." She shrugged off her coat. "He's stuck in his studio being angst-ridden about his new performance piece. It involves nudity"—she stuck her finger into a pot of hummus and licked it—"feathers and a bucket of self-raising flour."

Lara laughed.

"Yes, yes," Mia said darkly, "you can laugh, but this family has had its fair share of tortured artists." Her voice dropped to a whisper. "Katy's ex, Ben, spent forever trying to write a screenplay. Put it this way, a lot of angst was ridden."

"Lara's met Ben," Katy said evenly, without turning from the cooker.

"Really? When? How?" Lara flushed. But before Katy could answer, a plume of dark smoke rose from the pan.

Mia kicked off her shoes, hitched up her dress, climbed onto a chair and took the battery out of the smoke alarm. By the time she had climbed down again, she had forgotten all about her question.

They shared a platter of meze and dips and, for dessert, summer berries dipped in four kinds of melted chocolate. Lovers' food, Lara thought, watching Phil feed Katy a strawberry.

When she was married, she had made special trips to obscure ethnic supermarkets for Vietnamese rice pancakes and soba noodles. She had bought extra-virgin olive oil online from a tiny estate in Sicily. She had discovered celeriac and plantains and Jerusalem artichokes. She had sautéed and ceviched and fricasseed and brûléed. Now she ate like an astronaut. Packet soups and cereal bars and microwave pots that announced their touchdown with a ping.

After dinner, while the others were still clearing up, she slipped out to look at the small, overgrown garden. There had been a lawn once, but it had been claimed by dandelions and dock leaves and fool's parsley and the tiny blue stars of forget-me-nots and speedwell. What had been a flower bed was a riot of shepherd's purse and fireweed. Michael had waged an ongoing battle with weeds, but Lara had a soft spot for them. "Weed is just another word for flower," her mother used to say when they collected cowslips or sat on the lawn making daisy chains.

"It's all a bit of a mess, isn't it?" Katy was standing behind her.

Lara nodded, unsure whether she meant the garden or something else.

Katy pulled a waxy white bell from the creeper that had woven a thick carpet over the high granite wall. "What's this called?"

"It's convolvulus. Gardeners call it bindweed."

Katy looked down at the flower. It was already growing limp in her hand. "How did you become a florist? Did you do a course, or teach yourself along the way?"

"Both," Lara said. "And my ex-husband helped with the business side of things. He was—is—a landscaper."

They watched a wheel of starlings turn in the rectangle of sky overhead. Dusk was falling into the garden like a fine mauve dust. Katy pulled another convolvulus blossom and it glowed in her hand in the gathering darkness. "You're going to think I'm awful," she said softly.

"Why would I think that?"

"Because Ben called while we were on honeymoon. He asked for your number, but I didn't want to give it to him." She frowned down at the flower. "I don't have feelings for him, it's not that. It's just that you're Phil's sister. It seemed too close."

"It's okay. Really." Lara's heart had been perched high in her rib cage for a week. Now it fell through her chest cavity like a stone.

"But—"

"Really. I'm not interested in him. And even if I was, I'm not ready for a relationship." She wrapped her arms around herself and around the invisible weight that was still there, pressed against her heart. The baby she had dreamed of holding the morning her marriage ended.

"Let it go," Leo had said. But she didn't know where that dream ended and where she began.

"That's a shame"—Katy twirled the flower in her fingers—"because

Phil changed my mind. He reminded me of how happy we are. How selfish we'd be to rain on anyone else's parade. I called Ben back this afternoon. I didn't give him your number . . ."

"I don't understand." Lara's heart had stopped falling, but now it gave a sickening lurch.

It was too dark to see Katy's face, but there was a smile in her voice. "I promised I'd give you his. Leave it up to you to call him."

She took Lara's hand and folded her fingers around a torn piece of paper and a flower.

All week Lara looked for signs not to call Ben. She found plenty. The billboard on Dame Street was covered with posters for a charity called Alone. Her Dart ticket said "Adult Single." When she turned on the radio in the van, Natasha Bedingfield was singing "Single."

But on Friday evening, when she was locking up the shop, she heard a familiar voice behind her, or thought she did. "Just do it!" And when she turned and looked up, there was a perfect Nike swoosh of a contrail in the sky above the jumble of chimney pots.

"Subtle, Dad," she muttered. "Very subtle." But one hand was already reaching for the folded piece of paper with the flower pressed inside it, and the other hand was pulling out her phone.

She should have picked somewhere dark and quiet, but she had named the first restaurant that came into her head. Glitzy sunshine bounced in off the water through the floor-to-ceiling windows. Ben was already there. He stood up.

"You're early."

"So are you."

She moved around to the other side of the table before he could kiss her cheek or shake her hand. She had remembered him all wrong. His hair was more red than brown. The little scar on his chin was shaped like a catapult not a crescent moon. His eyes were gray not blue, and in the swimming-pool light from the water outside he looked even younger than she'd thought.

This is a mistake, she thought. What am I doing here? A waiter appeared and began to recite the brunch menu in a sitcom Spanish accent. "Botched eggs. Crumpled eggs. Fright eggs on toes. Egg and backcomb or," he added with a flourish, "the fool Irish."

They managed to hold it together until he had taken their order and gone back into the kitchen. Then, while the door was still swinging closed, they started to laugh. Ben leaned forward, bent over his knees; Lara lay back, helpless, tears of laughter blurring the watery reflections dancing on the ceiling. She wasn't someone who had ever laughed easily. Since her marriage had ended, she hardly laughed at all.

Ben talked as if he was afraid that if he stopped, she'd get up and leave. He talked about his job at the library and the screenplay he had just finished and his apartment, which had a handkerchief-sized view of Dublin Bay.

"Where do you live?"

"In Ranelagh," Lara said. "Near the rugby stadium."

"I used to go to the disco there when I was seventeen."

"Me too."

He grinned. "We could have met."

Lara moved a little pile of scrambled eggs from the plate to her fork and then back again. "I'm not sure they would have let me in," she said quietly. "When you were seventeen, I was nearly thirty."

Ben pushed his plate away. "Is that why you took a whole week to call me? Because of the age thing?"

"That"—Lara pushed the eggs under a limp corner of her toast—"and Katy."

"Age doesn't matter to me. And Katy is happy and she's history. If she's told you stuff about me, stuff that might put you off, then all I can say is I made mistakes in that relationship that I won't be making in this one." She looked up at him. "If"—he looked flustered—"this is one. Which I hope it is because"—he looked out the window and then back at her and she saw his pupils widen—"because I feel something here."

He put his hand over hers, and his fingertips covering her knuckles sent four little shots of warmth traveling up her arm and then down her spine, threading her vertebrae together like fairy lights. It was something she'd never had with Michael, with anyone. Chemistry.

Ben let go of her hand to pay the bill, but he took it again when they were outside. They walked along the sunny side of Barrow Street, past the sooty redbrick houses and the shiny office blocks that had nothing in common. Like us, Lara told herself. Ben didn't speak and she couldn't. Her mind was too busy listening to the steady hum of her blood to get around to words. By the time they turned onto Grand Canal Street, her palms were slippery with sweat. She didn't know whether it was hers or Ben's and she didn't care.

Boys were jumping off the lock gate at Mount Street Bridge. The canal was full of summer and sky. Ben led her by the hand down the narrow stone steps. They walked more slowly now and Lara's mind tripped ahead of them on the sun-splashed path, past the dog walkers and the children feeding the swans, looking for trouble.

Chemistry didn't last, she reminded herself. It was just a quick cocktail of estrogen and testosterone, serotonin and dopamine.

Ben stopped and turned to face her, looping his arms around her waist. His gray eyes moved from her mouth up to her eyes and then back down again.

Lara gulped back a little air pocket of panic. Her mind was fizzing with questions she couldn't bear to ask. *Why me? Why not someone your own age?*

He was leaning toward her now. "Wait!" She leaned back. There was one question she had to ask.

"Why did you come to the church the morning of the wedding? Were you going to ask Katy not to go through with it?"

"No." He looked over her shoulder as if he was trying to remember.

"We were friends for a long time. Better friends than anything else, you know?" Lara nodded. She and Michael had been friends too.

"Katy doesn't have a father. Well, she does, but he left when she was young, so I came that day to give her away, in my head I mean." He looked back down at her. "I'm not crazy. I wasn't planning on hanging around and walking her up the aisle or anything. It was a symbolic thing. I just figured that I had to find a way to let her go. And when I was sitting in that church, with my eyes closed, so if anyone walked in, it would look as if I was praying or something, I realized that what I'd been holding on to all those years with Katy, it wasn't real. Then I opened my eyes and there you were. And you were, *real* I mean. At least I hope you were. I hope I'm not just imagining you."

"Wait!" Lara said again. She could feel Ben's eyes on her back, the way she had in the chapel, as she stepped onto the grassy bank and closed her eyes.

She had been holding on to the idea of the baby she could have had with Michael as tightly as she'd held on to Ryan the night before he was buried. Now she opened her arms and held them there until she felt the weight leave her. When she opened her eyes, she saw two bright spangles of light dancing together on the surface of the water. She turned around and walked back to Ben.

"Where were we?" She looped her arms around his neck.

His arms crossed behind her back. "Here."

PHALAENOPSIS

Fragility and Strength.

Some people are just asking for it. That's what Baz says. Leaving their cars unlocked, their curtains open, their wallets and phones sticking out of their pockets, their bags hanging over the backs of their chairs. The woman in the flower shop is on her own and she isn't even close to the till half the time. Sharon has walked past twice now eating her chips, watching her.

Call that a job? she thinks, dropping the greasy chip bag and licking the salt off her frozen fingers. Sitting on your bum all day playing around with flowers, having a gab with some Southside Fanny who can drop fifty euros on a bunch of daisies without batting an eyelid.

Sharon pulls a packet of smokes out of her jacket, lights the last one and walks past for a fourth time, nice and slow. She stops in front of the window, looks inside, acting interested in the three skinny vases full of big, fat white roses, flicking her eyes up over them to scope out the shop beyond. The till is behind the counter on the left. The woman is on a stool in front of it, smiling to herself, sticking flowers in a jam jar. She is tall and skinny and she is older than she looked from the other side of the street. Old is good. If she catches Sharon with her hand in the till, she won't win a fight.

But if she does? Sharon rehearses it in her head. Quick jab in the eye or a sharp elbow in the tits. She shivers in her damp coat, folding one arm across her chest to hold the two sides of the broken zip together, taking a deep drag on her smoke, psyching herself up. She hasn't hit anyone, not ever, but Baz says she's more than capable. Women are dirtier fighters than men, that's a fact. Still, she's not going looking for it.

A taxi pulls up behind her. A blonde woman in a cream coat gets out and goes into the shop. Sharon crosses the street and stands under the awning of the pizza restaurant and keeps her eye on the door.

After a minute the woman comes out again with her arms full of pink flowers and gets back into the taxi. It does a U-turn and speeds up as it passes Sharon, churning up a puddle that drenches her leggings. She'll never get them dry now. The heating doesn't work in the flat. She's even started using the gas rings on the cooker to warm it up. Baz will kill her if he catches her.

Sharon glares after the disappearing taxi. Fucking bitch probably doesn't even know where the cooker is in her nice big, warm house. Probably has someone else to do all the cooking for her.

The rain is starting again and a waiter in a bow tie is eyeballing her from the other side of the restaurant window. The best chat line blokes used to give her was that she looked like Kate Moss but she hasn't had that in a while now and the waiter looks more annoyed than interested. She moves along the street a few doors, wishing she had another smoke. There's another customer going into the flower shop now. An old dear with a skinny gray dog in a coat that she's left tied to the lamppost outside.

Nick it? Sharon thinks. Get a reward? Too complicated. Anyway, the dog might get freaked, and she likes dogs. When Noah was only tiny, when they'd lived in the flat in Charlemont Street, he used to make this excited high-pitched sound when he saw a dog. He'd stagger over to it with his arms out, like a little drunk. He knew the names of all the dogs on every floor of the flats. The lift was always broken and he'd rattle them off like a mad poem when she carried him up the five flights of stairs. How did it go? Bambi, Chippie, Prince, Foxy and Pal.

God, he was sweet, she thinks, but too much for her to handle. Things got messy. She was gutted when Social Services took him off her. Cried for a week. But in the end they'd done her a favor, hadn't they? She was only a kid herself really.

Noah's long gone now and the Charlemont flats are gone too. Demolished last summer. She told Baz she was going to shoplift some stuff in the center but she hopped the Luas into Harcourt Street instead. It was like 9/11 or something, watching those big blocks collapse into a cloud of their own dust. She had to look away. Gone, everything gone. But fuck it, life went on.

The dog across the road is shivering and he's wearing a bloody coat: that's what kind of a day it is. Sharon's arm is starting to ache. It's done that in the cold since she broke it. She was selling Ecstasy outside a gig on Francis Street and some smart-ass grabbed four off her and done a runner without giving her the eighty quid. When she got home, Baz flipped. Grabbed her. Asked her what he looked like, the kid, but she couldn't remember, could she? She slipped and cracked her arm off the windowsill. He was gutted. Paid for a taxi to take her to St. James's Hospital. Sat out in the waiting room while they put five pins in her wrist. When they wouldn't give her any pain meds except bloody paracetamol, he sorted her out.

They have their ups and downs, but he loves her. He went out on the rob to get her a new coat last week. Black with gold zips and a fur-lined hood; she'd seen it in Zara. But he got caught, didn't he, and now he's in remand. Bail was five hundred euros and there was only three hundred and fifty in the balled-up sock where he keeps the cash. That's why she's standing here freezing her ass off, waiting for the old dear to come out of the flower shop so she can go in, rob it and get this over with.

The door of the shop opens and the old dear comes out with a bunch of bright pink daisies or whatever. She unties the dog and they totter off, the dog stopping to sniff the chip bag where Sharon dropped it.

Her palms start to sweat as she crosses the road. Her heart speeds up like she's halfway up an amyl nitrate high.

Don't take drugs, you're supposed to tell your kids. Don't drink.

Don't steal. Do your homework. Get a job. But kids aren't stupid. They have eyes. They'll copy you, like she copied her mam. Way of the world. The rain is coming down now: good. The street is empty. Just before Sharon gets to the door, the woman on the other side picks up an empty bucket and disappears through the doorway at the back of the shop.

There is a little jingle of bells as the door opens. Sharon's heart springs into her mouth, wet and trembling. She holds her breath and listens, then she hears the faint sound of footsteps from above. Better be quick.

The smell hits her first. The street outside smelled of car exhaust and litter and damp clothes, but in here it smells like fresh air. Then she sees the flowers. The floor and shelves are packed with them. Each bucket is full of one kind, one color, and the spotlights in the ceiling and the candles flickering make them look like stained glass in a church.

Sharon hurries past them, gets to the counter, slips around it. First thing she sees is a green leather handbag, the zip open. There's no wallet but there's an iPhone in a flowery cover; she fishes it out and slides it into her back pocket. She touches the release button on the till and the drawer slides open. Four fifties, a couple of twenties, a ten. She stashes them away quick.

Halfway to the door she hears the woman. She whips around and, keeping her face hidden, bends over a bucket of lilies.

"If you want a hand," a voice behind her says, "just ask."

Sharon nods, shoots a quick sideways glance from around the damp fur of her collar. The flower woman reminds her of that Pocahontas cartoon Noah liked. Long black hair, big dark eyes in a pale face, good-looking, though she's old, forty maybe. She's pouring tea from a big flask into a little red glass, not a cup. "Do you want some mint tea? It's nearly as cold in here as it is out there."

"Yeah," Sharon says, thinking, This'll get rid of her. "Yeah, I would like some." Bingo. She waits for the woman to go back into the kitchen, then goes to leg it. She has her hand on the doorknob when she looks up and sees it, high up on a shelf near the ceiling, and stops dead. That weird plant Noah tried to give her once. If she'd brought it home, Baz would have wanted to know where she got it and then there'd have been trouble.

She's sure this is the same kind. Big flat leaves, a tall straight stem and all the flowers crowded together at the top, big lush purple petals that look too perfect to be real. She should be well out of here by now, back on the street, but instead she stares up at it and it all comes back. The snowy day nearly a year ago. The last time she saw her son.

She hears the voice behind her again. The woman is back. "That's a phalaenopsis."

"Thought it was a moth orchid?" Sharon says.

"It is." The woman sounds a bit surprised, like how would she know? "That's the other name for it. I'll leave your tea here." She turns away and opens a drawer and starts tidying it, like she's giving Sharon space.

Run! Get out now before she gets a proper look at your face, Sharon tells herself. But instead—she just can't help herself—she rises onto her tiptoes and reaches up to touch the velvety tip of one of the big flat purple petals.

She kept Noah hanging about that day, hoping he'd be gone by the time she showed up. But there he was, stupid kid, snow in his hair, shivering on the wall by the bus stop. He'd bought her a flower. Nobody had ever done that before. Not Baz, not Noah's father. And none of the tossers in between.

He's sixteen now, Noah. Probably over six foot. How tall was he last year? All her memories of him are tangled up in a knot like the Christmas lights when you get them out again. She's only seen him ten times in twelve years. Big gaps in between.

In the moves from flat to flat, she's lost all the photographs she's ever had. She has only one left. Him at four, the year he was taken into care. And it's a picture she hates. She can see now what she was too spaced to see then. How scared he was.

She left him on his own for a weekend. That was why he was taken away. Well, she'd only meant to go to the pub for a few hours on a Friday night, but she got wasted, didn't she, and ended up going to a party in Kilkenny in a car someone stole. She was too out of it to know what day it was until Sunday.

Noah had yelled the place down. All Friday night, all day Saturday. Someone called the guards on Sunday morning. The fire brigade came too, broke the door down to get him out.

"I saw a fireman," he said when she was allowed to see him, like he was delighted with himself. He looked like someone else's kid then. Clean clothes, color in his face, clutching a Mr. Potato Head toy with little eyes and ears that popped off.

She fought it—they'd have thought there was something really wrong with her if they saw it in her face—but deep down she was relieved. Even if she'd been straight, there were too many lowlifes coming and going in her flat to raise a kid. She knew he'd be better off without her. That was the truth, God help her.

"They're easy to look after," the woman says, jolting Sharon back from memory lane.

"What?" She turns around.

"Moth orchids." The woman is looking straight at her.

Shit! Sharon digs her fingernails into her palm till it hurts. She's seen her face now. She'll be able to ID her. What's she still doing in the shop?

"The most important thing is not to water them too much. They're like cacti: sometimes they do best when you ignore them altogether." She walks over and stands next to Sharon, looking up at the plant. She smells of some kind of rose perfume and bleach. "Whatever you do, they still keep coming back."

She hands Sharon a little glass of tea and takes out a wooden crate. She climbs onto it, her back to her, and reaches for the orchid. All Sharon has to do is kick the crate away now and this woman will be flat on her face. She could nip out with the money and the phone and whip the orchid too. Jesus, she could take half the shop if she wanted a flat full of flowers. But she doesn't. Instead she watches the woman lift the plant down carefully and carry it to the counter.

"When all the flowers have fallen off, the flower spike will look dry and brittle. Orchids fool lots of people into thinking they're dead, but if you look after them, they'll come back. You cut it here . . ." She points at the stem. "Just below the place where the first flower was, and it'll bloom again." She looks up. "Do you mind if I ask how you knew it was a moth orchid? Most people wouldn't."

Sharon takes a sip of the tea. Feels the comforting heat travel down her throat. "My son bought one for me once," she says.

"How old is he?"

"Sixteen."

"You have a sixteen-year-old son?" The woman shakes her head. "You hardly look seventeen yourself. You look like Kate Moss's younger sister."

The heat travels back up Sharon's throat now, flushes her face. She's pleased. Who wouldn't be? And for a moment, she forgets that she's talking to a woman she has just robbed.

"What's his name? Your boy?"

The word has to squeeze its way up through Sharon's tightening throat. "Noah." She takes another gulp of tea. And then, for some reason, maybe because she can't remember the last time anyone paid her a compliment, maybe because if someone can read your mind you might as well say it as it is, maybe because she doesn't give a shit, she goes on. "He's in foster care. I lost him when he was four."

She looks up, hardening herself against the judgment that she knows will be in this woman's eyes. The look. But for once, it isn't there. "He must really love you," she says, "because I don't get many teenage boys coming in here to buy their mothers flowers."

"Really?" Sharon stares at the orchid, wanting this to be true, wondering if the woman is just softening her up to try to get her to buy it.

"No," the woman says thoughtfully, "that's not true. I don't get *any* teenage boys coming in here to buy their mothers flowers."

And suddenly Sharon wants the plant that she didn't let Noah give her before. Baz is in a cell in Mountjoy; she won't have to explain it to anyone. She can put it on her windowsill and look at it.

"I'll take it," she says.

The woman looks pleased. "I'll wrap it for you."

What am I doing? Sharon thinks, standing there like a statue, watching the woman folding a sheet of green tissue paper into a sheet of cellophane, wrapping the plant, taking her time to choose a thick silky purple ribbon, then tying it on around the cellophane and pulling it into a fat bow.

When she has finished, Sharon stands looking at it for a full minute, chewing her lip.

"Is that okay?" The woman looks worried.

Sharon nods. She puts her hand into her pocket and pulls out a twenty. The woman goes to take it, but before she can, Sharon pulls out the second twenty and then the ten.

The woman shakes her head. "It's only eighteen euros."

Sharon takes out the four fifties and lays them on the counter. The woman looks from the pile of money to her face and then back again. But Sharon can't stop now; something has taken over. She pulls out the iPhone still in the flowery cover and puts it beside the money. Finally the woman understands, and they both stand there for a while in silence, surrounded by flowers.

Sharon holds her breath, listening to a bus drive past outside, a tap dripping from a room in the back, piano music she didn't notice before playing softly in the background. She waits for what she knows will happen next. The woman will start shouting abuse; she's going to pick up the phone, to call the guards. But, weirdly, she doesn't. Instead she just says, "Thank you."

Sharon can't believe what she's just said. A laugh bursts out of her mouth, a harsh, hacking sound. "For what? Trying to rob you?"

"For changing your mind." The woman picks up the plant and holds it out toward her.

"No, no, no," Sharon says, "you don't have to do that."

The woman nods at the pile of money on the counter, and the iPhone.

"Neither did you."

Sharon shrugs and picks up the orchid. It gives her a thrill to hold it in her arms. Apart from Noah, she thinks, it is the most beautiful thing she has ever held.

"You'll look after it," the woman says, "won't you?"

Sharon wonders if it's possible for a person to start growing again, the way an orchid does. "I'll try," she says.

WHITE TULIP

Sorrow and Forgiveness.

Spring was coming. Lara could feel it hovering at the edges of the frigid air. The world was holding its breath. She loved to think of the smallest flowers making their way up through the frozen earth. Pale yellow celandines, pink-tipped daisies, the little white stars of the chamomile, the bright yellow faces of the dandelions.

It was Saturday morning. She had spent Friday night with Ben, and Thursday night and every night this week, and she was happy. So happy that the tips of her fingers fizzed as she set aside the flowers for Zoe's dad's bouquet—Ocean Song roses, waxflower, berried eucalyptus.

The temple bells tinkled above the door of the shop. She looked up and saw a beautifully dressed man in his seventies clutching the door frame. His face was pale above the collar of his white shirt; his mouth was open in a ragged O.

Lara dropped the flowers into a heap on the counter and hurried across the shop. "Do you need help?"

He shook his head. "My wife died," he whispered.

"I'm so sorry!"

"I need flowers." He looked around wildly. "I have to get the flowers sorted. That's the first thing."

Lara shifted a pot of African violets off a wrought-iron garden chair and took his arm. "You need to sit down. You've had a shock." He crumpled into the chair and put his elbows on his knees. "Just stay there!" she told him. "I'll get you a glass of water."

"Do you have anything stronger?"

Lara was shaking her head when she remembered an airplane miniature that Ciara had brought in once to make a hot whiskey when she had a cold. "Take some deep breaths," she said. "I'll be right back." She rushed into the kitchen and found the bottle in the back of the cutlery drawer. It was only a thimbleful but it was something. She hurried back.

He tipped the bottle to his lips, then clutched it in his fist, pressing his teeth against his knuckles. "It was so sudden," he whispered. A tear dripped off his chin, ran along his bony wrist and disappeared inside the sleeve of his navy coat.

She crouched down beside the old man. "What's your name?"

He looked at her for a moment, his eyes baffled and upset. "Maurice," he said.

"Maurice, you shouldn't be on your own." She squeezed his arm. "Is there someone I can call for you?"

He shook his head but pulled a mobile phone out of the pocket of his coat and passed it to her. She scrolled through his recent calls. "Would you like me to call Derek?"

"My son." Maurice looked shocked. "I haven't told my son!"

Lara's brother had been in the hospital cafeteria when their father died. Lara had waited for him outside the ward, and watched him amble along the corridor in his bike leathers, walking in and out of shafts of sunshine that streamed in through the dusty plate-glass windows. He was balancing two coffee cups in one hand and two plates of cheesecake in the other. The nurse at the station probably saw a handsome man, but Lara saw a little boy whose heart she was about to break.

She held the old man's phone in her hand and imagined his son out there somewhere, sitting on a sofa in Starbucks maybe, unfolding a crisp newspaper or walking through the sunny park on the way to brunch. She wanted Derek, whoever he was, to have another few minutes before his world fell apart. She typed out a quick text with the address of the shop. Please come quickly, it said. Your father is here and he has had a shock.

The phone buzzed back immediately. "He's on his way," Lara told the old man. "He'll be here in ten minutes."

"It was so quick," Maurice said.

"Do you want to talk about what happened?"

He stared down at his feet. He was wearing Nike trainers that looked odd with his cashmere coat and his dark wool trousers. "It was an accident." He pressed his lips together. "The driver lost control."

"I'm so sorry."

"She died instantly."

"She didn't suffer, then." Lara took his hand. That was the thing that comforted her about her dad's death. If it had been a stroke instead of cancer, he might have lived longer, might even still be alive now. But he wouldn't have been able to drive or play golf or look after his garden. He would have hated that.

"The flowers!" Maurice looked up, suddenly agitated again. "What am I going to do about the flowers?"

"Were you thinking of a wreath?"

"I hate those things." He shuddered.

Lara felt the same way. She had tucked a bunch of pansies into her father's coffin. They had always reminded him of her mother.

"What did your wife like?" she asked Maurice. "Did she have a favorite flower?"

Maurice rubbed the silver prickles of his stubble with his palm. "I don't know." He stared around helplessly, then pointed at a bucket of white tulips. "Those," he said. "She grew those in the garden." He pulled two ten-euro notes out of his pocket and put them on the counter. "Is that enough?"

"More than enough," Lara said.

He fell into a trance as she worked with the tulips, watching her hands as if he was hypnotized. She talked to him quietly, telling him the names of the greenery she was adding—evergreen viburnum for the primary foliage at the bottom, eucalyptus to fill out the gaps in the middle, tall bells of Ireland to add texture at the top.

As she was tying the flowers up with a white satin ribbon the door opened and a man in his thirties came in. He was wearing a mac that flapped open over a dark shirt and jeans and holding a little girl by the hand.

"Jesus, Dad!" the man said sharply. "What are you doing here?" Maurice blinked up at him and covered his eyes with his hands. The younger man sighed. "Go and look at the flowers, Molly!" He turned to Lara. "How long has he been here?"

"About fifteen minutes," she said, wanting to sit him down to prepare him for what was coming. "I think he's in shock."

"Really?" The younger man looked skeptical.

Lara glanced at Maurice, but she could see he was in no state to break the news. "I'm so sorry." There was no easy way to say this. "There was an accident." She lowered her voice so that the little girl wouldn't hear. "A bad one. I'm afraid your mother is—"

"Dead?" He sounded exasperated instead of upset. "Yeah, I know." Lara stared at him, confused.

He rubbed his face hard with his fingertips. "He told you that it just happened, right?" She nodded. "Mum died six years ago." He stuffed his hands into his pockets defensively, but she saw his jaw clench.

"It's the Alzheimer's," he muttered. "It's a nightmare. You probably think I'm callous, but you try living with him. Explaining to him every morning who you are." He shook his head. "Explaining who *he* is."

"That must be hard," Lara said.

"Half the time he doesn't even know his own granddaughter."

Lara looked at the little girl. She had collected a handful of pink gerbera petals from the floor and she was counting them out onto her grandad's knee. The old man was staring absently into space.

"You feel sorry for him, don't you?" His son was looking at Lara.

"Of course."

"Really." His eyes narrowed and his fists dug deeper into his pockets. "Did he tell you how my mother died?"

"He said she was killed by a driver who lost control of his car."

"Did he mention"—his mouth was set in a hard line—"that he was that driver?"

Lara shook her head slowly.

"It's convenient, isn't it, that he forgot just that part. It's not him you should feel sorry for. He'd just been diagnosed, the doctor had banned him from driving. She begged him not to, but he wouldn't listen to her—he never did. And now she's gone, and so is some poor eighteen-year-old kid, a boy who was cycling home from school."

"I'm sorry!" she said again.

He was fighting tears. She saw his Adam's apple jerk above the collar of his dark shirt. "I'm sorry too," he said when he could speak again. "That was rude. I should be thanking you, not giving you my sob story. I'm just having a bad morning." He walked over and put his hand on Maurice's shoulder. "Come on, Dad," he said gently. "Time to go."

Maurice looked up at him. "David?" he said.

"Derek."

Maurice stood up obediently, brushing the gerbera petals to the floor.

"Grandad!" the little girl sighed. "You ruined everything!"

It was only after they had gone that Lara turned back to the counter and saw the tulip bouquet. She stared at it for a moment, then picked it up and dashed after them, not bothering to lock the shop.

At first she couldn't see them, then she caught a flash of the vivid green stem of the little girl's dress as she climbed into the backseat of a blue Volvo. Lara ran along Camden Street. "Derek! Wait!" she called. He looked up as he opened the driver's door. "Your father forgot something."

He gave a short laugh. "That's an understatement!"

Lara put the tulips on the roof of the car as she caught her breath. "He asked me to make up this bouquet for your mother."

"You know, he never bought her flowers," Derek said bitterly. "Not once in the thirty years they were married. Not on Mother's Day, not on her birthday, not on their anniversary."

"Well, he bought flowers for her today," Lara said firmly. "He said she used to grow white tulips in the garden."

"Really?" Derek glanced down at the flowers, and when he looked back up at Lara, his eyes had softened. "He remembered that?"

It was a miracle, Ciara said later, that someone hadn't tried to rob the shop again when Lara left it unattended. But Ben saw the real miracle straight away. That a man who could not remember his own name had remembered the flowers that his wife had once loved.

SUNFLOWER

The Return to Joy.

Lara had pulled her jeans and cardigan off and was zipping up her dark green silk dress when Ciara popped her head around the door.

"Bridezilla's back," she groaned. "I've told her you have to be somewhere but she won't take no for an answer."

Lara checked her watch. The party at Phil and Katy's was starting in half an hour, but she couldn't send Emily away. "Tell her to come up. And can you put the kettle on?"

Most brides came to the shop just twice. Once for an hour-long consultation to discuss ideas and then a second time two weeks before the wedding, when the seasonal flowers were in, to see a test bouquet.

This was Emily's *fourth* visit. She was in her late twenties, milkmaid-pretty, with worried blue eyes in a heart-shaped face. At least, she had been pretty when Lara met her back in May, but she had lost so much weight now that she looked like a child wearing her mother's clothes.

"I've been having second thoughts," she said as she came up the stairs, "about the snowflake hydrangeas."

"*Fourth* thoughts," Ciara mouthed from behind her.

Emily opened a plastic folder that contained, Lara already knew, dozens of pictures clipped from bridal magazines.

"I just think they might look dusty with the new dress. Well, it's actually the same dress but I'm going for white instead of ivory and I've asked for a marabou trim on the sleeves. I think I need the flowers to be more romantic. White roses or lavender or lilac or agapanthus maybe?"

"Will you have a cup of tea?" Ciara asked her airily. "We have regular or mint or chamomile or Earl Grey. Or coffee? There's instant, but I could nip out for a cappuccino? Or a hot chocolate? Or would you prefer a latte?"

"Thank you, Ciara." Lara gave her a warning look. "Peppermint would be fine."

Emily sipped her tea while Lara scrolled through her Pinterest boards. "Everyone's tired of me," she said sadly.

"I'm sure Dan isn't tired of you." Lara was careful to sound casual. Emily had spent ten minutes talking about the alterations to her dress and another five explaining why she'd changed the main course from salmon to sea bass, but she hadn't mentioned her fiancé once. Lara was starting to wonder whether her indecisiveness might run deeper than flowers and menus.

"Oh!" Emily's face lit up with excitement and she pointed at the screen. "What are those?"

"Tuberose," Lara said, pinning the picture. "And they smell like heaven."

Half an hour later, she printed out a mood board of all the flowers they'd selected. White tuberose and two kinds of orchid, white dendrobium for romance, pale green cymbidium with pink-tipped lips for drama.

"Why don't you live with these for a while." She handed over the printout and a couple of sketches she'd drawn freehand. "If you're still happy, we can order a test bouquet for the beginning of June. But I want you to know"—she looked into Emily's eyes, trying to send her a message, tucking it in between her words, like a card in a bouquet of flowers—"it's okay to change your mind. It's not the end of the world."

The living room of Phil and Katy's flat was crowded with a peculiar mix of Phil's courier mates, in band T-shirts and beaten-up jeans, and glammed-up girls in cocktail dresses, Katy's friends from the wedding magazine.

That was weird enough, Mia thought, but weirder still were the two couples chatting by the fireplace: Katy and her husband, Phil; and Katy's ex, Ben, with Phil's sister, Lara. "Look at them." She jogged Ronan's elbow and one of the canapés slid off his plate. "It's like *Life Swap*."

Ronan retrieved his devil-on-horseback from the rug and popped it into his mouth. "I think it's pretty evolved."

"It's too evolved," Mia groaned. "It's plankton to Einstein and it's hurting my head."

"Where?" Ronan put down the plate.

She pointed at the middle of her forehead, where an ache was twisting itself into a tight knot. "Here!"

"Ah." Ronan pressed his thumb gently between her eyebrows. "Your third eye."

She rolled her first and second eyes at him but she didn't pull away, and after a few seconds the knot began to loosen.

"It's going away, isn't it?" Ronan said.

"No," she lied, "but I am. I can't look at them anymore. I'm going to open more wine." She brushed a few flakes of pastry from his beard. The beard was back. She pretended to disapprove, but deep down she felt a sort of proprietorial affection for it. It was her beard too.

Her mother caught at the skirt of her dress as she crossed the room. "Oh my God! They're talking to one another," she whispered. Phil and Lara had turned to chat to one of the courier types, and her sister and Ben had been stranded together. "What on earth do you think they're talking about?"

"Evolution," Mia said airily.

"I'm going to need another glass of wine." Her mother handed over her glass. "I'm finding this situation extremely awkward."

"Oh, get over yourself, Angela," Mia snapped and stamped off to the kitchen to find a corkscrew.

*   *   *

Ben and Katy stood beside one another by the bookcase, like two people who'd just met, not two people who'd previously spent thousands of nights in this very living room. Ben had seen Katy across the bar at the Christmas Eve drinks that Lara had organized, but this was the first time they'd really spoken since their breakup.

Katy looked different, he thought, thinner, her long dark hair cut shorter, her manner more self-assured. He ran his finger along the spines of the books and pulled out an anthology of Carol Ann Duffy poems. "I think this is mine."

"It's mine now," she said, looking at him steadily. "Statute of limitations and all that."

"Fair enough." He put the book back, stuffed his hands in his pockets and turned to look out the window. The three watercolors that used to hang by the shutter were gone. In their place were half a dozen framed photographs. A couple of Katy and Phil on their wedding day (or the day he and Lara had met, as he preferred to call it) and some holiday snapshots. His eyes slid past them to the photograph of Katy with her old dog, Pat. They were face-to-face, Katy laughing, the greyhound gazing into her eyes.

"You didn't invite Pat to the party, I see," he said. "Did you book him into a suite in the Shelbourne?"

"He's in there," Katy said, pointing at the tall white cardboard tube on the table by the window. "He died."

Ben stared at the tube, trying to imagine the immortal, the legendary Pat reduced to a little pile of ashes. "I'm sorry," he said sadly. "We thought he'd last forever."

"He did pretty well. We all did." Katy looked across the room at Lara. "She's a lovely woman, Ben," she said softly. "Try not to screw this up, okay?"

Before he could speak, she turned away and caught Phil's arm as he headed for the kitchen. "Hey! You can't go in there! You might see your surprise cake!"

"You mean my completely-predictable-and-expected cake?" Phil slung an arm around her shoulder.

"Oops!" She grinned.

"Happy birthday, bro," Ben said, immediately regretting the "bro."

"Thanks. I'm not big on birthdays." Phil looked at him coolly. "The party was Katy's idea."

Ben wondered whose idea it had been to invite *him*. He was guessing that neither of them had wanted him on the guest list, but they couldn't invite Lara without having him too.

Lara had wanted Ben to get on with her little brother (who turned out to be four inches taller than him). And that was what Ben had wanted too. But Phil had pushed his buttons from the start, and when he ran out of buttons, he pulled his levers and flicked a few of his switches for good measure.

He'd strolled into the Fitzwilliam Bar the night of the Christmas drinks in those ridiculous bike leathers as if he owned the place. He'd barely spoken to Ben but those big brown George Clooney eyes had never shut up. They were sending him a message now too, loud and clear. *Hurt my sister, pal, and you'll have me to answer to.* He didn't know what Katy had said to make Phil dislike him so much, but as long as she didn't turn Lara against him, he didn't care.

"Well, see you later." He backed away from them, raising a hand in a little wave that looked, he realized too late, a bit like a papal blessing, and crossed the room looking for Lara. She was talking to some bloke when he got to her, so he veered off and headed for the bathroom. It was a relief to be away from the party, to stop pretending, even for a minute, that the whole situation was not deeply fucking weird.

He looked around the small bathroom where he had showered every day for seven years. What had he been doing? He and Katy had been all wrong together. Why had he stayed with her for so long? He stared at himself in the gilt-framed mirror over the sink. Aptly named, he thought, as he saw his guilty expression reflected back at him.

Poor Katy. He had treated her badly. He could see that now. He could see all the little things he'd done to avoid serious conversation, anything that might have rocked the unsteady boat of their relationship.

He'd managed her mood with wine. He'd have a glass poured for her before she got through the door, but that hadn't worked for him, so he'd sneak off to the bathroom a couple of times every night to roll up a joint.

But that wasn't the worst thing he'd done. Katy used to tell him he was a commitment-phobe, and he'd ducked and dived, saying they'd talk about marriage in a year, or when he finished his screenplay, or when they'd saved enough to buy a place. Anything to avoid the truth. That she was right. That they were more like flatmates, not soul mates. That all the familiarity and friendship and affection in the world did not add up to love.

Maybe he hadn't known what love was back then, but he knew now. Love was intense and funny and deep and light and unfathomable. Love was wanting to jump into bed with someone when you were already in bed with them. Love was not needing to medicate himself with marijuana to get through an evening in someone's company. In the nine months since he'd met Lara, he hadn't been tempted to smoke a single joint.

He turned to go back out to the party. At the last moment, he went back to the sink and felt along the top of the mirror. His fingers found a little plastic bag tucked in between the frame and the wall. A stash he'd forgotten all about when he packed up his things.

Two cigarettes, a packet of Rizlas, a little nub of dope wrapped in foil. He flipped up the lid of the toilet to flush it away, then hesitated. It might float. Phil would just love that, wouldn't he? Evidence that his sister's boyfriend was still a stoner. He shoved the bag deep inside the inner pocket of his jacket, then he went back out to the party to prize Lara away from whoever she was talking to now.

"Was it a bit awkward for you?" Lara asked Ben as they were getting undressed.

He hung his shirt up in the wardrobe, which was still half full of her dad's things. "More weird than awkward. It made me realize some things about me and Katy that I'd tried to avoid before." He turned to look at her. "But to be honest, when I'm with you, it's kind of hard to believe there even *was* a before."

She smiled. "I know what you mean. Sometimes I look back on those ten years with Michael and I wonder if they were real."

"This is real"—he kissed the top of her head—"isn't it?"

She took his hand and kissed his fingertips. "Yes."

She watched him cross the room to the bathroom in his white boxer shorts. His broad shoulders dusted with freckles tapered to a narrow waist, his body smooth and taut.

She wished that she still had her twenty-nine-year-old body—more for Ben's sake than her own. The one without the dimples and creases and sags and folds that had arrived in her thirties.

There were tricks she could have used to hide her age—hair dye and facials, fillers and Botox—but they would be a lie. She had lived through a marriage where the truth was always covered up. She wanted nothing hidden with Ben.

She had locked her heart in a safety deposit box for safekeeping after her marriage had ended, but Ben picked the lock a dozen times a day. He scribbled lines of poetry and tucked them into her coat pocket. On mornings when she had to be in the shop early, he woke her with a cup of coffee, a plate of scrambled eggs and a dressing gown that had been warmed on the radiator. And every evening he asked her about her day.

Michael had never asked about the shop but Ben was fascinated by all her stories. So she told him about the customers, their romances and their anniversaries and celebrations, their special requests and their eccentricities.

About the man who had already proposed to four women. The artist who bought himself a hundred-euro bouquet every time he sold a painting. The girl who sent roses to herself to make her boyfriend jealous.

Ben was as happy to talk as he was to listen. Lara knew on any given day exactly what he was reading and writing and thinking. His past was an open book. He told her about his long-suffering mother and his unfaithful father. About the boarding school he'd run away from. About meeting Katy at college. He would have told her every detail of their relationship if she'd asked him, but she didn't. It was history: that was all she needed to know.

She told him things she hadn't told anyone, not even Phil. About the evening her father told her he had cancer and the morning Michael had told her he was gay.

The day after she had told him about losing Ryan, he arrived at the shop with twenty pink roses. He had done what no other man would ever think to do. He had brought flowers to a florist. Ben had already said that he loved her, but that day she had started to believe it, started to understand, maybe for the first time, what love was.

It was like his roses in the corner of her workroom.

A soft blur of color at the corner of her eye. A scent that she was aware of even when she was busy, even when her back was turned.

And then there was the sex. If anyone had told Lara that sex was supposed to be like this, she would have known there was something wrong in her marriage right away. But even if she had been told, she thought, she would have written it off as an unrealistic romantic fantasy. The sweat, the laughter. The stars falling through the dark heaven behind her eyelids.

Ben came back and sat down on the side of the bed and looked at her. "What are you thinking about?"

"You." She pulled him down, wrapped her arms around his neck.

Ben lay listening to Lara's steady breathing as sleep rolled away from him like a retreating tide. After an hour of staring at the ceiling, he gave up, pulled on a T-shirt and went quietly down the stairs. His messenger bag was by the hall table.

The living and dining rooms of Lara's father house, which she hardly used, felt abandoned and melancholy, but the big, comfortable kitchen was the heart of the house. Old-style wooden kitchen units, simple and functional. An oak table and six bentwood chairs. Big French doors gave out onto the lawn, where he could just make out the sooty silhouette of the water feature he'd installed for Lara.

He took a carton of orange juice from the fridge, sat down at the table and fired up his laptop. He had ditched his old screenplay and started working on a new idea. He had almost finished the first draft. The writing was easier and better than it had ever been before. It felt, like everything else, as if it had finally slotted into place when he met Lara.

A couple of his friends had been shocked when he'd told them that the woman he was seeing was forty-one. But most of them understood when they met her, except for Diane, who had always been a little in love with him herself.

But the age difference didn't matter. He loved that Lara had lived through so much. That she was a woman, not some girl still trying to find herself.

A shadow flitting past the window jolted him out of his thoughts. He stood up, went to the door and looked out expecting to see a fox or a cat, but there was nothing out there except the soft gray outlines of the bare trees and the shapes of flowerpots forming in the gathering light. He took the key from the hook by the door, opened it and went outside. The lawn was stippled with frost and the soles of his bare feet burned as he walked across the stiff grass to the water feature.

He was proud of that big lump of granite. It was a monument to Lara's dad, Ted, whom he hadn't known; it also felt like solid proof that Ben himself was part of Lara's life.

He felt a sudden chill that had nothing to do with the cold air. What if Katy was right? he thought, remembering what she'd said at the party. What if he was going to screw this up?

He put his hand on the cold, hard rock. He cleared his throat.

"Ted," he said. "I know we haven't met. I know you probably think I'm not good enough for your daughter and my track record is not that great. And I'm scared that I'm going to mess it up. Can you give me a hand here? Tell me what do?"

Ben slipped into bed and kissed Lara's bare shoulder. "I have an idea," she heard him say, through her dream.

"Have you?" she murmured sleepily, desire waking up before she did, humming through her veins. "Could you have it again in half an hour?"

She was still sleep-deprived after the mayhem of Valentine's Day, and Mother's Day was only two weeks away. She was going to need all the rest she could get.

He kissed her shoulder again. "I think we should get married."

Her eyes snapped open. He was propped on one elbow, looking down at her. "Well, that certainly woke me up." She yawned and looked up at him, waiting for the punch line, but he wasn't smiling.

"Ben . . ." She reached out and switched the bedside lamp on so she could see his eyes, and so he could see hers when she laid it bare. "Do the math. I'm too old for you. By the time you're my age, I'll practically be retired."

"You, retire? From your beloved shop?" He laughed. "They're going to have to take you out of Blossom & Grow in a box wrapped in cellophane tied with one of those curly ribbons."

She smiled. He was probably right.

"Look." He rubbed his jaw. "Maybe there's someone else out there for you, but you are as good as it gets for me. And time is moving on."

"It's only been nine months."

"Phil and Katy got married a year after they met."

"It's not the same," she sighed.

"Why not?"

Because Lara had been married before and she wasn't sure she wanted to go there again. Because people would call her a cradle-snatcher. Because she had never been happier in her life and she was terrified that getting married might ruin what they had.

"Because we can't all end up in happy-clappy couples," she said. "This is life, not *The Waltons*."

"The what-ons?"

She groaned. "Oh God! Are you so young you don't even know who the Waltons are? Please." She straddled him, then leaned down until her hair covered his chest and kissed along his collarbone till she reached his ear. "Can't we just keep doing this?"

"Sure." He gathered her hair behind her head in a knot. "For better for worse, for richer—"

She sat back up and pulled the duvet around her. "For goodness' sake, Ben! Will you think this through? If you're going to get married, you should be marrying someone your own age, someone you can have a family with."

He reached up and put a finger against her lips. "I've told you. I don't see myself with kids. I never did."

But Lara could. She could picture it as clearly as if she had seen a photograph. Ben walking along a beach with a little girl up on his shoulders.

"You'll change your mind," she said.

"No." He pulled her down again. Put his mouth against her ear. "I won't change my mind. So I'll have to change yours."

Afterward, just when she was about to fall back into the feathery depths of post-sex sleep, she heard his voice against her ear again.

"Good night, Mary Ellen."

It was the day before Mother's Day, the second busiest day of the year, and Blossom & Grow was under siege. Lara and Ciara had both been in the shop since 5 a.m. making up bouquets, but by mid-morning the combination of walk-ins and a sudden flurry of website orders had created an order list of impossible proportions. Lara was standing at the counter trying to make arrangements and serve customers while Ciara made up cellophane wraps and replenished the empty buckets and dealt with the ever-ringing phone.

"Look who it is," she whispered, sliding past Lara with an armful of dripping gladioli. Lara glanced up from the bouquet she was tying and saw one of her regulars slipping into the crowded shop. This woman was a mystery. For nearly six years she had come in every single Saturday and Lara still didn't know her name. She chose her flowers herself, always lilies, and hardly spoke except to ask for them to be double-wrapped in cellophane, then paid in cash so there was no card to read her name from.

She was not as old as she looked, probably only in her late forties, but her face was haggard. She wore expensive but mismatched clothes. What looked like a Chanel wool jacket with a trailing jersey skirt. Office trousers, their hems catching under the soles of ballet flats, with a zip-up sweatshirt. For a long time Lara had suspected that she was battling a serious illness, but since last summer she had started to look better. Today she had a little color in her face and a dab of lipstick on her thin, lined mouth, and for the first time, she wasn't alone. She was holding the hand of a small boy who, Lara felt, she must have seen somewhere before. He looked so familiar. If it had been any other day of the year she might have placed him, but she had made what felt like several hundred bouquets since five this morning, and her brain was almost as numb as her fingers.

"Goodness," the woman said, looking around at the empty buckets and the large queue of customers crammed into the shop, standing on the carpet of leaves that neither Lara nor Ciara had had time to sweep up.

"Sorry!" Lara stepped out from behind the counter and waved a tall white lily. "We're a bit all over the place. It's Mother's Day tomorrow."

She saw a tiny flare of pain in the woman's eyes.

Then a small voice piped up. "You have a pen in your hair!" It was the little boy.

"Do I?" Lara put the lily down and pulled it out, pretending to be amazed. "So that's where it went! Ciara!" She called across the heads of the waiting customers. "Someone just found the pen. We can write all those important messages now." She turned back to the boy. Yes, she thought, taking in the blue eyes below his blonde fringe, she had definitely seen him before, but when? "Thank you!"

"It's okay," he said, graciously. "I'm very good at observing. Do you know about Venus flytraps?"

"Josh," the woman said gently. "The flower lady might be too busy to play twenty questions."

"They eat all kinds of bugs," Josh said. "And some of them"—he lowered his voice—"the really mean ones, eat frogs. That's not right. Everyone loves frogs."

There was a ripple of laughter from the queue.

"I think that's just a rumor," Lara said. "Their roots are stuck into the earth and frogs are pretty good at hopping away."

Rita had been speechless the day she opened the door and saw Rebecca standing on the porch in a red lace dress beside what looked like a bunch of amaryllis with legs. Then the flowers had swayed to one side and there, behind them, was the boy. She might be standing there still with her mouth open and no sound coming out if Fergus hadn't stepped past her, opened the door wide, shaken Rebecca's hand, ruffled the boy's hair and invited them both inside. In the kitchen he found the tall crystal vase for the flowers, located a bottle of orange squash from the back of a cupboard somewhere and filled a glass for the boy, produced cups and saucers and plates and two kinds of biscuits, fed little capsules of coffee into the Nespresso machine and chatted about the weather.

He acted as if this was just some casual visit. As if the girl was a neighbor's daughter and not the reason why their only son, Gavin, was dead. It might have been the old man with Alzheimer's who had knocked him off his bike, but Gavin would not have been on Arran Quay in the first place if it had not been for this girl in the slutty red dress and the high shoes, taking a cup of coffee from Fergus, agreeing that the evenings were getting longer and that the lilac was lovely this year. Could she really believe, Rita thought, that showing up unannounced five years later with a bunch of flowers and this boy who could have been anybody's son for all she knew was going to make it all okay?

Rita sat like a statue, her own coffee untouched and cooling, waiting for her voice to return so she could open her mouth and tell this insolent girl what she thought of her.

"Why do you have two remote controls?" She looked up and saw the boy standing beside her looking at the two black controllers on the coffee table. "Is it because your telly is so big?" He gazed admiringly at the huge flat-screen on the wall at the end of the room. She would not look at him. What Fergus did was his own business; she had to tolerate it but she would not be part of it. "Do you have Cartoon Network?" he persisted. She shook her head. "Boomerang? The Nature Channel?"

"I don't know," she said coldly.

He came over to her chair. "If you like," he said very quietly, "you can come to our house and watch our telly." He set off across the wide room, heading for what Fergus referred to with gentle mockery as "the shrine."

She had hung a dozen photographs of her son on the wall between two tall white cabinets. Below it was an antique end table where she had lined up her most precious mementos. The trophy Gavin had won in a chess tournament in first year. His mobile phone. His key ring, a worn leather fob with a silver outline of a wolf's head, which had been in the pocket of his school trousers when the hospital had given his clothes back.

"Josh!" Rebecca called.

"It's all right," Fergus said. "Let him explore."

Rita got up and followed the boy across the long room, wanting to get away from her husband and the girl, intending to stop the child if he so much as touched anything. He came to a sudden halt and looked up at the photographs.

"Is that your swimming pool?" He pointed at a picture that had been taken the year before Gavin was killed, at the villa they'd rented in Aix. She swallowed hard and shook her head. Gavin was seventeen in the photo. His chest was tanned beneath the open shirt. She had asked him to take his sunglasses off and he held them in one hand. He was grinning at her, squinting slightly in the strong sunlight, telling her, she remembered, to hurry up.

"What's that for?" The boy had moved away but still kept on with his questions. He was by the conservatory door, pointing at the small bronze statue of the sausage dog on the floor.

"It's a doorstop." She hurried after him across the marble tiles. Behind her she heard Fergus asking Rebecca about summer camps. "It's for stopping doors."

"Stopping doors doing what?" The boy leaned on the brass handle of the glass door. "What's in here?"

"It's a conservatory." Rita tried to shoo him back into the kitchen but he stayed put. She sighed. "A sunroom."

And just as she said the word "sun," the glass room beyond the door filled with one last blaze of evening light. The boy was backlit by the setting sun and for a moment it seemed to Rita that Gavin, aged six, was standing in front of her again.

"What's your name?" he asked.

"It's Rita," she stammered. The light was leaving now as the sun fell behind the pine trees at the back of the garden, but her son was still there in the boy's blonde hair and his navy eyes.

"I'm called Josh," he announced.

Rita swallowed. She had refused to let Fergus tell her anything about the boy. She had threatened to leave when she found out that he was sending Rebecca money every month, but he refused to back down and she never mentioned it again. "Rita, he's your grandson. Have a heart." But the thing was, she had lost her heart when her son was killed, and she had carried on living without one until now.

Rebecca arrived with Josh the next Sunday and soon it became an established weekly visit. She brought him on his birthday and Christmas morning too. The house, frozen for all these years, seemed to thaw as he ran through it trailing Lego blocks and sweet wrappers and discarded garments—pitifully small socks, odd mittens, wet anoraks—and a never-ending stream of questions that flowed out behind him like bubbles in the air.

The florist was saying something.

"Sorry?" Rita said. "I was miles away."

"I was just saying that we're short on most things today, but if you give me a second, I can run down to the cold room. I think I might still have a wrap of lilies. It's the white ones you like?"

"Rita?" Josh had slipped away from her and was crouching by a bucket near the door. "Can we get these beanstalks?"

Rita went over to take a look at the handful of sunflowers that were left in the bucket.

"They grow from little seeds, you know," Josh said importantly.

They were happy flowers, she thought. Too bright, too cheerful.

"Are you sure they're the ones you like best?" she asked him doubtfully.

He nodded. "Will I count them in French?"

"All right."

There were six. One flower for every year since Gavin had died.

There was a lull in the constant stream of customers as Lara wrapped the sunflowers, and then the shop seemed to take a breath. Ciara, who had brought out all the remaining stock to refill the buckets, stared at the door as it closed behind the woman and the boy. "Five years of lilies, and suddenly sunflowers. What's going on?"

It was yet another unsolved mystery, Lara thought. Like the man who had a single red rose delivered to his girlfriend every day for ten months and then suddenly requested a white one. The married actor who had sent one hundred black tulips to a married actress. The woman who had wanted to send another woman a cactus, anonymously. "We'll probably never know," she said.

Rita left the sunflowers in their cocoon of cellophane in a sink half full of cold water. She put a frozen mini pizza into the microwave, poured a glass of milk, opened a bag of salad leaves and sectioned a clementine while Josh lay on his stomach on the rug, turning the pages of one of Gavin's old picture books about marine life.

The microwave chirped to tell her the pizza was ready, but she remained standing by the kitchen island, watching Josh. She had read somewhere, maybe in a women's magazine she had flicked through at the doctor's office, that the mother of a six-year-old was asked around a hundred and forty questions a day. Josh had already asked at least a hundred since this morning. There was another hour to go before Rebecca came to pick him up. Rita was sure he could pack the other forty in before then.

He looked up and caught her watching him. "Rita, why don't you put the beanstalks into a vase?" he asked, as if he could read her mind.

"They're for someone else." She opened the microwave door and slid a plate under the small disc of steaming pizza.

"Who?"

She took a breath. "They're for your dad." He could not, for some reason, connect his dad with the teenage pictures of Gavin, but when she had shown him the dog-eared photo in her wallet that had been taken when Gavin was eight, she thought that maybe he had come closer to understanding.

He inspected the plate carefully and transferred the salad leaves onto the saucer she had put under the milk glass.

"My dad is dead," he said in a matter-of-fact way.

"Yes," Rita said. It was strange to hear herself admitting the fact that she had fought so hard against for years.

Josh took a noisy slurp of milk. "Then how are you going to find him to give him his beanstalks?"

"I'm going to put them at the place where he died."

"He died beside a river." Josh put his glass down.

"Yes," she said softly. "On Arran Quay."

Rita had gone to the place Gavin had died the week after the accident and every week since, bringing white lilies and, at Christmas, a simple holly wreath.

The quay was one of the main busiest streets in the city, and she had to endure the curious eyes of the drivers as she kneeled down and opened her bag. She carried the same things every week. Scissors to cut the wire on the old, faded flowers. A sheet of newspaper to wrap them in. A roll of garden wire to tie the new bouquet on. A copy of Gavin's photograph in case the one in the plastic zipped pocket she'd taped to the lamppost had gotten wet in the heavy winter rain or faded in the June sunshine.

She had thought all these years that the flowers were a simple tribute, but now it struck her that they were something else. A way of prettifying bitterness. A performance for the audience of drivers in their cars who were watching the brokenhearted mother grieve for her son.

She had blamed Rebecca for the fact that Gavin was on Arran Quay that day in the rain, but he had cycled across the city to say good-bye to her because Rita was sending him to boarding school. If anyone was to blame, she was.

"Do you know how big a whale's heart is?" Gavin had asked her once, when he was about seven, as full of impossible questions and odd facts as Josh was now. "It's so big that a whole person can fit inside it," he'd told her.

She thought about her own heart. It had dried and shriveled as the years slipped past, until there was no room in it for anyone. Not even the son she'd lost.

The doorbell rang.

"It's Mum!" Josh leapt excitedly to his feet, scattering pizza crusts, clementine segments and salad leaves on the rug, and skidded along the polished marble in his socks.

Rita didn't expect Rebecca to accept her offer of coffee. They were still awkward with one another. But Josh accepted it for her, mostly, Rita thought, because he liked feeding the little capsules into the Nespresso machine. Rebecca wouldn't sit down. She stood behind the kitchen island with her mug in her hand while Josh filled his backpack and put on his coat. She and Rita talked carefully, avoiding one another's eyes, sticking to safe territory. Where Rita had taken Josh and what he had said and eaten.

"Okay, buddy," Rebecca said, "have you got everything?"

He nodded and ran over and took her hand. In her skinny jeans and hoodie and sneakers, with her long hair in a ponytail, she looked, Rita thought, more like his older sister than his mother.

Rebecca put her empty mug down on the draining board beside the sink full of sunflowers. "They're lovely," she said. "We tried to grow some last year, didn't we, Joshie? But we might have watered them a bit too much!" She smiled nervously at Rita over his head.

They were almost at the door when Rita stopped. "Hold on!" she said, and hurried back into the kitchen. When she came out again, Rebecca was kneeling on the floor redoing the toggles on Josh's duffle coat. She looked up and saw the sunflowers.

"Will you take them?" Rita held them out, not caring that the stalks were dripping onto the cream carpet.

Rebecca looked at her warily. "What for?"

"It's Mother's Day."

* * *

She watched them from the window, the tall girl and the small boy walking hand in hand to the gate. Rebecca was swinging Josh's backpack and her son was carrying the sunflowers, his arms wrapped around them tightly. She had the strongest, sweetest feeling that her own son was standing beside her. That he had come back to be with her for Mother's Day.

Lara was cashing up when Ben came in on a jangle of door chimes, a breath of icy March air.

"Will you turn the 'Closed' sign around?" she asked him, taking off her reading glasses, which she knew magnified all the little lines around her eyes.

"Does this mean I have you all to myself?" He came over and wrapped his arms around her.

She opened her mouth to tell him that Ciara was still upstairs but he closed it with his own. She tried to resist him for a fraction of a second, then stopped trying and fell into the kiss.

"Will you marry me?" he said, when they came up for air. He'd been true to his word, asking her every day for the last two weeks.

"I'm sure he doesn't mean it," Lara had said to Leo at their last session. "He'd probably run a mile if I said yes."

But when Leo gave her a thought record to fill out, the only proof she could find to support that was the age gap.

As if he had been anticipating this conversation, Leo was wearing a T-shirt that said: *Leap and the Net Will Appear.* "Maybe, just maybe, the age difference doesn't matter to him," he said.

Maybe, Lara thought, but maybe it did. Perhaps Ben had was keeping his doubts hidden the way Michael had kept his sexuality secret all those years.

"Why won't you marry him?" Ciara was standing in the doorway to the kitchen in her fluorescent yellow jacket, her cycle helmet in her hand.

"Yeah, why not?" Ben, who was still holding on to Lara, head-butted her softly.

"Because I don't have time for this nonsense. I've got work to do." Lara slipped out of her cardigan and escaped behind the counter.

"Tell you what, Ben!" Ciara said. "I'll work on her tomorrow if you help do the cleaning up." She waved at the floor of the shop, which hadn't been swept for hours. "I'm late for my Icelandic lesson again. They probably won't let me in."

"Deal!" Ben said. "What's with the Icelandic?"

"A medium told me that I would moving out of darkness into light," she said. "There are twenty-two hours of light in Iceland in summer, so I thought I'd go there at some stage, to shorten the odds."

"I used to work with an Icelandic bloke," Ben said, "at the library. I think he still does conversation classes. Maybe you should give him a call."

"Why not?" Ciara handed over her phone and bent to put on bicycle clips while Ben tapped a number into her contacts.

"You believe in all that psychic stuff?" he said, handing it back.

"I do, and so does Lara!" Ciara's eyes glittered with mischief. "The psychic she went to the Christmas before last told her that her soul mate would be along soon."

"Ciara!" Lara threw a roll of ribbon after her as she headed for the door.

Ben grinned. "Well, he's here now. Come on, I'll give you a hand." He took off his heavy jacket and draped it over Lara's shoulders and they set to work.

The Icelandic bloke had taught Ben a few phrases. He tried to remember them as he poured water out of buckets into the sink, sterilized them and stacked them while Lara swept the fallen leaves and petals into rustling piles.

"You work too hard," he told her when they were finished. She had been on her feet for nearly fourteen hours.

She was washing her hands at the sink. Her fingers were chapped and her wrists were dotted and dashed with thorn scratches. "It doesn't feel like hard work." She looked around. "It's tiring but it gives me more than I give it. It's good to get lost in other people's lives sometimes, to get away from your own."

He wondered if she still felt like getting away from her life now that he was in it.

"Oh!" Lara said suddenly. "We forgot all about this." She picked up a huge arrangement that had been left in a bucket by the sink. "It was ordered and then canceled. It seems a shame to take it apart. What about your mother?"

He shook his head. His mother didn't deserve them. She hadn't been nice to Lara the one time they had met. Ben was her only child and she had been counting on grandchildren. But he'd had a lifetime of pleasing other people; now he just wanted to please himself.

"Why don't you take them to *your* mother? We could go to the graveyard."

She looked taken aback. "I don't really go there. I've only been three times."

He counted them off in his head. Her mother, her father, the baby she had lost. "Well, let's make it four," he said. "It's about time you took me to meet the parents."

It was too cold for snow, that's what Lara's dad would have said. The air was sharp as a blade and the sky as black as spilled ink as they parked outside the graveyard. When they got out, Lara was relieved to see that the gates were locked.

She loved that Ben challenged all the old rules she'd made in her life, that he shook her loose from her past. But this was different. This was a place she had always hated.

"Come on!" He grabbed her hand. "We're not going to let a little padlock stop us, are we?"

Before she could stop him, he'd climbed onto the railings and swung himself over. He took the bouquet from Lara and she had no choice but to clamber up and follow him. He held out his arms to catch her, and she jumped and he lowered her carefully to the ground.

The moon came out from behind a cloud as they emerged from the avenue of yew trees into the open and stood looking at the vast field of gravestones.

"I like cemeteries," Ben said. "Every grave tells a story." He took her arm. "You're not afraid of ghosts, are you?" Lara shook her head. What she was scared of was seeing the names of the three people she had lost.

It took her a few minutes in the dark to find the right row. "This is it," she said to Ben at last. They stood and looked down at the headstone. Her dad's name was crisply etched in silver lettering. The silver on Ryan's name was softer. The gilding on her mother's name was almost worn away.

"You named your baby after your mother," Ben said quietly. "I didn't realize that."

Lara nodded. "Ryan was her maiden name." She bent down and put the bouquet on the grave. When she stood up again, Ben had his arms open waiting for her. He folded her into himself and held her tight, sheltering her from the wind that snapped at the cellophane around the flowers.

"You want to know something funny?" she said, her words muffled against the heavy folds of his jacket. "My mother chose this place because of the view. How crazy is that?"

"Not crazy at all," Ben said. "It's kind."

She looked up at him; his face was in shadow. "What do you mean?"

"The view was not for her, Lara." He turned her around so that she faced the bay. "Look. It's for you."

The lights of the city were strung around the semicircular bay like the fairy lights in her flower shop. The moon was spilling a shimmering silver path across the water, stretching all the way to the sooty silhouettes of the Sugar Loaf and Wicklow Head.

Her heart leapt. She turned back to look at Ben. "How on earth did you know that?" she whispered.

He shrugged. "She loved you. She knew that every time you turned away from her grave you'd see this beautiful view and maybe not feel so sad."

He might be twelve years younger than she was, Lara thought, but he was an old soul. They walked back to the gate and he helped her back over the railings.

"*Eg elska thig,*" he said, jumping down onto the pavement beside her. "What?"

"It's Icelandic for 'I love you.' It just came back to me. Amazing the things that stay stuck in your head."

Lara stared after him. Had she told him that her dad could say "I love you" in every language except English?

He turned his collar up against the cold. "Come on, let's get into the car before we freeze."

He walked back to the curb and began digging through his pockets, looking for the car key.

"Yes!" Lara said.

Ben looked back at her. "Yes what?"

"Yes, I'll marry you!"

"You will?"

And he walked back to her, his arms wide, his face lit up by the moon and the streetlights and by love.

HYDRANGEA

A Deep Connection.

Emily was early. She sat at their usual table in the Library Bar in the Central Hotel. Late-afternoon sunshine was flooding in through the tall sash windows, glancing off the gilt-framed mirrors and the crystal chandeliers, picking out the spidery gold lettering on the spines of a wall of books.

They should have thought about putting books in the guest rooms at the wedding, she realized. Romantic novels and volumes of poetry with personalized bookmarks so they fell open on significant pages. It was the kind of touch people would remember. Maybe there was still time to get it organized?

She'd opened her laptop to add a note to her spreadsheet, when Dan arrived, carrying his fold-up Brompton bike. His hair was damp with sweat. It was his day off and they were only meeting for half an hour, but still, Emily thought, he could have made a bit of an effort.

"You look hot!" she said as he bent down to kiss her nose.

"Thanks." He grinned and gave her a quick eyebrow flash. "So do you."

He waved at the waiter behind the elaborately carved wooden bar. "Half-pint of Guinness, extra cold. And?" He looked at Emily.

"I'm good," she said pointedly. They were both supposed to be on diets. The wedding was only two months away.

"So." Dan stashed the fold-up bike behind her chair and looked at her laptop the way a horse might look at a fence he had fallen at many times before. "You said there were one or two things to discuss?"

"It's more like three or four."

He turned back to the waiter. "Can you make that a pint?"

Emily had already changed the bridesmaids' dresses from eau de Nil to watermelon and back again. The number of tiers on the cake from three to four to two. The song for their first dance from "The Sweetest Thing" to "Falling Slowly," which was all wrong, she'd realized at four the previous morning. Falling was something you did by mistake, and "slowly" made them sound like learner drivers, not lovers, didn't it?

"What do you think of Van Morrison?" she asked Dan.

"I think he's old and grumpy and . . ." He saw her frown and changed course. "Incredibly talented."

"Really?" She hadn't been sure he'd know who Van Morrison was. "Would you mind if we changed our first song to 'Moondance'?"

"Is that the one about the brown-eyed girl?"

"No, Dan," Emily sighed. "That song is called 'Brown Eyed Girl.'"

"In that case"—he picked up the pint the waiter had put in front of him and took a gulp—"'Moondance' it is."

"Settled. Now I know we've paid the deposit for the flamenco guitarist, but can we go back to the string quartet? Classical music is just . . ."

"Classier?" Dan stifled a sigh.

"Exactly! I'll get to the canapés or hors d'oeuvres in a minute, but first, about the soup . . ."

"What about the soup?" His eyes were beginning to glaze over.

"Will it be too hot for soup? Would we be better going for something lighter?"

"Hmm?" He wasn't even pretending to listen now.

"I was thinking maybe a hedgehog sorbet."

"Sounds good." He licked the Guinness moustache off his top lip then his eyes snapped back to her. "Ah! That's a joke, right?"

"Yes, it's a joke." She shut her laptop decisively. "And so is this! You're not remotely interested in this wedding, are you?"

"Of course I am. I just don't have your level of . . ." He searched for the right word.

Go on, she thought, say it. Neurosis. Obsession. That was what everyone thought.

"Attention to detail." He waved his half-empty glass. Except that for Dan, it was half full. It was one of the things she loved about him, his optimism, along with all the other things. The way he paused Netflix to explain the plots of complicated thrillers. Listened to her father's nutty conspiracy theories, played Junior Scrabble with her seven-year-old nephew and let him win.

Dan put the glass down and picked up her hand. His fingertips were deliciously cool. She wanted to press them against her aching temples.

"Look, Em. I can see you're upset, but trust me, everyone's going to be far too busy having a good time to notice whether they're eating canapés or hors d'oeuvres. I'm not sure many of them will even know the difference."

Paul will know the difference, Emily thought.

"I met the love of my life by accident," Dan liked to tell people. Emily had wrenched her shoulder on the first day of her skiing holiday when she swerved to avoid a snowboarder and collided with a tree. Dan had sprained his ankle five minutes into his first lesson. They were both grounded from the slopes for a week.

He had smiled at her from the other side of the crowded waiting room at the resort clinic. Had she smiled back? He said she had but she wondered if he'd imagined it. The truth was, she had hardly noticed him. He was just an average-looking brown-haired blur at the corner of her vision. She had been miserable that day, as she sat waiting for her injured arm to be strapped up. She had been miserable most days back then.

The trip to Courchevel with her friend Lisa and her boyfriend was supposed to cheer her up. It had been eighteen months since she'd left

Paul, but he was like one of those exotic parasites people picked up in the tropics. Just when Emily thought she had finally gotten him out of her system, he flared up again, humming through her blood, making her sick with longing. She was beginning to wonder if she would ever get over him at all.

Lisa had wanted to stay behind at the hotel the next day and keep Emily company, but she didn't want to ruin her friend's holiday too. She'd be fine, she'd insisted. She'd find things to keep her occupied. But what? she wondered, after Lisa had finally given in and left. What the hell was she going to do for the next six days?

Having only one working arm meant she couldn't straighten her hair or put on her eyeliner or pop in her contact lenses. She couldn't zip up her jeans or balance properly in heels. The only thing she could comfortably wear with her sling, it turned out, were fleece leggings and an extra-large sweatshirt with one sleeve cut off, donated by Lisa's boyfriend.

She didn't want anyone to see her dressed like that so she sat on her bed feeling sorry for herself while the hotel emptied, listening to the laughter and excited voices, shouted instructions not to forget lift passes, the clatter of boots passing her door.

When she finally emerged, the hotel was deserted. She made her way down to the dreary, windowless breakfast room, a Tyrolean-style horror decorated with a mural of the mountain that looked as if it had been painted by a kindergarten class.

There was no sign of any breakfast now, and there were no waiters to be seen. She managed to coax a cup of coffee out of the ancient vending machine, then sat under the disapproving gaze of a stuffed moose head.

If Paul was to walk into the breakfast room, she thought, he probably wouldn't recognize her. In the two years they had been together, he had never once seen her without makeup. She used to get up half an hour before him so she could set her hair in Velcro rollers and brush her teeth before he woke up.

Paul had never seen her in a sweatshirt. He liked her in fitted jackets and tight pencil skirts and sky-high heels. He said she looked danger-ous in them. Emily, who had never considered herself even slightly dangerous, except when she was changing lanes on the M50, liked this new, dramatic version of herself. She had always worried that she was too timid, but Paul made her sound risky and exciting.

Her shyness was "enigmatic." Her girlish ticklishness made her "polymorphously perverse." This meant, he explained delightedly, that she could derive erotic pleasure from any part of her body. He said it when he nipped at her earlobe or nibbled the crook of her elbow and she shivered.

She felt as if she was turning into a character in a movie when they were together, but after it was all over, she realized she was just ordinary Emily after all.

She picked up her phone. She should have deleted Paul's number after what he'd done, but she hadn't. She wanted to call him so badly that it hurt more than her aching shoulder. She looked up at the moose. *Don't even think about it!* his weary, glassy eyes seemed to say.

She sighed, put the phone away and popped a codeine, which would have to do instead of breakfast. She swallowed her longing with a gulp of cold coffee. She tried not to think about whose elbows Paul was nibbling now and how perverse they were.

Half an hour went by before she heard a sign of life in the hotel. The faint click-clack of someone walking on crutches growing louder until a man appeared in the doorway. For a moment she couldn't place him, then she realized with a sinking heart that it was the guy she'd glimpsed at the clinic the day before. He lifted one crutch solemnly in salute, then limped toward her.

"All fun and games"—he sat down at her table and twiddled his thumbs—"till someone breaks a leg, then it's snow fun at all, is it?"

She shrugged without meeting his eye, as if not looking at him meant that he couldn't see her horrible glasses, her un-made-up face, her hideous outfit.

He gazed around at the pretzel-colored wooden beams and the chintz curtains and the cuckoo clocks, then did a comic double take when he saw the moose head. "You think he lost his head in a skiing accident?"

Emily glanced up. "He looks more like a snowboarder to me."

He smiled, and she felt oddly pleased.

"You have to keep your sense of humor," he said.

"Someone should have told me that," she sighed. "I left it in my room."

He smiled again. "Dan."

"Emily."

"Come on." He stood up and picked up his crutches.

"Where?"

He nodded at the mural. "If we're going to spend the rest of the week stuck looking at a mountain, it might as well be a real one."

Dan somehow persuaded the hotel manager, a man who looked even more disapproving than the moose, to take pity on them. Except there was no silky charm involved: Dan was just polite and direct. The manager's expression didn't change but he opened the dining terrace on the fourth floor, lit the burners and rustled up two plaid rugs and a hot-water bottle for Emily.

They settled into two wooden chairs and sat, bundled up, watching the enormous jagged white molar of the mountain appear and disappear through the falling snow.

"We don't have to talk," Dan said, on that first morning. "Or amuse one another. Deal?"

"Deal," Emily agreed.

They read their books in companionable silence. From time to time, when the view became especially beautiful or magical, one of them would look up from their book and point at the wall of falling flakes and hum a bar of "Let It Snow!"

And it might have been the codeine, or the majesty of the view or the easygoing company, but Emily forgot about her bad mood and the pain in her shoulder. For nearly a whole day, she forgot about Paul.

And next morning, she was waiting impatiently when the manager arrived to unlock the terrace. As she was sitting down, she heard the clatter of crutches behind her.

"Did you book?" Dan asked, looking around at the empty tables.

"No," she deadpanned. "I just showed up on the chance they'd have a cancellation."

"What do you and this Dan get up to all day?" Lisa asked, relieved that Emily had company and fishing for any scent of romance.

"Nothing much," Emily said, and it was true.

They played gin rummy, although they were both a little vague on the rules. They ate leathery omelets and drank hot chocolate. They filled in crosswords in old newspapers. They listened to his iPod, which had better playlists, with her headphones, which had better sound quality.

When they got caught up in Emily's glasses, Dan untangled them and polished the lenses carefully with a napkin before he handed them back. When her hot-water bottle went cold, he limped off to find an elusive hotel employee to get it refilled. When her rug kept sliding off, he thought to bring the safety pins from a hotel sewing kit and pinned it to the sweatshirt. Tiny acts of kindness, each one as light and inconsequential as a snowflake, but it was amazing what a lot of snowflakes could do when they got together, she thought. You only had to look at the mountain.

"Will you do me a favor, Em?" Dan was turning her engagement ring around and around with his thumb, an oval sapphire surrounded by a cluster of tiny diamonds. Emily had loved the ring when he'd given it to her, but now she wondered if it was a bit ordinary, a bit— what was the word Paul used to use? A bit *vanilla*. "Will you stop changing things that are already perfect?"

That's what everyone kept saying; well, some version of it anyway. Her mother, her sister Monica, Lisa, the caterer, the cake designer. The only person who hadn't said it so far was the florist.

Emily had called into the shop and changed her mind about the flowers four times so far, but Lara still always looked pleased to see her. She'd stop what she was doing and make them a pot of Moroccan mint tea and start again from scratch. Emily could sit there for hours—and had done—listening to her describing the sooty center of an anemone or the scent of white lavender or the tightly packed petals of a rose.

And every time Emily left, she was certain she'd picked the right flowers this time, until she woke up a day or a week later and realized that they were all wrong.

Dan ordered another pint. "Come on, Em, have a glass of wine. You look as if you need it."

"I can't." She had already lost ten kilos but the dress, a simmering bell of gauze, would look even better if she could lose another two. "It'll just undo all the work I'm going to do at the gym later."

"That's snow excuse." Dan smiled. They had started trading snow puns that first week and they still hadn't stopped.

"Snow pain, snow gain," Emily said, opening her laptop again.

She wanted a glass of cold white wine, though, and not just one. She wanted to sit here with him knocking back glasses of wine until her head spun. To saunter over to the Italian in Temple Bar and sit at a table outside and eat quattro formaggi pizza and lick the cheese off her fingers. To go home and get into bed and watch a box set and spoon-feed one another cookie dough ice cream until one of them decided it was time to have sex. But there was too much to do.

"Fire lanterns!" she said. "I think the red ones are a bit tacky. Do you mind if we go back to white?"

"Snow problem," Dan said sadly.

That night, Emily dreamed that she showed up for her wedding in a tracksuit instead of a wedding dress. That her dad did not arrive to give her away and someone else had to step in. That it was Paul.

She woke up with a jolt and couldn't go back to sleep. Instead she lay awake staring at the ceiling, worrying about the readings for the wedding. Dan's mother had chosen them and picked that one from the Song of Solomon that everybody used. "My beloved is like a gazelle or a young stag. Look! There he stands behind our wall, gazing through the windows."

"Whenever I hear that one," Paul had whispered at her sister Monica's wedding, "I always think the beloved sounds like a Peeping Tom."

Monica had choked on her coffee when Emily told her about the invitation she'd sent Paul.

"You invited him to your wedding? After what he did?" Monica mopped spilled coffee off her knees. "Have you lost your mind?"

"Dan is inviting two of his exes," Emily said. "It only seems fair."

The truth was that she wanted Paul to get the invitation and to read, in black-and-white on heavy gilt-edged cream paper, that she had moved on. That she was so madly in love with someone else that she wanted to share her happiness with everyone. Even him.

The possibility that he might decide to turn up had never occurred to her, but his was the first RSVP that arrived, and now, whenever she thought about the wedding, she saw it all through his eyes. The venue, the ceremony, the food. Most of all—worst of all—herself.

Paul's eyes were amazing. A startling blue that bordered on violet, so bright in his lean, dark, handsome face that they looked as if they had been digitally enhanced. Cowboy's eyes, Lisa had called them. He looked as if he should be spending his days roaming the plains beneath a vast empty sky, but in fact he was the marketing director of a low-fat yogurt brand and a part-time lecturer in advertising.

They had met when the PR company where Emily was working handled his new product launch. She had only sat in on the initial briefing because one of her colleagues was ill and her boss asked her to pad out the team so that Paul would feel important.

"You don't even have to listen," he'd said. But ten minutes into the meeting, she realized that Paul was addressing his PowerPoint presentation directly to her. She was first puzzled, then intrigued, then flattered. Why her?

Much later, she found out that this was a trick he used in his lectures. Get the interest of the least interested person in the room and the rest will follow. By then, Emily had realized that keeping Paul was far harder work than getting him, but she didn't care. She would have followed him anywhere.

"He really loves himself," Monica said, "doesn't he?"

But what was wrong with that? People were always saying that you had to love yourself before you loved another person. He was just putting it into practice.

Yes, Paul could be tricky. He didn't tolerate fools gladly, and he had a pretty broad definition of the word "fool." But on the other hand, waiters (Emily had always found waiters intimidating) took one look at him and gave him the best table in the restaurant. Airline staff upgraded him. He got what he wanted without even asking for it, and—here it was—he wanted *her*.

It was like being pulled from the audience onto the stage at a rock concert to dance with the lead singer. Whatever it was he'd seen in her, that was what she wanted to be. That was the price of admission. She didn't change for him; she did it all for herself. Upgrading like an operating system, losing all the old, annoying, clunky features and becoming a slicker version of herself.

She lost weight. Traded in her Citroën for a secondhand Mercedes CLK. Took a wine-tasting course. She ditched her M&S underwear for sexy Myla and beautiful Stella McCartney. She stopped buying clothes and invested in "pieces." A pair of shoes she'd seen in *Vogue*. A butter-soft leather dress that cost as much as a holiday used to. Her credit card was permanently maxed out but it didn't matter. She wanted to be perfect for him.

Then, as she got to know him, she realized that he wasn't as perfect as he looked. He used hair thickener to bulk up the spot where his blonde curls were thinning. He changed his clothes three or four times before they went out. He practiced his lectures, word for word, in front of a full-length mirror in his bedroom (she knew; she listened).

She loved him even more for these little flaws because maybe they meant that he wouldn't love her any less when he found out that she had flaws too.

Emily felt a familiar rush of dread as she pushed open the door of Blossom & Grow. She hoped that Lara would be behind the counter and not that stroppy blonde assistant. But the shop was empty and deliciously cool and quiet after the heat and clamor of Camden Street. It smelled like a forest—of ferns and greenery and moss.

"Emily!" Lara came out of the kitchen with a huge bucket of water in each hand. Her green apron was soaked and the sleeves of her pink T-shirt were damp to her elbows. She blew hair out of her eyes. "I was just giving the flowers a drink."

"I'm really sorry!" Emily began nervously. "I know you must be sick of the sight of me."

"You're just the excuse I need to put down these damned buckets before I drown myself, and make some tea. Make yourself comfortable and I'll be with you in one second."

Emily sat down at the wrought-iron table under a Moroccan lantern. Paul had been going to ask her to marry him on that holiday they had booked to Morocco, she was sure of it.

She had seen a link to a diamond dealer in Antwerp when she was having a sneaky look through his Internet browsing history on his laptop. There was no reason for it, nothing specific, he'd just seemed a little distant. Emily was ashamed of herself for spying on him, but if she knew he was losing interest in her, then she could take corrective action, couldn't she?

She'd grinned at the screen of his laptop, feeling light-headed with happiness. He wasn't losing interest at all. He was planning to propose to her in the souk or the mountains or the desert. It was going to be perfect. Except that it never happened. She had to go to the ER with bad abdominal pains one afternoon and it turned out that she needed emergency surgery to have a fibroid removed. She didn't tell Paul that, of course, she just said she needed to have a small procedure. She wanted to maintain the illusion that her womb was as perfect as the rest of her.

She hoped he'd cancel the trip to stay with her, but his mate James had just broken up with his girlfriend, so the boys decided to head off on their own. They weren't on their own for long. They met up with a pair of English girls and decided to take a tour of the desert.

They were just traveling together, Paul said, sharing the cost of the jeep and the guide, which made sense. Camping in the Sahara, white tents, candlelight, silver service. It sounded a bit romantic to Emily, but that was just her imagination again.

When she got an infection and had to stay in the hospital for another few days, Paul sent her four kinds of roses. He didn't have a good signal in the desert but he Skyped her when he got back to Marrakesh. The English girls had headed home and he and James were staying in a *riad* in the Medina. He held his phone up so Emily could see the stars and hear the sound of the drummers in Djema el-Fna.

After they said their good-byes, he pressed the wrong button and Skype stayed open on his phone.

"Paul," she whispered, in case she disturbed the other patients in the ward. "I'm still here!"

But he couldn't hear her over the sound of his own footsteps as he left his room with the phone in his hand. She saw dizzying fragments of the *riad* as he hurried past a fountain and down some steps into a courtyard. An intricately tiled floor, a window made of jewel-colored glass, a corridor lined with candles in huge glass lanterns.

The footsteps stopped and she saw a carved wooden door, heard three sharp taps. She smiled, waiting to see James's feet, but instead she saw high silver sandals, heard a voice—English, female, slightly annoyed—saying, "What kept you?"

He claimed that the girl was just a mate, that Emily was being paranoid. It killed her that he thought she was such a perfect fool.

Lara poured the tea into two tiny glasses and moved a plate of short-bread biscuits closer to Emily, who looked even thinner than she had a month ago. "Just stop me when you see anything you like." She began to scroll through her Pinterest board. Flowers blossomed on the screen. The golds and ochres first. Golden peonies, apricot honeysuckle, saffron, poppies the color of amber.

Emily gnawed at her thumbnail. The corners of her mouth were jittery. "I'm so confused." She turned to look at Lara. "If you were getting married, what would you choose?"

"I don't know." Lara flushed. She had to stare at the screen in case her expression gave her away. She *was* getting married, just a few days after Emily's wedding, but nobody knew.

Ben had wanted to have a party but Lara had managed to persuade him that it would be more romantic if they kept it just between the two of them. The truth was, she would have loved her brother to be there, but Ben was awkward around Phil, and having Katy there would just be too hard on him. They had so much history together.

So she had talked him into a registry office ceremony with strangers as witnesses. Afterward they were having lunch at Restaurant Patrick Guilbaud, then spending the night in the Merrion Hotel. The next morning they were going to fly to Greece for a honeymoon that everyone thought was just a holiday.

"You don't think it's a bit cloak-and-dagger?" Ben asked when everything was booked. "Not telling anyone at all?"

"I think it's a good thing," Lara said, as much to herself as to him. "Most weddings are about other people. This will just be about us."

Her wedding to Michael had felt oddly impersonal. The ceremony had been held in Michael's family church in Richmond in Surrey and the reception was at a hotel that overlooked the Thames. Lara was supposed to be involved in the planning, but she was in Dublin and in the end Michael's mother had taken over.

Only the flowers had felt like her own. She'd ordered them from a florist in Kew. Garden roses, sweet pea, chamomile, lavender and Queen Anne's lace. She wore a simple garland of ivy instead of a veil. Her dad had cut it from his garden and brought it over on the Ryanair flight in his suitcase.

Lara had lost sight of Michael at the champagne reception. She searched for him in the crowd milling around on the lush green lawn that rolled down to the river until she found him, finally, by the water, leaning against a tree, looking uncomfortable in his gray morning suit. He had smiled at her and let her lead him back up to the wedding party. Poor Michael, hiding even then, pretending to be someone he wasn't.

Who was this girl pretending to be? she wondered, looking at Emily's tense profile. What was she hiding? Lara wanted to tell her that if you went into a marriage with a secret, all the flowers in the world would not hide it. That when you committed to someone, you had to commit as the person you really were, not the person you thought they wanted you to be. But that was something she had to work out herself.

"What's wrong with me?" Emily whispered. "I'm looking at all these beautiful flowers but I can't decide which ones are right for me."

Lara closed her laptop. "Why don't you imagine you're buying them for someone you've known your whole life, someone you really love."

"Who?" Emily blinked at her.

Lara smiled. "You."

Emily had been trying to be all things to all people, she realized as she lay awake that night staring at the ceiling. The polished, elegant woman she'd turned herself into for Paul and the ordinary girl in the XL sweatshirt with her arm in a sling making snow puns with Dan. Which was the real Emily? There was only one way to find out.

When she arrived at the French restaurant he'd picked, he was already at the table, tasting a glass of wine, watched by an attentive waitress. He inhaled it, sniffed it, swirled it around his mouth. Emily knew that he'd seen her but he didn't look up till she reached the table. It was worth it, though, just to see those amazing blue cowboy eyes of his widen in amazement.

"Wow!" he said, looking her up and down.

She sat down opposite him. The waitress made as if to fill the glass in front of her but Emily covered it with her hand.

"Really?" Paul said, recovering his composure. "You're turning down a 1996 Cuvee Jean Gautreau?"

"I don't want it."

The waitress put the bottle and the menus down and left.

Paul leaned back in his chair, locked his fingers behind his head and smiled. "Well, what do you want, Emily? Why are we here? I'm intrigued."

She wanted to be the upgraded Emily, just for one more minute. That cool, confident version of herself whose hands wouldn't shake, whose voice would stay steady. But she wasn't that person so she would have to settle for saying the lines she had carefully rehearsed. She had taken a leaf out of Paul's book, prepared herself in advance.

She took a deep breath. "We're here because I made a terrible mistake," she said quietly.

Paul tipped his chair forward so suddenly that his elbow connected with his glass. He caught it just before it hit the table. A perfect save. "I knew it," he said. "The minute I got that wedding invitation. It wasn't you. All that swirly type and the gilt. And the venue? The Enniskerry Lodge? I was having visions of flamenco guitarists and Chinese lantern balloons."

Emily nodded. "You won't mind not coming, then?"

"What?" The smugness was gone in a flash.

"To the wedding."

"But . . ." Now he was flustered. Floundering. "You said you had made a mistake."

"Oh!" she said, pretending to be surprised. "You thought I meant that I'd made a mistake about *getting married*?"

"Well"—he swirled his wine, trying not to look as uncomfortable as he obviously felt—"naturally, I thought . . ."

"What I meant was that I'd made a mistake inviting you."

She had never seen him blush before, but as she watched, he turned puce. He was still the handsomest man in the room, in the country, maybe, but now he was also the most annoyed.

Emily picked up her bag and upended it, and all the souvenirs of their time together scattered across the table. She'd kept them in a box all this time, at the back of the wardrobe, where she knew Dan would never look.

Her key to Paul's apartment. A shower cap from the hotel where they'd first had sex. Ticket stubs from an opera at the Gaiety. An empty bottle of Gucci Pour Homme. The wishbone charm he had given her.

He glared down at them and then up at her. "What's all this crap?"

He was right, it was crap, and she'd been giving it head room and house room and heart room along with all the other crap. The idea that she had to reinvent herself to please another person.

She hadn't ever been polymorphously perverse. She'd hated it when Paul had nibbled her earlobes and her elbows. She didn't want to be enigmatic or dangerous. What did that even mean in the real world? Hiding the cutlery in the laundry basket? Using a 120-volt device in a 240-volt socket?

"You know what I think?" Paul said. "I think you're still in love with me."

"I don't think I was ever in love with you. I think I was in love with me, except it wasn't the real me."

He snorted. "And this is?" He pointed a finger at her.

Her hair was lank, she wasn't wearing makeup and she had dressed carefully for this meeting. Fleecy leggings. Crocs. An XL sweatshirt with one sleeve cut out.

"Yes," she said. "I think it is."

Emily was fast asleep when Dan came crashing in after his stag party. He crawled onto the bed with all his clothes on, smelling of tequila and garlic mayonnaise.

"How was it?" She sat up.

"Pretty tame." He hiccuped. "No strippers, no lap dancing, but I think I might have done the funky chicken in Abrakebabra. How about you?" He looked at her carefully. "Was it okay seeing your man?"

She had thought about not telling Dan she was going to see Paul, but then she had thought again. She wanted not to have any secrets.

"He's not my man." She head-butted him softly. "You are. And it was okay."

"Did you get closure?"

She smiled. "I did."

"Where is it?" He frisked her through the duvet. "I want to see this closure you got."

"Wait!" She giggled, pushing him off. "Just one second. I've decided on the flowers."

"Fascinating!" he mumbled into her neck.

"I'm going back to the snowflake hydrangeas. And I've had another idea about our first song."

He lifted his head. "Oh, Emily! Not again."

"What about 'Let it Snow!'?"

"I like it!" He grinned at her. "But in June? Will everyone think we're unhinged?"

"Who cares? It's our song, not theirs!"

"That's snow true!" He laughed.

And they both began to hum the tune.

LILY

A New Life.

Lara was working three kinds of ivy together, weaving them into cascading strands. Tomorrow, after she'd pinned them into place on the tables, she'd work in the little knots of white roses and the scented vines. When the wedding guests came in from the garden after the champagne reception on the lawn, the dining room would smell of jasmine and honeysuckle.

It was midsummer's day and the height of the wedding season that had begun in May. So far the flowers for every bride had somehow worked out perfectly, but there was always the lurking fear that the next one would not. The possibility that the wholesaler would leave out the most important bloom for a bouquet. The business of moving stock from the cold room into the warmth of the workroom and back again, so that every rose and peony had the perfect degree of openness, was fraught with danger. And that was nothing compared to dealing with the brides themselves, who needed even more careful handling than their flowers.

There were three weddings in the book for tomorrow, another three lined up next weekend, and then—Lara felt light-headed with excitement as she bent down to pick up another strand of ivy—there was her own wedding, a week from Monday, just ten days from now. After weeks of secret searching, she had finally found the perfect dress in a vintage boutique owned by Ciara's flatmate.

She hated to lie, so she had said that she needed something for a summer wedding; she just hadn't mentioned it was her own. Suzanne had brought out a 1930s blush-pink silk tea dress with a skirt that fell softly to the knee like poppy petals. Lara had been daydreaming about the bouquet since April, but she had finally ordered the flowers this morning. White O'Hara roses with pale pink hearts, and white veronica.

Two weeks from now, she and Ben would be married and in southwest Crete, where her parents had honeymooned. Ciara, who had been surprised when Lara told her she was taking a week off, had now decided that it had all been her idea in the first place.

"I told her she had to take a break," Lara had heard her tell Becca, the intern, this morning. "She hasn't had a holiday in six years!"

The guilt Lara had felt about leaving Ciara on her own for a week disappeared after Becca had come on board. She was only twenty-two but a natural, intuitive with people and flowers. Lara was already thinking of offering her a job.

She had finished the ivy garlands and was sweeping up the fallen leaves when she heard someone bounding up the stairs, taking the steps two at a time. She was already smiling when Ben stuck his head around the door.

His cheeks were flushed and his eyes were glittering with mischief. Sometimes he looked so boyish that it scared her.

"Hey! What are you up to?"

Lara leaned on the brush. "My eyes," she said. "In weddings."

"Any wedding in particular that I should know about?"

"Sssh." Lara put her finger to her lips and pointed at the floor. "Ciara might hear you!"

He came over and took the brush. "Come on, Cinderella," he said. "I'm taking you to lunch. I've booked Guilbaud's. I know we're going there on our . . ." He dropped his voice to a comic whisper. "*Wedding day*, but this can be a sneak preview."

"What about your work?"

"Software upgrade!" He twirled the brush. "All the computers are out of action. I'm supposed to be proofing a manuscript at home, but

I'd much rather hang out with you!" He took her hand. "Come on, grab your things."

"Ben," she said carefully, "it's a lovely idea, but I can't go anywhere. I've got three wedding bouquets to make by the end of the day, plus two sets of table arrangements. Damn! I forgot! Hang on a moment!" She hurried to the door and called down the stairs. "Ciara, can you take the agapanthus out of the cold room?"

When she turned back to Ben, he was taking out his phone.

"Let's have an early dinner then. I'll call and see if they have a table."

"I'll be working late, but I'll come home early tomorrow evening, I promise."

Ben stuffed his hands into his pockets and his fingers closed around the little red leather box as he walked along Camden Street. Lara hadn't wanted an engagement ring, and the wedding ring she'd picked was a plain rose-gold band. But he'd asked the jeweler to design a flower-shaped diamond cluster, and had been planning to give it to her at lunch.

Surely she could have spared an hour? Ciara and the new intern could handle things.

He'd hardly seen Lara since the start of May. She was gone from six most mornings and back late every night. Ben hadn't been that bothered back in March when she wanted to keep the wedding secret. She'd had a big showy wedding before; he got it that she didn't want to go there again. But now he wondered if there was some other reason for all the secrecy.

Was Lara ashamed of telling people she was marrying him? Was she having second thoughts? Was she using work as an excuse to avoid him?

A knot of worry gathered in his stomach as he turned toward St. Stephen's Green.

"Save me!" A tall blonde woman wearing a cream dress and carrying a briefcase stepped into his path. "Save me from twats and lying bastards!"

He laughed. "Hello, Mia."

Katy's sister was coming from a meeting with the Revenue, where she'd found out that one of her clients had stashed away five hundred grand. She leapt at the chance of lunch.

"Very posh!" she said as a waiter in black tie walked them to their table. "Do you have five hundred grand stashed away somewhere as well?"

"I wish," Ben said. He flicked through the leather-bound wine list, his eyes widening at the prices. "House red okay with you?"

"House Dutch Gold would be okay. That's how desperate I am! God"—she bit her lip—"how long is it since we've hung out together?"

"Must be two years."

"I've missed you! Maybe now you're all playing happy-ever-afters we can be friends again."

"I'd like that."

By the time they were finishing their starters, the knot of worry in Ben's stomach had dissolved. Lara was busy, that was all. She had a lot to get organized before they went away. Two weeks from now, he thought as he emptied his glass, they'd be married and he'd have her undivided attention.

"Another bottle?" Mia asked. "I'm buying. I can't bear to go back to work. I'm too hammered now anyway."

He smiled. "Go on!"

Mia kept him entertained with wickedly funny stories about her work colleagues and Ronan's pretentious arty friends before moving on to her favorite subject, her mother, Angela.

"She went into a total decline when you left. Pined for you like the dead parrot in that Monty Python sketch pined for the fjords. Then— you're not going to believe this—she got off that lovely little ass of hers and went out and met a man!"

"You're joking!"

"Nope. They've been together for nearly two years. We haven't met him yet. She's keeping him secret." She took a spoonful of her strawberry parfait. "My theory is that he's younger than her. Can you imagine it! Mum and a toyboy!"

Ben winced. "Would that be such a bad thing?" he asked drily, but she was too tipsy to make the connection.

"You were always too easy on her, Ben. You know she thinks you're on the rebound from Katy. She told me at that party back in the spring that she gives you and Lara a year." She loaded her spoon up and held it out to him.

He pushed it away and the parfait slopped off onto the white tablecloth. A waiter swooped in to clean it up. Anger rose in Ben as he sat, unable to speak, while the man first fussed with the stain, then covered it with a clean napkin.

"A year? Bullshit!" he said when the waiter had finally gone.

"Course it is," Mia agreed cheerfully. "Mum's full of it, you know that."

"Well, if you see her, tell her that Lara and I are getting married." It was out before he could stop himself.

"You are?" Mia dropped her spoon on her plate with a clatter.

"Yeah, but you can't tell anyone. Nobody knows. It's classified information. Seriously!"

But she had turned away and was waving the waiter over. "Two glasses—no, make it a bottle of champagne. We're celebrating!"

She turned back to Ben, her lovely face lit up with excitement, and said the one word that nobody had said to him.

"Congratulations."

They were both drunk at half past five when they left, but Mia was the drunker by far. They hugged outside on the pavement, watched by the white marble statues above the gate of the Dáil and the equally impassive doorman on the steps of the Merrion Hotel.

"You look after yourself!" Mia said, thumping his back. "And you look after that gorgeous woman." She staggered a little in her high sandals. "I'm due at Katy's for dinner. She's going to kill me for showing up drunk but I don't care. I'm so happy for you both. So, so, so"— she waved at a cab—"happy!"

She folded herself into the taxi gracefully and turned around and waved at him till it turned the corner onto Merrion Row. She wouldn't tell Katy about the wedding, he told himself.

Phil came home at eight thirty. He'd done a run to Kildare and back and he'd been caught in a summer shower. Raindrops glittered on his leathers and his fringe was damp when he took his helmet off.

"Mia gone already?" he asked.

Katy looked up from her book. "Home. Drunk as a skunk. So," she said, folding her arms, looking annoyed, "when were you planning to tell me the news?"

He kissed the top of her head then went over to the table. "What news?" The frangipani tart that Mia hadn't touched was on a cake stand. He broke a piece off.

"The news about Lara and Ben getting married?"

Phil's hand stopped midway between the plate and his mouth, which was gaping with astonishment.

Katy knew that she herself had probably looked exactly like that when Mia told her. Ben, the most commitment-phobic man on the planet, was getting married. Ben, who had avoided any mention of marriage when they were together. Who had said, when anyone asked, that Katy art-directed "a magazine," carefully omitting the word "wedding" as if saying it out loud might make it happen.

After the news had sunk in, she had probed her emotions carefully, looking for a raw nerve ending. It was not particularly flattering that Ben had avoided marrying her for seven years and then proposed to someone else within nine months, but what had happened between them felt like ancient history. She was happy now; why shouldn't he be happy too?

Phil put the pastry down and sank into the chair by the window. He was staring straight ahead, rubbing his dark hair slowly with the flat of his hand. "Mia told you?"

"She bumped into Ben. He told her." Katy decided not to tell Phil about the boozy lunch. He already thought that Ben was a stoner.

"She must be winding you up," Phil said grimly.

"He showed Mia a ring. You really didn't know? Lara didn't drop any hints?"

"No." Phil's jaw was set.

"Mia did say it was supposed to be a secret," Katy began.

"Really?" he snapped. "Well, remind me never to trust your sister or your ex with *my* secrets."

It was after eleven when the three wedding bouquets were finally finished and Lara blew out the candles, switched off the fairy lights and locked up for the night. It had been raining all evening. The puddled pavement shivered with blue and pink neon from the nightclub across the street.

She had forgotten to text Ben. She hoped he hadn't been watching the clock, waiting for her. She scanned the street for a taxi but there were none so she decided to walk home instead. Every step was an effort. She didn't remember ever feeling this tired, not even when she was pregnant.

At the Bleeding Horse, she had to thread her way through the crowd of drinkers who were milling around on the street. Young people, she thought, then realized that most of them were Ben's age. She would never admit it to him, but she still felt self-conscious when people clocked that they were a couple. Awkward when she was with his friends, especially Diane, who looked at her as if she thought anyone over thirty-five was a candidate for a bus pass. She had almost died of shame the one time she met his mother.

"Nobody would think twice if the age gap were reversed," Ciara had pointed out. That was true, but it didn't make Lara feel any better.

The light was on in the living room. Ben was watching the TV, a beer in his hand. He didn't look up when Lara opened the door.

"Sorry I'm late."

"It's okay." His eyes didn't leave the screen.

"Do you want to come up and have a shower with me?"

He took a gulp of his beer.

"I'll just watch the end of this movie," he said flatly. "I'll be up in a bit."

Poor Ben, she thought, turning on the shower. It wasn't just brides, she thought ruefully as the water finally began to ease the tension in her shoulders. Bridegrooms needed careful handling too. She brushed her teeth and slipped into a cream lace nightdress that Ben had given her on Valentine's Day. As she crossed the landing to the bedroom, she heard the swell of a soundtrack from the TV. The movie was ending. Ben would be up soon.

She must have closed her eyes for a moment, and when she opened them again, her 6 a.m. alarm was ringing and Ben was sleeping beside her, turned away on his side, snoring softly. She slipped out of bed and dressed quickly on the landing so as not to wake him.

Lara forgot about her exhaustion as she made her deliveries. Three very different bouquets for three very different brides, but the pre-wedding chaos at each address was identical. The roar of hairdryers that could not drown out the laughter and chatter of women together. Mothers and aunts crying and hugging one another. Sisters and friends helping one another into their dresses. Brides in Velcro rollers and waffle robes, their faces Kabuki masks of foundation, their eyes blazing with excitement when they saw their bouquets.

Lara disengaged herself from hugs of gratitude, declined several glasses of champagne and dashed back to Blossom & Grow to give Ciara and Becca a hand with the reception and church flowers.

Phil's motorbike was parked outside the shop. That was strange, Lara thought, pulling the van into the space behind it. He wasn't due in this morning, but she could certainly do with an extra pair of hands.

She loaded her arms with the stacked Dutch buckets and the rolls of Bubble Wrap she'd used to keep the flowers steady and went inside. She knew, before Phil turned around, that something was wrong. Saw it in the stiff angle of his shoulders before Ciara gave her a warning eyebrow flash from behind the counter.

"I need to talk to you." He was stony-faced.

"I'll just dump this stuff and put the kettle on." It must be something bad, she thought. Her mind began to race. Was Katy okay? Had one of the couriers been injured?

"It can't wait," he said sharply.

Ciara turned and clattered out into the kitchen.

Lara dropped everything on the floor by the door and went to him, her arms out. "What is it, Phil?"

He put his hand up to block her. "You and Ben, sneaking around behind everybody's backs. I just found out that you're getting married in less than two weeks."

She flushed. This was not how she'd planned to tell her brother.

"Is it true? What Ben told Mia?"

Ben told Mia? she thought, stunned. Why would he do a thing like that? "I'm sorry. I wanted to tell you, but it was complicated with Ben and Katy and everything and I didn't want a big fuss."

"Right." He folded his arms and nodded—a quick jerk of his chin. "Because I'm the sort of man who'd make a big fuss."

"Of course not."

"Maybe I would have made a fuss." His dark eyes, always so warm, were hard. "Told you to think twice about the person you were marrying this time around." His words were like a slap. "I know Ben is a charmer, but I'm not so sure that he's husband material and I don't think you're that sure either or you'd be celebrating this wedding instead of hiding it."

"Sorry." Lara held up her hand. "Did you say I should think about who I'm marrying *this time around*?"

"That was harsh."

The door opened with a soft jingle and a blonde woman in a yellow summer dress stepped in. She took a look at the two of them and then backed out again.

"I have a business to run here," Lara said quietly. "Can you leave now, please?"

"Listen to me." Phil put his hand on her arm. "When Dad was dying, I promised him I'd look after you. How am I supposed to do that if you don't even trust me enough to tell me who you're marrying?"

"You? Look. After. Me?" Lara's voice rose on every word. "I can look after myself!" She pointed at the door. "Get out!"

He strode past her, clattering into a bucket of flowers as he slammed out of the shop.

Water spread across the floor, pooling around the scattered white foxgloves. Lara's hands were shaking as she bent down to pick them up. She didn't know which one of them she was angrier with, her brother or her fiancé.

Lara could hear Ciara talking to customers in the shop below. Voices she recognized asking for her. The bright chirrup of Zoe, in with her father for their usual Saturday bouquet. The deep bass of Charlie the artist, who must have sold another painting.

She stared numbly at the white flowers she had carried up to the worktable—nigella and dahlia, astrantia and viburnum for the table arrangements for a christening party—then she pushed them away and pulled out her phone.

She called Ben for the fifth time, but it went straight to voice mail again. She threw her phone into her bag in frustration. How could he have been so careless? Had he any idea of the trouble he'd caused between her and Phil?

She picked up her jacket. It was no use sitting here going over it in her head. She might as well ask the girls to make up the christening arrangements and go out and get the deliveries done instead.

She calmed down a little as she delivered the bouquets. One to a woman in her forties whose eyes filled with tears when she saw her roses. Sunflowers to a house where one excitable small girl in Dora the Explorer pajamas danced with delight on the doorstep while her sister, in a ladybird sleeping bag, hopped down the hall shouting for their mum.

But her heart sank as she drove into the hospital multi-story. Ciara had insisted on doing all the hospital runs since Lara's father died. She carried a bouquet of delphiniums and lilies up to the third floor and then hurried back down the stairs rather than wait for the lift. When she came out of the stairwell, it was into a department she didn't recognize, and she found herself lost in a maze of corridors that led, eventually, to the door of the ER.

An ambulance was parked right outside, blue lights still whirling, and two men in high-visibility jackets were unloading a body strapped to a gurney as Lara passed by. Something about the shape, cocooned in pale green blankets, made her look back. By then, the ambulancemen were rushing through the doors into the ER, but as they disappeared, Lara saw the sole of a scuffed leather biker boot and, stuck to it, the flattened bell of a white foxglove flower.

And within the space of a single heartbeat, the fire of her anger was extinguished and in its place was an arctic chill of fear.

"Phil!" She shouldered past the ambulancemen and ran alongside the trolley.

Someone tried to pull her away, but she hung on to the metal bar. Phil's eyes were open but out of focus. His skin was the dusty gray of withered lilac, his lips almost blue. A gurgling noise came from under the oxygen mask.

"Phil! It's me. It's okay, I'm here."

A swinging door opened with an electronic beep and the trolley was rushed through. A nurse grabbed Lara's arm.

"You don't understand! He's my brother!" She watched the door swing shut, then let herself be led to the waiting room. Her legs buckled as she sank into the plastic chair.

"Is there someone you can call?" the nurse was saying.

But Lara couldn't hear her; she was talking to God in her head. *I'll do anything*, she was telling him. *I'll give up everything I love. Blossom & Grow. Ben. Just don't let Phil die.*

What was the big deal? Ben thought, digging the small plastic bag out of the bottom of his jacket pocket. He used to do this all the time when Katy thought he was working on his book. Have a joint with his morning coffee, go for breakfast in Bewley's, then stroll across town to Cineworld on Parnell Street. He took a Rizla and glued it onto another one, then began to rub one of the cigarettes between his fingers. It was stale but it would do the trick. He'd show Lara that she wasn't the only one who could play at being unavailable. He deliberately left his phone behind so that if she called she'd get the message.

An hour later he was settling himself in the velvety dark of the cinema. He watched two movies back-to-back. When he emerged into the bright late-afternoon sunshine, he felt queasy. He was dreading telling Lara that he'd told Mia about the wedding. She was going to be livid but she was the one who had insisted on keeping the whole thing secret in the first place. Ashamed, probably, of what her bloody brother would think.

His anger built as he crossed the Ha'penny Bridge and walked along Dame Street. By the time he got to Camden Street, he had convinced himself that it was Lara who should be apologizing to him. But when he tried to open the door of the shop, he found it was locked. He banged on the door and peered through the glass. It wasn't even five o'clock and Lara never closed before six thirty on Saturdays. What was going on?

He hailed a cab and went back to Lara's place. That was empty too. He took the stairs two at a time, knowing in some deep part of him that none of this was good. He grabbed his phone from the bedside table and saw the text messages flashing on his screen. They were all from Mia.

Ben, bad news! Call me!

Phil's had an accident. Not sure how bad. Lara's at St Fintan's. On way with Katy. Call when you get this.

Ben?!!!? Where the hell are you????

"It's my fault." Katy clutched Lara's hand and stared at her, wild-eyed. "We had a fight last night. Our first fight. I stormed off to bed and left him to sleep on the sofa. He was upset with me, Lara. That's why this happened."

"No," Lara said quietly, remembering the look on Phil's face when she'd told him to get out. The bucket he'd knocked over as he slammed out of the shop. "It's my fault."

When the doctor came through the swinging doors, they all stood up. Lara and Katy, Mia and Ronan and Ciara and her boyfriend, like children, Katy thought sadly, in a classroom when the teacher arrived.

The doctor checked his chart. "Which one of you is Phil Kiely's next of kin?"

Lara took Katy's hand and they both stepped forward, looking like two terrified little girls.

Katy was having trouble understanding the words but she could tell from the doctor's face, from the urgency of his voice, that Phil was in a bad way. He had six broken ribs. There were four fractures to his pelvis and both his legs were broken too. But the real danger was the collapsed lungs.

There were all sorts of complications they would have to get around, the doctor explained, but until they drained his pleural cavity and repaired his lungs, nothing was clear. "If we can stabilize him tonight," he said, "there's a possibility we can do that surgery tomorrow."

"And if you can't?" Lara whispered.

The doctor pressed his lips together. "Let's cross that bridge if we come to it."

"Wait." Katy put a shaking hand on his arm. "What are his chances?"

The doctor looked down at her hand. "Without the surgery, not good. With it, I can't really say . . ."

"You have to!" Katy plucked at his sleeve. "You have to say! I won't hold you to it, I promise, but I need to know. Does he have an eight percent chance? A fifty percent chance? Tell me!" Lara tried to pull her hand away. But she had seen the look on the doctor's face. "It's less than that, isn't it?" she whispered.

Mia and Ronan were standing in the corridor outside the waiting room of the ER.

Beyond them, Ben registered a row of chairs, a line of worried faces, Lara at the very end, between Ciara and Katy, looking paler than he'd ever seen her.

"Jesus, Ben!" Mia shook her heard. "Where the hell have you been?"

"I got here as soon as I could. How is Phil doing?" he whispered.

"It's touch and go." Mia's eyes glittered with tears and annoyance and Ronan put his arm around her. "Go and talk to Lara. She needs you."

But Lara barely seemed to see Ben. She stood up to let him hug her and it felt as if she was made of wood.

"Lara," he said, conscious of Katy only a few feet away. "I'm sorry I didn't get here earlier. Will he be okay?"

"We don't know," she whispered. She stepped back and slid shakily into her chair and took Katy's hand. "We have to wait."

"Katy." Ben bent down and put his hand on her shoulder. "Do you need anything? Is there anything I can do?" She closed her eyes and shook her head. He wondered if she could smell the dope smoke on his breath.

Lara was right. All they could do was wait. Two long days before Phil was strong enough for the surgery. Eight nail-biting hours while a team of three surgeons operated on him.

Afterward, Katy and Lara were allowed to go in to see him for a couple of minutes. Phil was unconscious. His head was bandaged and his face was black with bruises. A thick raised line of stitches ran down his jaw. Both of his legs were in traction. There was a cage over his chest and his mouth was covered with a mask connected to the machine that was breathing for him.

He had been put into an induced coma to give his lungs time to heal, and it could be another week before he could safely be brought around. The trauma to his head had been minimal but there was still a chance of brain damage. He had survived, he was alive, but the waiting wasn't over yet.

"Dad! Dad!" Phil thrashed around in the thumping red-black darkness. "Daaaaad!"

When he was five, he used to point his bike down the steep hill outside the house, stand on the frame and let go. He'd shoot down and at the last minute lock the back wheel with his foot to stop. How many times had his dad come running down that hill to pick him up and patch him up? Why wasn't he coming now?

The hospital was a parallel universe, Ben thought—a world of fear and uncertainty that made the intensive care units in TV dramas look like a walk in the park—and Lara was lost in it.

All he wanted was to be useful in some small way, but she didn't need anything from him. The few occasions when he managed to persuade her to go home to get some rest, she spent most of the time on the phone whispering to Katy. At the hospital, the two women were inseparable. They huddled together, their dark heads touching, comforting one another, swapping little shreds of hope, shutting everyone else out. Even him; especially him. Whenever he did manage to get close to Lara, Katy was always there, her eyes watchful, suspicious. Ben felt as if he was playing the part of the supportive partner rather than actually being it, as if his concern for Lara was fake. As the days dragged on, and the date of the wedding drew closer, he felt her slipping farther and farther away from him.

Four days after the accident, he came into the waiting room and saw Katy and Lara holding on to one another. He knew, from their faces, that the news was good. The consultant had just done his rounds. He was pleased with Phil's progress. He was going to start reducing the sedation with a view to bringing him out of the coma over the next few days.

Lara smiled up at Ben and for the first time since the accident, he felt as if she could actually see him. "I'm so relieved," she gasped. "I'm so happy I could . . . I don't know what I could do."

Could you get away from here for half an hour so we can talk about the wedding? he wanted to ask her. The wedding was the elephant in the waiting room. It was Wednesday. They were getting married next Monday, but Lara hadn't mentioned this once since the accident. Nobody else had mentioned it either, though Ben suspected that they all knew.

But Katy was listening and he guessed that Lara would not want to leave the hospital, so instead he asked, "Could you eat something?" She had been surviving on coffee all week.

"I don't know. Maybe."

"I'll go across the road and get you a sandwich."

On his way back from the café, he passed a bookshop. He went in and picked up a guidebook for Crete. It might be too soon to bring the wedding up, but at least he could remind her that this would be over soon and that they'd be on their honeymoon.

Lara took the sandwich he handed her, then slid the book out of the bag. She stared at the white church on the blue cover.

"Oh!" she said, turning to look at him. "Oh, Ben, I'm sorry. I thought you realized, we can't go ahead with the wedding."

Ben's heart sank. "What do you mean?"

Katy, sitting in the next chair, was fiddling with the wrapper on the sandwich he'd brought her, pretending not to listen.

"We have to put it off," Lara said.

"I don't understand." He lowered his voice. "You said the consultant was pleased with Phil's progress."

"But he's not out of the woods yet. And when he is, he'll need me."

What about me? Ben thought. I need you too. He stood up quickly, wanting to get away before his feelings showed in his face.

"Okay, I'll go and give the registry office a call."

"Thanks." She lifted her hand to take his, but he pretended that he hadn't seen it. He had to get out before he was humiliated any more by the woman he loved in front of the woman who used to love him.

What could Lara give Phil? she wondered. Flowers were not allowed in the ICU but she wanted him to have something, so she dug out her dad's watch. An old Timex with a brown leather strap that had started to split. The face was the color of milky coffee. The date slowly changed in a tiny window. She would put it on his wrist when they brought him safely out of the coma. She would do anything, she reminded God, to make that happen. To give her brother time.

Phil was pulling a rickshaw through the cobbled streets in thick fog, trying to find his way back to Katy. He could hear her voice ahead of him sometimes, but he could never quite catch up with her. Then he was flat on his back, pinned down by a heavy animal that was lying on his chest. He couldn't open his eyes, but when he put his hand up, he felt Pat's ears, soft and velvety between his fingertips. But Pat was dead. Did that mean he was dead too?

Phil was still unconscious but now his eyelids flickered as if he was dreaming. Lara and Katy were allowed to see him for a few minutes on Thursday and when Lara arrived on Friday, Katy was already sitting by the bed, holding his hand.

"I think he can hear me," she whispered.

There was a muffled groan.

"Phil!" Katy took Lara's hand and put it on top of their joined ones. "We're here. Don't be scared. You're okay, it's just a couple of broken bones!"

Lara flashed her a look of amazement. Dozens of broken bones. Phil would have to have at least two more surgeries and it would be months before he would be back on his feet again.

Phil's hand twitched twice and then he sighed. "Wait!" Katy gripped his fingers. "Don't go back to sleep yet. Say something, anything, just so we know you can hear us."

He took a long, shuddering breath and grunted two words.

Katy turned to Lara. "I didn't understand him. What did he say?"

Lara lifted their three hands and grinned. "He said, 'Hand sandwich.'"

Lara and Katy were hugging one another again when Ben arrived at the door of Phil's room with a coffee for Lara. He watched through the window as they broke apart and started to laugh, then hugged one another again. When was the last time Lara had laughed like that with him? Something flipped.

He turned and walked quickly back down the corridor and took the lift down to the cafeteria. The doors opened onto a concrete wheel-chair ramp and a sunlit square of grass. He bummed a cigarette from a guy in scrubs, then found a quiet spot between two trees and rolled the last tiny nub of dope into a skinny joint.

He closed his eyes and held the sweet smoke deep in his lungs until a fog rolled in over his frantic feelings, then he went back inside and waited for Lara. He was still sitting in a corner of the cafeteria with the cold, bitter coffee in front of him when she found him.

"I was wondering where you were." She sat down opposite him. "I was hoping you'd come up to the ward."

"I came." He didn't look up. He was making an origami bird from a till receipt. "But I felt like I was kind of superfluous to requirements."

"I know what you mean," Lara said. "I worry that I might be in the way when I'm in there with Katy. But I'm glad I was there just now. He said two words, Ben! Isn't that amazing?"

Ben nodded. He ran his nail along a crease in the little square of paper. "Listen," he said. "I've been thinking about the wedding. I don't think we should postpone it."

"What? But I thought you were going to call the registry office—"

Ben cut her off. "I did. Now I think we should cancel it altogether."

"What do you mean?"

Ben looked up. She was staring at him, her expression unreadable.

"That it was a mistake to rush into this." He looked down at his hands, made another paper fold. "Maybe the whole thing was a mistake."

He waited for her to contradict him, to protest, to tell him he was crazy, that they loved one another, that she loved him, but she didn't say a word.

Lara could hardly believe what Ben had said. Her mind flashed back to the last week. She had been so frightened that Phil was going to die that she hadn't been fully present, hadn't seen what she suddenly saw now. That Ben had been attentive at the beginning, then a bit distant, then absent. Slipping away from her a little more every day. She had looked away, and when she looked back, she had lost him. She wanted to reach across the table and take his hands, but his hands were busy with the little paper bird and his eyes were flat and expressionless.

"Are you sure about this?"

That was it? Ben thought dully. He told her they should end their relationship and that was her response. No fight, nothing?

"Absolutely!" he said, hurt, wanting to hurt her back. "I've had doubts about it for a while, to be honest." He had doubted that Lara really wanted to marry him. "I know you have too."

She felt the heat of tears behind her eyes and blinked them away. "I just worried about the age difference." She had doubted that it mattered as little to Ben as he'd claimed but she had been willing to marry him anyway.

"You were right. I should have listened to you."

He wouldn't even look at her. He was busy finishing his origami bird. She watched him pull the tail, but only one wing flapped. It was broken.

He had known it all along, Ben thought triumphantly. She had never really wanted to marry him. Then the sadness hit him and all he wanted to do was take back what he had said. To go back to the night outside the graveyard when she'd said yes.

He looked up at her bent head, the curve of her cheek, the waves of her dark hair around her pale face. He was afraid that he was going to reach over and touch her, make more of a fool of himself than he already had.

He crushed the bird in his fist and stood up.

Lara put her hand out to stop him, to pull him down beside her, so they could talk, hold one another, try to salvage this. Then she remembered the deal she'd made with God the day of the accident. She'd said she'd give up everything she loved if Phil lived, even Ben.

Ben took her hand and looked at it. So many flowers had passed through Lara's fingers and all that beauty had left its mark. Her skin was chapped, her nails were thin, there were thorn scratches on her wrists and bumps on her fingers from all the hours she spent working with scissors.

He had loved all of her, but what he'd loved best were her hands.

"Good-bye, Lara," he said, and then he walked away.

Phil rose up through a blur of watercolors. Sunlight from behind a green curtain. His legs, for some reason, floating before him. The fuzzy outline of a person leaning over him. A woman? Sounds. People chattering from another room, the slam and clang of a trolley, the steady hum of a motor. Slowly it all began to swim into focus. He was in a hospital room. A nurse was elevating the bed he was lying in. He tried to lean up on his arm but it was too heavy to move. His breath was shallow, as if there was a ton weight on his chest.

"What day is it?" he groaned.

The nurse smiled. "It's Saturday." She pumped up the blood pressure cuff she had attached to his arm. "Day seven," she said in a Newcastle accent. "In the Big Brother house, or St. Fintan's University Hospital, as it's commonly known!" She let air out of the cuff with a hiss.

He licked his cracked lips. "Remind me what I'm doing here?"

"You and your motorbike had an argument with a bridge a week ago." She took the cuff off and stuck a thermometer into his ear. The sharp beep made him jump and a searing pain tore through his pelvis.

She frowned down at his face. "Pain?" He managed to nod. "I'll get you something for that."

He closed his eyes, tried to steady his breathing. *Last Saturday.* He and Lara had had a row and then he'd stormed out of the shop. He'd been too angry to go home. He'd gone for a burn on the bike. He remembered flashing past the gate to the graveyard where his parents were buried. He'd thought about pulling over.

He went there sometimes to have a one-sided conversation with his dad and to look at that view. It was the closest place you could get to heaven while you were still standing on Dublin soil. On a sunny day, there was no line between the wide, flat sea and the vast sky. The red and blue container ships and ferries coming out of Dublin port seemed to float suspended on air. Sunlight burnished the steel jumble of the docks and turned the glass office blocks of the distant city gold.

But that day, he didn't stop. He was trying to get away from his guilty conscience but it had caught up with him by the time he got to Howth. What had come over him? He had been obnoxious to Katy, then he'd had a go at his sister. All he had to do was decide which one of them to apologize to first.

He rode straight through the village over the summit and down onto the sea road, had to stop himself from breaking the speed limit in his rush to get back into town.

The journey was a blur. The last thing he remembered was pulling away from a red light along the Ranelagh Road. Then there was a blank. As if his mind had been full, like a memory card, and there was no room left for what happened next.

The nurse was back. He felt the pinch of the needle as she found a vein, then his eyes closed. It seemed like a few seconds later that he opened them and, floating up on a cloud of morphine, he saw his sister at the door with an armful of wildflowers.

"Flowers?" he croaked. "Am I on the way out?"

"They're not for you." She grinned. "You're not allowed to have flowers. They're for Katy."

Same old Lara, he thought, still looking after everyone else.

"It's so good to see you! I want to hug you!" She had tears in her eyes now. "But I'm afraid I'll hurt you."

"Hold my hand," he said. "It seems to be the only part of me that isn't broken.

"Listen," he said, after a while. "What I said about you and Ben getting married. I was way out of line."

"It doesn't matter."

"I should have been happy for you and I wasn't. I was a tosser. Not just that day, the whole time. I never gave the poor bloke a chance. But now that we're going to be related"—he squeezed her fingers—"I'll do lots of manly bonding shit with him. Snooker. Fishing. Golf."

She shook her head.

"Maybe not golf." He smiled. "I hate golf. I only played it to keep Dad company."

"We're not getting married," Lara said quietly. "Ben broke up with me."

"The two of you must have had a week from hell with me in here. He's probably just having a wobble."

"His things were gone when I got back to Dad's last night."

"Shit!"

"It's probably just as well. It was a bad idea all along." She sounded as if she was trying to convince herself as much as him. "I got carried away. I told myself that the age difference didn't matter, but of course it does. At least it does to him."

"Maybe getting married is too much pressure. Maybe you should just go on as you were."

"Ben doesn't want to. And if I was ten years younger or he was ten years older, I'd probably try to change his mind. But I can't." She turned away, hiding her face behind the dark curtain of her hair. "I've done it again, Phil. Let myself believe that something was right because I wanted it so badly. How could I have been so stupid? I even booked our honeymoon to Crete. To that place Mum and Dad went after they got married."

"Oh, Lara. I'm sorry." Phil wished he wasn't tied to the bed with tubes so he could reach his sister to comfort her.

"Don't be," she said. "It's better this way. I'd rather know he has doubts now than wait eight years to find out."

He couldn't argue with that. The door swung open and Katy stood there, her eyes blazing with happiness.

"They told me you were awake."

Phil faked a yawn. "I was but I got tired waiting for my wife to arrive. So I'm going back to sleep now."

"Don't you dare!" She half ran to the bed and bent over him, her hair falling around his face.

"You can kiss me," he said softly. "I don't care if it hurts."

"I'll kiss you on one condition," she whispered. "That you never leave me like that again."

Lara made up a story about needing breakfast so she could leave them together. She went down to the hospital canteen. She should be making last-minute preparations for her wedding in two days, she thought, poking at a plate of dried-up scrambled egg; she should be packing for her honeymoon. That future without Ben stretched ahead of her bleak and empty, starting with the week that she should have spent with him in Crete. She couldn't face going back to the shop yet. She had no idea what she was going to do with that time. But Phil did.

"Lara," he said the next morning, when she came into his room. "Will you do something for me?"

"Anything," she said.

"Swear on my life that you'll do it?"

"That's not funny, Phil."

"I'm serious."

"Okay," she sighed, sinking into the chair by the bed. "I swear."

"Will you go away?"

"What?"

"Will you take that week in Crete?"

Her dark eyes widened. "Go on my honeymoon on my own? You're joking."

"Look, if you stay here, you'll just be haunting the hospital." Or sitting in their dad's house staring into space, Phil thought, slipping into depression, the way she had two years ago. He couldn't let her go back to that dark place, not when he wasn't in the whole of his health, able to pull her out again.

"I can't go away, Phil. You're down to have surgery on your pelvis."

"Katy will look after me. And she'll be able to if you're not here to get in her way."

"I'm not getting in her way, am I?"

He hardened his heart against the hurt in her eyes; he had to make her do this, no matter what it took. "I know you don't mean to. But it's hard for her to take the lead with my big sister around. We need time together now, me and Katy. Just the two of us."

"I know."

"You swore on my life that you'd do anything for me. Well, this is it, Lara. This is anything."

Lara spent the day of her wedding working at Blossom & Grow. She couldn't face the customers so she scrubbed out the cold room, conditioned the flowers, checked the stock to make sure that nothing would run low while she was away. Ciara dropped her home and stayed for a few hours, cooked a meal that neither of them ate, opened a bottle of wine and then another one.

After she left, Lara went upstairs to pack a case. The drawer in the bedroom where Ben had kept his clothes was empty. There was a question mark of brown hair caught on the duvet. The ghost of a heart shape he'd once drawn in the condensation on the bathroom mirror.

Where was he now? she wondered. What was he doing on their wedding night? The wine she'd drunk with Ciara had softened her resolve. She could just send one text, couldn't she? Just to tell him that she was going to Crete, to leave the door open in case there was any way they could ever make things work again.

* * *

Ben was in the men's room in Doheny & Nesbitt's pub. If he walked outside and threw a stone, he could hit the Merrion Hotel, where he should be right now with Lara. He went over to the sink and leaned his forehead against the mirror. He wondered where she was tonight. Probably in the hospital with Katy, he thought. Comparing notes on what a waster he was.

Ben's phone buzzed on the bar. Diane put her drink down and picked it up. A text, from Lara. She looked over her shoulder, then opened the message. She read it quickly and, with another quick glance over her shoulder, deleted it.

Lara had made Ben just as miserable as Katy had. Diane ordered another round and waited for him to come back and realize that *she* was the one he'd really wanted all along.

Ben didn't text back. He didn't call. Lara lay awake with the phone in her hand all night, waiting. She was still waiting when the taxi arrived to bring her to the airport the next morning. It was only when she was sitting in her seat on the plane and the air hostess asked everyone to switch their phones to flight mode that she realized that he wasn't going to call, and she finally let go.

She slept all the way to Crete. She slept again in the cab from Chania Airport to the south of the island, only opening her eyes after two hours as the driver slowed to take the hairpin bends down the hill into the small port. Sugar-cube houses spilled down the last slope toward the sea. A full moon floated above the inky water; the air from the gardens they passed smelled of gardenias and jasmine.

She slept as soon as she put her head on the pillow of the small white hotel room. When she opened the creaky blue shutters the following morning, brilliant sunlight fell in through the window and the hum of the bees on the vines below filled the room. The sea was every color of delphinium and larkspur. The smell of food drifted up from the small restaurant below her balcony. Bacon, fresh bread, coffee, cinnamon. All she wanted was to feel Ben's arms sliding around her waist. To sit with him under the white awning below her window and eat breakfast. But she couldn't have that. So she forced herself to gather her things and go downstairs and eat alone.

She almost missed the ferry scheduled to leave at 10:30 a.m. She got confused trying to find the cubicle that sold tickets and had to run down the slipway, bumping her carry-on case along behind her. Twenty minutes later, she dragged it off again in a village called Chora that was hardly a village at all, just a couple of dozen whitewashed buildings and a narrow shingle beach. She couldn't bear to stay in the hotel she had booked for the honeymoon so she had picked the most remote place she could find out of the guidebook Ben had given her.

She walked the length of the village twice, looking for a sign that read "Room for Rent," then, tired and hungry again, she ducked out of the sun and sat under the awning of a café and ordered a second breakfast.

The man who served her had murderous eyes and a bushy black beard with a pen stuck through it.

"Do you have rooms?" Lara asked him.

"No," he said contemptuously, as if any inquiry about rooms from a tourist was the stupidest thing he had ever heard.

But as she paid her bill, he picked up her case without asking her, slung it over his shoulder and took off, giving Lara no choice except to follow him. He set off down a narrow alley that led to a winding backstreet. They passed a mini market and a walled church with a huge palm tree and climbed some shallow whitewashed steps scattered with the litter of bougainvillea blossoms.

He stopped at the gate of a small garden. Lara saw lilies and carnations, a terrace covered over with a tangle of vines and jasmine and a vegetable garden with neat rows of tomato plants, zucchini and herbs. An old woman was sitting in the shade crocheting. Her silver hair had been plaited and wound around her head like a garland. A kitten was tumbling in the dust beneath her chair.

The bearded man spoke to her in a rapid babble of Greek, then dumped Lara's suitcase unceremoniously on the terrace. "Stavroula." He pointed at the woman. "Rooms!" Then he turned on his heel and marched away.

The old lady put her crocheting aside and stood up, pushing her swollen feet into shoes with the backs worn down and shuffling into the house. Lara dragged her case inside into the cool dark. Stavroula nodded several times, pointed up the stairs and took a key on a white ribbon from a hook on the wall.

Lara climbed the marble steps to a narrow room with a single bed and one window that opened onto a handkerchief-sized flat roof backing onto a dusty hill dotted with olive trees. She closed the shutters, climbed into bed and slept again.

She was woken every morning by goat bells. She allowed herself to check her phone just once a day, before breakfast. Ciara fired through an occasional reassuring update about the shop, but she skimmed over these, concentrating instead on Katy's messages about Phil. He was improving every day. He had started reading the newspaper; he had asked her to smuggle in a roast chicken sandwich. The consultant had confirmed that the operation on his pelvis would go ahead on Monday. There was nothing from Ben.

No matter how early Lara woke, Stavroula was always awake before her. She came down every morning to find breakfast laid out on the wooden table under the vines. Yogurt with a pot of honey or a peach. Boiled eggs and a thick slice of bread. Coffee.

While she ate, Lara soaked up the peace of the garden. Bees buzzing in and out of bean flowers, a kingfisher skimming in low over the sea, the sound of the old lady counting the stitches under her breath as she bent over her crochet hook.

One morning, Lara found a small, rusty metal palette of paints and a dog-eared watercolor pad on the table waiting for her when she came down to breakfast.

"For me?" she asked Stavroula.

The old woman shook her head. "*Ne.*" Although it seemed like "no," Lara had learned that this meant "yes" in Greek.

It was years since she had drawn anything other than designs for flower arrangements. She made quick sketches of the flowers in the garden, then more detailed ones, mixing colors on an old cracked plate that Stavroula brought her, trying and nearly making the exact shade of magenta for the bougainvillea.

After breakfast, she walked to the beach along high dusty goat trails, tiny blue butterflies flickering in the sage and thyme flowers she brushed with her boots. By the time she laid a sarong she'd bought at the mini market under a feathery tamarisk tree and tied her lunchtime picnic in a plastic bag to a high branch out of the reach of goats, she was ready to sleep again.

She dreamed that Ben was lying beside her. She could see his face a few inches from hers, his green eyes watching her, the sunshine picking out sparks of copper on his stubbled chin, but when she reached out to put her hand on his shoulder, she woke up. It all seemed unreal now. Ben, the year they'd had together, the life they'd planned. Sometimes she wondered if she had dreamed the whole thing.

At night, the small taverna in the village was crowded with tourists, so Lara sat with Stavroula watching the moths dancing around the bare bulb by the gate and the fireflies around the jasmine.

Sometimes, on the walk back from the beach, she took a fork in the goat track and climbed up the hill to the tiny whitewashed chapel. Cicadas rattled like a thousand sets of tiny maracas as she walked around to the back to look at the tangle of passionflower that grew from the window above the altar. She picked one and carried it home to put in the water glass next to her bed.

The peeling wooden door of the church was closed with a double length of rope attached to a nail. One day she went inside. The floor was littered with goat droppings. A cardboard box of candles sat beneath a crooked brass candelabra. Red and gold icons gleamed from the painted panels in front of the altar.

She closed her eyes and let the memories she'd locked away pour back. The sound of Ben's footsteps hurrying up the wooden stairs to the workroom. The moonlit night he'd held her in the cemetery and turned her around to see the view, telling her it was a gift from her mother. A glimpse of him in the garden, his T-shirt sticking to his back with sweat as he dug a hole for the water feature. The look in his green eyes the day he'd kissed her by the canal. The first time she'd seen him, in a very different chapel, in a different place, a year ago.

On her last night at Stavroula's, Lara gave her landlady a jar of fig jam, a tin of fancy biscuits that the mini market owner had unearthed from somewhere and the sketchbook filled with paintings. The old lady's rheumy eyes were serious as she turned the pages, examining every picture.

"*Galfallo*," she said, pointing at a painting of red flowers.

"We call them 'carnations.'" Lara smiled.

The arthritic fingers turned another page.

Stavroula looked down at the blossoms that were not really blossoms at all but clusters of magenta leaves around the pinhead-sized flowers. "*Boukamillia*."

"Bougainvillea." Lara nodded.

"When?" Stavroula looked up at Lara.

"When am I going? Tomorrow." Lara had decided to take the bus up the coast to hike a gorge her father and mother had visited on their honeymoon. She would spend the last night at a hotel near the airport. "Tuesday. Chania!" she said, hoping the woman understood.

"*Ochi!*" The old lady nodded, which meant "no." "When?" She pointed at Lara and then patted her own stomach.

Lara shook her head, embarrassed. "No, I'm not pregnant—"

"*Ne!*" the woman insisted. Which meant "yes."

Suddenly Lara froze. She looked up at the vast frozen firework of the Milky Way above the vines. I couldn't be, she thought, could I?

The old lady turned the page again and pointed down at the last painting, a watercolor of a lily growing in a green and gold olive oil tin. "*Krinos*," she said.

Lara looked at it, her eyes widening, her hand going to her own stomach. "Lily!" she whispered.

Phil swam up to consciousness after the anesthetic. It seemed like only a moment ago that he was lying on the operating table and the surgeon was asking him to count backward from ten, but now he was back in his bed, trussed up to his pulleys again, connected to a new set of tubes. Moonlight was flooding in through the window of his room.

There was someone standing near the end of his bed. He thought it was the old man from the end of the ward, who was allowed to use the bathroom instead of a cardboard bedpan. Sometimes he hobbled past the door on his crutches, Phil guessed, just for the thrill of it.

But as the man moved closer to the bed and into the light from the window, Phil saw his face.

"Jesus!" he said.

"You're the one who looks like Jesus!" his father said. "You let them wash you and dress you and cut up your food. Could you not let them shave you while they're at it?"

Dad, Phil thought, but he held the word at the back of his throat, afraid that if he said it out loud, he would cry and wake himself up.

His dad snorted with frustration. "I knew this was where that bloody bike would take you in the end! You're like a turkey trussed up for Christmas."

Phil knew it was just the drugs they'd given him for the surgery. But bloody hell, they were pretty good. It was as if his father was actually there.

He was wearing a golf jumper he had loved. Dark red, with the Slazenger logo, a tiny springing puma, appliquéd on the chest. He was clean-shaven and his gray hair was neatly cut. The tiny scar the size of a match head at the side of his right eyebrow, where he'd had a mole removed, stood out against his tanned skin.

"Philip"—his dad shook his head—"you plonker. You were going way too fast."

"Was I?" Phil stammered, finding his voice. "I can't remember."

His father sat on the side of the bed. "Forty miles an hour on the Ranelagh Road. In a thirty-mile-an-hour zone. You'd no time to react."

"To what?"

"To that bloody election poster that blew into the road."

Phil saw it suddenly, clearly. The lightweight board lifted by an updraft from a passing car. It had come slicing at him from the left. Some part of his brain had confused the printed face for a real one and he'd braked abruptly, spooked.

The rest came back in a rush of broken flashbacks. He'd pulled sharply to the right. Swerved across into the other lane. The bike had slammed into the curb, spun ninety degrees and tossed him into the air like a toy. He had been almost weightless for a few seconds as his body somersaulted once, twice, three times, then he'd slammed down on his side on the tarmac, a few inches from the curb. If he'd landed on his back, he would have broken his spine.

"You'd be dead," his dad said as if he could read his mind. "And you and me would be having a whole other conversation."

A lump of emotion caught in Phil's throat. "Dad, I know you're just a hallucination, but it's so good to see you."

"Philip!" His dad leaned over him, his eyes glinting with irritation. "If I'm not really here, then kindly refer to me as *an* hallucination, not *a* hallucination."

This was his dad all right: the same person who rang supermarket managers to tell them that the sign at the checkout that said "Ten items or less" should read "Ten items or fewer."

"Jesus, Dad." Phil gripped the rail of the bed, trying not to laugh. He had a feeling that laughing would hurt a lot. "Only you," he gasped, "would come back from the afterlife just to give me a grammar lesson."

"Somebody has to do it," his dad said gruffly. "Well." He stood up. "I'd better go before we wake the hospital."

Phil wanted to lift his arm, to catch his father by the sleeve, to keep him by the bed, the way he had when he was a child and it was time to turn the lights off. "Dad, are you okay? Are you happy?"

"Stop worrying about me," his dad said. "And stop worrying about your sister while you're at it. We can look after ourselves."

"Lara's in Crete," Phil said. "On her own."

"She's not on her own," his dad said, looking very pleased with himself. "She has Lily."

Lily? A wave of exhaustion washed over Phil, pulling him under. He looked up into his father's eyes and saw, past the love, the pain of loss, the ache of longing. They miss us, he thought, the dead. They miss us as much as we miss them.

"Love you, Dad," he mumbled.

His father cleared his throat. "*Agapi mou*," he said.

He touched the fading bruise on Philip's cheek. "That's Greek," he whispered, "for 'I love you,'" but his son was already asleep.

Lara got out at a dusty bend in the road. The driver pointed at a jumble of boulders clinging somehow to the steep slope that fell away from the road and shrugged. The bus rattled off in a hot breath of dust and diesel fumes. She put on her hat and looked for the first waymark: a pile of stones a foot high that marked the path leading down into the deep, high cleft.

There was a sign—well, what was left of a sign. A metal rectangle pockmarked with bullet holes bearing one word just about legible: "*Dragula*." Lara had loved the name when she was a child. The story of the wild, deserted beach her parents had found at the end of their honeymoon on a long hike through the gorge.

A herd of slant-eyed goats perched on ledges on the sheer rock face watched as she picked her way carefully down the winding track. She was soaked with sweat by the time she reached the bottom. She rested gratefully in the shade, ate some bread and an apple, refilled her water bottle at the small stone trough, then began the long walk beneath the oleander trees that followed the line of an invisible underground stream the same way she was following the invisible footsteps of her parents, who had walked here forty-two years ago.

The canopy of trees ran out and for the last kilometer she walked in full sunshine. It was midday, and heat hammered down on the crown of her head through her hat. She trudged on, too hot even to stop for a drink of water. Finally the walls of the cliff opened up and she was on the long, dramatic deserted beach. Beyond the stretch of shingle, the sea was breathtaking: crystalline, aquamarine, feathered with whitecaps.

She unlaced her walking boots and threw off her backpack and waded out into the glittering water in her shorts and T-shirt. Bubbles of colder water escaping through the rock into the sea from the underground stream fizzed up between her feet as she ducked under the surface.

She floated on her back, looking up at the sheer red and gray cliffs and the huge tent of blue sky above. A bright pink flower bobbed up beside her, followed by another. Two bougainvillea blossoms that she had tucked into her pocket in Stavroula's garden.

"We swam in the sea and we lay in the sun," her dad used to tell her. "Me and your mother. We were like Adam and Eve. The only two people in the world. Except there were three of us! You were there too, we just didn't know it yet."

Lara watched the two blossoms drift away, and said a prayer to the sea and the sky that Stavroula was right. That she really was pregnant and that this time her baby would make it. And that she—she had a feeling that this was a she, this child she might be carrying—would come back to this place someday, like Lara herself had.

She waded back onto the shingle beach and lay out in the sun till her clothes had dried, then she put on her boots and began the long journey home to Blossom & Grow.

Acknowledgments

Thank you so much.

To my wonderful agent, the one and only Mr. Jonathan Lloyd. And to Lucia Rae, Melissa Pimentel, Alice Lutyens and all the team at Curtis Brown.

To my lovely American editor, Julie Mianecki, and all the team at Penguin Random House.

To fabulous fellow writers Marian Keyes, Cathy Kelly and Kate Kerrigan for all their kindness and encouragement. For reading early drafts and for being there for me every step of the way.

To Helen Falconer, who helped me to see the wood for the trees.

To my friends and family for their support. Especially Susan McNulty, Wendy Williams, Frances, Bernard, Mimmi and Mel Griffin.

To my favorite florists who shared their secrets and their stories with me. Bronagh Harte at Ginkgo, Ruth Monahan at Appassionata, Eilis Gaughan at the Garden in Powerscourt Townhouse. And Jill Whyte, whose heartbreaking tale of the guitar-shaped wreath appears in this book.

To Mags McLoughlin, Trevor Harte, Orlagh Daly, Cathal O'Flaherty, Brian Toolan, Helen Seymour, Bernice Barrington and Doug Lee for all their help along the way. To Una Hand, whose beautiful wedding proposal story I have borrowed.

And to my husband, Neil Cubley, who deserves a medal for the hours he spent reading, editing, guiding and coaching me. And a halo for pep talks, dog walks and all-around saintliness. Who has filled my house and my heart with so many flowers. And who does to me what spring does to cherry trees.

The *Flower* Arrangement

READERS GUIDE

Discussion Questions

1. Flowers are part of every significant moment in our lives. Of every birth and wedding. Every joyful celebration and heartbreaking funeral. They can shout out our happiness or speak our sympathy softly. Seduce a lover or comfort a friend. Express feelings we cannot put into words. Why do you think that is?

2. Every story begins with a flower or plant. Ivy for tenacity. Daffodil for new beginnings. Pansy for remembrance. Did the flower meanings add to the stories for you?

3. Lara lost her mother when she was a child and then loses the baby she longed for. How do you think her losses shaped her as a character?

4. Lara is intuitive about flowers and people. She seems to understand exactly what every customer needs. Why then is she so blind to her own needs? Do you get the sense that she is using her work to hide from the sadness of her life?

5. Discuss Michael. Why do you think he married Lara? Do you think he ever really loved her? Was it selfish or selfless of him to try to make the marriage work?

6. The book deals with loss and grief. Did you feel that the author was writing from her own experience? Did any of the stories bring up a loss you have suffered in your life?

7. Lara's family, friends and customers all play a part in the book. They are a mixed bunch. What do you think of the way their stories are interwoven?

8. Were you surprised that the woman who was visiting Ted was his wife, Margaret? Do you think she was real? Or a hallucination caused by the morphine he was taking?

9. Katy is ready to start a family with Ben even though she realizes that they are more like flatmates than soul mates. Why do you think she has stayed so long in the relationship when he seems so unwilling to take it to the next level?

10. Mia has a very clear idea of the kind of man she is looking for, but she ends up falling for his complete opposite. Do you think that's true to life? Do we really have a choice about the people we fall in love with?

11. Lara struggles with the fact that she is ten years older than Ben. Do you think it would worry her if the age gap was the other way around? Why do we still have a problem with older women dating younger men?

12. Lara's story isn't tied up in a neat bow at the end. We are left with unanswered questions and unresolved situations. What do you think happens after Lara goes back to Dublin? Do you think that she and Ben will get back together?

13. Lara expresses her customers' feelings through flowers. If you were to make a bouquet that expressed who you are, what flowers would you include?

Photo by Bryan Meade

Ella Griffin always wanted to be a writer, but before she got around to it she was a waitress, a movie extra, a pickle factory worker, a travel writer and an award-winning advertising copywriter. Her debut novel, *Postcards from the Heart*, was published in 2011. *The Flower Arrangement* is her third novel. Visit her online at ellagriffin.com, facebook.com/EllaGriffinAuthor and twitter.com/EllaGriffin1.